Honoria

MARION
FITZGERALD

POOLBEG

This book is a work of fiction. The names, characters, places, businesses, organisations and incidents portrayed in it are either the product of the author's imagination or are used fictitiously. Any resemblance to actual persons, living or dead, events or locales is entirely coincidental.

Published 2019
by Poolbeg Press Ltd.
123 Grange Hill, Baldoyle,
Dublin 13, Ireland
Email: poolbeg@poolbeg.com

A catalogue record for this book is available from the British Library.

ISBN 978178199-319-4

www.poolbeg.com

About the Author

Marion FitzGerald was born and grew up in Sandymount, Dublin. She went to school locally and then to University College Dublin where she did a BA degree in English and Spanish. After she left college she got some part-time work with a trade journal and eventually went on to work for the *Irish Times*, first as a secretary and then as a full-time journalist. She wrote for various newspapers and magazines over the following years and did a bit of television in RTÉ's very first days. She also did some radio work and loved it.

Marion enjoys travelling and has always enjoyed meeting people and hearing their stories. She counts herself lucky to have met many of the most interesting people of her time in her role as journalist.

Acknowledgements

My thanks ...

First of all, I want to thank Paula Campbell of Poolbeg, who answered my submission in six days, and said she would take on *Honoria* for consideration. How lucky was I!

I want to thank Gaye Shortland, my editor, who has been hugely supportive and encouraging – and patient – all along the way.

I want to thank my daughter, Emer, for being at my side all through the writing of *Honoria*, rapping my knuckles when she thought some of my writing was lazy, being sharp with me when she thought I wasn't depicting a character properly or fairly. I would go down to Kerry or she would come up to Wicklow, and I would rewrite and rewrite. We had our arguments. But almost always we would agree – and mostly she was right.

I would like to thank my son Donal for the painstaking historical research he did on my behalf.

Also my husband Brian and the rest of my family for their patience with me and *Honoria* over very many years.

I would like to thank the late Gordon St. George Mark, whom I met when I came across his book on

Tyrone House and its family, and also his mother, Victoria, who had never missed the Galway races since the age of seven – she was eighty when I met her and heading off to the races the next day. Gordon was passionate about the history of the St. George family, and provided me with a wealth of information, written and oral.

I would like to thank Gordon's cousin, the late Mary Keegan, whose father had spent his childhood in Tyrone. Over many years Mary had collected a huge volume of information, and she was incredibly generous to me, sending me copies of so much of the material she had collected in her lifetime.

I would like to thank the writer Brendán Ó Cathaoir – whom I've never met. His *Famine Diary* was my constant companion and signpost through the famine years.

Most of all I want to thank Honoria who inspired me to write this book in the first place.

To Emer, without whom this book would never have been finished

Chapter 1

1827

Honnie enjoyed milking. She loved the feel of Nóinín's warm flank against her face and the way she turned around and looked at her, with big brown eyes, full of curiosity and intelligence. She enjoyed the flexing rhythm of her fingers as she watched the milk froth into the pail between her knees.

It was the month of November in Maree in County Galway.

Honnie was almost eighteen years of age. It was more than four months since she had given up her position as kitchenmaid to Mrs. Dolan, the priest's housekeeper in Oranmore, to come home and care for her sick mother and younger brothers and sisters.

She had been happy enough to come home when her mother had been taken ill, but now that she seemed to have recovered there could be no question of just staying at home. Another girl had taken her place in the priest's household. She had to find a new position.

Her mother was talking about Honnie going to work in the kitchens of Tyrone House.

"If you're offered the chance you must take it," she had said. "You came back here to take care of things while I was sick, and I'm right grateful to you. But now it's getting time for you to move on. I'm stronger every day and inside a week or two I'll be able to manage fine. Your father has been talking with Mrs. Smith, the cook in Tyrone. They need somebody to help in the kitchens. It's a great chance for you."

"What sort of chance is that?" Honnie had said. "To work all the hours God gives me in a dark, steamy kitchen, where I'll never see the light of day? Some chance that is, for sure."

Honnie stopped milking for a moment as she considered the idea again. She didn't want to work in Tyrone House, in the kitchen, or any other part of it. No matter that it was seen as a great opportunity for her, a chance to learn about good food and good cooking, a 'fine position' as her mother had said.

Nóinín, who had been rhythmically chewing the cud, looked round at this break in the momentum and decided to remind Honnie to concentrate on the business in hand. She flicked her tail across Honnie's face with expert aim, catching her across the eyes. Her tail was dirty and thick with mud and cow dung. Honnie cursed her roundly – truly Nóinín was nothing like the meek daisy she was named after. She wiped her forehead with her apron and finished the milking, then set off across the field with the pail swinging gently in her hand.

She had never been inside Tyrone House but her best friend Bridget Fahy had been working there for the past two years. Bridget and Honnie had grown up together in Maree and had been friends since they were very small children. Bridget said that Tyrone House was "very splendid".

"There's a massive big hall, with festoons and medallions and all sorts of plaster decorations. There's a big dining room and a lovely drawing room, and a morning room, and they all have these plaster ornamentations on the walls, on the ceilings."

Honnie put her pail of milk down on the grass and stood, looking at the fields around her, remembering Bridget's excitement about the idea that she might come to work alongside her.

The countryside around her was almost flat, with just the odd hill or slope. There weren't many trees. Those which were to be seen were bent double from the winds which thrashed in from the Atlantic for most of the year. The parish of Maree hung near the ocean's edge though Honnie couldn't actually see the sea from where she stood. The sky was wide and luminous.

As a child she had explored all the fields and lanes, the hills and hollows around her home. She knew where the best clumps of pale primroses were to be found in the springtime, and where the sweetest wild strawberries were hidden in summer. She knew the lushest blackberry bushes, the secret places where white clusters of mushrooms sprang up on cobwebbed autumn mornings. The freedoms and pleasures of childhood were long gone, but there were times when she still managed to visit her favourite places.

She heard her mother's voice calling and, picking up her pail of milk, she walked quickly back to the cottage.

Her mother was standing at the half door.

"What kept you so long, Honnie? You could have milked three cows in the time you were away."

"I was thinking," said Honnie. "About Tyrone. I don't want to go there."

"That's too bad," said her mother. "Because it's there you'll be going – that is, if you are fortunate enough to get taken on."

There were six children younger than Honnie. The Kanes were better off than many of their neighbours but the last few years had not been easy. The bit of land they rented just grew enough potatoes and vegetables for the family, provided grazing for a couple of cows and their calves, and for the horse, Packie, as well as space for the sow and her litters. But when the potato crop failed as it had done a few years previously, when their best cow died as she had done just one year gone, when Mary herself fell ill, life was very hard.

"But we're still very lucky," Mary said to her friend and neighbour Eileen Kelly, who called later that afternoon to see how she was.

"Of course you are, Mary. Haven't you a good strong house, always enough to eat, and doesn't Bartley bring in quite a bit of extra money from the painting work? And isn't he very handy? Look at the lovely room he built on for yourself and himself."

"He is very handy," Mary replied. "Mind you, the work isn't as easily got around here as it once was – these days he's working on the other side of Galway, but not too far away. He gets home now and then. With mouths to feed, we're lucky he can earn the money."

Later in the evening Mary came back to the subject of Tyrone House.

"I don't want to go there," said Honnie.

But Mary Kane was adamant.

"It's a chance, Honnie, to better yourself, to go up a bit in the world and learn the ways of a really good kitchen. Think of it – if you work hard you might end up as cook in some really grand house."

"From what I've heard of Mrs. Smith, I can't imagine she's going to waste her time teaching me how to cook," said Honnie. "It'll be 'do this, do that, get the other', and a scolding if everything isn't exactly as she wants."

"Everyone has to learn," said her mother, "and sometimes people have to be scolded."

"Bridget says she's a right slave-driver," said Honnie. "And that she likes her drop of port too, only it isn't just a drop she takes, more like a bottle."

"One of these days, Honnie, your tongue will get you into serious trouble," said her mother.

Mary Kane was weary. She had been trying to do things round the house in recent days, and return to her old routine. She was annoyed with herself for being so weak. But she had nearly died when she got pneumonia some four months before. The threat of consumption hung over all the family. Consumption had killed her own mother, two of her brothers, and two of her children – a boy, Eoin, who had been next in age to Honnie, and a girl, Ellen, some years later. As a fit of coughing overcame her, she wondered, not for the first time, if it was going to take her too.

Her mother's coughing struck fear into Honnie's heart.

"You've been trying to do too much, *a Mhamaí.* You're not ready yet. Come on now, sit down and rest. There, sit you down beside the fire, and I'll have the supper ready in no time at all."

In the daytime and unless the weather was bad, only the lower half of the door was closed. That way light got in, the animals were kept out and passers-by could bid you the time of day. Now the sky was darkening and a wind had begun to rise. Honnie closed the upper door.

Mary Kane shivered as she sat down beside the fire.

"I feel as though somebody is walking over my grave," she said. "And where are William and Seán? They went out fishing with Martín Breathnach this morning. They should be home by now."

"*A Mhamaí*, Mairtín Breathnach has been fishing these waters since he and I were children together," said Honnie.

Mary said nothing, just drew closer to the fire.

"Kathleen!" Honnie called her younger sister."Would you ever go out and get more turf from the rick, and maybe a few twigs as well?"

"You're always telling me what to do. We managed fine without you while you were away in Oranmore," said Kathleen crossly as she went out the door to get the firing.

Honnie drew the dying embers to the front of the fire on the open hearth and, when Kathleen came back in with a basket of turf and twigs, she put some kindling at the back, and then some sods of hard black turf. Within minutes there was a brisk blaze.

She filled a pot with potatoes and hooked it onto the iron crane hanging over the fire. The family had eaten rabbit stew for their midday meal and there was a good share of it left for her brothers. She hung the stewpot alongside the potatoes so that it would be hot when they returned. William was good at snaring rabbits and they made a stew which was rich and nourishing.

She separated nine-year-old Maureen from eight-year-old Thady, who was crying bitterly because Maureen had been telling him he was a very bold boy when he hadn't done anything at all. Thady was easily risen and Maureen took pleasure in rising him, especially when she was bored. Honnie told her sharply to make herself useful by cleaning Joseph, a good-humoured five-year-old who seemed to delight in playing in every muddy spot or dirty pool around the house.

She asked Kathleen to tidy the kitchen and went to straighten the bedclothes in her parents' room. A muttered "bossy-boots" followed in her wake.

Mary Kane was proud of her room, which Barney had added on to the house about ten years earlier. "And wasn't it very clever of your father to build it against the chimney wall?" she often said. "It's always warm. Truth to tell, I think this is one of the best houses around Maree."

Honnie knew her mother was right when she said they were lucky. And it was true that they very rarely went hungry and could usually find something for those who came begging for help. There were times, though, when Honnie thought her mother was too *flaithiúlach* with beggars, far too generous in fact. She thought so once again when she answered a knock at the door and found Mairéad Rua had come calling.

"*Dia duit*," said Mairéad. *God be with you.*

"*Dia is Muire duit,*" said Honnie rather crossly. *God and Mary be with you*. She opened the door to let her in.

"Mairéad? Is it you? You're very welcome," said Mary. "Come and sit down and tell us all your news."

"You're a kind decent woman, Mary Kane," said

Mairéad, "and you've always been good to me. These aren't easy times, and I've been out of my mind with worry over my poor Cáit. She's been laid low this six weeks past, coughing and wheezing from morning to night, frightening me out of my mind. It's only in the past few days she's taken a turn for the better, but she's still very weak, and so thin you could blow her away. You're a mother yourself, Mary – you know how important it is to build up an invalid's strength. I've been thinking, Mary, that she'd be the better for eating some of the good eggs laid by your hens, if, in the generosity of your heart, you could spare some?"

"Of course you can have some eggs, Mairéad," said Mary. "You're more than welcome. Honnie, go and wrap up some eggs in straw, carefully, so that they can be safely carried."

It so happened that Mairéad had a wooden noggin with her, and if Mary could spare a little milk as well, she would say a prayer for her every day. When she left a while later, calling on all the saints in heaven to witness Mary's goodness, she was also carrying half a round of brown soda bread which Honnie had baked earlier that morning, and a stone or so of potatoes.

"And if she'd been able to carry any more," said Honnie, "she'd have asked for a few carrots, maybe, or a slice or two of bacon, and maybe a shawl to keep the child warm – and she's just one of the regulars! Do you ever think, *A Mhamaí,* that these people are taking advantage of your kindness?"

"We can afford to give,' Mary said. "Poor Mairéad. She has no husband, and Cáit is an awful worry to her."

It was getting dark and the wind had started to work

up to a gale by the time William and Seán returned. Mary Kane's relief was palpable. But while she didn't have to worry about her sons for the moment, she now worried about the wind taking the roof off the house.

"Do you remember how that big gale took the roof off the Mannions' house up the way? If that happened to us, what would we do – with your father away working? How many nights have I been listening to the savagery of the wind, waiting for it to take the roof away?"

"It's not going to happen, *a Mhamaí,*" said William. "It's well weighted and secure. *Daidí* and I went over it again the last time he was home."

During the weeks that followed Mary got stronger, and Honnie could see a place in the kitchens of Tyrone fast approaching. Her mother busied herself making two dresses for her – one to wear and one to wash, as she said. Honnie stitched too, to her mother's instructions, but she knew she would never make as good a needlewoman. She hadn't the patience.

Eileen Kelly came to help. Her son Tom was just a year older than Honnie, and himself and Honnie had spent much of their childhood together roaming the countryside, fishing in the small streams and little inlets at the sea's edge. The Kellys always had a couple of horses on their land and Tom had encouraged a love of horses in Honnie, until she became as fearless as he was, riding bareback along the strand or across the fields whenever she got the chance. But last September Tom had gone to Maynooth in County Kildare, to study for the priesthood.

"He knew so much about so many things," she said to

Eileen, as they stitched the dresses. "He knew which birds stayed all year round, and which ones visited in the summer. He knew where the badgers lived. He knew where you could see young fox cubs playing in the early morning. He could tell great stories of happenings past and present."

"He was certainly a great lad for learning," said Eileen. "He read every book he could get his hands on, and he never forgot anything he read."

"I miss him," said Honnie.

"Think of all the fine people you'll see in Tyrone, all the comings and goings, the parties and the entertainment!"

"I know exactly what I'll see," said Honnie. "I'll see the scullery sink, and no end of work from dawn to dusk. At least in the priest's house the work wasn't too hard. We did what we had to do, but there was time to talk and some time for yourself."

But Mary Kane was adamant.

Honnie's father Bartley, home from a painting job in Galway, agreed with her.

"Your mother has the rights of it, and the sooner you go the better."

Then, one Sunday morning Bartley announced, "I've talked to Mrs. Smith. She needs someone as soon as possible. I told her I'd take you over there tomorrow."

Suddenly everything seemed to be happening very quickly.

That evening Honnie called in to the Breathnachs to say goodbye.

Sarah Breathnach wished her luck, taking in Honnie's downcast face.

"Sure you're only going down the road," she said comfortingly.

"And isn't your friend Bridget Fahy over there? " said Peig, Mairtín's younger sister. "Won't she be great company for you?"

Mairtín Breathnach put his strong arms around her and hugged her.

"I'm going to miss you, Honnie," he said. "I really am."

She looked into the grey eyes gazing down at her, at the fair hair flopping across his forehead, and gently pulled away.

She knew that Mairtín had warm feelings for her. She just wasn't sure how she felt about him.

"I'm going to miss everybody here," she said.

Walking to Tyrone House the following day, Bartley Kane tried to cheer his glum-faced daughter. Maree was about five miles from Tyrone, and it was a road Bartley knew well. Mick Murphy, who was head groom in the stable yards at Tyrone House, was a great friend of his. They both shared a passion for horses, and the horses in the Tyrone stables were among the finest to be seen in the county. Bartley and Mick often spent a happy hour or so discussing their various merits, their form, their performances, and their potential at upcoming race meetings.

"Mrs. Smith's bark is worse than her bite," Bartley said to Honnie. "She can be a bit contrary, but she's not got a bad heart. You can learn a lot from her. Just think of it as a step upwards. You don't want to get married to some poor lad with an acre of land and find yourself living in a mud cabin with six children before you're thirty, do you?"

"I don't want to end up as a cook in somebody else's kitchen either," said Honnie. "And I don't particularly want to marry anybody at the moment – but, if I do, it certainly won't be to somebody who'll keep me in a mud cabin. I want more than that. I'd expect some sort of a decent house at the very least."

Bartley Kane thought, not for the first time, that his daughter had notions above her station – not that she wasn't fit for better things. She was a fine-looking girl, handsome rather than pretty, tall and slim but well-built, with a confident carriage. Her hair was a rich chestnut, curling around her face, and she had fine brown eyes – now scowling under dark brows as Tyrone drew nearer. But she was still only the daughter of a tradesman and tenant farmer. She had intelligence, but little education apart from some spells with a hedge schoolmaster, and what she had learned from Tom Kelly as his education progressed. She had always wanted more from life than she could reasonably expect.

Wanting was one thing, thought Bartley, getting was another thing altogether.

"Who built Tyrone?" asked Honnie.

"Christopher St. George, the father of the present owner Arthur, had it built almost fifty years ago," said Bartley. "You'll remember he only died the year gone by. He gave the house to Arthur when Arthur married Lady Harriet in 1801, and went to live in Kilcolgan Castle. Arthur's eldest son is another Christopher. They own a lot of land, the St. Georges, close on 30,000 acres of land spread over Galway, Queen's County and Roscommon."

The land around Tyrone was mixed. There was a great deal of shallow, rocky soil, but there were stretches of decent pasture as well. Beside them as they walked, in a lush green field, a group of young horses galloped to and fro, tossing their heads, their manes flying, glad to be alive.

"Just look at them!!" said Honnie, leaning over a fence. "Aren't they splendid!"

But it was the sheep that dominated the landscape, big sturdy animals with deep woollen coats, hundreds of them.

"Tyrone sheep have quite a reputation in Galway," said Bartley. "Stockbreeding is Arthur St. George's passion. He loves his sheep."

Even in the distance Tyrone House presented an imposing aspect. It was a great stone house, three storeys high, standing dark against the skyline, surrounded by tall trees. The nearer they got, the more apprehensive Honnie became.

"It used to be one of the liveliest houses in Galway," said Bartley.

"Well, it certainly doesn't look very lively today," said Honnie.

"Do you not remember how we'd often look at the lights blazing across the bay of a summer evening?" said Bartley. "An invitation to a party or ball in Tyrone would always be eagerly accepted. But not any more. The Mistress hasn't been that well of late."

Looking out the window of the library, Arthur French St. George watched father and daughter coming up the rear avenue and paused. He recognised Bartley. He had often seen him round the stable yards, but he had never seen Honnie before. A good-looking girl, he thought.

He had been sitting at his desk, looking with a sense of despair at the sheaves of paper in tumbling piles around him, when he stood up to stretch his legs and look for some distraction in the November landscape. Every month, it seemed, the piles grew higher – demands for payment, threats of foreclosure on loans taken out. His debts were mounting relentlessly. Times were grim. Some years ago he had hoped it was all only temporary, but things were getting worse rather than better.

The estate was big, and there always seemed to be part of it sucking up money. With bad summers and crop failures, even the best of tenants found it hard to feed their families and pay their rent. He himself had eight girls and two boys. True, two of the girls were no longer with him, but they were still entitled to support from the estate.

His father had lived in happier times, he thought, his eye lighting on copies of his father's account books, immaculately kept, every farthing accounted for. But then he was his father's only child. Raising ten children was very different to raising one.

He looked at a portrait of Lady Harriet, smiling down at him from the wall above his desk. As master of Tyrone he had a position to keep up. He owed it to Lady Harriet, a daughter of the Earl of Howth. He owed it to his standing in society. He owed a great deal of money.

He looked forward to the day when Christopher would take over the running of the estate. It couldn't come soon enough. But Christopher had only begun his studies in Trinity College in Dublin. Arthur would have to battle through the next few years as best he could.

As Bartley and Honnie drew near the steps to the basement of Tyrone House, fear clutched at Honnie's stomach, but she was determined not to be overcome. It was only a building, after all, and the people in it were only people – not that different from herself, only luckier in that they had been born to better circumstances,

With a closed face she followed her father down the outside steps to the basement kitchens.

"Mrs. Smith, this is my daughter Honoria," said Bartley. That was his job done. "Honnie – I'll be on my way now. Mind yourself. Be good."

Bartley headed out to see Mike Murphy in the stable yard. Mick had told Bartley about a new colt bought recently by young Christopher St. George – "a horse who could clear a six-foot gate or a dozen stone walls as easy as a swallow can fly". Bartley was keen to see it.

Mrs. Smith, who was Scottish, had probably been a good-looking woman in her day, but now she was decidedly plump. Her once blonde hair was almost all grey, her skin was reddened with fine lines from years in the kitchen and too much indulgence in her own cooking – not to mention her predilection for port.

It was not one of her better days. She looked Honnie up and down without much enthusiasm, registered the set expression, and decided that this was a young person who would need a firm hand.

As her father disappeared up the steps, Honnie held herself tall and waited for Mrs. Smith to speak. The vaulted kitchen was very hot, and full of steam. Along one wall was a huge open fire, with pots suspended above it and a creel of turf beside it. From the corner of her eye Honnie could see Bridget in a room alongside the kitchen. She was standing on a wooden box, her hands plunged deep into a large stone sink.

"So you're Bartley's daughter," Mrs. Smith said finally. "Honoria, is it? I think Honnie will do well enough for the likes of you. Well then, Honnie, I hope you're a good worker. All the cooking for the house and the servants is done down here, but of course a young person like yourself wouldn't have any idea of the kind of cooking that goes on in the house of a gentleman like Mr. St. George, so you'll have a lot to learn. We keep a very good table here, I can tell you. Some nights there might be thirty or more people for dinner. That means ten or fifteen chickens or pheasants to be cleaned and readied, joints to be roasted, puddings to be made, cakes to be baked. Lady Harriet is very particular about the food she serves. So don't get the idea that you'll have an easy time here, my girl, for you won't."

I certainly won't, thought Honnie.

"This is the range and the fire has to be kept well reddened at all times. I expect it to be ready for me to use at any time of the day. Seamus here brings in the turf, but it will be your job to see the fire is kept going."

Seamus was a tall awkward boy, with a head of red hair and huge hands and feet. He looked Honnie over with an appreciative eye.

Mrs. Smith continued with her instructions. "You're here to help Bridget. You'll get up at six of the clock and get the fire going, fetch water and put it on to boil so it's ready when the mistress and Mr. St. George need to wash. There must always be plenty of water boiling come breakfast time. Then you can bring me a cup of tea in my room. You and Bridget will wash the dishes after every meal, and scour and clean all the saucepans, stew-pans, kettles, pots and kitchen utensils. I expect everything in the kitchen to be clean, dry and fit for use – at all times. You'll help Bridget and the kitchen maids whenever they need help. They'll show you what needs doing. Now, when Bridget has finished preparing the vegetables she can take you to your room and show you where to put your things. You'll be sleeping with the other girls, upstairs at the top of the house."

She paused and fixed her eyes sternly on Honnie's.

"One last thing – there's to be no gentlemen callers. I expect all the servants to be in bed by eleven o'clock at the latest. My own room is nearby, just down the corridor from the kitchen and, believe me, I know everything that goes on. But don't worry, you'll be so tired at the end of a day's work here you'll be glad to fall into bed. Have I made myself clear?"

Gentlemen callers indeed! What kind of a girl does she think I am, thought Honnie.

"Yes, Mrs. Smith," she said.

While she waited for Bridget, Honnie looked around the kitchen. It was full of smells, noises, voices, talk, and laughter. Bells rang, and people were coming and going through several doors. The gardener's boy arrived with a basket of fresh vegetables. Another man was arguing with Mrs. Smith over a basket of fish.

"That fish wasn't caught this morning, Paddy, and don't try to tell me it was. That fella's eyes haven't seen the sea these two days – they're sunk in his head. Bring me nice, firm fresh fish that smells sweet, and then I'll talk to you."

And even though Paddy swore by the Virgin Mary, his ancestors, and all the saints in heaven that he had come straight from his boat to the kitchens of Tyrone, Mrs.

Smith had him out the door before he knew what had happened to him.

At one end of a long table a girl in a plain blue dress and white apron was beating a creamy yellow mixture in a large bowl. At the other end another girl with a pink-and-white complexion and a head of yellow curls was rolling out dough. She gave Honnie a warm smile. Her strong plump forearms were dusted with flour.

"I'm Kate," she said, wiping her hands on a wide white apron. Her grasp was warm and reassuring. "And that's Josie there at the end of the table."

She nodded towards the small, wiry girl with frizzy black hair beating the mixture, then leant closer to Honnie.

"We're always at Mrs. Smith's beck and call," she whispered. "But it's not all as mad as it first seems. I remember what it was like when I first came here three years ago – you'll get used to it, I promise."

Bridget arrived.

"Come on," she said. "I'll take you upstairs, and you can put your things away. The sooner I get help in the scullery the better."

As they passed the range where a number of pots of different shapes and sizes were steaming and hissing, Bridget paused.

"See, there's an oven at both sides of the fire," she said, "and the turf is kept beyond in the turf-hole beside the steps – so when the creel is empty there's always more turf at hand. Mrs. Smith likes the range to be piping hot in the morning. And I can tell you that range has its vagaries. Some days it's very easy to get going, other days no matter what you do it sulks and sulks – but don't try explaining that to Mrs. Smith. Then there's the spit, over the open fire there, for when we want to cook a *banbh* or maybe a side of beef. That'll be your job too, to turn the spit so that it cooks nice and even. And it's our job to wash all the plates and dishes, and the saucepans, the stew-pans and the kettles – and clean the servants' hall, and the housekeeper's room and the steps outside the front door, and clear away after Mrs. Smith and the kitchen maids. There are days you think you'll never finish, and your legs ache and your hands are red raw."

Outside, Bartley had made his way to the stables. Some said that the St. George horses were better looked after than the St. George tenants. Nothing was too good for them. When old Christopher St. George had built Tyrone, very special attention had been paid to the stables.

"That man knew all about horses, I can tell you," Mick constantly proclaimed. "A good horse deserves a good stable, he always said. No horse likes a damp home – it kills the heart in him. The floor of the stables should always be kept higher than the ground outside – it's for drainage, you see. But there shouldn't be too much fall of ground on it either. If there's a bad slope, the poor animal's legs can go astray under him."

Barney would nod impatiently. He had heard Mick on countless occasions going on about the Tyrone stables.

Today was no different. "These are the best stables in the whole of Galway. A horse needs space, enough space to be comfortable. He needs fresh air – but no draughts, mind you –"

"The new fella, the new horse, man, where is he?" interrupted Bartley.

Horses looked out of the stalls on either side of the yard, whinnying at a passing groom or stableboy, tossing their heads, blowing steamy breaths out into the cold November morning.

Mick strode off, beckoning him on. "Mind how clean them stables are," he said, as they passed men mucking out. "Every morning each one of them stables is cleaned out, any dirty bedding is taken away, the floor is swept and the air let in, until everything smells sweet and fresh as newmown hay. These horses live like kings, I can tell you."

"You've told me that so many times I could put it to music and sing it to you," said Barney. "Where's the bloody horse?"

From the last stall on one side of the yard, a loud whinnying and clattering could be heard.

"The devil take him!" said one voice. "Even if he is the finest horse that ever came into our stables, he has the temper of a devil!"

"Come on, you fiend!" said another voice. "Easy does it, come on now, come on."

A furious whinny was the only answer.

Bartley and Mick stood watching as a tall black horse was slowly persuaded out into the yard.

He was certainly impressive – a gleaming, plunging force of nerves and energy.

"He's a bit high-spirited all right," said Mick, "but he's still very young, and it's early days yet."

The horse reared, eyes rolling, as he glimpsed two more people in his line of vision. One of the grooms tried to calm him, leading him slowly along the stable yard, talking to him and stroking him as he went. Good breeding was obvious in every line of the animal's body –

almost too much breeding, some might say. Temper and temperament shivered over the glossy coat. But he walked beautifully – lightly and easily. As the groom gentled him along, he picked his paces over the cobbled yard with elegance and style, the groom alongside him.

Looking at him, Bartley felt that particular surge of pleasure that he always felt at the sight of a fine horse.

"He seems a bit wild all right, but then he's not properly broken in yet," said Mick. "You mark my words – in a few years' time he'll be winning races all over the country."

"That's if Master Christopher doesn't break his neck and the horse's neck first," said one of the young grooms standing by. "If that horse is wild, Master Christopher is wilder."

"Ah sure, they're both very young and young blood is hot," said Mick. "But they work well together, and they'll cool down in time. Besides, Christopher doesn't get much chance of riding these days, Bartley. Mr. St. George has put a stop to him. He's sent him off up to Dublin, to Trinity College, and I hear tell he'll be there for the next four years."

"He'll still be back to hunt," said the groom. "No power on earth could keep Master Christopher away from the hunt for long."

Bartley's eyes were still on the horse. "And what is he being called?" he asked.

"Necromancer," said Mick.

"*Necromancer.* What kind of a name is that for a horse?" said Bartley.

"It's the name Master Christopher gave him," said Mick. "It means wizard, he says."

Over in the Big House Honnie had been shown the

bedroom she would share with Josie, Kate, and Bridget. It was a spacious room, with windows on both sides. There were four beds, immaculately made up, and a chest with four drawers – "One for each of us," said Bridget.

"A real bed," said Honnie, who had spent her life sharing a settle bed with Kathleen, "and all to myself. And a drawer of my own – not that I have much to put into it."

There were a couple of plain wooden chairs, and not much else. There were no clothes lying round, no untidiness, no disorder.

"Mrs. Hunt, the housekeeper, inspects everything," said Bridget. "If everything isn't absolutely tidy we get a right telling-off. Not that it bothers Josie – she always leaves things lying around."

On this November day the room was cold. The windows on one side looked out over lawns and flowerbeds, to the steel-grey waters of Galway Bay and the Aran Islands beyond. From the other window you could see the hills of Clare. Through thick shrubbery a path led down to the kitchen gardens, walled in brick, with a glasshouse caught in a chance ray of sunshine, and beyond that again lay the sea.

Honnie hadn't brought much with her. Just a couple of changes of underwear, some stockings, a shawl, a brush and comb, some other bits and pieces, two aprons and the two dresses she, her mother and Eileen Kelly had made together. The dress material was tough and hardwearing. The sleeves could be easily rolled up which was important, her mother pointed out, because Honnie would be doing a great deal of washing.

"It makes me look like a stuffed goose," Honnie had complained to her mother. "And it's scratchy."

"It will last, it will wash well, and these are the kind of dresses scullery maids wear," said her mother.

"Come on, Honnie," said Bridget now, "put on one of those dresses and an apron and let's get downstairs."

It was mid-morning, and the kitchen was a hive of activity.

"It's coming up to luncheon time," said Bridget, "when we're always busy. There's lunch first for the family upstairs, and then we have ours. And I still have a pile of dishes to wash. You'd better wait here 'til Mrs. Smith tells you exactly what she wants you to do. If I take you into the scullery now, she'll probably say I'm getting above myself. Then she'll find something else for you to do, and I'll be back on my own."

Bridget bustled off, leaving Honnie standing uncertainly just inside the kitchen door. What was she supposed to do? She stood, moving from one foot to the other, and trying to keep out of the way of people hurrying past.

Steam swirled from the pots on the range. The oven door was opened, and a rich meaty smell wafted across the kitchen. Every so often Mrs. Smith issued an order, and someone scurried to obey. Honnie stood, watching, and trying to remember the names of all these new faces.

Mr. Scott, the butler, made a brief appearance, and was treated with deferential respect, which Honnie thought he obviously felt was his due. He was a tall man with iron-grey hair and a rather severe expression, and to Honnie he seemed aloof and forbidding. The only person to whom he spoke in the kitchen was Mrs. Smith.

As he left, Mrs. Smith glanced at Honnie. "I'll deal with you in a minute," she said.

Honnie could feel her stomach knotting. Never, ever, she thought, would she be able to belong here.

After a few minutes Mrs. Smith called her over.

"You'll be working in the scullery. Now is as good a time as any to get you started. Bridget will show you what to do, but I'll be keeping my eye on you. We'll see how you get on."

The scullery was dark and steamy, but warm. There were two huge stone sinks. In each sink stood a wooden tub and in front of each sink stood a low wooden box.

"The washing is done in the tubs," said Bridget.

Dirty delph was stacked high, large plates and small plates alongside each other. The glasses were ranked separately. And there seemed to be scores of pots and pans of all shapes and sizes.

"One sink is for vegetables and suchlike," said Bridget, pointing, "and the other is for washing the pots and pans, and all the crockery we use down here. The sinks are so deep it's hard to reach down into them. You mightn't need the box to stand on, Honnie, but I definitely do."

Bridget stood not much over five feet in height. She was a slender girl, with long fair hair caught in a plaited loop at the nape of her neck. Without the box she would have had no hope of reaching into the sink.

"We may as well get started. Soft soap and soda, that's what we wash with and everything has to be well rinsed. I'll do some of the pots and you can dry, and then you can wash for a while and I'll dry. The plates go into this rack here."

The pots were copper.

"Mrs. Smith says they're the most beautiful pots of all

to cook with," said Bridget. "They heat easily and if you want them to lose heat, then they cool down quickly too. They *never* wear out either. There's just one thing we have to remember. Do you see the inside of them? It's tin, and Mrs. Smith says we are to tell her immediately if it looks as though it's wearing out. If you leave food in the saucepan and the tin has worn, a kind of poison can escape from the copper, and you *die* if you eat from it the next day. Can you imagine? Mrs. Smith says there were two gentlemen she knew in England whose cook gave them stew that had been in the pot from the day before. And they died!"

After the washing-up, there were the potatoes, a huge basin of them waiting to be peeled. Bridget took one sharp knife herself and handed one to Honnie who watched Bridget as she peeled quickly and deftly. It looked easy enough but when she tried doing it herself she found her fingers seemed to be all over the place, and she was taking a lump of potato with every bit of skin she peeled away. Bridget peeled four potatoes in the time it took her to do one. Honnie's nervousness was not helped by knowing Mrs. Smith was keeping a watchful eye on her from the kitchen doorway.

When Honnie had about ten lumpy-looking peeled potatoes in her bowl, alongside Bridget's pile of smoothly round ones, Mrs. Smith came over.

"I can see you haven't had much experience of peeling potatoes, my girl!"

"At home we always cooked them in their jackets," said Honnie. "The best part of the potato is just under the skin, my mother says."

"I don't want to hear what your mother says, I want you to listen to what I'm telling you!" said Mrs. Smith sharply. "The best part of the potato could still be there, if you didn't take half of it with you every time you put a knife to it. Look. Don't dig the knife in, just slide it barely under the skin ... like so." And a delicate curl of paper-thin skin fell from Mrs. Smith's hands into the colander in the sink. "It's all a question of practice. And don't worry – you'll get plenty of that."

Almost half an hour later Honnie looked at the pile still unpeeled beside her with a sense of despair.

"I'll never be able to do it as well or as fast as you can," she said to Bridget, who had moved on to scraping carrots. "And how many people are there to *eat* all these potatoes? An army? Why can't they eat them in their jackets anyway, like other good Christians?"

"Well, there's sixteen upstairs tonight," said Bridget. "And we could have as many as fifteen people in the servants' hall. I can't imagine a potato being served in its jacket to Lady Harriet!"

Then there was more washing-up.

"Last thing of all, every night, we have to scrape off every bit of fat from around the sides of the wooden tubs," said Bridget. "Otherwise maggots can get into the wood. They like the fat that's come off the dishes. And if there's one thing that puts Mrs. Smith into a rage, it's maggots."

"It seems quite a lot of things can put Mrs. Smith into a rage, from what I've heard," Honnie said.

It was after ten in the evening before everything was done. The scullery had grown cold and, as Honnie leant over to put the last pot away, she slipped and fell on the wet floor. She got scant sympathy from Bridget, once she was sure Honnie had no broken bones.

"That's all I need. You to be away with a broken leg, and you only here half a day. It's good you're so well padded!"

"God, I'm tired," said Honnie, as they climbed up the stairs to bed. "But I don't think I'm going to be able to get to sleep easily. My head's too full."

"You'll soon get over that," said Bridget. "Besides, you didn't start working until the day was nearly half gone. Wait and see how you feel tomorrow night."

Honnie had never slept in a feather bed before. There was a magic about sinking into the soft folds. Bridget stayed awake long enough to tell her that the feathers from all the fowl killed for the table were saved to make mattresses and pillows and cushions. Then she laid her head on the pillow and fell instantly asleep.

Honnie had grown up sleeping with Kathleen beside her in the settle bed, and even in Oranmore she had shared a bed with the other maidservant. At home she was used to hearing the murmur of her parents' voices in the nearby room, the occasional fluttering of her mother's hens in the yard, Bran the dog barking from time to time at a passing fox.

She felt very high up at the top of this tall house, far away from family and home. As she lay there, listening to the regular breathing from the girls in the other beds, she could feel her throat tightening, and tears coming salty, until she had to bury her face in her pillow to smother her sobs.

Then somebody took her hand and squeezed it hard. Honnie could just make out Kate in the darkness.

"The first few nights are the hardest," she whispered. "Everything seems so strange. But it'll pass, I promise.

Now try and get some sleep. You need all the rest you can get. You have a hard day's work ahead of you tomorrow."

Chapter 2

It seemed to Honnie as if she had just closed her eyes when Bridget was shaking her awake.

"It's gone six. Come on, get up quick or nothing will be ready when Mrs. Smith comes down."

It was pitch dark as they crept down the stairs. Outside there was a sharp wind blowing, and the kitchen was cold.

Bridget turned her attention first to the fire. The deep bed of smouldering embers just needed some fresh fuel. She threw some sods of turf on it and the fire sprang quickly to life. Then she filled some pots with water and hung them over it. Next she turned to the range.

"I don't think it's in a good humour today," she said. "The wind is from the wrong direction and that's sure to make it contrary. Honnie, bring me over some sods of turf from the creel beyond."

Bridget raked out the ashes, and quickly put thin sticks onto the embers in the grate, then some bigger pieces of wood, and topped the pile with hard black sods of turf.

"It eats turf," said Bridget. "We have to fill it every hour. Mrs. Smith likes the heat to stay steady."

The small pile of turf embers flickered fitfully.

While she waited for the range to warm up, Bridget applied some blacklead with a brush to its front and sides.

"Now, Honnie – here's two cloths. Polish it off with this one and finish it off with the softer one. If the range is warm the shine comes up faster. This is what you might call a lick and a promise. Once a week we give it a really good going-over."

But the range had decided to sulk. It was definitely one of its off-days.

"The ovens aren't heating because the flues haven't been cleaned out properly this week," said Bridget. "We'll do it tomorrow. Come on – I'll do the kitchen table and floor, you do the larder and the scullery. If you sweep the servants' hall, I'll do the housekeeper's room, and if you scrub the back steps, I'll do the front ones. Then we can bring Mrs. Smith her tea."

It seemed to Honnie that the clock handles jumped to half past seven while her back was turned, and there was barely time to blink before Mrs. Smith arrived in the kitchen.

"That oven seems to be very slow getting going," she said. "It's barely warm. You know I want it ready to use at all times. When did you last clean out the flues, Bridget?"

"I'll do them tomorrow, ma'am, first thing."

"You will indeed, Bridget. And yourself and Honnie

can get up an hour earlier to be sure you have plenty of time to do it properly."

The rest of the day passed in a blur.

It was still black dark when Bridget shook Honnie awake the following morning. All she wanted to do was burrow under her blankets and go back to sleep.

Cleaning out the flues was a nasty, dirty job. The only way of removing the soot was with a long narrow brush with a bent handle which had to be pushed up and down, up and down, up and down, until the soot broke free. By the time they had finished cleaning the range and got to black-leading it, they were both nearly as black as the range itself.

Bridget looked at Honnie and laughed. "If you could see yourself!"

"You're not looking too pretty right now either," said Honnie.

Cleaning themselves up before Mrs. Smith appeared meant carrying water up three flights of stairs to the top of the house so that they could wash and change and come back downstairs looking clean and respectable again. Which, as far as Honnie was concerned, meant that she had one dirty dress and one dirty apron, and one clean dress and one clean apron.

"What happens if my other dress gets dirty before this one is washed?" she said to Bridget.

"You can cross that bridge if you come to it," said Bridget. "Now, come on, Mrs. Smith will be looking for us."

After breakfast and the washing-up, there were the vegetables to be prepared for luncheon and dinner. The gardener's boy arrived at nine o'clock with a basket of cabbage and turnips and carrots. It had been a cold, cold night. Honnie could feel the ice in the carrots and turnips and see the particles on the cabbage. When she tried to peel and chop the vegetables the cold clawed into her fingers. The knife was slippery and kept slewing off at an angle.

"There now," a voice behind her said, making her jump.

A large young man, wearing a filthy jacket and muddy boots, stood smiling at her. From his arms hung various dead animals and birds – rabbits, hares, pheasants. He dropped them on the scullery floor. "Rabbit stew, jugged hare, roast pheasant. Mrs. Smith will be pleased."

He bid them good day and left, the rich odours of the farmyard trailing behind him.

"That *amadán*!" said Bridget furiously. "He's been told again and again not to do that. Mrs. Smith will *not* be pleased. She likes to see the game when they first come in, decide which ones are good enough for the kitchen, and then oversee the hanging of them."

Honnie had often raised pheasants from their hiding places when she went walking in the woods near her home in Maree, but she had never seen them close up before. The colours of the feathers were really beautiful.

"Lovely feathers, but empty heads," she said to Bridget, remembering the flitter-brained squawking they always made when you surprised them.

When Lady Harriet asked for pheasant to be cooked some ten days later, the pheasants were brought in to Bridget and Honnie to be plucked.

"Chicken and ducks and turkeys and geese are

plucked out in a house in the yard," said Bridget, "but Mrs. Smith likes us to pluck pheasants. She says they need more care and attention. The sooner we start, the sooner we finish. They're for eating tonight. Careful now – you have to pull out those little quilly things at the bottom of the feathers – the trick is to pick them low down. If you don't get every single one out Mrs Smith will make us pluck all over again."

Honnie had just taken a pheasant in her hand to start plucking when Mrs. Smith called Bridget away to help her in the kitchen. She was on her second bird when the scullery door opened and Josie hurried in, looking for a particular stew-pan. The feathers in the pot at Honnie's feet flew up in the air, into the sink, onto the prepared vegetables, onto the newly washed pots and pans.

"Oh! Sorry, Honnie – I'd stay and help only Mrs. Smith will have my life if I don't get back to her this minute – but that's not the way to do it, you know? That old pot you're using isn't half big enough. You should be plucking into a box or a pail. Didn't Bridget tell you?"

And with that she was gone.

Honnie stared in stunned disbelief at the chaos created in just one instant. The longer it took her to clean up the mess, the crosser she got with Josie.

"I'd like to wring her neck," she told Bridget when she got back. "I'd like to shake her 'til her teeth rattle. I'd like to cover her in smelly feathers –"

"None of which you're going to be able to do," said Bridget. "Besides, it's not her fault – she just came into the room. It's really my fault. I should have told you to pluck the feathers into that bucket over there. That way, if somebody opens the door, they don't fly all over the place. Come on – it's not that bad. We'll clean it all up and then we'll finish them together."

Half a dozen pheasants later, Honnie's fingers were red raw.

"Don't worry," said Bridget. "When you've plucked a couple of dozen of them every few weeks, your fingers will get used to it."

Honnie was still silently cursing Josie when she became aware of the gathering noise of horses and barking dogs in the distance.

"That's the hunt," said Bridget. "I'd forgotten it was meeting here today. Come on – Mrs. Smith always lets us go out and have a look at them setting off. It's a powerful sight."

Men from the stable yard and servant girls from the house had gathered outside to watch. On the steps stood the various members of the St. George family.

"Look, there's Mr. St. George with young Master Arthur – he's fourteen – and Miss Anne and Miss Harriet and Miss Matilda," said Bridget. "Master Christopher must be missing the hunting something awful, and he up in the college in Dublin with his books. And there's Lady Harriet."

Lady Harriet was tall, thin and pale. She shivered in the cold November air, and her husband wrapped her shawl more tightly around her shoulders. She didn't look very happy, and she certainly didn't look very friendly, thought Honnie.

On the sweep of gravel in front of Tyrone House were thirty or more horses and their riders, wheeling and circling, discussing the hunt ahead of them. Circling excitedly around the horses were the hunting dogs.

"Master Christopher's been building up that pack of dogs for the past couple of years," Bridget whispered to

Honnie. "He calls them the St George Hounds. Wouldn't he love to be here today!"

A long table had been set up just below the entrance steps with glasses and jugs of hot punch laid out on a crisp white tablecloth. As the horses pranced in anticipation, the riders chatted, reins in one hand, a glass in the other.

Honnie took deep breaths of the crisp fresh air. It was good to be out of the kitchen and the scullery, even for a little while.

"That old dog fox has been killing chickens for miles around," said one of the riders. "He's been causing devastation. And not only with the hens – he got two of our fine geese as well."

"He's escaped us three times this season already," said another rider. "A stop must be put to him – but not before he's given us a good run."

The hounds had worked themselves up into a frenzy of excitement. The hunting horn was sounded, and the hunt set off, the Master and hounds in front, the horsemen following behind in the direction of a rounded clump of woodland two fields away.

"Look at them!" said Honnie, as a group of horsemen swept to the front, ahead of the main body of the hunt. "They'll overrun the hounds and destroy the whole hunt! The Master will have choice words to say to that lot."

"They'll be back in a matter of hours, hungry and thirsty," said Kate, who was standing next to Honnie.

"And covered in dirt and mud," grumbled 'Biddy the Wash', the large woman who did all the laundry in an outbuilding at the back of the house.

With the stables almost deserted, Honnie decided to slip

off and see for herself if all the talk she'd heard from her father about the new colt was true. With Master Chrstopher away, she knew he wouldn't have been ridden out – no one else would dare to ride him, by the sound of it.

She found Bartley in close conversation with Mick Murphy.

"I mighta known you'd find your way out here," Bartley greeted her.

"Where is he?" Honnie said.

A roar came from the far end of the yard.

"There's your answer," Mick grinned.

Bartley and Mick followed Honnie across the yard.

The hammering of hooves grew louder as they approached. He was black as pitch, and powerfully built, and he was putting on an expressive display to make it clear what he thought of them.

"Well, Honnie, what do you think of Necromancer?" said Bartley.

"I think he's one of the most splendid horses I've ever seen," said Honnie."But he's almost too powerful, and he seems very ill-tempered. I'm very glad I have the stable door between himself and myself. I think he could be dangerous."

Next morning Lady Harriet came down to the kitchen to discuss Christmas preparations with Mrs. Smith. As word of her imminent arrival was whispered downstairs, aprons were smoothed, stray wisps of hair were tucked in under caps. Even Mrs. Smith looked anxious. You could almost hear backs being straightened, thought Honnie.

From the scullery where she was preparing vegetables, she was able to watch Lady Harriet's arrival – and listen as she told Mrs. Smith what she wanted done. The list was long and Lady Harriet's instructions very precise.

"The mistress is always very clear about what she wants," said Mrs. Smith, after Lady Harriet had departed. "We must do our best to observe her wishes and see that everything is properly prepared, and in time."

"Or else we'll know all about it," said Josie under her breath. "Her ladyship will be on the warpath and Mrs. Smith will get an earful, and then all our lives will be miserable."

"Why has Lady Harriet got a title, and the Master hasn't?" asked Honnie that night as she and the other girls were settling down to sleep.

"Because her father was an earl, and Mr. St. George's father wasn't," said Bridget. "Lady Harriet's father was the second Earl of Howth. His first wife died and he married again, and had a son – Thomas – who is now the third Earl of Howth."

"He's only five years older than Master Christopher, and they're the best of friends," said Josie.

"The St. Lawrence family have a castle and a big estate in Howth, just outside Dublin," said Bridget. "Mick Murphy has been up there and he says it's absolutely beautiful, and the St. Lawrence famly have lived there for hundreds and hundreds of years."

"I've been told there are eight St. George daughters," said Honnie. "I know there's Miss Mary, Miss Anne, Miss Olivia, Miss Matilda, Miss Harriet, and Miss Louisa, but that's only six. Who are the others?"

"Miss Emilia, but they don't talk about her," said Josie. "Or Miss Isabella. Miss Emilia eloped with a man called Robinson who worked here as a gardener, and off with them to America! Miss Isabella ran off with Patrick Joyce of Drimharsna. Can you imagine – to lose not just one daughter, but two within months of each other? And them barely out of the schoolroom."

"I came here only a short time after Miss Emilia went and then Miss Isabella," said Kate. "It was very hard on the whole family."

"When Miss Emilia went the whole house was thrown into disarray," said Josie.

"Doctor Veitch had to be called to the Mistress, she was that upset," said Kate. "She stayed in her room, and neither the Master nor any of her daughters could console her. But when Miss Isabella went she seemed to give up altogether. She stayed in her room for weeks, with the curtains drawn, and turned away any meals that were brought up to her. But she came downstairs in the end and took hold of the reins more firmly than ever."

"What about the Master?" said Honnie.

"He took to the library," said Kate, "as if nothing had happened, reading and rummaging among old papers."

"They say he spends all his time now sending letters to high-up gentlemen, trying to prove that Lady Harriet has a right to more titles," said Josie. "He's hoping for a peerage himself. He loves titles, does the Master."

"My father said there was great entertaining done here in Tyrone," said Honnie.

"That's true, surely," said Josie, as she burrowed down under her blankets. "I've been told there used to be grand supper parties, and balls, and music and dancing. And people would come in fine clothes and splendid carriages, and the whole house used to be so lit up you could see it blazing right across the bay. But the Master and Lady Harriet haven't the heart for any of that any more. After their daughters eloped I think they felt disgraced. I fancy both of them suspect that people are laughing at them. Maybe they're right. There would be those who feel that the St. Georges set themselves up too high and aren't that displeased at their misfortunes."

"That would be unfair," said Bridget with a yawn. "The Mistress may look proud but she isn't. She's really a very good person. Look at all the hours she spends in her herb garden, where she grows all the special plants, and in that special room where she makes medicines from receipts she brought with her from her own home, and receipts she has learned over the years. People come to her from all around Tyrone, people who could never afford to go to a doctor. They have great faith in her, and they're very grateful to her."

"But she seems very strict to me," said Honnie, "even with her own daughters."

"Wouldn't you be strict if two of your daughters had eloped?" said Kate drowsily. "She worries all the time about the daughters she still has with her. I think she came from a very orderly house. She likes things to be orderly, everything in its own place. But she's really a very kind person."

They all fell silent at that point, and Honnie lay there staring into the darkness, wondering if she had perhaps misjudged Lady Harriet.

Preparations for Christmas started early in Tyrone, and even if Lady Harriet didn't seem to be looking forward to it, she knew that for the young people of the house it was a time for feasting and fun, and she did her best to see that long-established practices and traditions were observed.

Many head of stock had already been killed so that the spicing of the rounds of beef could be done in time for the Christmas festivities.

"We always have spiced beef at Christmas," said Bridget. "I like it better than goose or even turkey. But Mrs. Smith is very fussy about how it's spiced. The spices have to be rubbed into the meat. She always says *into* it, not just *onto* it. And the meat has to stand in barrels, in a special mixture of spices and porter, for at least six weeks before Christmas. But that's one messy job we don't have to do, thanks be to God – that's a job for the men. And then there are the turkeys and chickens, the geese and the ducks. They're being fattened up for the past two months, so they'll be good and plump come Christmastime."

"But they'll be plucked outside, won't they?" said Honnie anxiously. Her fingers still showed the marks of the pheasants she had plucked.

"Rest easy," said Bridget. "The women in the yard will do that."

"Then there are the oysters," said Josie.

"You must know all about oysters, Honnie. Don't your brothers, Seán and William, work on the Ballyinacourty oyster beds betimes? There are thousands of them taken out and kept in tanks on the shore so that the lords and ladies above can have them any time they want for luncheons or supper."

But what intrigued Honnie most of all was hearing about the men being locked in the cellars.

"Locked in?" she said. "Why so? So that they can get well and truly fluthered?"

"No," said Bridget. "They're in there bottling wines and ales for drinking over the Christmas. And if they're not locked in half the drink disappears, given out to their friends and all the people hereabouts who are fond of their gargle – and there are a lot of those, I can tell you. If Mr. Scott goes in to check and finds there are only six dozen bottles instead of seven, or ten dozen instead of twelve, he gets right furious. Of course everybody always says that they don't know anything, they didn't take anything. And Mr. Scott says he doesn't want to know who didn't, he wants to know who did. Locking them in while they're bottling is a way of trying to put an end to all that."

Honnie got a chance to take a peek at the rooms upstairs one afternoon, when the family had gone to visit the Wallscourts in Ardfry, and Mrs. Smith had gone to visit Mrs. Hunt, the housekeeper, for a cup of tea and a chat.

"Come on quickly, Honnie, before anybody sees us," said Bridget.

Of course somebody did see them as they crept up the stairs from the bowels of the kitchen to the main floor. But Hannah, one of the housemaids, was a good-natured girl, and she offered to show them around.

There was a high hall with a tiled floor. The lower part of the walls and the doors opening off the hall were panelled in a deep, dark wood, which had been lovingly polished. Honnie ran the tips of her fingers across the gleaming wood. It was silken smooth to the touch. In contrast the walls above were white, with plaster decorations of ribbons and leaves and flowers. It was all as Bridget had described it.

"There's an office and library on one side of the hall, and the morning room is on the other. But my two favourite rooms are the dining room and the drawing room," said Hannah.

Honnie could see why.

The dining room was a beautiful room, full of afternoon sunshine glimmering off the sea, lighting up the big polished table set with silver candelabra and the glowing wood of the floor. Even the gilded white fireplace seemed to reflect the sun.

But Honnie liked the drawing room best of all. The beribboned plaster figures decorating the walls looked elegant. The sofas and the chairs were upholstered in soft, gentle colours. The paintings hanging around the room were mostly of country scenes. Altogether the room had an air of gracious quiet and ease about it.

The noise of a returning carriage brought them quickly to their senses. Bridget and Honnie scurried downstairs, which was just as well, because Mrs. Smith had returned from her afternoon chat with Mrs. Hunt and was asking Josie where they were.

Honnie was able to see the kitchen gardens a few weeks later when she was sent down with Bridget to collect vegetables for the next day's meals from Johnny O'Connor, the head gardener. It was a quiet time in the garden, but there was still work to be done. There were men hoeing paths, removing moss, raking up the last of the autumn leaves. Another man was working on a seedbed. More men were in the greenhouse, scrubbing pots, preparing compost, cleaning down the sheets of glass. Bridget was very informed about activities in the gardens, and always glad of an excuse to go down there. Jimmy Ward, one of the under-gardeners, conveniently appeared as they walked down one of the paths.

"So how's Bridget today? D'you still love me as much as ever?"

"Love you? Indeed an' I don't," Bridget replied. "Why on earth would I fancy you, with so many other more handsome men around?"

"Ah Bridget, you shouldn't judge a book by its cover. I may not be the best-looking man around, but I'm a great dancer, and a greater singer, and I tell wonderful tales. There are men who can make music better than I can. But are there many men who can make you laugh the way I can?"

"Enough of your nonsense – Mrs Smith wants carrots and parsnips," said Bridget. "Onions and shallots – a few turnips, and some celery – parsley and thyme and a bit of sage, and some bay leaves. She says this is the weather for a warming stew. She wants leeks for soup, and she wants some potatoes, good sound ones. She said the ones you sent up the other day were damaged."

As they walked back to the house with their baskets piled high, Bridget stopped at the herb garden.

"We call this Lady Harriet's garden – the one I told you about," she said. "Being the time of year it is, most of the herbs have died down for the winter. But you should see it in spring and summer. You can pick a leaf and rub it in your hands and hold it up to your nose, and the smell can be so sweet. And each plant smells differently.

"Miss Olivia helps her a great deal. Everyone is very fond of Miss Olivia. People usually come to her first, and she talks to them, finds out what's bothering them, then talks to her mother to see what's best."

Honnie thought of her own mother and of the many remedies she had. She wondered if any of them were the same as Lady Harriet's. How interested her mother would be to talk to her!

When they came back in with the vegetables, Mrs. Smith eyed Bridget shrewdly. "I suppose you were out there chatting to that chancer Jimmy Ward? Have sense, Bridget. He has a great gift of the gab, but I wouldn't trust him as far as I'd throw him. He's always on the move. He worked at Ardfry before he came here, and before that he was working over beyond in Gort, and somewhere else again before that. He's got itchy feet, that young man. Don't let him fool you."

"He's not fooling me," said Bridget. "I've no feelings about him one way or the other. I just think he's funny."

"Go on out of that!" said Honnie when Mrs. Smith had gone out of the kitchen. "Admit you have a soft spot for him. "

But Bridget wasn't having any of it.

Christmas was fast approaching. There was a great feeling of anticipation in the house, but the servants had to work hard. Friends and relatives came to stay, others came calling. There seemed to be something cooking all day and half the night in the big kitchen, and the nearer it got to Christmas, the more hectic it got. And of course the more cooking that went on, the more washing-up had to be done.

Tipsy cake, plum cake, porter cake, cherry brandy, orange brandy, ginger cordial, milk punch, plum pudding, devilled fowl: Honnie got dizzy looking at all the food and drink.

On Christmas Eve there was the Christmas pie to be made. This pie was very special, Kate explained to Honnie as she laid out a turkey and a goose on a chopping board on the kitchen table.

"It's always been a tradition in Tyrone. First you bone out the turkey like I'm doing now. It's tricky enough to do. You have to keep some shape on it, because you are going to put stuffing in the empty places where the bones were. The first time I tried to bone out a turkey I made a terrible mess of it. There were bits of turkey all over the place. But Mrs. Smith said she could make a fricassee out of it and brought me another turkey and told me to try again. She stood over me while I did it, and I learned. I've got better at it over the years."

Honnie watched carefully as Kate worked. It certainly looked difficult.

"Then you do the goose the same way," said Kate as she finished stuffing the turkey, and reached out for the goose. "We use forcemeat stuffing, or bread stuffing like I'm using here, and we truss the meat and the stuffing together, like so."

She took a big flat-bottomed dish out of a cupboard. The turkey first, then a beef tongue, then the goose, were laid in it side by side. A thick gravy was poured over it all and the dish was covered.

"Now it goes into the oven to steam for two hours."

While they were waiting for the meats to cook Kate made pastry. She had a very light touch, barely handling the dough, deftly turning it and rolling it.

"We need to leave the pastry to rest for a while before we make the pie."

When the meats were judged properly cooked, they were taken out of the oven and allowed to cool.

"I won't roll out the pastry until the meats are really cool because if I put them hot onto the pastry it will make it soggy," Kate explained.

When she felt the meats had cooled sufficently, she began to roll out the pastry, one piece to line a huge pie-dish, with enough left over to put on the top. Into the lined pie-dish she put the turkey, then the tongue, and then the goose, again side by side. Beef jelly filled in the spaces, and it was all covered with a pastry crust and brushed with beaten egg

"Now we'll bake it in the oven 'til it's a nice brown," she said. "On Christmas morning it's served cold. The important thing is that it's cut lengthways, so that each person gets a little bit of tongue, a little bit of turkey and a bit of goose on their plate. And it's so big that there is usually a little bit left for us as well."

On Christmas Day, after the St. George family had returned from church, the servants were called to receive their presents in the drawing room, where the whole family was gathered.

Master Christopher had come back from Dublin, and he was standing laughing and joking with his sisters who were all looking pretty and pleased with themselves in their best finery. Master Christopher was tall, gangling, with a head of dark hair. He was seventeen going on eighteen, so Josie said, but he certainly didn't look it. He was still very much a boy, Honnie thought. His mother clearly doted on him.

Honnie, for her present, got two pairs of fine woollen stockings, presented by young Arthur with a big grin and a bow.

It was a Christmas the like of which she had never seen before, but she missed her own family sorely. She kept imagining them round the table, the excitement as they waited, the rich aroma of corned beef as her mother carried it to the able. Later in the evening the Breathnachs and the Kellys would come round. There would be storytelling around the fire and singing, and maybe a bit of dancing if Ned Breathnach, Mairtín's father, brought his fiddle – which he would of course. Not all the fine fare in the world, none of the grandeur of the big house, made up for not being at home.

Honnie wept a little in her bed that night.

The celebrations carried on into the New Year, with several midnight oyster suppers in the kitchen. The oyster suppers were another family tradition and were regarded as a particular treat of the Christmas season. The servants were less enthusiastic about it. They had worked hard over the weeks just gone, and had more than their fill of Christmas fare and Christmas festivities.

The last supper was particularly uproarious. The kitchen had been invaded by a crowd of young family members and friends. Each person was given a knife, a chunk of bread and a glass of beer, and told to help themselves. The kitchen table was covered with oysters and people ate until they could hardly see each other across the room behind the piles of empty shells. There was much laughter and joking, and even a bit of singing.

Christopher St. George seemed to be the life and soul of the party, thought Honnie, watching two young lady visitors hang on his every word.

When Christopher turned and caught her watching he smiled and raised his glass. Furious with herself, Honnie put her head in the air, and turned the other way.

It was the early hours of the morning before everybody finally left, full of oysters and drink and good humour, wishing everybody a Happy New Year.

As he passed on his way out, Christopher slipped an arm round a surprised Honnie, and kissed her on the cheek.

"Happy New Year," he said, "to the best-looking scullery maid we've had in a long while!"

Furious, Honnie raised her hand to slap his face. She was too late.

Amid cheers of merriment Christopher and his friends were already halfway up the stairs on their way out of the kitchen.

Honnie raged. "How dare he! He wouldn't do that to one of his fancy lady visitors. He thinks he can do what he likes with me because I'm a servant girl. That's the trouble with the gentry. They think they own everything, the people as well as the land. If he *ever* so much as puts a finger on me again, I'll – I'll ..."

"He shouldn't have done it," conceded Mrs. Smith. "It was the drink talking. He's normally a mannerly boy."

"Mannerly!" said Honnie. "He doesn't know what manners are."

"Pay no heed to him," said Mrs. Smith. "He was just

a bit foolish with the drink." And she went off to bed.

"And who is left to do the tidying and the washing-up?" said Josie. "Us."

Josie started tidying the kitchen while Bridget and Honnie brought the glasses, mugs, plates, and knives into the scullery to be washed.

"And it's us who will have to get up at the crack of dawn tomorrow – or should I say today – not like some people," said Josie sourly.

"Oh well, I hid a few oysters away for ourselves," said Bridget. "And some beer."

"I, for one, don't want any oysters," said Honnie. "So you can have my share. They always taste like seaweed to me. But I'll take the beer surely."

"Some people just don't understand that oysters are a taste you have to acquire," said Josie. "The more you eat, the more you like them."

"Well, I've tasted them over in Ballinacourty a number of times," said Honnie, "and I've never acquired a liking for them. The beer, now, that's a different matter entirely."

But, as Bartley Kane had said, Mrs. Smith's bark was worse than her bite. In the middle of January, when all the festivities were over, she had Kate make a big plum cake and, wrapping it firmly in a linen cloth, she told Honnie she could have a day off to take it home to her mother.

"Just mind you bring me back the cloth," she said.

Kate smuggled her some raisins and nuts "for the little ones" and a few sweets she had saved from a Christmas present. And Mrs. Smith gave her some beer for her father.

Honnie was overjoyed and hardly knew how to thank them for their kindness.

It was good to see her family again. It felt longer than two months to Honnie since she had left home. Bran jumped up, then rolled over on her back so that Honnie could scratch her tummy. Everybody asked questions at the same time.

William and Seán wanted to hear all about Tyrone.

"Do you have to work very hard? Is Mrs. Smith as cross as people say she is? How much will you be paid?"

Kathleen and Maureen wanted to know about the house.

"Is it very grand inside? Do they all wear very fancy clothes? Do you get all sorts of good things to eat? Did you bake the cake yourself?"

Her two youngest brothers, Thady and Joseph, were more interested in what she'd brought with her.

The day passed quickly, and it was getting dark when she started back, with her brother William to keep her company.

It was a slate-grey evening. The clouds loured above them, sleet-filled. The countryside looked barren. Leafless thorn trees crouched eastwards, their backs to the prevailing wind. As they passed through Kilcolgan the weir murmured sullenly, but voices and the sound of laughter came from the candlelit window of Moran's Inn.

They talked about William's life and what he would like to do with it. He could see no future for himself in Ireland.

"I'm grateful to Mairtín for giving me the chance, but I don't want to spend my life going out fishing day after day, in all kinds of weather. I've no appetite for it. I want to grow things, work on the land, but on my own land. That's never going to happen in this benighted country. It's Canada for me, or maybe America as soon as I can scrape the fare together. That's going to take me a year or more."

"Mammy would be heartbroken," said Honnie. "And so would I. We'd never see you again."

They were silent for some minutes before moving on to talk about their mother and her joy in growing things, and their father and his love of horses.

"He's been over a good few times since I've been in Tyrone," said Honnie. "Himself and Mick Murphy are as thick as thieves. They spend hours talking about the different horses, their good points and their bad points."

"I've heard you're not too far behind yourself," said William. "Even Father has respect for your judgement of horseflesh. And I hear Mick was impressed as well."

"They're beautiful animals," said Honnie. "I love the awkward grace they have about them when they're born, and watching them with their mothers, and the way the mares mind them. And Mick is a marvel the way he can handle young animals. They seem to take to him immediately."

"Mick does seem to have a magic touch with horses all right," said William.

"He's been kind to me," said Honnie. "He lets me spend time in the yards the odd minute or two I can get away. I can tell you, it's wonderful to get out of those hot, steamy kitchens, even for a short while."

They had almost reached Tyrone House.

William stopped and turned to Honnie.

"Mind how you go, Honnie," he said. "Your place is in the kitchens, not in the stables. Mammy is pleased you've got a start in Tyrone. She thinks you can better yourself, move up in the world. You won't disappoint her, will you?"

"You know I won't," Honnie said.

"Mind how you go now," he said again and, giving her a quick hug, he set off for home.

Chapter 3

As the months passed Honnie became adept at peeling potatoes and preparing vegetables in the sculleries of Tyrone House. She learnt how to pluck a bird neatly and cleanly, but it was never one of her favourite tasks. She mastered the intricacies of the range, and the pots and pans shone from her attention. Her hands were so sore from all the washing and the soda in the water that they cracked and bled. She tried soaking them in buttermilk at the end of the day, but it never got time to work properly because next morning she would have to put them back in the water again.

"And there isn't much you can do about that," said Bridget.

Honnie learned to listen carefully to any requests that came down from Lady Harriet, because she knew there would be recriminations if they weren't met promptly.

Lady Harriet was known to have a short temper.

"But then," as Mrs. Smith said, "she's never been the

same since Miss Emilia and Miss Elizabeth ran away. She doesn't talk much about them, but she worries about them all the same. And she worries about this big old house and all the people in it. She's near wore out with worry. The Master's a nice man, but it's the Mistress does the minding and the managing and the worrying. She was used to things being done properly where she grew up. And you have to remember her father was an earl ..."

"As if we are ever let forget," muttered Josie, her voice getting louder as she continued. "She's just plain stiff with pride. If she hadn't thought that nobody was good enough for her daughters, maybe Miss Emilia and Miss Isabella wouldn't have run off the way they did. And now the Master is looking for more titles –"

"Josie! Don't ever let me hear you speak about the Mistress like that again," said Mrs. Smith sharply. "Or you'll find yourself looking for another place, and without a reference. Your tongue will be the ruin of you yet."

"But it's true what I said about the Mistress," said Josie later that evening when she and Honnie and Bridget were on their own. "If any of her daughters so much as look twice at a man, she's there, hovering over them."

"But Lady Harriet seemed happy enough to see Miss Mary marry Mr. Cuff of Creagh," said Honnie. That was just a few months after she came there. "I know it was a quiet wedding, but Lady Harriet and Mr. St. George seemed pleased."

"That's as may be," said Josie. "The Cuffs were old family friends. But Lady Harriet has higher hopes for her other daughters."

After a really hectic day in the kitchen, Honnie would

escape out to fresh air, the stable yard and the horses, for even a few minutes. She often thought longingly of the days when she had been able to ride out on one of the Kellys' horses. A good gallop across open country was one of the best pleasures life could offer.

When they saw her coming, the horses in the stables would neigh in greeting. She sometimes managed to smuggle them a carrot, or an apple or two, from under Mrs. Smith's sharp gaze. If she was feeling annoyed with Mrs. Smith, or cross with Josie, or just plain tired, a soft nose nuzzling her hands, a horse's warm breath on her face, immediately soothed her.

Some horses were special. She had a great fondness for Cowslip, a particularly gentle and sweet-tempered chestnut mare ridden out on occasion by Miss Olivia. She was the mare on which learner riders were first mounted. She seemed to sense their nervousness and do her best to make learning easy for them, yet once someone had learned to ride Cowslip could go at a brisk gallop. She was a good mother as well and had produced some worthwhile foals.

And then there was Barebones, a three-year-old chestnut horse, full of energy, with life and spirit. Honnie thought he would surely go on to win important races in the years to come. She felt he was special – you only had to look at the way he moved, with such freedom and ease, and the real power in him when he got going. Mick Murphy was disposed to agree with her and reckoned he'd go far. And Barebones was Christopher's favourite horse, the horse he rode most of the time.

The only horse that Honnie disliked was Necromancer, whose temper had not improved. The only two people who seemed to have any control over him were Mick and Master Christopher. Even Mick, who was disposed to like most horses, and who had been so impressed by Neromncer in his early days, had grown to dislike him. But Christopher was determined to win him over, show him who was master. Whenever he came home on holiday from his studies, he was straight out to the stables to Necromancer.

Honnie worked hard and learned a great deal. She learned to enjoy food the likes of which she had never tasted before. She learned how to eat in what Mrs. Smith called "a mannerly fashion". Sitting at the lower reaches of the table in the servants' hall, she quietly watched what the others did, how they ate, the cutlery they used and how they used it. She tasted good wine and, once, champagne, bubbles rising up through the hollow stem of delicate glass, sneaked out to her after a family party by Robert, one of the footmen.

"Robert is quite fanciable in a 'broth of a boy' kind of way," Honnie said to Bridget, "but he flirts with almost every pretty girl who crosses his path. I might flirt a little with him myself, just for a bit of fun, but nothing more. He has no interest in me nor I in him."

"He comes from Cork, just down the road from the Blarney Stone, and he's full of blarney all right! But he has a way with him," said Bridget. "And he's had his way with more than one girl in the parish. But you'd want to watch yourself there. You must know Josie has a bit of a *grá* for Robert. She likes to think of him as her property – not that he's ever given her any reason. She'd be less than pleased to hear that he was bringing you glasses of champagne."

"I never asked him to," said Honnie.

But Bridget was right. Josie knew Robert never saw her as worth his notice, but that didn't stop her dreaming. When he threw her a chance smile her heart leapt. She thought about him as she lay in bed at night. She looked forward to her first sight of him each morning.

Josie fancied Robert, and Seamus the kitchen boy fancied Honnie.

Every day Seamus was in and out of the kitchen on various chores. It seemed to Honnie that she was always tripping over him. Nothing seemed to discourage him. One day he came up behind her, as she stood at the sink, and put his arms around her in a very familiar fashion.

Honnie jumped away as though she'd been bitten.

"You do that once more and I'll *puck* you, really hard!" she said angrily.

But nothing appeared to dim Seamus's ardour. Every chance he got to visit the kitchen, he was there, hanging around at Honnie's heels, making sheep's eyes at her, as Bridget said.

Everyone else in the kitchen thought it was funny, and kept teasing her about her "admirer".

"One of these days I really will clout him," she said. "I'm finding it harder and harder to resist the temptation."

Josie was the only one who was not amused.

"Man-mad, you are, Honnie, and no mistake. Wherever I turn you're there flirting with anything in trousers that happens along. If it isn't Robert, it's Seamus, or the garden boy or Paddy who brings the fish."

"The garden boy!" said Honnie. "Paddy who brings the fish! I can't believe my ears. What rubbish!"

"Don't mind her," said Bridget. "She's just jealous."

What fascinated Honnie more than anything else was cooking. Any spare minute she had, she spent watching Mrs. Smith and Kate and Josie and Bridget preparing the different meals of the day – Bridget had been promoted from scullery maid to kitchenmaid. But Mrs. Smith could see that Honnie wanted to learn, so she let her help the other girls from time to time – though she was always reminded that her real place, for the present, was in the scullery.

Chapter 4

Then in the New Year of 1829, just a year and a bit after she had first come to Tyrone, Mrs. Smith told Honnie that she was going to be a kitchenmaid. Kate was leaving to marry her childhood sweetheart, Muiris Rooney, a fisherman who lived near Kilcolgan Weir, a few miles down the road from Tyrone. Honnie was to be the third kitchenmaid. She was delighted.

"Becoming Mrs. Smith's *peata,* aren't you?" said Josie. "Pretending you're mad to learn all about cooking. Well, she may be taken in by you, but I'm not. Maybe you think if you make up to Mrs. Smith you'll have an easier life and get off some of the worst chores. Well, you won't. You're going to be making the bread, beating the eggs for cakes – and that's some job I can tell you. You'll be in charge of all the stock-pots – oh, and you'll be skinning eels – you'll love that. They're all the jobs I had to do as third kitchenmaid."

"You're not going to take the joy out of it for me,"

said Honnie. "I want to learn and I'm going to learn."

She was determined to work hard. But, if she worked hard, Mrs. Smith worked just as hard. She had to admit that Mrs. Smith wasn't one of her favourite people, but she was developing a certain respect for her.

Honnie often came to bed completely exhausted. Bridget would chide her.

"What are you trying to prove? That you can work harder than anyone else in the house?"

"I just want to show her that I may be an Irish countrygirl without much education, but it doesn't mean I'm not able to learn as well and better than any of those girls in the Big Houses across the water she's always talking about," said Honnie.

The fact was that Honnie loved trying her hand at making some of the things she had seen the others make. She loved the lemon sponge cake that Josie sometimes made. It had a light, delicious sweetness that creamed against the roof of your mouth, and melted with a sharp sting of lemon. Now she learned that, simple and all as it looked, it cost quite a bit of work. The yolks and the whites of ten eggs had to be beaten with a whisk for up to an hour, with three quarters of a pound of sifted sugar. As the newest kitchen maid – just as Josie had said – she had to do most of the beating, and it felt more like ten hours than one.

"That's one of the reasons I've fine strong arms – small and all as I am," said Bridget. "But if you don't get the mixture really stiff and creamy before you add the flour, then you get a sponge cake that isn't a sponge cake at all – more like a tough pancake."

The plum cake was a different kind of hard work.

First there was a long list of ingredients.

"Six pounds of currants have to be washed and dried before the fire, because if they're not dry they'll make the cake heavy," said Josie. "You have to stand a half pound of almonds in boiling water for a few minutes, and then they have to be peeled and chopped. You need two pounds of butter, two pounds of sugar, two pounds of flour and twenty eggs. Then a half-pound of candied peel and a half-pound of citron peel have to be cut into tiny strips. And the butter has to be beaten with the sugar until it is a light cream colour."

She handed a big bowl with the sugar and butter in it to Honnie.

"And that's where you come in," she said and went to gather up more ingredients.

During Honnie's first days as kitchenmaid there seemed to be visitors above stairs every second day. If it wasn't butter and sugar she was beating, it was sugar and eggs she was whisking. Every evening her right shoulder ached.

"It's because you're using your whole arm, girl," sad Mrs. Smith. "Beat from the wrist, whisk from the wrist."

The eels were a worse task. They were brought into the kitchen and then laid on a slab of ice in the larder until needed. When Josie first asked Honnie to fetch an eel from the larder she got the fright of her life. She picked up what looked like a dead creature, and the eel, revived by the heat of her hands, began to wriggle frantically. Mrs. Smith quickly grabbed it before it fell to the floor.

"You weren't to know," she said. "I'm sure you've

never handled an eel before and you couldn't know what to do. Josie should have warned you."

Expertly she secured the eel to a block of wood with a fork and split the skin around its neck. Then she gripped the skin tightly and pulled downwards until the whole of it came off. It clearly took muscle and strength, but Mrs. Smith seemed to do it in a matter of seconds. Honnie didn't think she'd ever get used to skinning eels.

There were the special meals which had to be prepared for Lady Harriet. "She's eating like a bird," said Bridget. "She'll ask for something, and then when she gets it she has no appetite for it. I don't know what's wrong with her but she's not a well woman."

One day it was calf's foot jelly Josie was making, and the next something called "A Strengthening Medicine". She read out the recipe.

"'*Put two newlaid eggs without breaking them into a bowl. Squeeze over them the juice of two lemons, and cover close for two or three days till the shells are almost dissolved. Then beat up well and take out any skin or shell that may remain. Add a pint of good old rum, a quarter pound of sugar candy, well pounded, and two tablespoonfuls of the finest salad oil.*'"

"That sounds truly horrible!" said Honnie.

"'*Strain the mixture and put into a bottle,*" Josie continued. "*Shake well before using. Take half a wineglass with a little cold water every morning.*'" Then Josie feigned an accent similar to Lady Harriet's. "*It is really most excellent for loss of strength!*"

"But none of her treatments seem to be doing her any good," said Honnie.

Dr. Veitch came out from Galway and prescribed

various other medications. But she seemed to be getting weaker rather than stronger.

Her daughters all helped to care for her, but Olivia was especially attentive, sitting with her when she felt particularly unwell, reading to her in the evenings when she found it hard to sleep.

Honnie liked Miss Olivia. Of all the daughters in the house she was the one who had shown her particular kindness. She smiled when they met in passing, and once when Honnie had a bad cold she had come down to the kitchen with a cough bottle she herself had made up from a receipt of her mother's.

And she had given Honnie one of her old shawls, which wasn't really old at all, but Miss Olivia said the deep purple colour suited Honnie's looks more than it did her.

"That colour is too strong for me. It makes me look pasty. I want you to have it."

Mrs. Smith didn't approve.

"Don't start giving yourself airs and graces, now, my girl," she said, "just because Miss Olivia has been kind to you. She's kind to everybody, God love her. That shawl is to be put away and worn only when you are going to church or visiting your home."

But in the shared bedroom that evening Honnie couldn't resist showing the shawl off to the other girls.

'It's the nicest thing I have ever had to wear," she said, twirling around. "Everything my mother made for me was fine, but it was always made to be practical and hard-wearing. This is so beautiful. It's as light as a feather but still so warm and the colour reminds me of spring violets!"

Josie looked on sourly. "If you want my honest opinion, I don't think the colour suits you particularly well. It makes you look ... showy."

Chapter 5

The Christmas of that year was not a happy one. It was normally Lady Harriet's favourite time of year, and in the weeks leading up to Christmas Day she had done her best to give instructions from her daybed. But when the day came, although she made a special effort to come down for dinner, she had picked at her food, taken two sips of champagne, then asked Olivia to help her back to bed.

Almost daily now, Dr. Veitch came out from Galway.

In the New Year, 1830, at the end of January, Christopher was summoned home from Dublin.

Coming into the sickroom one evening with a bowl of beef tea which Mrs. Smith had sent up, Honnie heard Lady Harriet asking again and again for Isabella and Emilia.

"Where are they? When will they come?"

Anne and Olivia, sitting at either side of the bed, looked at each other uneasily and wondered what they should say.

"They'll be here soon, Mother," said Olivia finally.

"They didn't understand," she kept saying. "They thought I was being too strict, but I only wanted the best for them. They were flighty. I only wanted to save them from hurt ..."

Looking at her, Honnie could see that death was near, already sucking her life away.

She died early in February, as the first snowdrops and crocuses were coming up on the lawns beneath her bedroom window.

Arthur St. George was devastated. He and Lady Harriet had been married for almost thirty years. For most of that time she had never been seriously ill. True, she had occasionally suffered from chest inflammations but she had always recovered rapidly.

"You know, I don't think the Master ever believed that she was going to die," Honnie said to Bridget. "He kept telling himself that she would get better. Now he can't believe she's dead."

"Poor man," said Mrs. Smith. "She looked after him so well, attending to his every need and shielding him from domestic concerns. Now he's left alone to worry about his children and their futures."

"I suspect he is also cross with Miss Isabella and Miss Emilia for the hurt they caused her," said Bridget. "She worried so much about them. That kind of worry can make you sick."

"Poor man," Mrs. Smith said again. "There he is, wandering around the house like a lost soul, telling everyone how much he's going to miss her."

Out in the yard Biddy the Wash had her own story to tell.

"I knew it for days," she said to any passer-by who stopped to listen. "Didn't I hear the banshee the other night, and she keening away. She was sitting on that pile of rocks forninst the water below the house, keening away and combing her hair. A terrible sound it was, I can tell you."

"What was wrong with you was too much poteen, and what you saw was a trick of the moonlight," said Mrs. Smith who had come out to see what all the hubbub in the yard was about. She knew the girls in the kitchen would be disposed to believe every word. They would soon be seeing things themselves, if she didn't put a stop to it. "What you heard was a fox calling to its mate."

Biddy's great bulk shook with rage. "'Twas no fox," she said. "I saw what I saw, I heard what I heard. And it's very unlucky to be casting aspersions on the banshee. You'll be bringing bad luck on yourself surely, mark my words."

"Away with you, Biddy!" said Mrs. Smith. "Away with you and your *banshee* nonsense!"

"What happens, happens," said Biddy. "Doesn't everyone know that when there's a death in the St. George family, the swans from Kilcolgan are seen standing near the family vault? Waiting for the mourners. And weren't they waiting there the day Lady Harriet was dying, a whole flock of them? Explain that to me now. And weren't the carrion crows perched on the windowsills of the house, and neither man nor mortal could frighten them away. How do you explain that?"

"There's no explaining to be done," said Mrs. Smith. "The crows were there because they're gathering for nesting. And I'm sure the swans gather there many a time, only nobody notices until somebody dies. Now off with you, Biddy, and go easy on the poteen you have hidden in your apron pocket, or you never know what you might see crossing the yard."

Biddy left, muttering to herself.

One day, a week after the funeral, Honnie felt she had to get out of the house for a while.

"Mrs. Smith has gone to her room for a rest. She's still tired after all the work with the funeral," she said to Bridget. "I just need some fresh air and a bit of space to myself. I won't be long."

In the trees the birds were in a bustle of nest-building. The sap was rising in the hedgerows, and the grass was greening.

Honnie walked down behind the house, to where the Kilcogan river flowed into the sea, and sat down at the end of the little pier where the turf-boats came in from Connemara. She gazed out towards Ballinacourty on the far side of the bay. Her home was over there, towards the north of that peninsula.

"You're enjoying the day, I see," said a voice, and Honnie swung around to find Christopher St. George looking down at her, his dog Rua, a Red Setter named for his red coat, by his side.

She scrambled quickly to her feet and said the first words that came into her head.

"I'm sorry for your trouble, Master Christopher. There is nothing I can say that can make any difference … but I'm sorry, real sorry …"

"She suffered a lot," he said. "If I had known she was so bad I would have come back from Dublin sooner. I feel I missed out on time with her ... and now the time has gone. But at least she isn't in pain any more. I still find it hard it believe that she is dead."

Honnie could think of nothing to say. She felt awkward and embarrassed. If Mrs. Smith heard she'd been talking with Master Christopher she'd be in for a scolding.

"I'd best get back," she said, "or Mrs. Smith will have my life. But I'm right sorry again about your mother."

And she turned away and walked quickly towards the kitchen.

Somebody had seen her. Seamus, the kitchen boy, had followed Honnie from a distance. He was back at the house before her – with a somewhat exaggerated version of what he'd seen.

"Honnie is down below there, alongside the water, talking away to Master Christopher as if she's known him all her life," he told the kitchen at large. "Just talking away to him, she is, as though she'd nothing else to do."

"Well, there's plenty for her to do," said Josie. "While she's out there making a fool of herself, there's soup to be made, and a sponge cake, and a fruit cake, and biscuits are needed in case we have more visitors, and dinner still has to be prepared. And she's out there disporting herself."

Honnie heard the last of this tirade as she returned to the kitchen.

"Disporting myself?" she said. "Is that what you call it? I went out for ten minutes to get a breath of fresh air. You can do nothing in this place. Were you following me, Seamus?"

Seamus had the grace to look ashamed.

"I might have guessed. Have you nothing better to do with your time? I'm sore sick of you *haunting* me."

He mumbled something and went out of the kitchen.

Mrs Smith, returning from her rest sooner than expected, caught the end of Honnie's response.

"What's all this about?"

"She was out there talking to Master Christopher," said Josie. "Seamus saw them himself."

Mrs Smith's mouth tightened. "I hope, Honnie, that you aren't going out looking for trouble. Because if it's trouble you want, it's easily found, and nowhere more easily than with Christopher St. George. He's had an eye for the girls since he was a boy, and he's still not much more than one. There's many a girl around here who's had her head turned by him and been sorry afterwards. I hope you're not going to be silly enough to fall for an easy manner and a handsome face."

"Don't worry – he'll be married off soon enough to some high-up lady," said Josie. "Mr. St. George has big hopes for young Master Christopher. He was a long time waiting for him, with six little girls coming before him. I've heard his parents were so happy that at his christening they gave a great party for their relatives, their friends, their neighbours and all the tenantry. There were upwards of eight hundred people present and the tables were laden with beef and mutton and porter and ale and all kinds of good things, as much as anybody could eat or drink. His Grace the Duke of Leinster was one of the sponsors. I can tell you, Mr. St. George wouldn't be at all pleased to hear that Master Christopher was dallying with a kitchenmaid."

"That's quite enough, Josie," said Mrs. Smith. "Get on with your work."

"He was not *dallying* with me!" Honnie said furiously. "He said it was a nice day. I said I was sorry about his mother. And that was an end to it. I never heard such silly *raiméis* in my life. There's no doubt but people have little to talk about when they can make up stories like that. And from *Seamus*! You'd think the lot of you would have more sense."

"Keep a civil tongue in your head, my girl," said Mrs. Smith. "And mark my words. I want to hear no more stories about you, or you'll be out of here in the blink of an eyelid. Now go and prepare the hares for tomorrow's soup. It needs doing straight away so that they can be put on to cook first thing in the morning. They have to cook for four or five hours. Mind you save the liver and as much blood as possible for flavour."

She just gave me the hares to do because she knows I hate skinning them, thought Honnie angrily, but she had enough sense to bite back the retort that sprang to her lips.

Josie had to have the last word. "Master Christopher will not be around to dally with for a while anyway," she said. "He has to go back to the college in Dublin to finish his studies."

After the fuss had died down, and Mrs. Smith had gone to talk to Mrs Hunt, Bridget came and put her arm around Honnie.

"Pay no heed to the lot of them," she said. "Mrs. Smith is just in a bad humour today. Josie used to upset me, but now I take no notice. Try not to let her get to you. She hasn't had much happiness in her life. Her mother passed away when she was born, and her father died of consumption soon after. She was reared by an uncle and aunt who were very hard on her. They didn't show her much kindness, just put her out to work, day in, day out. She was lucky to get a position here, and she spent five years in the sculleries before she became a kitchenmaid. I don't think any man has ever paid her any attention. Josie is … curdled. Now, come on, I'll help you with the hares."

Chapter 6

Christopher's career in Trinity had been somewhat chequered. After a brilliant first year the Provost and Senior Fellows of the College awarded a prize ***"to a noble young man of great hope, Christopher St. George, on account of his outstanding progress in Classics in attaining a first class at the examination held in Trinity Term 1828".*** But after that first year the delights and diversions of Dublin proved more attractive than poring over books. For him, and other like-minded young men, free and on their own in a big city, the distractions were many. His grades went down. But in his final year he decided to put his head down and try to make up for the lost years. With one exception – he would go home for his 21st birthday celebrations. A big party was planned for the 15th March. His father said it was only right that it should be celebrated. "His mother would have wished it so, and she will be here with us in spirit."

"It will cost a pretty penny and a lot of work," said

Mrs. Smith. "I hear half the county is being invited. And you can be sure the Master will see to it that some suitable young ladies are invited to attend – marriageable girls from good families who are known to have a nice fat dowry. But, sure, it will be nice to have a bit of jollity in the place again. We haven't had a party here for years, her Ladyship being unwell."

As plans for the event got under way, Tyrone became a bustling hive of activity. The house was cleaned from top to bottom, furniture examined, refreshed, repaired, menus discussed. Garden paths were hoed, gravel spread, early grass trimmed back, flowerbeds weeded and tidied.

Mrs. Smith spent a great deal of time conferring with Christopher's sisters, Miss Anne and Miss Olivia in particular, about the food to be served. Mr. Scott retired to the cellars to choose the wines.

In the days immediately before the event the house was decorated with garlands, and the night before the party with spring flowers.

The night of the party the whole house was lit up with thousands of candles.

"I'm sure it can be seen the far side of Galway Bay," said Bridget, "like it used to be."

Naturally, Honnie and Bridget wanted to see the guests arriving, and as carriage after carriage drew up on the gravel sweep in front of the house, they worked out a way to escape in turn and creep up the back stairs, so they could peep through the door to the hall and see the guests in their finery.

It must be wonderful, Honnie thought, to dress up in splendid clothes and spend a whole evening being waited on hand and foot, and served fine food prepared by somebody else, and never have to worry about cleaning up afterwards.

But there was so much to be done in the kitchen that Honnie and Bridget's brief expeditions up the stairs were few and far between. Mrs. Smith had got three local girls in to help prepare the birthday banquet, and the extra help had been well worthwhile.

The evening was clearly a success. After the guests had dined and wined, the dancing started. The sounds of music, merriment and laughter floated downstairs to the kitchen.

"And now we can have our own party," said Bridget.

The tables in the servants' hall were laden with good food and drink and, when everyone had eaten their fill, all the furniture was pushed back to the sides of the room, and the dancing began.

Halfway through the evening Master Christopher came down to join them. He helped himself to a glass of wine and raised his glass.

"Let's drink to a great day and a great party!" he said.

They all wished him a happy birthday, and he thanked them for all their hard work.

Honnie watched as he talked in turn to everyone in the room. He paid particular attention to Mrs. Smith, telling her what a wonderful cook she was and how lucky they were to have her.

The boy Honnie had first seen more than three years ago had become a man. He had filled out. He was tall, broad-shouldered and his dark hair and very blue eyes were – she had to admit – very attractive.

She was not to know that Christopher had been

thinking similar thoughts about her. The girl he had first admired three years ago had become a woman, tall, straight-backed, full-bodied. Her dark chestnut hair was still curling out of her cap and her brown eyes still had a flicker of the fire he had seen that New Year's Eve three years ago.

When he had gone back upstairs, the dancing started in earnest.

Robert asked Honnie if she would like to dance. But Honnie thanked him and said her feet needed a rest, and she needed something to quench her thirst. Robert got her a drink, and then turned to Josie who was sitting nearby.

"How about a dance, Josie?" he said.

Honnie watched them as they joined in a set dance and saw the look of pure bliss on Josie's face.

Later that night, as they were going to bed, Honnie could see Josie was still in a whirl of happiness, no doubt remembering her dance with Robert, his hands touching hers, his face smiling down at her.

What must it be like, Honnie wondered, to feel like that about somebody? Josie didn't need any more unhappiness in her life. But Robert wasn't going to bring her happiness, of that Honnie was sure.

Next day, catching Josie on her own for a few minutes, Honnie decided on impulse to try to talk to her.

"Josie, I want you to know that whatever you might think I honestly and truly have no interest in Robert, and I know he has no interest in me. And I know you like him, Josie. But I don't believe he's the right man for you."

Josie looked suspiciously at her. "Why are you telling me all this, Honnie? I don't need your advice or concern. I can take care of myself, thank you. It's very easy for someone to get a bad reputation. That doesn't mean they deserve it."

That evening, as they discussed the party after the day's work was finished, Mrs. Smith asked Robert if Christopher had shown any preference for any of the lady guests at his party.

"More than a few of the lady visitors were casting an eye over Master Christopher. He danced with them all, but showed no special favour for anyone," said Robert. "And some of them come with good dowries. Mr. St. George must be hoping that young Christopher will make a good match. A sizeable dowry would be most welcome, and much needed, here in Tyrone."

The spring of 1831 was good. The days grew longer, the sunlight came warm and luminous from the sea. Everywhere there was new life – skittish lambs playing their elaborate games, doe-eyed young calves, trees exploding into pale green leaf.

Honnie's visits to the stable yards continued and were a source of considerable amusement in the kitchen.

"You'll be wanting to go horse-riding yourself next," said Bridget. "Should we all save up to buy you a riding habit for next Christmas?"

Mrs. Smith was more indulgent. "Leave the girl alone," she said. "There's nothing wrong with admiring fine creatures."

"That would depend on whether they were animals or men," said Josie.

In fact, Bridget had come nearer to the truth than she realized. Honnie's visits to the stables had taken a different turn in recent months. There was a new groom in the yard, called Nicky Reilly. He was, Mick Murphy said, a natural with animals. He was rather taken with Honnie, and it was he who suggested one quiet May afternoon that Honnie might like to see what it felt like to ride one of the St. George horses.

"Cowslip there would give you a nice gallop," he said. "And nobody need be the wiser. Master Christopher is above in Dublin, the Master has gone in to Galway, and Miss Olivia's not riding at the moment because she's not been so well. Cowslip needs the exercise. You can meet me in the field at the far side of the copse beyond. Nobody'll see us over there."

Honnie could not resist such an offer. She ignored the voices in her head which told her that this was a very unwise course on which to embark, and that news of her exploit was sure to get around. On this occasion she felt that temptation was not to be resisted. She embraced it with open arms.

That afternoon was the first of a quite a few similar afternoons. Up on a horse's back, Honnie felt free. It was good to be alive. But in her heart she knew that each time she went out riding she was taking a huge chance. There was very little you could do in Tyrone that wasn't noticed and talked about.

Chapter 7

Christopher was back in Tyrone for good in June. His studies had been completed, not with the promise of his first year, but he had managed to get a BA degree.

His father met him in the big front hall one morning, some days after his return.

"It's so good seeing you back home, Christopher," said Arthur. "And this time for good. It gives me great ease of mind to know that you are going to be here with me, and we can try to deal with all the problems and affairs of the estate together. I'm afraid there are a lot of debts, money borrowed, loans to be repaid . . ."

"Father, I'm really sorry, but just at this moment I am about to go off with three of my sisters to a picnic party at Ardfry. They're waiting for me. They are very excited. I'm not trying to get out of helping you, but could we talk about it another time?

"Of course – of course we could," said his father.

Afterwards, when Arthur thought about it, maybe he

had been a bit premature. Christopher was only a few weeks home from college and he was enjoying his newfound freedom. It would be unfair to load him down immediately with worries about all the responsibilities he would have to face in the future. He was like a young colt let out on new grass. He was still only a boy, out to enjoy himself. He'd put these matters aside, wait 'til the boy was more settled.

But Chistopher couldn't sleep that night, thinking about his father and his problems. He couldn't remember a time when his father hadn't been worried about money. There were always loans to be paid, money being borrowed. Debts seemed to be mounting up all the time. The death of his mother had hit his father hard. He had relied on her completely. He was beginning to look like an old man. He wasn't able to go out and about his estates as he had been accustomed to do.

Christopher thought of all the mounds of papers in his father's study. The idea of having to go through them, trying to find a way out when there was no way out, made his heart sink. Nor did he want to listen to the vicissitudes of bygone years, the difficulties his father had experienced. He had heard it all before, many times. But he would have to help his father. The question was how.

He had enjoyed the picnic party. He smiled in recollection. It had been fun, even if he had – perhaps – drunk a little more wine than he should have.

He rolled over and went to sleep.

The picnic party had been given by Colonel Hales and the officers of the 28th regiment, who were stationed in Galway. As the *Galway Independent* reported: "A select

number of the beauty, rank, and fashion of Galway and its vicinity were invited. The band of the regiment were in attendance and occasionally executed some beautiful pieces of Italian music."

"Doesn't that sound really grand?" said Josie after Mr. Scott had read out the piece from the paper next day.

"I heard there was too much drinking altogether at that picnic," said Mrs. Smith. "It wasn't a place for the likes of Miss Anne and Miss Matilda and Miss Harriet. I doubt if the Mistress would have let them go, certainly not on their own."

"But they weren't on their own," said Mick. "They had Master Christopher with them. He'd see they came to no harm."

"Master Christopher is hard put to mind himself, never mind look after anybody else," said Mrs. Smith. "When he came back here after the picnic he'd had a right skinful, I can tell you."

"Arrah, 'twas all harmless fun for the most part, just young people enjoying themselves," said Mick. "And Master Christopher was celebrating getting free of all that studying he had to do in the college in Dublin. And wasn't he up bright and early this morning, exercising Barebones? Now there's a horse that'll go places! He's got the makings of a true winner. Not like that brute Necromancer – that horse could bring him harm."

"Master Christopher is not long back from the races in Howth, and now he's off to more races, in the Curragh, and probably in Cahir," said Mrs. Smith. "And whatever other race meeting there is after that, until the hunting season starts again. If only his poor mother was alive – but there, she's gone, poor lady, more's the pity.

Master Christopher never thinks of anything but horses. If he spent half the energy and time about the business of his estates that he spends on horses, the Master would be happier, and the place would be better off. And he treats the men in the yard like his own kith and kin. No good can come of that."

But Christopher had not forgotten about his father. He thought a lot about him. One day at the end of July, he decided to seek him out and ask him him in what way he could best help him. He found him where he was always to be found – in his study, surrounded, as usual, by papers.

"Father, I want to help you, but I'm not sure how. You have run this estate for many years, travelled around from one part of it to another, for one reason and another for most of your life. But you are not really able for these chores any more. Nor should you be expected to travel hither and thither tryng to sort out problems, many of them probably simple problems, which I could learn to handle."

"I've been thinking too," said Arthur. "You need to learn about the running of the estate. You need to get to know the tenants, and all the other people who live and work here – you need to talk to them, listen to them. The best way you can do it is by travelling around with Danny Murray, who has been my right-hand man for many years. He knows this estate inside out, he knows all our tenants, and they like him and respect him. He is a fount of information and local knowledge. I have spoken to him, and he is happy to help."

And so it was arranged that Christopher would ride out with Danny at least once a week – a learning experience – something he soon began to enjoy and even look forward to.

Chapter 8

July had been very wet. August turned the tables. It was very dry and very hot.

Then William came to see Honnie at Tyrone. At first she was alarmed but he quickly assured her all was well at home. With Mrs. Smith's permission, she walked with him in the grounds for a short while. They walked down past the walled vegetable garden and the orchards, past the big ricks of turf brought in from Connemara and out onto the little pier near the mouth of the Kilcolgan river.

When William didn't volunteer an explanation as to why he had come to see her, she became increasing uneasy, an unwelcome suspicion lurking in the back of her mind. She was puzzled when he began to talk at length about Christopher St. George who, he argued, had an overabundance of good fortune.

"There he is," he concluded bitterly, "with all the time and money in the world, and nothing to do but enjoy himself. He can get up of a morning, and go horseriding, or fishing or shooting – or do nothing at all. He can take himself off to a race meeting, or go on a jaunt to Dublin, or take his pick of any girl hereabouts. When he wants something, all he has to do is put his hand in his pocket or ask his father."

At this, he halted and turned to her.

"And what's facing me, Honnie?" he asked. "The emigrant ship. I came to tell you that I'm off next month."

Her heart sank.

"Things are very bad in Galway town, Honnie. You're hardly ever in there, but you should see the people in the streets, not just old and sick people, but young people like yourself who can't get work. Things are bad all over the county. They say there's close on a hundred thousand people and more living on public bounty now. You're lucky, Honnie, to be here with a roof over your head and plenty of food to eat."

"I work hard enough for it," said Honnie sharply. "I'm up at the crack of dawn, and hardly sit down the live-long day, always at Mrs. Smith's beck and call."

"Honnie, I'm telling you, there is many a girl walking the roads of Galway who would be happy to have the work you have, to have food to eat and a bed to sleep in. There are people out there, families, living on cabbages and weeds. There are people selling every possession they've got to get food for their children. I've been able to earn some money myself, but it hasn't been easy. I'm just fortunate that father's work as a painter means he's been able to raise most of the rest of the money for my passage to America."

"Things must get better," pleaded Honnie. "Maybe

Mick could get you a job here in the yard? You've always been good with horses. Who knows, you might end up as head groom one day."

"I don't want to be somebody else's groom," said William. "I want to work for myself. I want to own my own horse, have my own place, my own bit of land. In America they say everybody has a fair chance if they work hard enough. I've got a cheap passage on a ship called the *Venus* and she's sailing from Galway in two weeks' time. She's for St. John's in Newfoundland off the coast of Canada. It's right close to the boundary of the States – so I can stay in Canada or go on to the States. They say there's great trade in St. John's, a power of building going on, good money to be made and no shortage of work. Donie Fahy, Bridget's brother, is out there this two years. He's sent money home to his family and saved some as well. He says you can get land out there at low cost, with a long time given for payment, and in some places you can get a grant of land for free. You'll see, Honnie – I'll end up a landowner, but in the New World. And I've promised Seán I'll send for him as soon as I've found my feet."

Once William went to Canada, Honnie knew she'd never see him again. She had seen enough young people around her take the emigrant ship to know that, once gone, they hardly ever returned. To lose one brother was bad enough, but the prospect of losing two was worse, along with the feeling that if two went, even more might follow. She had a sudden vision of the house at Maree empty of all her brothers and sisters. Her mother must be sore at heart.

They were approaching the back of the house. There

seemed to be no more to say. Honnie could feel the knot forming in her throat.

"I suppose we had better say our goodbyes here," said William, coming to a halt.

Honnie grabbed him and gave him a hard, fierce hug.

"Promise you'll write, William. Promise. And come and see me again before you go. *Please.*"

"I'm not as good as you are at the reading and writing, but I'll do my best. And I'll try to see you again before I go. But, before I leave you, Honnie, what's this about you and Nicky Reilly?"

"I can see that my father doesn't come over to Tyrone just to see the horses – he comes for the gossip as well," said Honnie tartly. "I can tell you straight out there's nothing in that story, and absolutely nothing between us. I like horses, Nicky likes horses, and he lets me visit the horses in the yards when I can get away and there's nobody round to object."

"From what I've heard, you're doing more than looking at them," said William. "I've heard stories about you riding round that back field beyond, as though you were training for a race meeting. Poor Nicky must be badly smitten. You'll land him in trouble, and yourself along with him. Have some sense, Honnie. I don't want to get a letter in Canada telling me you've lost your place. They have enough to worry about at home."

He put his arms around her and kissed her.

"Take care, Honnie, take care."

And he turned and walked away. Honnie watched as he disappeared around the corner of the house. He didn't look back. She knew he wouldn't come back again. William had always hated goodbyes.

She walked back down to the water's edge, and sat on a rock beside the pier.

What William said was true. She buried her face in her hands. It wasn't fair that one young man should have everything he could ever want, and another have to travel so far and work so hard just in the hope of getting some of the world's good things. She felt sick at heart at the thought that she would probably never see her brother again, and at the thought of the others who might follow him out.

Just two weeks after he had visited her, William left aboard the *Venus*, bound for Canada and a new life. A little bit of Honnie had hoped that in the end he mightn't go, that something would turn up to change his mind.

The day her father came to tell her that William had really gone, her world seemed very dark. She went to talk to the horses, but even the horses didn't lift her spirits.

"What do you think of it all, Barebones? Will I ever see William again?"

She rubbed her tearstained face against his soft nose.

It was a dead August day. The countryside was panting in the hot heavy weather and the flies were thick and tormenting around the horses' heads.

Honnie knew what she needed. She knew she had been reckless in availing of Nicky Reilly's suggestions over the past months that she should take "a quick canter around the field beyond". But just one more time, she said to herself. One more time. She went to Nicky Reilly and asked him if he could take Cowslip out.

On this particular occasion it was against Nicky's better judgement.

"Master Christopher could be back soon," he said. "He rode out with Danny Murray some hours ago and I expect him back shortly. There'll be murder if he finds out what we've been at."

But all Honnie could think of was the prospect of the reins in her hands, the horse answering the call of her fingers, and the sheer liberation of riding full out.

"Just ten minutes, Nicky, please!"

Reluctantly Nicky gave in.

Minutes later, Honnie was cantering off, her mind empty of everything except sheer exhilaration and physical pleasure, when another horse drew up beside her.

Someone grabbed the reins and pulled Cowslip up sharply.

"*Just what in hell do you think you're doing?*" said Chrisopher St. George in a voice of steel.

Honnie opened her mouth, but no sound came out. She could feel a guilty flush spreading over her face. But her first thought was for Nicky.

"I'm waiting," said Christopher.

"Don't blame Nicky," she said. "Please. It wasn't his fault, truly. I talked him into it. He didn't want to let me. Don't blame him."

"I presume that Nicky can speak for himself," said Christopher. "Now get off that horse. And get back to the kitchen. I can promise you that Mrs. Smith will hear of this."

All that evening Honnie waited for Mrs. Smith to call her and demand an explanation of her behaviour. The likelihood of being dismissed loomed large. Her brother

William's words came back to haunt her. How would she explain things to her mother and father? Would she also be responsible for Nicky Reilly's dismissal? How could she have been so foolish?

But nothing happened.

That night, Honnie didn't get a wink of sleep.

Even Bridget had little sympathy for her. "It was bound to happen sooner or later," she said. "All you can hope is that Master Christopher doesn't ask his father to let you go. They're sure to let Nicky go."

Honnie waited the next day and the next, but nothing happened.

As the days passed, and Mrs. Smith said nothing, Honnie began to relax ever so slightly. But she still worried about Nicky Reilly until Mick Murphy set her mind at rest.

"Master Christopher gave him a severe ticking-off and said no man should allow his sense to be put astray by a pretty face. But no, he didn't give him his walking orders. No thanks to you, Honnie. Now stay away from the yard, from the horses and from Nicky. Or you'll land me in trouble as well."

Then, quite unreasonably, Honnie began to feel cross. Christopher St. George was trying to torment her. He must know that she would be out of her mind with worry, waiting for Mrs. Smith's wrath to descend on her.

Still, Mrs. Smith said nothing. And, whenever Honnie encountered Christopher over the next few weeks, he merely nodded to her and passed on.

Chapter 9

Olivia St. George got sick quite suddenly one day towards the end of September. She had a pain in her stomach and lost her appetite. But she had suffered similar turns before, and always recovered. She assured everybody that she would be better "by the morrow". But this time was different. The pain got worse instead of better.

Dr. Veitch was fetched out from Galway to see her but when he tried to examine her stomach it was so sore that she cried out in pain. He prescribed some medication, but didn't look too hopeful. He had seen cases like this before.

Her sisters sat beside her bed, sponging her forehead, holding her hand, talking to her soothingly. Honnie visited her bedroom many times a day, bringing cool drinks, broths and different dishes prepared especially to tempt her. But there were times when she cried out with pain that was clearly agonising, and her cries struck mortal fear into the hearts of those hearing it. As each day passed those cries became more frequent.

"She's going to be all right, isn't she?" Honnie said to Mrs. Smith. She couldn't believe that Miss Olivia wouldn't recover.

Mrs. Smith was non-committal. "We can only hope for the best," she said.

But hope wasn't enough. Five days after she first fell ill, Olivia St. George died.

"She can't be dead," said Honnie. "Only last week she was out gathering herbs in Lady Harriet's garden. She was going to make up medicaments against the winter using her mother's receipts. I remember thinking how young and pretty she looked." Tears flowed down her face. "How can anyone who seemed so well and healthy be here one day and gone the next?"

Honnie remembered how Olivia had been good to her in many little ways, as she had been to many people in her family and outside it.

"All those people she used to visit, the old people and sick people she used to bring food and medicines to are going to miss her sorely," said Bridget. "She always had a soft word for them, and a smile for them. She was a very kind person."

Arthur had been shattered by his wife's death, but it had not been unexpected. Olivia's death came out of the blue, like an awful unreal nightmare. One day she seemed alive and well. Six days later she was dead. She had always minded him, looked after him. She had been so good to him after her mother died. In ten days he seemed to age ten years.

Christopher seemed at first stunned, then angry.

"Olivia was always his favourite sister," said Mrs. Smith. "Whenever he had a problem, he'd go to her. She would stand up for him when he got into trouble and his parents were annoyed with him."

"Yes," said Honnie, "and he would talk to her about his horses and their exploits on the racecourse and the hunting field, and she would be interested, Mick Murphy says. Now it seems that one way he is dealing with it is by riding out, mostly on Barebones, but sometimes he even takes out Necromancer."

"And rides him as if all the hounds of hell were after him," said Bridget. "Mick says one of these days he'll kill himself."

"Everything comes in threes," said Biddy, who had just come to the kitchen door with a load of kitchen cloths. "I just hope we're not going to have a third funeral the way Master Christopher is riding."

"What a prophet of doom you are, Biddy!" said Honnie. "I sometimes think you want bad things to happen."

Christopher was now riding all day, every day, from early morning until late in the evening, until both he and Barebones were utterly exhausted. To distract himself further he poured all his energies and mind into the organisation of the County Galway Hunt. His enthusiasm was noted and commented upon by the *Connaught Journal.*

Mrs. Smith read out the piece in the servant's hall one evening. It was after supper and Mr. Scott and Mick Murphy, along with Josie, Bridget and Honnie, were having a cup of tea. Outside, it was a raw October evening, with no moon to be seen, no stars, just low clouds and a bitter wind winding down from the north. But the kitchen was warm, and the day's work was done.

"'*The gentry of the county are indebted to that excellent and patriotic gentleman, Christopher St. George, Esquire, of Tyrone House, for the establishment of the County Galway Hunt*,'" read Mrs. Smith, "'*through whose instrumentality and exertions it has already enrolled, amongst its original members, upwards of forty of the most respectable and influential gentlemen of the county. Mr. St. George may be justly described as the Nimrod of this society, having diffused much pleasure and amusement through various parts of the county, to whose gentry he afforded, exclusively at his own expense, and the subs required by the advert being merely a trifle from each member for the preservation of the country, the purchase of foxes, and the fencing of coverts, in order to ensure the continuation of amusement of the manly and delightful sport of hunting. Mr. St. George is deservedly much esteemed and popular amongst the gentry of the county of Galway and continues to support the hounds*.'"

"He's certainly spending money all right," said Mr. Scott. "He's spending it like it comes out of a well with no bottom to it. He'd be better employed paying heed to the land and the estate. There's much needs doing."

"Ah, sure you're only young once," said Mick Murphy. "And isn't it a fine sight to see a hunt away on a winter's morning, with the horns sounding, the hounds in full flight, and the prospect of a good day's sport. There's no other sight like it."

"Hounds cost money," said Mr. Scott dourly. "And

horses even more, especially if you think nothing is too good for them, like Master Christopher."

"I can tell you that he has been looking after things for his father," said Mrs. Smith. "I've seen him myself riding out, and he had that satchel thing with him."

"Well, all I can say," said Josie, "is that I think it's a very strange way to behave when your sister's not cold in her grave. For all his ranting when she died, he seems to have forgotten all about her now."

"Maybe it's because he finds he can't stop thinking about her that he's gone mad on the hunting," said Honnie.

"Don't tell me you're making excuses for him," said Josie. "And I wonder what could be the reason for that? You wouldn't have a bit of a *grá* for him, now, would you? I've sometimes thought you had."

"I've never heard anything so silly in my life," said Honnie crossly. "Me, nursing a *grá* for Master Christopher? I said what I said because I think it's very hard to know what anybody is really feeling. I mean, just because somebody doesn't show what they're feeling, it doesn't mean they're not feeling."

"And you know what Master Christopher is feeling, I suppose," said Josie acidly.

"Well, I know what I'm feeling myself," said Honnie, "and I only knew her for a few years. Master Christopher has known her all his life, and they were very close. What can it be like to lose your mother and your favourite sister in not much over a year?"

"Enough of that talk now," said Mrs. Smith, glancing sharply at Honnie. "Master Christopher's feelings are no concern of either of you."

Chapter 10

The month of October went quickly, and Hallowe'en seemed to come in a flash. Outside the sky was a steely grey, and the evening darkened early in the kitchens of Tyrone. Nobody was in the humour for marking the day. Olivia's death hung heavy over the household.

"I used to love *Oíche Shamhna* at home," said Honnie as they sat around the table drinking tea.

"I never liked it," said Bridget. "It's fine if you're safe inside with a lot of people. But I used to have to visit my grandmother who lived a good mile down the road, and I was always so frightened I couldn't get home quick enough. They say the little people will lead you astray that night if they get any chance at all. And the Púca is abroad. And the spirits of the dead are everywhere. It's their special time."

"Some people say that all the people that ever lived in a house come back at Hallowe'en and sit around, and look at what everybody is doing," said Josie.

"There'll be great sport here altogether, then," said Rory, a young groom who had just come into the kitchen with Mick Murphy. "We can expect to see Miss Olivia come back to see how we're all getting on, and Lady Harriet herself."

"And Matt the pedlar man who died in this very kitchen some twelve years ago," said Mick Murphy. "And don't forget old Christopher St. George who built this house over fifty years ago. And maybe even *his* uncle, another Christopher, a priest, who often said Mass here. He'll likely be looking for a body to serve Mass for him."

"A priest, you said?" said Honnie. "What kind of priest?"

"A Catholic priest."

"But the family is Protestant," she said, surprised.

"Ah, they weren't always," said Mick. "And they weren't always St. Georges either. The family's name used to be 'French' – they were Normans of course originally. But in 1774 they changed their name to St. George – which was the name of the other side of the family. It was something to do with land and inheritance. And they became Anglicans along the way but some of them stayed Catholic – like that priest. Anyway, as I was saying, if a priest has taken money for a Mass and dies before he can say it, he comes back to say it and looks for a living creature to help him – and, if nobody helps him, he'll keep on coming back 'til Judgement Day."

"What I'd like to find out is who I am to marry," said Bridget. "One Halloween, when my mother was a girl, she wanted to find out who she was to wed. My grandmother told her the way to find out was to eat a salt herring, and then not to speak to anybody for the rest of the night, and when she went to sleep she would dream of the man she'd marry. So my mother ate a salt herring, and didn't speak at all for the rest of the night, and when she went to sleep she had a dream, and 'twas my father she dreamt of."

"Or you can put two hazelnuts together in front of the fire, one to be you and the other the man you fancy," said Josie. "If they stay together and burn away slowly, you'll marry him. But if your hazelnut jumps away or his hazelnut jumps away, then it's not going to happen."

"Well, there'll be no carry-on of that kind hereabouts this evening," said Mrs. Smith.

Honnie was still thinking of the Hallowe'ens in her own home. "We always have a big dish of colcannon, and my mother makes apple-and-blackberry pies – the last blackberry pies of the year because of course you can't pick any more after the Púca spits on them on Hallowe'en night. And she makes oatcakes and pancakes and we play Snap Apple, and roast nuts. And we're always allowed to drink some punch. I'm sure they're getting it all ready this very minute," she said wistfully. "We always had powerful fun ..."

"Well, there isn't much of a feeling of fun in this house tonight," said a voice behind them.

Nobody had heard Christopher St. George coming down the stairs, and all heads turned.

"But I think we'd all be the better for a couple of glasses of Mrs. Smith's milk punch," he continued. "I know I'd like some. Would you be good enough to make some, Mrs. Smith?"

Mrs. Smith rolled her eyes to heaven, unabashed by Christopher's appearance in the kitchen. "Master Christopher, have you any idea how long it takes to *make* milk punch? It's not something you throw together at a moment's notice. You need lemons, and a great many of them – now where would I get lemons at this time of night? You need quantities of the best rum, and the best whisky, and you need Seville oranges. And it takes at least three days to ready itself before you strain it and bottle it."

"It was just a notion I took, Mrs. Smith – truly, it doesn't matter."

"But it just so happens," said Mrs. Smith with a smile, "that I made some of it the week gone by, and I have a bottle or two hidden away."

Mrs. Smith had a soft spot for young, handsome men, and a special affection for Christopher, who she had known since he was a boy – even though she felt that at times he lacked "a proper sense of responsibility". She departed, rattling her keys, in the direction of her room.

The other servants shifted uncomfortably. Christopher stood in front of the range, his hands out to the warmth.

"My sisters have gone to visit friends," he said to no one in particular.

He began to wander abstractedly around the kitchen, lifting up a teapot and putting it down again, picking up a teaspoon off the table, stirring the sugar in its bowl round and round. The kitchen cat, fat and spoiled, rubbed itself against his legs, and he bent down to stroke it. Then, taking it up in his arms, he sat down on a nearby empty chair.

Mrs. Smith bustled back with two bottles.

"Honnie, get you a glass for Master Christopher – quickly now."

"And for everybody else as well," said Christopher, looking around.

But there was only Mrs. Smith, Josie, Bridget and Honnie left. The two grooms had slid quietly out of the kitchen as soon as Christopher appeared, and Mr. Scott had already departed to his own quarters.

Honnie took over the glasses to Mrs. Smith and, taking the first one that was filled, she carried it over to Christopher. Their hands touched as he took the glass from her with a wide, warm smile that caught her by surprise.

"Thank you," he said. "I feel the need of a drink after a day with the horses. You should try horse-riding yourself some time, Honnie," he continued, with a bland expression on his face as he glanced up at her.

Honnie could feel a blush spreading from her neck up to the top of her head. During the past weeks, what with Olivia's illness and death, she had pushed Nicky Reilly and her exploits with Cowslip to the back of her mind. Now she bitterly regretted them. She could see Mrs. Smith looking at her acutely, and she was sure that Josie had noticed her confusion as well. She turned away and pretended to be tidying some of the pots alongside the range.

She could feel Christopher's eyes on her and was annoyed to find herself worrying if her hair was tidy, or if her face was overbright from working in the hot kitchen, to say nothing of blushing.

She turned to see he was smiling at her. She smiled back at him tightly. She found she was getting angry. But there was nothing she could say or do. What she wanted to do most of all was thump him. She told herself to remember she owed him a great deal. Clearly, while Mrs. Smith may have heard some rumours about the riding,

Christopher himself had not said anything to her.

Honnie sat and tasted her punch. The mix of flavours was delicious.

Christopher sipped his drink, stroking the cat on his knee and talking to Mrs. Smith about other Hallowe'ens.

"You used to make a special cake for my mother," he said. "She always said nobody could bake a cake like you. And do you remember, when we were small, you used to make us stampy cakes at Hallowe'en ... and we'd duck for apples in the barrel of water with our teeth or try to bite them as they hung from a string."

By the time he had finished his third glass and stood up, the effects of the day in the open air were beginning to show.

"Goodnight all and thank you. I'm for bed."

On his way out, he rested his hand lightly on Honnie's shoulder as she sat at the kitchen table.

"Goodnight, Honnie," he murmured, and was gone.

Honnie could see the glances Bridget and Josie were exchanging. She got up quickly and started clearing the table.

It all went over Mrs. Smith's head. She was thinking of her bed.

"I'll be saying goodnight too," she said.

And off she went, taking the remains of the milk punch with her.

Honnie, Josie and Bridget were left to tidy up the kitchen. Honnie waited for Josie to make some comment, but Josie's mind was full of Robert. He had paid her some attention recently. He had smiled at her when their paths crossed and yesterday he praised a cake she had made. A few weeks ago he had commented on her appearance, and told her she looked very well, and that he liked the new way she was doing her hair. And just yesterday when she was on her own in the kitchen late in the evening, he had produced a bottle of wine and two glasses and told her she had earned a drink. So, as she helped Honnie and Bridget clear the table, wash the glasses and sweep the floor, all she could think of was Robert.

"We never tried out any Hallowe'en ways to see who we'll marry," said Bridget.

"Mrs. Smith said we shouldn't," said Josie.

"I've noticed that Robert has been very nice to Josie lately," said Bridget. "Maybe she should have tried to find out his intentions. Maybe she should eat a salt herring and see if she dreams of him."

"One thing you can be sure of with Robert," said Honnie tartly, "is that whatever intentions he may have, they are never good."

Josie's face reddened with temper. "How *dare* you talk about Robert like that," she said. "I don't know how well you think you know him, but he's been very nice to me."

Honnie knew she'd spoken out of turn. "I'm sorry, Josie, I shouldn't have said that."

As they finished their chores, a low wind whined through the slightly open window and blew out all the candles except one, which Honnie took to light them up the stairs.

In their room, Bridget was very jumpy, imagining strange noises, thinking she heard voices.

"I tell you I can feel Miss Olivia here," she said.

"Don't be such an *óinseach,*" said Honnie, even as she

felt the hairs prickling at the back of her neck. "And even if she *is* here what harm would she do to you? She never did anybody anything but good in her life. So what harm would she want to do anybody now?"

Once in bed, the others fell quickly asleep – but Honnie lay awake, remembering a smile, a touch.

On All Souls' Day, the special day of prayer for all those who had died, Honnie decided to pay a visit to Olivia's grave. She wasn't the only one to do so. Christopher and Rua were already there. Honnie was about to turn back, having seen him, but Rua barked in greeting and Christopher swung round and saw her.

She reluctantly walked towards the graveside as Rua pranced over to greet her.

The earth still looked newly turned. Someone had left flowers there.

"She really liked you, did you know that?" He didn't look at her as he spoke, just kept looking down at the grave.

"She was very kind to me," Honnie said.

"She said you were always interested in what was going on," said Christopher. "She heard you asking Mrs. Smith about cookery receipts and she saw you talking to Johnny O'Connor in the garden. She said you always had a smile on your face."

"I'm sorry," Honnie said, "really sorry," and walked quickly away before he could see her tears.

Chapter 11

Christmas was a subdued affair. Last year had been their first Christmas without their mother, this Christmas the St. George family would be without Olivia too. Still, preparations went ahead. Chickens and turkeys and geese were plucked, beef was spiced, and drink bottled in the cellars. But there seemed to be no heart to the house. Christmas was a time when Lady Harriet had always been at the centre of the preparations. After her death Olivia had tried to fill her mother's place. Now she, too, was gone.

"Things just aren't the same," said Mrs. Smith. "There are servants getting above themselves, and nobody to stop them. The Master, God help him, never had to think of how this place was run, and Master Christopher has nothing on his mind but horses. I suppose Miss Anne and Miss Matilda do their best, but I think Miss Harriet lives in a dream world, and Miss Louisa is still only a child. The servants don't have the same respect for them."

It's true, Honnie thought.

She remembered her first Christmas in Tyrone when there had been so much gaiety, with hordes of visitors, and relatives who came to stay. She remembered all the hard work too, but this year it seemed that nothing could lighten the gloomy atmosphere.

But something did.

About two days before Christmas, when Bridget and Honnie came down to ready the kitchen for the morning, they heard piercing screams from the yard. They rushed out and were just in time to see three obviously terrified girls disappearing out of sight as though the devil was after them. In pursuit was a huge fluffy, bird-like creature, covered in feathers, shrieking and squawking. Seconds later the bird fell and was suddenly silent.

"In the name of God, what is it?" said Bridget. "'Tis a sign surely, of something bad going to happen!" And she blessed herself.

But Honnie didn't think so. She had caught sight of Biddy the Wash's red skirt sticking out from under all the feathers.

The other girls in the kitchen had come out to see what all the fuss was about, and they fell around the yard laughing at the sight that met their eyes.

The wash-house was a big building in one of the yards at the back of the house, where all the laundry was done, and washerwomen came in every day to work under Biddy's temperamental eye. On the floor above there was a large room for cleaning feathers to stuff pillows and feather beds. With all the fowl that had been plucked for Christmas there were large piles of feathers waiting for attention.

"I was wore out with all the work I've been doing these weeks past," croaked Biddy crossly as she struggled to her feet. "I'm not able for it at my age. I made myself a nice big mug of honey and tea with a few sups of the crathur to give me a bit of strength and comfort, and wasn't I so tired I must have fallen asleep on a pile of feathers, and I didn't wake up 'til I heard these young wans coming this morning and sure wasn't my mug empty and my clothes covered with honey and feathers."

"A few drops of the crathur indeed!" said Mrs.Smith. "More like a mug."

"Sure it's one of the few pleasures left to me," Biddy said.

On Christmas Eve, Kate Rooney, the kitchenmaid who had been so kind to Honnie when she started working in Tyrone House, came to call. She hadn't been back to visit very often since her marriage and Honnie was pleased to see her. With her she brought her new daughter, born just two months before, a bonnie and bright-eyed baby called Ellie, with Kate's soft skin, and a head of downy light-brown hair.

She smiled and gurgled as people cooed over her and admired her.

Honnie touched the little hand and marvelled at the tiny fingers. Then she held out her little finger and the baby took firm hold of it.

"Now there's a young lady with a good hold on life," said Mrs. Smith.

On Christmas Day the St. George family went dutifully to church and, keeping to custom, when they came home the servants lined up in the drawing room to receive their gifts.

It was Christopher who handed Honnie a pair of warm gloves, tied together with red ribbon. "For when you go walking, or to church, or to pay a visit home," he said.

Later, in her bedroom, in a quiet moment, when none of the other girls were around, Honnie took out her gloves to try them on, and felt something inside a finger of one. She pulled out a pendant with a delicate blue stone in a silver setting. She remembered seeing it on Miss Olivia.

She was astonished. Had all the servants been given tokens of remembrance of Miss Olivia? She hadn't heard the others mentioning any such thing. But why should she be singled out? And why hadn't Master Christopher said anything about it? Or . . . was it a secret gift? From him to her? She blushed at the thought. It couldn't be . . . If it was, she would have to give it back.

She held it in the palm of one hand, and lightly rubbed her fingertips over the smooth metal, admiring the gleaming stone, the detail on the linked chain. She had never owned jewellery of any kind, much less any made of silver. She put it against her neck and tried to see how it looked in her reflection in the window. A shaft of evening sunlight caught it in the hollow of her throat, and for a moment it gleamed like something magical.

Then she heard somebody coming, and quickly slipped it under her pillow.

St. Stephen's Day, the day after Christmas Day, was bright and crisp. Some of the family had gone out hunting, and the younger members of the family had gone to follow the hunt. During the afternoon the house was quiet and Honnie asked Mrs. Smith if she could slip out for a short walk.

Mrs. Smith had grown fond of Honnie. She was a quick and willing worker, she had an appetite for learning, and an ability to learn quickly. She could well end up as a cook in some Big House. She knew that Honnie came back refreshed after a spell in the open air. If you spent every hour of the day down in the kitchens of Tyrone, you could get to feel you never saw the light of day.

"Off with you, then," she said. "Just mind you're back in time to get things going for tea."

Honnie headed for what she thought of as her special place, especially since the day she had been there with William. She went down past the gardens at the back of the house, past the walled vegetable garden on one side, and the orchards on the other, past the big ricks of turf brought in by boat from Connemara and out onto the little pier.

She sat there, slipped the pendant from her skirt pocket and held it in her hand. She turned it over, feeling it cool against her fingers. Suddenly she heard snuffling and felt a dog's wet nose against her neck. It was Rua and where Rua was, Christopher had to be.

"Do you like it?" Christopher asked

Honnie shot to her feet, closing her fist on the necklace.

Turning around, she said the first thing that came into her head.

"I thought you'd gone hunting!"

"I'm back," said Christopher. "I saw you slipping out of the house. So how do you like the pendant?"

"I like it," said Honnie. "I like it very much, but I can't keep it. It wouldn't be right for me to take things like that from you. If anybody heard about it, they might get the wrong idea." As soon as she spoke, she knew it was the wrong thing to say.

Christopher looked down at her, smiling, a gleam in his eye.

"What would they think?"

"That ... you know well what they'd think ..."

"I give you a little trinket that belonged to my sister, because I know you were fond of her," said Christopher. "What harm could there be in that?"

"People like you don't give presents to the likes of me," said Honnie. "And, besides, I could never wear it. How could I explain where I'd got it? What would your sisters say if they saw me wearing it? Or Mrs. Smith? Or my family?"

"Well, *I'd* like to see how it looks on you," said Christopher. "And I know you have it there in your hand. Give it to me."

He caught her two hands and gently prised them open. She was very aware that her hands were rough and reddened from all the kitchen work. The little pendant sparkled in the sunlight.

He opened the catch and, standing behind her, he hung it round her neck.

She could feel his fingers on the back of her neck, then on her shoulders. She could feel his breath on her cheek. She spun around and away from him.

"This isn't fair, Master Christopher, and you *know* it

isn't. You'll cost me my place, so you will. Thank you for the gift, but you may take it back!"

She tried to undo the catch, but her hands were all fingers and thumbs and her hair caught in the chain.

He watched her with his hands in his pockets, and a smile on his face.

"Keep it – please. Forget it was I who gave it to you. Pretend you got it from Olivia."

He smiled at her again and, calling to Rua, went off whistling.

Honnie watched him go. It would be nice to wear something that had belonged to Miss Olivia. And, after all, who was to know she had it? Maybe she could wear it under her dress, and nobody would be any the wiser except herself?

She disentangled her hair and tucked the pendant down inside the collar of her dress but, as she walked back to the kitchens she could feel it against her skin, and as she worked to prepare the evening meal she felt someone was sure to see the chain.

"What's wrong with you this evening?" said Bridget. "You're in danger of letting the potatoes boil dry, and you've forgotten to put on the carrots. You're all astray in yourself."

"I'm fine," said Honnie. She pulled herself together and concentrated on her chores.

But Josie had seen the gleam of silver on Honnie's neck.

"Maybe somebody should ask Honnie about the fancy necklace she's wearing," she said.

"What's that about a necklace I hear?" Mrs Smith asked.

"She's wearing it under her dress," said Josie. "Maybe she'd like to tell you where she got it."

Honnie blushed and stumbled frantically for words.

Mrs. Smith's face sharpened. "I would like to see the necklace, please."

"It was a gift," said Honnie. "A Christmas gift."

"*At once*," said Mrs. Smith.

Reluctantly, Honnie pulled the little pendant out from under her dress.

"Who would give a girl like you such a gift?" said Mrs. Smith.

"That necklace belonged to Miss Olivia," said Josie. "She wore it all the time."

There was a deathly silence.

"So where did you get it?" asked Mrs. Smith.

"I didn't steal it," said Honnie. "Truly, I didn't steal it."

"Seamus saw her just a while ago," said Josie. "She was with Master Christopher and he was putting it round her neck."

"Is this true?" asked Mrs. Smith.

"Why don't you ask Josie what she's been doing meeting Robert on the sly?" said Honnie furiously.

"This isn't about Josie, it's about you," said Mrs. Smith in an icy voice. "I can't believe what I'm hearing. I will talk to you in my room – *now*." And she turned on her heel and walked out of the kitchen, looking back just once to see that Honnie was following her.

In Mrs. Smith's room, with the door closed firmly behind her, Honnie stood, her hands clasped in front of her, her eyes on the ground and fear in her heart. She couldn't think what to say.

Mrs. Smith looked at her severely and then she spoke.

"I want to hear the whole truth. I want to hear *exactly* how you got this ... pendant."

She waited while Honnie stumbled for words.

"Master Christopher gave it to me," she said.

"He had no business giving it to you, and you had no business taking it from him," said Mrs. Smith.

"But it wasn't like that," said Honnie. "I didn't know he had given it to me. I found it in one of the fingers of the gloves I got as my Christmas present yesterday. I didn't know who had put it there."

"But you kept it just the same."

"But who was I going to give it back to?"

Mrs. Smith said nothing.

"I didn't know that it was Master Christopher who had put it there until today. I told him I couldn't take it. I told him I'd be in trouble. But he just put it round my neck and said he had given it to me because I had always been fond of Miss Olivia, and she had been fond of me. He said what harm could there be in that ..." Honnie's voice trailed off miserably.

"I don't know what I am going to do about this," said Mrs. Smith. "I am not sure who should be told, nor to whom I should go for advice. This may not be entirely your fault, Honnie, but I am warning you now, as I've warned you before – keep away from Master Christopher. You may go. And mind you take that thing off and put it away somewhere safe."

What would Mrs. Smith do, Honnie wondered. Would she tell Mrs. Hunt who had very strong opinions about most things? Would she feel that Christopher's sisters should be told? It was well known in the kitchen that Mrs. Hunt felt that Christopher should be more disciplined and, as for Honnie, while she would grudgingly admit that Honnie was a hard worker, she felt she was inclined to get above herself. Would Mrs. Smith talk to Mr. Scott, who would surely say that Arthur St. George should be told?

Honnie worried and wondered, until Mrs. Smith told her some days later that, for the time being, she was going to take the matter no further. She had decided to keep her concerns to herself, for the present at any rate. She didn't want to see Master Christopher in trouble. She just hoped that word of it wouldn't spread back to his father, or to his sisters, especially to Anne who had been heard to say that she thought Honnie was a bit flighty.

"But I'm warning you, and I mean it, that if I hear any more about any goings-on between yourself and Master Christopher, I will have to take it very seriously indeed."

Honnie heaved a sigh of relief. She couldn't be seen to wear the pendant again, but she sewed a tiny pocket into the waistband of each of her two dresses, where she could always keep it, safe from curious hands and eyes.

Chapter 12

Honnie was glad to see the back end of Christmas – not that she welcomed the New Year of 1832 with great heart. She had always felt wary of new years. The old one, at least, had the advantage of being familiar. A new year was unknown. She always worried about the bad things it might bring.

Early in January she went to visit her family. She was very happy to see how well her mother looked. They had received a letter from William, carried home by the *Venus* on one of its return trips to Galway.

He wrote that he had not gone on to the United States but had stayed in Canada.

There is plenty of work in Canada, and a smart young man can earn between four and five shillings a day along with his board. Land is to be bought here for seven shillings and sixpence an acre, but if you are prepared to go some distance inland you can get land free. I've got a grant of land in the interior, thirty miles from St. John's in New Brunswick, where I landed last summer.

The soil here is good and fertile, with beautiful trees of every description, particularly the maple, which makes elegant sugar, and is sought after in towns. There is at the back of the farm a small lake, and around its borders masses of cranberries, which are sold at a dear rate in towns. They grow strewn along the ground, about the size of gooseberries and a reddish colour. This lake is called Cranberry Lake.

They are all wooden houses here except a few brick ones – they build their cellars under them. Whenever a new settler takes a farm it is the custom that the neighbours gather and build him a snug house in the course of a few days, with the expense of only giving them five gallons of rum, but they expect the same help when required.

It might take me a little time to get the money for your passage together, Seán, but I can't wait to welcome you to the New World.

"This is the man who told me he would be no good at letterwriting," said Honnie. "I call that a really splendid letter."

Mary Kane was very quiet in herself. Honnie knew it was breaking her heart to have one son lost to her, and another on the way to leaving her as well – even though she knew it was probably the best thing for them. Honnie could think of nothing to say that would comfort her mother. She put her arms around her and held her tight. She could only hope that things would improve in Ireland before Thady and Joseph were old enough to take the emigrant ship as well.

The one thing that gave Mary Kane cause for cheer was that Tom Kelly had called to see her.

"He was back from his studies in Maynooth, on a visit to see his parents. And though he's nearly a priest now, he hasn't changed a bit. He was in great form, full of ideas and plans and schemes, like always. He was inquiring about you, Honnie, and wondering how you liked Tyrone."

"Oh, I wish I had been here when he came," said Honnie. "I'd dearly love a chance to talk with him again. Tom and I, we could talk about anything together. I miss him."

Chapter 13

February brought the news of the Penny Post Offices which were to be opened all over Ireland.

"That may be good news," said Mr. Scott, as they sat drinking tea one evening in the kitchen, "but what about the bad news? It says here in the *Connaught Journal* that the cholera, which they had in Russia and Poland last year, is making its way west. It is certain to get here."

"Poland and Russia are a long way from Ireland," said Mrs. Smith. "It may never come here. I must say, Mr. Scott, that you are a terrible man for always expecting the worst. Let's not trouble trouble 'til trouble troubles us."

But the news troubled everyone.

In the following months, through to the summer, people went about their everyday lives as they always did. But in their heads, and for ever growing, was the fear of cholera.

Honnie took Mrs. Smith's warning seriously and stayed

away from the horses, the stables and Nicky Reilly.

She had to admit that Nicky lay heavy on her conscience. He was a nice young man and she had not discouraged his overtures. She wanted to go horse-riding and he had made it possible. He had put his position in Tyrone in danger just to please her, and to be absolutely honest she hadn't give much thought to the risks he was taking. She had used him.

She was collecting vegetables from the garden one day when Nicky appeared at her elbow.

"Amn't I lucky to catch you?" he said. "You've been doing everything you could to stop me having a word with you. You were happy enough to see me when you wanted to go horse-riding. I thought you were fond of me, Honnie, I really did. You certainly led me to believe so."

Honnie squirmed. She knew there was truth in what Nicky said. She struggled to find the right words to answer him. But, of course, there were no right words, because she had behaved badly.

"I'm sorry ... truly sorry," she said. "I never meant to hurt you . . . "

"Sorry is cold comfort to a man," said Nicky. "Anyway, I thought you might like to know that you'll soon be rid of me. I'm going up to Dublin with Master Christopher to work for Lord Howth. It's a great chance for me."

"I can only wish you well," said Honnie.

The next day, in the kitchen, Mrs. Smith was in an unusually talkative mood. She was pleased to hear that Nicky was going away. There could be nothing more between him and Honnie.

"You know that Master Christopher's uncle is the third Earl of Howth?" she said to Honnie. "Master Christopher is very fond of his uncle. And they're both horse-mad. Thomas St. Lawrence is the son of his father's second marriage, and he was only a boy when his father died. He is only five years older than Master Christopher. They're always competing with each other, to see who can take the highest jumps in the hunting field, who can cover a course the fastest, who has the best horse. Not but that Lord Howth should have more sense, him being older than young Christopher. It's a good example he should be giving him, instead of leading him on wilder feats of derring-do."

Afterwards, Honnie approached Mrs. Smith and asked to have a private word with her. With Nicky out of the way and Christopher up in Dublin, she felt she could safely pay her first visit to the stable yards in months. But she needed to first ask Mrs. Smith's permission.

"I know I behaved badly in the past, and I still feel very sorry about that, but I promise you I will never do anything like that again. But I do miss the horses. Is it all right if I go to see them? Please?"

Mrs Smith hesitated. Nicky Reilly had gone up to Howth, and she didn't think any of the other grooms would dare to let Honnie go horse-riding. Nor did she think that Honnie would ever attempt such a venture again. And she knew that Honnie was genuinely fond of the horses.

"Well ..." she said, "I suppose there can't be much harm in going to see them. I hope I can trust you. But mind, if I hear one word of bad behaviour on your part, I will not be forgiving."

Honnie went thankfully out to the stable yards. The

horses seemed to remember her, and they certainly appreciated the apples she brought them. She thought longingly of her past pleasure in going for a canter. Those days are gone, she told herself sternly. She had got away with one piece of bad behaviour. She dared not tempt the fates again. And, anyway, none of the grooms in the yard would ever allow her take out a horse.

From then on, Honnie visited the horses whenever she could. One evening at the end of April when she was happily talking to Barebones in his stable, Christopher walked into the yard, with Rua at his heels.

"Still horse-mad, I see, Honnie. How would you like me to take you out one day? I could give you some lessons. Such devotion deserves reward."

He clearly couldn't be serious – he had to be teasing her. Something about the casual way he treated her annoyed her.

She drew herself up straight.

"I don't think so, thank you very much," she said primly. Out of the corner of her eye she could see one of the stable hands smirking broadly. "I'm quite happy to be able to come and visit the horses from time to time – that's if you have no objection, of course. But I have no desire to go riding."

"Lies, Honnie, lies," said Christopher. "You know perfectly well that the highest notion in your head is to go for a good gallop across the fields and over the fences. But there ... if you won't take up a good offer ..."

He smiled derisively at her, turned on his heel, and was gone.

Uppermost in everybody's mind was the fear of cholera.

It had spread rapidly to London, to Belfast, to Dublin and finally to Galway.

"I hear that many cases of it have been reported. It seems to be very serious indeed," said Robert, who was reading the *Connacht Tribune* in the Tyrone kitchen one summer evening. "It says here that it's raging in Galway, and that the inhabitants of nearby towns have cut off all communication with the city in the hope of avoiding the infection. Country people are afraid to bring their produce into the city for sale. It says '*Various remedies and treatments have been recommended in local newspapers but people continue to die*'."

Outside a beautiful summer day was drawing to a close. The sun was sinking, and around it the sky was ablaze, all red and gold. The scent of roses drifted in from a bush that had bloomed for many years near the back steps leading down to the kitchen.

But Honnie and the others listening to Robert sat silent, feeling only a dreadful, cold fear clutch at their hearts.

"Galway city is like a desert," Robert went on. "A child died after being sick for only twelve hours, a woman died after ten, others after sixteen, eighteen, twenty-one and thirty-eight. Two priests who were working with the poor and sick in Galway have died, and one of the doctors –"

"I think that's more than enough, Robert," said Mr. Scott. "We don't need to know any more."

"And it's in Limerick, in Clare, in Dublin, and even on the Aran Islands –"

"Robert! Mr. Scott is right," said Mrs. Smith. "We don't need to know any more."

But Bridget spoke up fearfully. "What way does it take people?" she asked.

"They lose control of their organs, top and bottom," said Robert. "They get diarrhoea and vomiting."

"And they get pains all over them, and their heart gallops," said Josie with relish. She had been hearing about it from Paddy, who brought fish to the Tyrone kitchens. "They get weaker and weaker, and their eyes sink back in their heads. And in very young babies that soft spot on top of their heads sinks right back down. Then they go into a coma, and then they die."

"In the name of God, Josie," said Mrs. Smith angrily, "be quiet! Get back to your work and let me not hear another word out of you or you'll be sorry!"

Scowling, Josie left the table and the others silently rose and went back to work.

For a brief period in the summer the cholera subsided. But Arthur St. George felt that travelling should still be avoided, while the threat remained.

He talked to all the people in the house, and said he felt that nobody should go in to Galway city unless they had a serious reason to do so.

"So far Tyrone House and places around us have escaped, but I think this is because we are largely self-sufficient. We can provide for all our own needs and can manage well without going to Galway or elsewhere for supplies."

Later that day Bridget heard him talking to his daughter Anne.

"I must insist that Christopher doesn't continue to make these excursions to Dublin. We've known cholera before, but I have had letters from friends in Dublin who tell me that this is a much more virulent form of the disease. It comes from the East, which is why it's sometimes called Asian cholera. Dr. Charles Orpen, a man much respected for his knowledge and experience, says that a third, or even more, of the people who get it will die. Millions have already died in Europe and Asia. Although I hope we are safe here in Tyrone, there's no point in taking chances. I will forbid Christopher to travel to Dublin."

And for some months at least Christopher was excused from going round with Danny.

But confined to the fields of Tyrone, Christopher got bored. Thomas had written to say that cholera had subsided almost completely in Dublin and it had never come to the St. Lawrence estates. So, against his father's wishes he went up to twice for race meetings in Howth.

"He's not just gone for race meetings," said Josie. "There will be some fine lady up there he fancies. You'll see – the next thing we'll hear is that he's going to be married."

"I'm sorry to disappoint you, Josie," said Mick, who had travelled up to Howth with Christopher in July, "but from what I saw and heard in Howth, Master Christopher was more interested in his cousin's horses than he was in any of the women to whom His Lordship introduced him. Lord Howth has a powerful stable up there. You could see Master Christopher's eyes lighting up. He wants to become a member of the Turf Club, and go racing at the Curragh of Kildare."

"There's no one says he can't get married and go racing as well," said Josie.

"Arrah, give over," said Mick, "and leave the lad alone. I can promise you marriage is not on his mind at the moment. Mind you, that's not to say that he's averse to a bit of diversion. I hear he's been seen chatting up Máire Conneely over at Kilcolgan."

"That redheaded hussy!" said Josie. "What would he want with the likes of her? Now *there's* a young wan who spells trouble for sure. Master Christopher would do well to steer clear of her."

"Maybe that's why he likes her," said Mick. "And she's a fine-looking piece as well."

Honnie said nothing but this was one of the few times where she had to agree with Josie. She had never liked the look of Máire Conneely.

In late September there was a particularly bad outbreak of cholera in Galway.

"And to make matters worse, the potato crop has failed," Arthur St. George said to Anne. "As you know, the potato has been the main food crop for most of the people in this country. What are they going to do now? First they were looking at pestilence, now they are looking at hunger *and* pestilence."

In November the weather turned grey and stormy, and there was an outbreak of cholera at Kilcolgan. The malady made its appearance there one Friday at the beginning of the month. Within days, six people had died, and died quickly.

"I hear they were dead within hours of being taken ill," said Mick Murphy.

"Big Johnny Duffy, him that was said to be the strongest man for miles around, he was drinking in

Moran's one night, boasting that the pestilence would never get him, and the following night he was dead. His wife died the next day, and their son, a boy ten years of age. People are in fear of their lives, I can tell you, afeard for their families, their children, themselves. Kilcolgan is like a deserted village. People are afraid to go outside their own doors."

The people listening to Mick in the kitchen of Tyrone that grey November evening shivered. Kilcolgan was very near Tyrone. How could they possibly escape?

"Kate and her baby," said Honnie, dread rushing into her head. "Mick, did you hear tell anything about them at all?"

"No – I only know what I hear from talk in the yard," said Mick. "I haven't been over in Kilcolgan, nor do I intend to go there. Mr. St. George says nobody is to go there, nor anywhere else either while this pestilence is around."

"And what about Maree, and Ballinacourty? Did you hear anything about my family?" asked Honnie.

But Mick had heard nothing.

That night Honnie lay long awake in her bed, remembering all Kate's kindnesses to her, remembering her little baby girl. She'd be over a year old now. Such a bonnie, good-humoured, smiling baby. Honnie remembered holding out her little finger to her, and the strong grasp of the tiny hand. She remembered Mrs. Smith saying she was a young lady with a good hold on life. She lay awake and prayed, over and over again, for their safety. When she let herself think of her mother and father, her sisters, her brothers, even for a second, her heart sank even further and she shuddered.

Over the following days the news from Kilcolgan wasn't good. More had died. The people were terrified. Some people were so terrified that they were afraid to bury their own dead. Bodies were lying in houses, in cabins, unburied, rotting, smelling. The stench was said to be dreadful.

But Mick Murphy was able to tell them that some people *had* survived, thanks in part to Arthur St. George.

"The Master has employed a physician and apothecary from Galway to come out every day to visit the afflicted," said Mick. "He's employed nurses to attend the sick. He's paid men from Galway to come and bury the dead. Master Christopher was working along with him, trying to organize things.

Honnie went on praying for Kate and her husband and baby. No news, she told herself, was good news.

Then, just when the outbreak in Kilcolgan seemed to be on the wane, the word came. Kate and her baby were dead. And Mairéad Rua and her daughter had also passed away.

That night, and for nights afterwards, Honnie cried herself to sleep. But she gave fervent thanks to God when Mick Murphy told her he'd heard that the Kane family in Maree were alive and well. The cholera hadn't spread its murderous fingers quite that far.

The year of 1832 drew to a close. And the spectre of the cholera receded somewhat, but everyone knew somebody who had died – a cousin, an aunt, a friend of a friend, or a relative of one kind or another. Christmas was a sombre affair. Nobody had much heart for it.

Chapter 14

Early in the springtime of 1833, Christopher returned from a trip to Howth and announced that he had invited a party of friends down to Tyrone. They were following on behind him with Thomas St. Lawrence.

"Master Christopher wants to show them what real huntng is like," said Mick Murphy. "He thinks a couple of days over Galway stone walls will soon separate the men from the boys. He says he threw in a couple of wagers as well. And he has a few splendid jumps in mind."

Mrs. Smith had heard rumours. "I'm told that the Master has hopes of marrying Master Christopher off to the daughter of a friend of Lord Howth's family," she said. "She's a Miss Cecilia Mitchell, and they say she's quite an heiress. She's coming to stay."

"Is she beautiful?"asked Josie.

"How could I know if she is or she isn't, never having seen her?" said Mrs. Smith.

Josie was filled with curiosity. In the evening when she heard a carriage coming up the driveway, she managed to find an errand which took her up to the big hall. She came back bubbling with her news.

"She's really beautiful. She's got flaxen hair, and a lovely complexion. And she doesn't look a day over eighteen. She's wearing a lavender gown, cut very low. It's made in satin, I think, and it has short white sleeves, with a kind of gauzy stuff over them – you can see her shoulders. And there's a velvet trim on the skirt –"

"That's enough," said Mrs. Smith. "The visitors will be hungry after their long journey. The Master won't be pleased if they're kept waiting. Stop chattering and get on with your work.

Robert, one of the footmen, came down to the kitchen later that evening.

"Robert, I was telling them about Miss Mitchell. Isn't she beautiful?"said Josie. "Like a china figurine!"

"Well, I wouldn't go so far as to call her beautiful," said Robert. "She's a pretty little thing. But she hasn't much go about her. She hasn't said two words all evening and she only picked at her food. She ate hardly anything at all – just a few spoonfuls of the oyster soup, a piece or two of the fricassee of chicken, and a small helping of pudding."

Mrs. Smith looked distinctly ruffled. "And I spent all day slaving over the range!"

"There's some as don't know good food when they see it," said Robert. "You know I always appreciate your cooking, Mrs. Smith. Sure everybody knows you're the best cook for miles around."

Mrs. Smith looked somewhat mollified.

"Well, I wouldn't go that far," she said. "But while I don't think I'm the very best, I must own I think I'm one of the best."

"Now that little girl up there, she could do with a good feed," said Robert. "She's like a bird. You could blow her away. Myself, I prefer women to be more full-bodied, with some curves on them." He smiled at Honnie.

Josie observed his look with bitterness. The little kindnesses he had tossed her way over the past months suddenly seemed meaningless. "Well, I think Miss Mitchell is the height of style and beauty," she said. "She looks refined, the kind of lady any man of taste must admire." She cast a catty look at Honnie.

That's meant to make me feel like a big fat lump, thought Honnie. "Well, I'm not going to rise to that, Josie."

The weather was not kind. Day after day, a wet grey mist rolled in off the sea, so that it was impossible to see more than a few fields from the house. The hills of Clare vanished, and so did the Aran Islands. And if it wasn't the mist, it was the wind, the familiar southwest wind wailing in off the Atlantic, driving the rain before it, across the sodden fields and dripping stone walls.

Over her years in Tyrone, Honnie had observed that the weather had never put a stop to Christopher's activities. He had grown up with the West of Ireland climate and for the most part he was oblivious to it. He didn't regard a little rain, or a bit of a wind, as a reason not to ride out. His guests were less enthusiastic, however, and largely confined themselves to the house. During the ten days they stayed, the sun came out only occasionally, and then with a pallid, lack-lustre glimmer. It might appear for twenty minutes or half an hour, but with little enthusiasm, disappearing behind the clouds as though it couldn't wait to get away from the desolate scene below.

It was on one of the sun's rare appearances that Christopher decided to show Miss Mitchell the horses and the stables. Honnie saw them on her way back from the kitchen garden. She had been sent there by Mrs. Smith, who needed potatoes, and carrots and onions from the autumn's store, some bay leaves, and some parsley and thyme for a warming stew.

Miss Mitchell, wrapped up against the elements in a burgundy cloak with a fur-lined hood, was picking her way across the mud and muck of the yard with an expression of distaste.

Christopher was talking and, as always when on the subject of horses, he was talking compulsively.

He's telling her the breed, seed, and generation of every horse in the stable yard, thought Honnie.

Miss Mitchell didn't look too impressed.

It began to rain.

Peeking from a sheltered vantage point, Honnie watched as Christopher stopped at each stable door in turn, and called to each horse, and talked to them, and stroked them, and elaborated on all the features of each individual animal, their temperaments, their histories, and what they might achieve in the future.

Miss Mitchell's burgundy coat was getting quite wet. The fur on the hood around her face had a wet, ratty look, and the blonde curls that escaped from it were beginning to droop. The dainty little shoes she wore, complete with silver buckles, were not ideal shoes for a visit to a stable yard. But Christopher seemed quite oblivious, talking, gesticulating, explaining every detail of his horses and his hopes.

Honnie couldn't wait to watch the full tour. Mrs. Smith was waiting. But Josie saw them returning to the house some time later.

"And poor Miss Mitchell was soaked to the skin. If she gets the pneumonia out of it, he'll be to blame. He has no sense at all, that boy. I don't know where he was when brains were being given out."

Robert had overheard Miss Mitchell say that she never wanted to see Galway again.

"She said that Christopher was quite a good-looking young man but cared about nothing but horses. She thinks we are an uncivilised lot over here, compared to what she's used to in Dublin. She thinks it's forever raining, the countryside is wild and barren, and she's heard enough about horses to last her a lifetime."

Chapter 15

With cholera reappearing again in Dingle and Tralee in County Kerry, in Tipperary, and also in Clare, Honnie couldn't help thinking of her family. Clare seemed horribly close. But thankfully Tyrone continued to escape.

On Mothering Sunday, the fourth Sunday in Lent, Honnie was given the day off to visit Maree, and this time she was able to take a special cake which she had made herself. She set out early in the morning. It was a 'pet' day, more like late April than March. She took deep breaths of the sun-warmed air, filled with sheer pleasure in the world around her. The banks were starred with primroses, and when she looked more closely there were little clusters of violets too. There was a smell of new growth and the blackthorn hedges were flushing white. The swans were sitting on their nests on the banks of the Clarin River.

Her parents were happy to see her. Mary Kane looked

well, but she was concerned by a letter they had just received from William in Canada. He was prospering, he wrote, and looking forward to being joined by Seán in the next few months. She had known that it was inevitable, but the thought of losing another son was dreadful to her.

Sitting listening to her mother, to Honnie the house seemed smaller than she remembered, and a bit shabby. It needed a good coat of limewash.

An hour or two after she'd arrived, a knock sounded on the door and Tom Kelly walked in. He'd been allowed home again to visit because his father had been sick. He was as pleased to see Honnie as she was to see him, and when she felt his strong arms hugging her, Honnie's heart flipped. She wondered – not for the first time – what might have happened if Tom hadn't chosen the priesthood. And when she looked up at him, she thought she saw – just for an instant – an answering flicker in his eyes. Then it was gone, and he was smiling down at her in an ordinary, friendly way. Honnie pulled her head – and her heart – back from bygone days and listened as he talked.

As always he was full of ideas, and plans, how the poor and distressed could be helped, how people emigrating could be properly advised. He was particularly enthusiastic about the new National schools, and how important education was, especially to the poor.

"Protestants say that the Catholic population is half savage, ignorant and lazy. Maybe some of them are, but if they are, whose fault is that? How could poor people ever rise up when they had no education? But now that the opportunity is there, it warms my heart to see how eager people are to learn. The rising generation will not be like the present one. They are our hope for the future. These new National schools will be the making of the country."

"I wish I had been given the chance of more education myself," said Bartley Kane. "I count myself lucky that at least I was given a chance to learn a trade."

"What people here need is more fire in their bellies," said Seán, who had been standing in the open doorway, listening to all the talk. "People need work, but there's no work to be had. As for land! Land is never sold in small plots and, even if it were, the ordinary Irishman wouldn't have a hope in hell of buying a piece. There's no way he'd have the money. Instead people rent a piece of land from a landlord and, if they make any improvements or any profit, the landlord puts up the rent. What's wrong with this country is the landlords."

"Not all landlords are bad," said Mary Kane mildly.

"Look at the way Mr. St. George got a physician and an apothecary from Galway to come out every day to visit people with the cholera in Kilcolgan last year," said Honnie.

"Because he was afraid the cholera would get to Tyrone," said Seán.

"*Shush*, Seán," said Mary Kane. "Many of the landlords are in real difficulties themselves."

"Difficulties, is it?" said Seán. "I've yet to hear tell of a starving landlord."

"Maybe when Dan O'Connell gets a repeal of the Union, when we can govern ourselves, things will be different," said Bartley.

"And pigs will fly," said Seán. "William has sent me

my fare. I sail in three weeks' time. I can't wait to leave this wretched country behind me!" And he stormed out the door.

In her chair beside the hearth, Mary Kane wept.

There was silence for a few minutes. Then Tom spoke.

"Speaking of landlords, I hear young Christopher is as keen on horses as ever. And talking of horses, Honnie, you must see the new mare I've bought. I think she's the best mount I ever had. She seems to know what I want her to do before I know it myself. Just the merest touch on the reins and she responds. She's sure-footed, and fast as well. And she has a really good-natured disposition. When I saw her I knew she was the right one for me. I'll soon be ordained, and then I'll be back to minister down here. I'll need a good horse to go about my work."

Tom stayed talking for an hour or more before bringing Honnie out to look at his horse and going on his way. The mare was a fine animal. Honnie congratulated him on his purchase.

"I knew you'd like her, Honnie," he said. "You always had an eye for a good horse."

Honnie stayed on at home for some hours longer, but she left to return to Tyrone while it was still light. Seán set out on the road with her to keep her company, but after they had gone more than halfway she told him to go back.

"It won't take me above an hour to go the rest of the way, and the evening is still very bright. I'll be fine. You go off home. You've left them upset."

He protested about leaving her, but Honnie insisted.

"Just promise you'll come and see me before you go," she said.

"I will," he said and embraced her.

She stood and watched him go, wondering if she would ever see him again. Then she continued on her way, her heart heavy.

She had about two miles to go when the evening suddenly became overcast. The rain clouds were hastening in from the Atlantic. It had begun to rain when she heard the noise of a vehicle coming up fast behind her. As she stood in under a tree at the side of the road to let it pass, a phaeton drew to a halt a few feet from where she stood.

"Jump up," said a voice. "I'll carry you the rest of the way."

Christopher St. George held out his hand.

Honnie hesitated, then shook her head.

"Thank you, but I'm perfectly happy walking, and there's only a short way to go."

"Don't be silly," said Christopher. "It's raining and bound to get worse. I'll have you back at the house in minutes."

"Mrs. Smith has warned me," said Honnie. "She found out about the necklace, and was very annoyed. She said she wants to hear no more rumours about you and me."

"What rumours?" said Christopher. "I gave you a trinket that belonged to Olivia who was fond of you. I'm offering you a lift home because it's raining. What could possibly be wrong with any of that?"

"Mrs. Smith said –"

"I don't think I want to know what Mrs. Smith did or didn't say," Christopher interrupted. "Have you decided whether you want to get drowned wet, or are you going to be sensible and climb up here beside me?"

"Don't talk to me as if I were six years old," said Honnie crossly.

Christopher held out his hand again.

"Come on, Honnie. Jump up."

Honnie's desire to preserve her dignity was fighting with the fact that it was now raining very heavily, and her nice purple shawl was going to be ruined. Deciding that sense was preferable to sensibility, she reached and took his hand which was firm and warm. He pulled her up easily.

Sitting beside him in the phaeton, she could feel his thigh, strong and muscled against hers. She sat very straight and tried to compose herself.

For a few minutes they travelled in silence before Christopher spoke.

"Mick Murphy tells me you're quite a judge of horseflesh. Would you like to give me your opinion of this animal?"

Honnie was familiar with the bay colt called Jasper trotting smartly between the shafts of the phaeton. She had made up her mind about him quite some time ago, when he first arrived in the stable yard in Tyrone.

"He's a nice enough looking animal," she said. "But I think he steps too high when he's trotting. I know people think that a high-stepping animal looks good, but horses that step too high get tired more easily. And then they stumble."

Christopher said nothing.

"I think his head is just a little too big. Horses with big heads can be heavy to handle."

He still said nothing.

"And, truth to tell, I think he's not got the nicest

nature. His eyes are a bit small and mean-looking." She looked at Christopher to see how he was taking her criticism.

"What very pertinent observations."

Christopher's face seemed perfectly serious, but Honnie thought she detected an amused gleam in his eye.

As they rolled along, Honnie glanced at him surreptitiously from the corner of her eye. His grip on the reins was firm but gentle. His dark curly hair was overlong and untidy. She was thinking how blue his eyes were when he turned and caught her looking.

Honnie looked quickly away.

The rain had stopped and the last rays of the setting sun were breaking through when Christopher stopped abruptly, wheeled the phaeton round, and set off at a brisk pace down a boreen that ran round the back of the St. George land. After a mile or so he pulled up again, and dropped the reins in Honnie's lap.

"Let's see if you can handle a phaeton," he said.

Honnie looked at Christopher and then at the reins.

Jasper, who was young and excitable, started to move off.

"So what are you going to do? Let Jasper do what he likes?" said Christopher. "As you said, he hasn't got the nicest nature."

Honnie grabbed the reins and found herself driving at a spanking pace, with her heart in her mouth, and Christopher St. George sitting back, grinning.

After the first few minutes of fear, she began to relax.

It was good to sit up on a well-sprung phaeton and feel a horse respond to the reins in her hands. It was pleasant to ride high above the muddy roads and lanes, with the gorse hedges glowing in the twilight, and the moon rising in the light-dimmed sky of the spring evening. She felt a surge of exhilaration.

It was Christopher who eventually said it was time to turn back. He took the reins and neither of them spoke as they drove home at a more moderate pace. In no time, it seemed they were almost at the back driveway leading into Tyrone, and Honnie's common sense asserted itself. She hoped it was dark enough for nobody to have seen them.

"Please, I'd like to get out here," she said. "It's better I walk the rest of the way."

Christopher didn't argue with her, just pulled the horse up short, and waited until she got down.

"Thank you very much for the lift," she said.

He smiled down at her. "We must do it again."

What was she supposed to say to that? Flustered and off balance, Honnie threw another "Thank you" back at him as she hurried away.

Chapter 16

A three-day race meeting was announced for Headford at the end of June. Headford was some distance away from Tyrone, on the other side of Galway, and Christopher decided to organize a family outing.

"Mrs. Smith, we'll need to take a picnic with us to the race meeting," he said as he walked into the kitchen one bright June morning some weeks before the outing. "We'll be inviting friends, of course – I'll let you know about numbers closer to the date. What about some of your chicken and ham pies, Mrs. Smith, and some veal cakes? And some of your nice plum cake, we must have that, and perhaps some strawberries and cream? But, Mrs. Smith, you don't need me to tell you how to make up a good picnic basket. Everybody knows the food is bound to be wonderful. I'll leave it in your skilful hands."

Mrs. Smith glowed in Christopher's praise. Even though she knew it was flattery, she enjoyed it.

Christopher turned back at the door.

"Oh, and I thought it would be a good idea to take Bridget and Honnie with us. They can look after the food while we're watching the racing. You don't mind, do you?"

He left without waiting for an answer.

Mrs. Smith did mind.

As she told Mr. Scott that evening, she didn't approve of taking flighty young kitchenmaids to race meetings, even if they were going there to work. The Lord alone knew what trouble it might lead to. She was very fond of Master Christopher, but she was under no illusions about him. She had observed his partiality for Honnie.

"He likes a pretty face, does Master Christopher – well, what young man doesn't? But I'd prefer he found his amusements elsewhere, and not among my kitchenmaids. I know who will get the blame if anything untoward happens."

Mr. Scott was sympathetic. "But there's not much I can do about it," he said. "It's more in your domain than mine."

"I so wish the mistress was still alive," said Mrs. Smith. "Should I mention it to Christopher's father, do you think? But, on the face of it, there's nothing wrong with asking that some of the household servants should go along with the food. I don't feel I can say anything to Christopher himself. It isn't my place to tell him what he should or shouldn't do."

Honnie had been making a pudding at the far end of the kitchen when this conversation took place. She went on beating the mixture and tried to look as if she wasn't listening, but her heart was pounding. She was gripped by both embarrassment and excitement. She had heard about race meetings from other people but she had never been to one herself though she had long wished to go. Her mind filled as she imagined the occasion – some of the best horses in Galway, and the races they would run. Barebones would surely be running, and probably some other St. George horses as well. There would be people from all over the county there, and fine ladies and fine fashions. She would be there to work, but she would be able to work and watch as well, wouldn't she? She couldn't wait to tell Bridget.

Bridget was as excited as Honnie by the news.

"They can't eat all the time and, once they've finished, I'm sure we'll be able to have a bit of time to ourselves. What'll I wear? What are you going to wear, Honnie? There'll be all sorts of people there, from all over Galway. Oh, I can't wait!"

"We'll wear what we wear here," said Honnie. "Our dresses and aprons and caps. And even if Mrs. Smith doesn't insist, the fact of the matter is that we haven't exactly got a wardrobe of clothes from which to choose. But it would be lovely, wouldn't it, to be able to wear a fine dress instead of a uniform?"

"But what if the weather was very bad? Would they have to cancel the picnic then?" asked Bridget.

"I suppose so," said Honnie dolefully.

The Tyrone kitchens were very busy the day before the big excursion, but Honnie and Bridget worked with singing hearts as they thought of the great day out ahead of them. There had been a long hot spell of weather which showed no signs of breaking, and the girls were confident that it would be fine on the morrow.

They helped Mrs. Smith make chicken and ham pies and veal cakes. They made plum cake. They cooked two joints of beef, and a shoulder of lamb and two lamb ribs, and a ham and a tongue, all to be eaten cold. They roasted four good fowl. They made bread and biscuits, puddings and fruit tarts. Quite a number of friends were going to join the family at the races.

Honnie and Brudget went to bed bubbling with excitement and found it very difficult to sleep.

They were up not long after dawn the next morning, and immediately looked anxiously out the window to check on the weather. To their great delight it looked to be another fine dry day. They cheerfully got to work to get everything packed in the big wicker baskets which had been used for Tyrone picnics for many years. Mrs. Hunt, the housekeeper, along with Mrs. Smith, were both there to see that everything was done properly. Care had to be taken with the strawberries, newly picked from the gardens. The cream needed to be packed in with ice from the Tyrone icehouse. Salads needed special attention. Nothing must be forgotten. Had the horseradish sauce been packed? The bottle of mint sauce – well corked? The vinegar, the mustard, the oil, the pepper and salt? The tea, the teapots, the milk, the lemons, the sugar? Baskets were opened to be absolutely sure.

Then there were the wineglasses and tumblers, plates and serving dishes, knives and forks and spoons, teacups and saucers, not to mention the tablecloths and napkins.

Mr. Scott had packed the beverages – ginger beer, soda water, lemonade, sherry, claret, some light wine, and a few bottles of brandy.

There was quite a large party travelling from Tyrone. As well as friends and neighbours, there were also some visitors who happened to be staying with the family. The servants who were going along had also to be accommodated, so a variety of conveyances were called into use. There was the big St. George shooting brake which could carry quite a number of people, and two more provided by Christopher's friends who were going to the races with them. There were a couple of traps, and a number of jaunting cars too.

The women of the St. George family, and as many of their friends as could be accomodated, would travel in the St. George brake. Honnie, Bridget, Robert, the grooms and men servants would travel in one of the other brakes along with the food.

Mrs. Smith came out to supervise – she wanted to make sure that her food was being properly loaded. Mr. Scott was anxious to see that the wine and beer and cordials were being carried as they should be – he'd had strict instructions from Christopher. And the Misses St. George made sure that rugs, parasols and similar creature comforts were being put in the vehicles.

Finally, they got under way.

Josie watched them go with envious eyes, before returning to the kitchen, which was in a state of some disorder. It would be her job to tidy everything up.

"You have to feel a sorry for Josie," said Bridget as they drove away. "She would dearly like to come on this excursion."

The journey to Headford was a leisurely one, and Bridget and Honnie enjoyed it. The sky was a pale blue, the ground bone dry. It was pleasant to sit high and at ease on a fine day and look at the passing scene, the little whitewashed cottages, the stone-walled fields, the grazing cattle and sheep. It was quite a big procession, and people came out to look at them and waved as they went by.

Honnie turned her face up to the sun.

"Somebody's been cutting hay," she said. "Can you smell it?"

Christopher had ridden over to Headford the day before with Mick Murphy, taking Barebones on a leading rein, and had stayed the night with friends who lived close by. Barebones was running in the second race, and Christopher wanted to have him near the course, ready and well rested.

The Tyrone entourage moved slowly, through Kilcolgan, and Clarinbridge, and Oranmore, around Galway city itself, rather than into it, and then north, near the shores of Loch Corrib. The closer they got to Headford, the more people they met. There were people on horseback, in carriages and carts and gigs and traps, people in all manner of contraptions. There were beshawled women carrying babies, barefooted children, shabbily dressed men. They were a good-humoured lot, even if some of them had started celebrating their day out a bit in advance. And why wouldn't they be thirsty, as the sun beat down on them, and the dust rose in clouds from the dry roads and paths?

Mick Murphy was there to meet the Tyrone party as they arrived at the course. He led them to a field a little distance away from crowds, where he had arranged a place for them. Mick told Honnie that there were much grander race meetings in other parts of the country but, never having been at a race meeting before, Honnie found herself completely caught up in the excitement of the event. She and Bridget were given a little time to look around before they got to work unloading and readying the picnic.

There were so many people, and they all seemed to be talking or shouting or calling out at the same time. There were tents and stalls selling drink and crubeens and other delicacies. There were big cauldrons of boiling tea.

"Father Matthew, the temperance priest, wants to see people drinking tea instead of whiskey," said Bridget, "so the stallholders have been told they should try to sell 'tay'."

"But I'd say there'll always be people who want whiskey and not 'tay'," said Honnie, "and there will always be people who are happy to sell it to them."

There was the three-card-trick man inviting people to "find the lady" – the Queen of Hearts – in the cards laid face down in front of him.

"I'm sure I could find her just as well as that man," said Honnie.

"And I'm sure you couldn't," said Bridget, who had been at race meetings before. "The one who is so good at finding her is a friend of the trick man – everyone knows that. It's all a lure to part you from your money."

There was the trick-the-loop man. He had a long, narrow piece of leather, which he doubled over in a loop, and then wound it round itself, so that the loop was hidden in the length of coiled leather. He invited passers-by to find the loop by sticking a thin piece of wood in it.

"And you're going to tell me that isn't as easy as it looks either," said Honnie.

"Why do you think it's called a trick?" said Bridget.

"I can only say I'm glad you've no money to spend, or you'd end up throwing it away."

There was the man in a barrel. Only his head was to be seen, while people threw balls at him – soft balls, made of rags tied up in old socks. His head had to be above the barrel when the ball was thrown, and he had to be quick enough to duck down before it hit him. There were acrobats, who tumbled and somersaulted, and did all manner of extraordinary feats. There were pipers and fiddlers, calling to people to join the dance, while the military were in a separate tent making their own music.

There seemed to be a remarkable number of pretty girls to be seen – fresh-faced girls with long glossy locks, red-haired, raven-haired, and golden. Some wore red petticoats, and many of them were barefoot. They walked in groups, laughing and chattering together. Boys called out to them as they passed by, and the girls pretended not to hear, though one young man got his face slapped when he tried to steal a kiss.

The better-off lady visitors wore silk gowns and shoes with silver buckles, and were usually escorted by gentlemen.

Everywhere there were people sprawled along the banks, sitting on top of the ditches, lounging by the surrounding hedges, enjoying the sport, the conversation and their day out.

It seemed like only minutes later that Bridget and Honnie had to return to prepare the picnic, which was to take place after Barebones' race. If they had everything laid out and ready, they knew they would be free to watch the race itself.

The flies were a problem, buzzing, droning, zooming

towards everything edible. But Mrs. Smith had made sure they had packed an ample supply of cloths and napkins, and as they unpacked each basket they were careful to cover the food.

"Picnics seem a great idea," said Honnie, "but the flies can make things miserable. And, God, how I hate bluebottles! They give me the creeps. My father always says if you have a lot of bluebottles, there's something dead not too far away."

"It's the horseflies I can't stand," said Bridget. "You don't hear them coming, and then suddenly you've been bitten."

Robert turned the glasses upside down on a cloth-covered tray, and unpacked bottles of wine, beer and cordials, before standing them in cooling buckets of ice. From the way he went about the task, Honnie suspected he had been sampling some of the drinks before they arrived.

The races were run in heats, each heat over a mile and a half, and over three four-foot walls. A horse had to defeat his rivals in two heats before he was declared a winner.

There were only four horses entered in the second race and Christopher was riding Barebones himself. A crush of people gathered to watch.

Honnie stood up on her toes to look. She had to admit that he and Barebones made a fine sight.

Will it ever begin, she thought impatiently.

As Christopher and the other three competitors rode up to the starting point Honnie cast an experienced eye over the other horses. A grey colt she dismissed immediately. Of the other two, there was a bay colt which certainly looked lively and free on his feet, and might be a serious challenge.

Still, she decided, if Christopher didn't try to push Barebones too hard at the beginning, and if Barebones didn't spend too much of his energy in the first heat, then they should win.

She found herself in a knot of anxiety as Christopher rode Barebones up to the starting post.

"So, do you think that horse of Christopher St. George's is going to win, Honnie?" said a familiar voice behind her.

She turned to see Tom Kelly – now Father Tom in his black priest's clothes and white priest's collar.

"Tom! I heard you were back, and back to stay now. How good it is to see you!"

A loud cheer signalled the race was about to start.

"Tom, I'm sure Barebones can do it," she said. "That's if Master Christopher is patient with him and doesn't try to rush him. He's full of heart and spirit, is Barebones, but the thing is not to let him use it all up at the beginning."

Once the horses got under way, Honnie clutched Bridget's arm so tightly that she yelped in protest. But Barebones won his first heat easily, several lengths ahead of the other horses.

Honnie had been right about the grey colt. It was obvious after the first heat that he didn't have a chance, and he was withdrawn.

Barebones came second in the second heat. Christopher had written off the bay colt on his performance first time round and was overconfident in the second heat, Honnie decided, when the bay showed a remarkable burst of speed towards the end and finished up winning by half a length. By the time the third heat got underway, Honnie was beside herself with excitement.

"*Come on, Barebones, come on, Barebones! Come on! You can do it!*"

"For heaven's sake, Honnie," said Bridget, "will you take it easy? People are staring at us."

Tom laughed. "It's good to see you haven't changed, Honnie," he said. "You're as easily carried away as ever."

Barebones came in first again in the third heat and, having won two of the three heats, he was deemed the winner.

Honnie could hardly contain her delight. "I knew he could do it! I knew he could!"

Then it was time to say goodbye to Father Tom, and get back quickly to look after the picnic. They had to have everything ready to serve when people arrived.

The women came first, followed by Christopher and his friends. Flushed and jubilant with his success, he demanded glasses of champagne for everyone.

"For you, too, Robert, and for Honnie and Bridget. There's cause for celebration. I've won my bet with my friend Richard Blake. And this is only the beginning. Did you see how easily he won? He didn't even have to try very hard. He just sailed along, as if he had all the time in the world. He won those heats like a champion, and that's what he is, a future champion. Wait until he gets to the Curragh of Kildare!"

His sisters, sitting on rugs around the picnic cloth, smiled fondly at his enthusiasm.

"A toast," he said, "to Barebones! And may this be

only the first of many victories."

Everyone raised their glasses.

"*To Barebones!*"

Christopher smiled at Honnie, who was standing with Bridget a few feet away.

"I heard you cheering for Barebones, Honnie – it would have been difficult not to. Didn't I deserve some support as well?"

All eyes turned on Honnie, who felt the blood rising in her face.

Let the ground open up and swallow me, she thought.

Then the company was distracted by a very lively horse resisting being led by a young groom a little distance away from them. The horse was winning the struggle.

The awkward moment had passed.

But Honnie could feel Christopher's sister, Anne, watching her. Honnie tried to avoid her eye – not, she told herself, that she had any reason to feel at fault. But she could still feel Anne's eyes on her, boring through her shoulders even when her back was turned.

Bridget had noticed it too. "I don't think you're one of Miss Anne's favourite people," she said.

"Nor is she one of mine," said Honnnie tartly.

For the most part it was a very good-humoured occasion, though towards the end of the day, when some of the race-goers had consumed more drink than was good for them, there were a few brawls. One brawl broke out quite near them. It seemed to be about money at first, and then the smaller of the two men started shouting about a woman and suddenly both men were rolling around in the straw and the dirt, furiously punching each other. Each man had his own supporters yelling encouragement from the sidelines, until a race steward arrived on horseback wielding a huge hunting whip, at the sight of which the brawlers, and their supporters, scattered in all directions.

It was time to pack up and go home. After a day in the open air, with the sunshine, the food and the wine, everyone was relaxed and happy. One of the grooms was bringing Barebones back, so Christopher travelled in the big shooting brake with his friends, with Honnie and Bridget and Robert in the other brake behind them.

Christopher called back to Robert.

"*Robert! How about giving us a song or two? I've heard you have a great voice, and a big repertoire of songs. So, come on, Robert, let's hear you!*"

Robert demurred at first.

"But we all know he'll not need much persuasion," Bridget whispered to Honnie.

"And we know what he's going to sing too – doesn't every Corkman sing 'The Bells of Shandon'?" said Honnie.

"And for an encore it'll be 'The Rakes of Mallow'!"

She was right. Robert sang a few more songs, and Honnie had to admit that he had a good voice, and it was pleasant listening to him as they rolled home under the clear, still, evening sky.

After Robert ran out of songs, the party grew quieter, with just the occasional burst of conversation. Honnie half listened to Robert talking to Bridget, about race meetings in his native Cork, about other race meetings he had been to in Galway, about Galway people and Cork people, before moving on to local gossip.

"I hear Master Christopher's taken a fancy to Ellen

Connors, over at Drumacoo," he said.

By the time they got back to Tyrone everyone was very tired.

"But not everyone has to clear up," said Bridget to Honnie as they wearily brought the wicker baskets, with all the china and cutlery, the platters and plates, the glasses and bottles, the tablecloths and napkins, into the kitchen.

Before she went to bed that night Honnie crept out to see Barebones. It was a bright warm night, with the moonlight flooding over the gardens and the stable yard. The scent of roses lingered in the air and, more strongly, the sweet delicate scent of wild woodbine.

But Honnie also liked the rich pungent smell of the stables. She went to Barebones who whickered when he saw her. She stroked his nose and told him what a fine fellow he was. She had brought him a quartered apple which she fed to him bit by bit. Then she heard a sound behind her.

"What a nice surprise! I didn't expect to find you here. Did you enjoy the day?"

It was Christopher.

"Very much," she said without turning round.

"He'd have won the second heat too, but for my foolishness. I was too sure he'd walk it. But he won anyway, despite me. He's a fine horse, isn't he?"

"Yes," said Honnie. "He is."

Christopher came closer. Honnie could sense him standing tall behind her. He reached out to stroke the horse's head. He smelt of brandy and cigars. After a minute he dropped his hand and slipped his arms around her waist.

Still Honnie didn't turn around.

Very gently he kissed the back of her neck. His hair fell forward across the side of her face, the smell of it oily and masculine. She could feel her whole body answering his. It would be very easy to go along with her feelings. But it would be a mistake.

She tried to break free, but Christopher's grip tightened.

"Don't you like me, Honnie? I'm almost sure you do."

"Let me go," said Honnie, struggling to break free. "I'll lose my place, that's what will happen. I've heard too many stories of girls like me who listened to soft words from handsome young gentlemen like you. Well, it's not going to happen to me!"

Christopher reluctantly loosened his hold and Honnie turned to go. She stopped to look up at his flushed face.

"I hear that Máire Conneely has gone the way of your other fancies," she said, "and that your latest fancy is Ellen Connors at Drumacoo. You might find her more willing to accept your advances than I am."

Christopher laughed, making Honnie want to punch him.

"You're *jealous,* Honnie," he said gleefully. "That's what you are – *jealous.*"

"*Jealous?*" said Honnie furiously. "Over you! I never heard anything so ridiculous in my life. You think any girl is yours for the taking. Well, I'm not."

She spun away, just catching Christopher's last words.

"I might just take your advice, though, about Ellen Connors."

Bridget was in bed when Honnie came into the room.

"Where on earth were you, Honnie?" she said in an anxious whisper.

The other girls in the room looked asleep, but you

could never be sure.

"Oh, I just wanted to say goodnight to Barebones," said Honnie. "I was so proud of him today."

"You seem very flustered for a girl who was just talking to a horse," Bridget whispered.

"Go to sleep," said Honnie.

Lying in bed, unable to sleep, Honnie went over the events of the day. Life had seemed much simpler when she and Tom were growing up together. With Tom, you knew where you were. Though she had sometimes wondered if they might spend their lives together, he had always behaved almost as a brother would. She now realised that he had intended to become a priest all along. She thought of her neighbour in Maree, Mairtín Breathnach. She knew he had feelings for her, and that his mother hoped she might feel the same towards him. But she didn't. Mairtín was a fine-looking fellow, and a kind one, and hardworking too, but he lit no light in her heart. She had never known the way the touch of a man could make her feel until now.

Chapter 17

Two days later, Christopher left for Dublin and Howth Castle to stay with Thomas St. Lawrence. Honnie only saw him a couple of times before he went, when he saluted her politely, but with a gleam in his eye. He stayed away for most of July, returning in the last week to get involved in the preparations for the Galway Races which were to be held at the beginning of August. After that he spent most of his time away from Tyrone, for he was one of the stewards of the races.

No sooner had the Galway Races finished than Christopher was off to the races in Tuam. After they finished, he was taking part in the Galway Regatta.

Despite herself, Honnie found she was listening for bits and pieces of news about his whereabouts and, when Mr. Scott found a piece in the newspaper about Christopher's part in the Regatta, she listened avidly.

"It seems Master Christopher rowed quite a bit when he was up in Trinity College," said Mr. Scott. "But, not surprisingly, he and his friends couldn't compete against fishermen who spend the whole year round in boats. They only came third."

Arthur St. George was beginning to feel a bit disgruntled. When the cholera epidemic was at its height it was obvious that Christpher couldn't go riding to the different parts of the St. George estates. But this wasn't so any more. Christopher was not making many journeys with Danny. He was always going somewhere else. He was going to race meetings all around the country, he was going up to the Curragh of Kildare. He was going up to Thomas St. Lawrence very frequently. He was looking forward to the hunting season. Yes, thought Arthur, Christopher would definitely have to be called to order. But how? And when?

The betrothal of one of Christopher's sisters was announced in the middle of August. Matilda was to marry Colonel Charles Pepper of Ballygarth at the beginning of December.

In the last week of August Christopher was back once again in the stable yards of Tyrone, spending all day with the horses, from early morning to nightfall. He was keeping a watchful eye on two foals which had just been born and, with one of the grooms, he stayed up all night with a mare who was about to foal. He took out some of the young horses for schooling, and he rode out older horses to test them and try them out.

Christopher still held on to Necromancer, who was – it seemed to Honnie – as bad-tempered and willful as he had always been. It was as if Christopher was determined to bend the horse to his will. It was when he was excercising Necromancer that the accident happened.

The first Honnie knew about it was when she heard a

commotion in the yard outside and Mick, the head groom, calling for help.

"They're bringing Master Christopher up from the stream field!" he said breathlessly as he arrived at the kitchen door. "He's had a bad fall and he's unconscious! The weather's been so good, the ground was dry, and he fell hard. Somebody should tell the Master."

But Arthur St. George had already been told and had sent one of the grooms off on horseback to fetch Dr. Veitch from Galway.

Honnie was surprised at the overwhelming clutch of fear that caught at her heart. She found herself racing out to the stable yard, to the sound of approaching voices shouting advice, warning of obstacles in the way.

"*Take it easy now, easy does it!*"

"*Mind them cobbles, there's dung on them – you don't want to slip!*"

A small crowd had gathered in the yard, all looking towards the group of men carrying Christopher on a makeshift stretcher made of a field gate with some coats thrown over it.

"He looks very pale, poor lad. God grant it's nothing serious ..."

In the hall, Honnie watched as he was taken to the morning room and laid down gently on a chaise longue.

Anne, leaning anxiously over him, looked up and saw Honnie at the door.

"For heaven's sake, girl, make yourself useful! Go down and fetch some warm water, and some soft cloths."

By the time Honnie came back Christopher had opened his eyes and was looking looked around him in a dazed way.

"I feel as though I've been bashed by a bull," he groaned. "Christ! Every bone in my body is aching." He moved first one leg, and then the other, gingerly. "Well, they seem to be working anyway. What happened to me?"

"You were trying to make Necromancer jump that high ditch in the field beyond and he stumbled and you both fell," said Anne. "Necromancer came out the worst of it. Mick Murphy says he told you there were bad potholes in that field, but of course as usual you didn't listen. Now lie still, Christopher, and let me clean you up a bit. Just try and do what you're told for once and stay quiet!"

"Necromancer!" said Christopher, as memory came coursing back. "Is he all right?"

"No, he isn't," said Arthur St. George, who had just come on the scene. "He broke his leg. He had to be put down. It was always going to be either you or him. Count yourself lucky it wasn't you."

"Oh, God, no!" Distraught, Christopher tried to sit up and gave a howl of pain. He clutched his left arm and lay back cautiously.

Dr. Veitch's verdict, when he came, was a dislocated shoulder. He manipulated it as gently as he could to the accompaniment of several loud yells from Christopher. He then put the arm in a sling.

"You did a fine job on yourself, young man. You must have hit the ground with some force. You have a nasty contusion on your head, and it's growing into quite a big bump, so you probably have a touch of concussion. And you put that shoulder out quite badly. I think I've got it back in. What you need now is rest. So, rest up, keep the shoulder in that sling, and no horse-riding for at least six weeks."

Christopher groaned. "But Howth Park races are on in a fortnight's time, and I promised Thomas I'd be up there at least a week beforehand ..."

"Be sensible," said Dr. Veitch. "That shoulder needs time to heal if you don't want it to come against you in years to come. Give it a chance. And mind that head."

And he packed his bag and bid them all goodbye.

Honnie, hearing about Necromancer, was surprised that she felt a twinge of sorrow for the dead horse. She remembered how powerful, how handsome he had looked the first day she had seen him. It was hard to believe he was dead.

Christopher was not a good patient His shoulder was painful, and for two days after the accident he felt quite groggy and his head hurt. For some days at least he would be confined to the house.

His father saw this as an ideal opportunity to do what he had been trying to do for two years – have a good long talk with Christopher about the affairs of the estate and all its problems, and its future. Despite Christopher's initial good intentions, every time he had tried to talk to him before, he had always managed to escape on some pretext or another. Now he couldn't escape.

He found him in the drawing room.

Christopher said he didn't feel able to deal with such matters in his present condition. He said he had a bad headache, and couldn't think straight. Couldn't they postpone any talking for a few days, until he felt better? He feigned faintness.

But his father was not to be thwarted this time.

"I'm not suggesting a long talk," said Arthur, "but we

need to make a beginning. When your mother and I got married in 1801, and your grandfather transferred Tyrone House and all the lands accruing to me, it came with a big debt. It had cost close on £30,000 to build Tyrone. And then he built Kilcolgan Castle, and more was borrowed to do that. We have accrued many more debts over years. We have a large family – eight daughters who have entitlements, and various other people who can make demands on the estate. Ireland looked like having a prosperous future in 1801. We thought we would be easily able to pay off the debts over the years. But prosperity never came. Instead things have got worse and worse. There are many landowners at their wits' end."

"I know all that," said Christopher irritably.

"Let me finish," said his father. "I don't think you are ready yet to take over ownership of the estate. I had hoped that would happen when you got married –"

"But why would I want to take ownership of an estate that is laden down with huge debts?" said Christopher. "None of which are of my making."

"Which brings me to my next concern," said his father. "I have expected, hoped, you would make a good match. What about that nice Miss Mitchell? She's very pretty and I've been told she would come with a good dowry."

"Miss Mitchell!" said Christopher. "She isn't particularly nice and she isn't particularly pretty. She's a bit like a china doll. We have nothing in common. She hated Galway. She's a city woman through and through."

His father rose to go. "I think that's enough for one day," he said. "Perhaps when you feel a bit better we can make more progress."

Seeing his father looking somewhat disconsolate, Christopher felt guilty.

"Father, I know I've been remiss in attending to our affairs. I'll start going out again with Danny but the doctor says I can't get up on a horse for six weeks. Just as soon as my shoulder heals I'll start again. But I will *not* take ownership of anything! I don't want all those debts hanging across my shoulders."

"We shall see," said his father as he left the room.

Meanwhile he was thirsty, he was hot. He wanted milk punch, he wanted lemonade, then he wanted a glass of wine, and he wanted Honnie to bring it up to him. And, as Honnie herself said, it wasn't even part of her job as a kitchenmaid. She knew that Mrs. Smith was less than pleased but hadn't quite the nerve to forbid it.

"Things are getting out of order in this house and I don't like it one bit," she said to Mr. Scott. "The Mistress would never have allowed such carry-on. She must be turning in her grave."

But Christopher didn't get away with it for long.

Three days after his accident he asked for some lemonade. When Honnie brought it up he spilt it.

"I'm very sorry, Honnie," he said. "It's just that I can only use one hand and even that's a bit shaky."

He looked so genuinely upset that Honnie reached forward to hold the glass to his mouth. Christopher's good hand was anything but shaky as it closed over hers. He was smiling up at Honnie when Anne came into the room.

"That will be all, Honnie," Anne said. "Now get back to the kitchen and stay in the kitchen. If Master

Christopher wants anything he can ring the bell and Bridget can bring it up to him. I shall speak to Mrs. Smith."

Honnie scurried out of the room, but when she heard Anne speaking sharply to Christopher she stopped to listen outside the door.

"I have been doing my best," Anne said. "Yet as hard as I try I am aware that the standards in this house have sunk sadly since Mother died. But things are sinking very low indeed when the eldest son of the house openly flirts with a kitchenmaid because he is bored and can think of nothing better to do."

"Oh, for heaven's sake, Anne, don't be such a stickler!" said Christopher. "It was only a bit of harmless fun. You're making a mountain out of a molehill."

"It may seem like a bit of harmless fun to you," said Anne. "And we all know that you are more than ready to take your fun wherever you find it. But it is totally inappropriate behaviour in your own home. It isn't fair to Mrs. Smith, and it isn't fair to Honnie either – though I must say that Honnie's own behaviour leaves a lot to be desired. A flighty piece she seems to me, with ideas above her station. I can't say I ever liked the girl."

Christopher's temper flared. "As you have said, Anne, I am the eldest son of the house. I am not answerable to you. And I will not be spoken to like a small boy, even if you are my older sister, my *much* older sister. The trouble with you, Anne, is that you're too prim and proper by half. No wonder you never married – you never met any man as straitlaced as yourself."

"If everybody ignored the proprieties of living, the way you do, we'd all be in a sorry mess," said Anne. "I can only imagine what Mother would think of all this –

but then none of this would have happened if she were alive. If I hear any more talk about yourself and Honnie, I shall feel it my duty to tell Father."

"Off you go," said Christopher. "Tittle-tattle to whomever you like. I don't care."

"That's the trouble. You don't care about anything – except horses, and having fun."

Outside, Honnie hurried downstairs. She had heard enough, enough to make her absolutely furious. A bit of harmless fun, indeed!

Later in the day Anne sent word down to Mrs. Smith that she wanted to see her in the drawing room.

In some trepidation Mrs. Smith made her way upstairs.

Anne bluntly told her that something had to be done about Honnie's behaviour with Christopher.

"I've been worried about it myself. But what was I to do, Miss Anne?" she said. "Master Christopher insisted he wanted Honnie to look to him. I told him it wasn't proper, but he said it was his house, and if he wanted Honnie to attend to him, then he'd have her attend to him."

"My mother would never have tolerated this kind of behaviour," said Anne. "And I cannot but think that much of the blame lies with Honnie for encouraging my brother. I know you have found the girl to be a very hard worker, but I am beginning to believe she should be let go. This kind of behaviour cannot be tolerated."

That evening in her bedroom, as she sat on the window seat looking out over the gardens of Tyrone and the grey sea beyond, Anne was still smarting over Christopher's remarks.

She had meant what she said. She had been trying to run things in Tyrone as her mother would have wished, but nobody seemed to notice or care. When her mother was alive the house had run like clockwork – or so it seemed to her, looking back. Her mother had been firm, even strict, with the servants, but not unkind, and they had respected her. Anne could not feel that they had the same respect for her.

Her mother had always said that the housekeeper was one of the most important people in any house. It was her task to keep a watchful eye on almost everything involving the running of the house and ensure good and orderly management. Her mother and Mrs. Hunt had always seemed to deal harmoniously with each other, and she knew that Mrs. Hunt had greatly respected Lady Harriet. She felt she herself would never command the same respect.

Three days earlier, she had tried to talk to Mrs. Hunt about a dinner party to which she had invited six of her friends the week before. She didn't often have dinner parties, and this had been arranged specially to celebrate the engagement of one of her friends. She had put a lot of thought and planning into the occasion. The guests seemed to enjoy themselves, but she herself hadn't been happy. Certain pieces of cutlery had been missing from the table, one silver serving spoon was clearly in need of polishing, and some of the glasses didn't sparkle as they should. Even the food was disappointing. A dish that was supposed to arrive hot had arrived lukewarm. And the whole appearance of the table was lacking in style.

Mrs. Hunt had listened with tightened lips.

"I'm sorry you were disappointed," she said. "I do my

best with the maids I have, but young maidservants today are hard to train. They have to be watched all the time. And I can't be everywhere at once. Things were different when the mistress was alive. She kept a sharp eye on everything. I do think Mrs. Smith is too lenient with the kitchen servants. And the food is more Mrs. Smith's concern than mine."

Anne inwardly bristled at the implication that part of the problem was her own lack of control, and decided that Mrs. Hunt should be stopped before she went on to criticise Mrs. Smith any further. She couldn't be party to one senior servant criticising another – whatever the rights and wrongs of it were.

"Thank you, Mrs. Hunt," she had said very firmly. "That will be all for the present."

Stopped in mid-flow, Mrs. Hunt had looked considerably put out. She opened her mouth to say more but, looking at Anne's severe expression, she thought better of it and left.

That had been three days ago. Now Christopher was making more trouble, flirting with that girl, providing the servants with easy food for gossip. The sooner Honnie was let go the better, thought Anne.

Feeling helpless and dispirited, she wept. She wished her mother was still alive. It was no use looking for help from her father or Christopher. Not only did they not notice what was happening around them, they didn't care too much if they did. Her father spent most of his time in his study. Christopher was always out and about with the horses, or away racing, or hunting. When he was at home, provided he had sufficient food and drink, he happily took each day as it came. Neither seemed to notice that without the care and attention it needed, the house had become quite *rackety*.

She was still weeping when Louisa came into the bedroom, looking for help with the repair of a gown. Anne told her about her disagreement with Christopher.

"Don't pay any heed to him," said Louisa. "He's just being odious, and nobody can be more odious than Christopher when he is in a bad mood. Mind you, I had thought on a few occasions that Christopher might have a fancy for Honnie. But with Christopher his fancies never last that long. But of *course* he shouldn't behave that way in his own house. Should we talk to Father about him?"

"Let's wait a while and see what happens," said Anne. "You know Father. He hates having to deal with family disagreements. He puts his head down and hopes it will all go away."

"Well ... all right," said Louisa, "but if things get worse, we shall have to talk to him, and he will have to call Christopher to order."

"And they will both lose their tempers, and shout at one another, and it will all be very unpleasant," said Anne.

"As to the house," said Louisa, "you're being too hard on yourself. You can't be responsible for every little thing that goes wrong. You can only do your best."

"Well, my best doesn't seem to be good enough," said Anne.

A chambermaid tidying a nearby bedroom was able to hear the exchanges between Anne and Louisa and recount it back later to the other servants – though not when Honnie was around.

Josie found it exciting.

"It's just like a story," she said, "only it's happening in front of you, and you want to know the latest bit. Miss Anne has certainly put manners on Honnie. She's very quiet in herself these days."

In the morning room, Christopher tweaked irritably at his sling and looked out gloomily at the heavy rain that had begun to fall outside. His brother had come to keep him company but he had quickly become irritated with him and told him to go. He picked up a book and started to read, then dropped it, and flittered through a newspaper lying on the table. He was regretting his remarks to Anne. He knew he had gone too far. He was beginning to feel ashamed of himself when Louisa came into the morning room, fresh from her talk with Anne.

"How *could* you talk to Anne like that?" she said. "You've thoroughly upset her. I found her upstairs, weeping. And how could you behave in that irresponsible way with Honnie?"

Christopher quickly forgot that he had been feeling ashamed of himself.

"Anne is a bossy, tiresome ninny," he said. "It's a lot of fuss about nothing. I've already had a telling-off from her. I don't need you to come along and berate me as well. Go off and do your needlework, or read your book, or press your flowers, or whatever else you were doing before Anne set you on me."

"Do you know what's wrong with you, Christopher? You're thoroughly spoilt. If you had listened to Mick Murphy, you would never have tried to make Necromancer jump that ditch and fallen and hurt yourself in the first place. But then, when did you ever listen to anybody? But still we were sorry for you, and we have looked after you, and read to you, and tried to divert you, and now you are behaving abominably."

Louisa left the room quickly before Christopher could answer back and when he tried to follow her, enraged, he knocked his injured shoulder against the door and gave a yelp of pain.

He was cross with himself for hitting his shoulder, cross with his sisters, cross because in his heart he knew that he had behaved badly. And he was also very, very bored.

After a few more days confined to the house, Christopher couldn't stand it any longer. Besides, he decided, his shoulder felt much better and his head didn't hurt any more. Soon he was back to his old form, out in the yard with the men and the horses. But he had sense enough not to try to get up on a horse for the first few weeks at any rate.

The susurrus of gossip which had been travelling around Tyrone House had subsided, but not gone away. People were watching Honnie, none more so than Mrs. Smith. Since Anne had spoken to her, Honnie had hardly been allowed out of the kitchen. But it was September, and September was blackberry time. Mrs. Smith decided that it should be safe enough to send Honnie off on a blackberry-picking expedition. She couldn't spare Bridget and she didn't trust Josie enough to let her off on her own – not with Robert around.

Every year since she had come to Tyrone it had been one of Honnie's more pleasurable chores to spend two or three afternoons gathering the rich dark fruit for pies, tarts and jam-making. She set out happily one warm afternoon for the bramble bushes that grew abundantly around the edge of the woods alongside Tyrone.

She brought two wooden pails with her, one hung over each arm, and a bottle of water as well. Blackberry-picking could be thirsty work. She was enjoying being out in the fresh air after her weeks confined to the hot dark kitchens. She felt relaxed and at ease.

She had one pail half filled when Rua suddenly appeared beside her.

She swung around to see Christopher gazing at her.

"What do you want?" she asked, completely taken aback. "What are you doing here?"

"What kind of a welcome is that?" said Christopher. "I'm not supposed to ride out or work with horses yet, so I came out for a stroll. I'm here because I saw you picking blackberries and I thought you'd be glad of some help."

"You won't be picking much with only one good arm," said Honnie. "You need to hold the pail as well as pick."

"I'll manage," said Christopher. "Besides, I don't really need this sling any more."

"I'm sure you could find something more entertaining to do," said Honnie.

"Now what could be more entertaining than picking blackberries on a lovely day like this with a pretty girl?" said Christopher, turning the full force of his smile on her.

I'm not going to fall for that, thought Honnie.

"You'll have to think of something more original than

that if you're trying to engage my attention," she said.

Christopher stepped closer, and Honnie backed quickly away.

"You'd want to be careful with that shoulder," she said. "I wouldn't like to see it being knocked out again."

"Now could that be a threat, Honnie?" said Christopher.

"Make what you like of it."

"You're a hard woman," said Christopher.

He put the empty pail at his feet, grinned at her and started to pick.

They moved slowly along a wide stretch of bushes at the woods' edge while Rua stretched out on the grass and dozed, occasionally opening an eye to check their wereabouts. Honnie felt the sun warm on her face and her arms. From a field nearby came the gentle sound of cows chewing the cud. The bees were out, collecting the last of the summer's honey. A pheasant called, shrill.

Christopher remarked idly how much he liked blackberry-and-apple pie. He talked about the harvest. He talked about Barebones. He talked about Father Tom.

"I like him. He is a powerful man on a horse – he can clear a stone wall better than most men in the field."

Honnie answered in monosyllables.

"You don't seem to be in the mood for conversation today, Honnie," he said. "Have I done something to offend you?"

"I dislike the idea that I'm being used for diversion," she said crossly.

"Now that's unkind," said Christopher. "It's a lovely afternoon, and when I saw you picking the blackberries I wanted to help. Is that such a bad thing?"

"I heard what you said about me to Miss Anne. You said I was 'just a bit of fun'. Well I don't intend to be *anybody's* bit of fun," said Honnie. "Leave me alone, stop making trouble for me, and go find your pleasures elsewhere."

"You think I've dishonourable intentions towards you, do you, Honnie?" said Christopher in a half-joking tone.

Honnie flushed a bright pink. "No ... that is ... if you do ..." she stammered, "you should know that I've never been with a man, and I never will be until I'm married."

"Good God, Honnie," he said, suddenly angry, "what kind of a man do you take me for?"

Honnie turned to look at him. His eyes were blazing.

"I'm getting very tired of people attributing the worst of intentions to me," he said. "Apparently I'm not capable of any decent feelings."

"You must admit you haven't exactly got a blameless reputation."

"I know what people say about me," he said. "I'm the landlord's son who tries to have his wicked way with any girl he fancies, a heartless womaniser who doesn't care about anything except his own pleasures, someone against whom every respectable girl should be warned. But that is just not true. What about you, Honnie? Do you really believe I'm that bad?"

"Well ..." said Honnie, "you can't honestly say there's no truth in the stories."

"A little, maybe," said Christopher. "I like pretty girls. I flirt with them. But I don't go round trying to destroy their lives or their reputations. Yes, I've been with some women of doubtful reputation, but their reputations were doubtful before I ever took up with them. But you're different."

Neither of them spoke for a while.

Then, because she was thirsty, and she couldn't drink without asking Christopher if he would like a drink, she offered him the bottle.

Christopher took a good draught and as he handed the bottle back to her their fingers touched.

Honnie raised the bottle to her lips, aware of his eyes on her as she drank. Then, laying the bottle on the grass, she turned away to pick more berries. The pail was almost full. She was reaching for some particularly fine fruit, high up on a bush, when her hair got caught in a bramble.

"Don't move," Christopher said.

Honnie felt his fingers on her shoulder and as he untangled her hair it fell loose down her back. He turned her round to face him and kissed her, at first gently, then more insistently. Honnie had never been kissed like that before. She was stunned at the force of the feelings which flooded through her. But her instinct for self-preservation also surfaced.

"*No!*" She pulled away, pink-cheeked and flustered. "My pails are full and Mrs. Smith will be wondering where I am. I have to go back."

She turned to walk away but Christopher caught her arm.

"Meet me this evening, down beyond the walled garden, in the copse at the edge of the water."

Honnie hesitated.

"I'll be there at nine," he said. "I'll wait until you come."

"Well, you'll be waiting a long time, then," said Honnie.

"I'll be there," he said.

Later that evening, as she was making a blackberry-and-apple pie, Honnie told herself she had no intention of going out to meet Christopher. It would be the height of foolishness. She warned herself that she'd be just heading down the same road as many another silly girl, and she promised herself sternly that down that road she would not go.

At nine o'clock things were quiet down in the kitchen, but it was still close to ten before everything was tidied and put away and Bridget and the other girls could take their ease.

"It's very stuffy in here, isn't it?" Honnie said to Bridget.

"No more than it ever is," said Bridget.

"Well, it seems to be getting to me this evening," said Honnie. "Maybe I'm sickening for something. I think I might just slip outside for a few minutes."

Bridget was concerned. "Are you sure you're all right? Would you like me to come with you?"

"Not at all," said Honnie. "You enjoy your cup of tea. I'll be back shortly."

"I'll go with you," said Bridget. "I'd like a bit of fresh air myself."

"The truth is I'd really like a few minutes on my own," said Honnie.

And before Bridget could say another word, she went out the door and walked swiftly away.

She hurried through the grove of trees below the house, past the walled garden and down to the copse at the water's edge.

If he's there, he's there, and if he isn't, then that's an end to it, she thought, trying not to walk too fast.

Christopher was waiting, for once without Rua.

"This is a mistake," Honnie said. "And I can't stay. I'll be missed. I told Bridget I didn't feel well and I was going out for a breath of fresh air. She wanted to come with me. If I don't get back directly, she'll come looking for me."

Christopher drew her arm through his and led her to a hidden woodland path that ran along the outside of the walled garden. Honnie could feel her heart thumping. Every nerve in her body seemed to shiver.

She couldn't think of anything to say. But Christopher talked.

"I really enjoyed spending time with you this afternoon, Honnie," he said. "It seems I can't stay away from you."

"We can't do this again," said Honnie. "The few times we've been together have caused trouble not only for me, but for you too. We can't be together."

They walked together for another moment until Christopher stopped and turned Honnie round to face him.

"Oh Honnie!" he said, his voice low and rough with feeling.

He put one hand at the back of her neck and ran his fingers up into her hair as he bent to kiss her.

Honnie felt herself yielding towards him until the noise of breaking brushwood brought her back to her senses abruptly. She stepped quickly away.

"What was that? There's somebody there. I'm sure I heard something."

Christopher tried to gather her to him again, but Honnie pulled away.

"There's somebody there," she said. "Listen – that was a branch breaking. Why was I ever so foolish as to come out here?"

She turned to run away, but Christopher caught her arm.

"It's just a fox or a badger," he said.

A bird squawked, disturbed in sleep.

"No," Honnie said, wrenching herself away and running as fast as she could up the path towards the house.

It was difficult to do anything in Tyrone without somebody taking notice. There were so many people in and around the house at almost every hour of the day or night. That afternoon Honnie had been seen picking blackberries with Christopher by one of the other maids who had slipped out to meet her gardener sweetheart. That evening a groom, sitting in a stable with a horse about to foal, had heard distant voices and had gone to investigate. Biddy the Wash was on her way back from a visit to the stable yards in search of some poteen from one of the stable boys who always had a supply when she saw Honnie hurrying back from the darkening trees. Biddy was sure that Honnie had been "up to no good".

By the following day there were numerous accounts of what Honnie had been up to the night before, and none of them lost anything in the telling.

Mrs. Smith took her to task.

"I'm hearing stories about you, Honnie, and I would like to believe they're not true, but I've no reason to doubt the people who told me. It seems you were seen picking blackberries with Master Christopher yesterday afternoon, that you went out on the sly to meet him last night, and that you were seen walking in the woods with him. What in the name of heaven has got into you, girl? Have you no sense at all?"

"I didn't ask him to pick come picking blackberries with me, Mrs. Smith," said Honnie. "He just happened along, and insisted he wanted to help. What could I say to him? As for last night ... I didn't feel very well and I went out for a breath of fresh air, and he appeared out of nowhere ..."

Even to her own ears, this sounded like a pretty farfetched story, and the expression on Mrs. Smith's face told her she wasn't taken in for one minute.

"How dare you try to fob me off with such nonsense, girl! Do you think I'm a complete fool? Now – I would like to know what exactly you think you're playing at?"

Honnie opened her mouth, but no sound came out. She knew Mrs. Smith had the rights of it. There was no way she could justify her behaviour. She could think of nothing to say.

"You've worked hard here, and you're becoming quite a good cook," said Mrs. Smith. "And while I wouldn't like to lose you, I had hopes of you bettering yourself, getting a good position in another house, thanks to all the training I've given you. And now you're behaving like a common hussy. What would your poor mother say if she heard about all this? I've grown fond of you, Honnie, and I'm considering giving you one last chance. If I were to do the proper thing I'd get rid of you straight away. I may still have to do so, because if Miss Anne hears about the goings-on yesterday afternoon and yesterday evening, she will certainly tell me to dismiss you. We'll have to wait and see."

Later, upstairs in their bedroom, Bridget tried to talk to Honnie.

"Honnie, I don't understand what's come over you. You seem to have lost the run of yourself altogether. Have you lost all reason? You're becoming a laughing stock. People are saying that Master Christopher is out to have his way with you, and that you are more than willing. Myself, I don't believe you'd be so foolish but I hate the feeling that Master Christopher is playing with you. I don't want to see you hurt."

"I'm not going to be hurt," retorted Honnie. "It's the whispering and the gossiping that's caused all the trouble. People hereabouts can't keep their noses out of other people's affairs, and when they can't find anything bad, they make it up."

"They haven't had to make it up," said Bridget. "You've given them plenty to gossip about!"

"All right, maybe I have been a bit silly on a few occasions," said Honnie, "but ..."

She shivered in dread at the thought of her mother hearing and how such gossip would affect her. Her mother was so proud of how well she was getting on in Tyrone.

Then they heard Josie coming up the stairs to bed.

"I hear you're in trouble, Honnie," she said in the most dulcet of tones as she came in. "And I'm sorry, but Mrs. Smith asked me where you were and I had to tell her you'd gone out. I'm surprised at you, Honnie. I would have thought someone like you, with such a high opinion of yourself, wouldn't be led astray by the soft words of a philanderer like Master Christopher. I thought you've have had more sense than to join the ranks of the Máire Conneelys and Ellen Connors of this world."

"Stop it, Josie," said Bridget loyally. "She's upset enough already, without you making her feel worse.

"As if I care what Josie thinks of me," said Honnie. "I never have and I never will."

"Well, maybe you should care about what everybody else thinks of you," said Josie. "And I can tell you now – not much."

The next day when Christopher followed her into the vegetable garden and tried to talk to her, Honnie would have none of it.

"I've nearly lost my place," she said. "Through foolishness. I may still lose it if your sister hears the gossip that's going round. I daren't talk to you. Mrs. Smith said if I misbehave again, she'll send me packing."

And she hurried away.

Chapter 18

At the beginning of October the weather changed for the worse. There was a week or more of hard frost, and the evenings were shortening. The long hot days of the summer seemed very far away. The leaves fell early from the trees, flailed by gale-force winds. Glowering dark rainclouds rolled in from the Atlantic, and the rain came in icy sheets, day after day.

Inevitably, the tales about Honnie and Christopher reached Anne's ears, and the tales lost nothing in their travels.

Honnie would have to go, Anne decided.

She came down one morning to tell Mrs. Smith of her decision. But Mrs. Smith was able to tell her that Honnie was going anyway.

"Her sister came over from Maree just yesterday It seems their mother is very unwell and her father is away working in Limerick. She's asking for Honnie. The family need her. I told her I could perfectly understand that she had to go home. She's leaving this afternoon."

"I hope you told her she needn't come back," said Anne.

Mrs. Smith made no answer to this remark. She was happy to have been handed this solution to her problems with the girl. She had given Honnie her blessing. What she knew of Mary Kane she liked, and she had every sympathy with a mother who wanted her daughter with her when she was seriously ill. And even though she had to admit that Honnie would be missed in the kitchen on the occasion of Miss Matilda's wedding in a few weeks' time, she felt a great sense of relief. Now she would no longer have to watch and worry about Honnie and Christopher. Nor would she have to tell Honnie that Christopher's sister, Anne, had decided, before ever word came of her mother's illness, that she was to be let go. Now Honnie needn't know.

With Honnie out of sight, away home in Maree, Christopher being Christopher would soon fix his interest elsewhere. From what she had heard, it seemed that Mary Kane was very ill indeed, so Honnie could be taking care of her for quite a while. With the passage of time a lot of things could change.

But Honnie had happened to be coming down the stairs to the kitchen when Anne was talking to Mrs. Smith. She knew Anne meant what she said. She would never be welcome in the Tyrone kitchens again. Already worried about her mother's illness, a chill descended on her at the icy look on Anne's face as she passed her by on her way back upstairs. How would she be able to explain to her mother that she had lost her place? She decided not to tell her, for the time being anyway.

Mick Murphy was taking her home in a pony and trap. It was late afternoon by the time they left Tyrone and dusk was falling. In the half light the moon was rising. They were about five minutes on their way when a hurrying figure emerged from the trees along the side of the driveway – a girl, with a shawl wrapped closely round her. They had gone past her when Honnie realised that she looked familiar.

"Mick, that girl looked a bit like Josie, what I could see of her. But what would she be doing out here, on a darkening evening, all by herself?"

"I don't believe it was Josie," said Mick. "Just some chance passer-by."

Chapter 19

It was some months since Honnie had seen her mother, and she was shocked by her appearance. She was painfully thin. And she was tearfully pleased to see Honnie.

Mary Kane's complexion at first glance looked nicely pink and white, but the rosy cheeks were due to fever, and her cough struck terror into Honnie's heart. She had heard it before. As she propped her mother up in bed, she remembered her uncle's shuddering cough as he lay dying. She wished her father was at home, but he was away working in Limerick. The house seemed small and cramped and, as she had noticed on her last visit to her mother, in need of a good whitewash.

Honnie called on everything she had learned in Tyrone to tempt her mother to eat, in the hope that she would gain strength. She made gruel, she made milk pudding, she made egg custards. She made drinks and draughts and soups. She killed one of her mother's chickens to make a delicate stew and used the carcass to make a rich broth. Mary Kane always said how good everything looked, how wonderfully it smelt. But she usually ended up just pushing the food around her plate rather than eating it, and apologising to Honnie because she felt guilty.

Honnie's days were long and busy, with her heart and mind and energy concentrated on her mother. And though Christopher stayed in her thoughts, she felt a sense of relief being away from the nervous tension he created around her. She remembered what Bridget had said, that she would only end up getting hurt. What could she possibly expect from him anyway? What could any girl like her expect from a landlord's son? Josie was right – he had just been amusing himself with her. She firmly resolved to be sensible and put him out of her mind.

Over in Tyrone, Christopher had been wondering where Honnie had gone. When he realised that she was nowhere to be seen, he taxed Anne about it.

"I haven't seen Honnie around for days," he said. "Is she sick? Don't tell me you have banished her because of a bit of mild flirtation?"

Anne looked at him coldly. "I didn't have to. She's gone off to mind her mother, who seems to be dying by all accounts."

"She never told me she was going," said Christopher.

"And why on earth should she tell you?" said Anne. "Kitchenmaids are none of your business – or shouldn't be."

"I was curious, that's all," said Christopher. "I'd liked to have wished her well."

And, whistling for his dog, he went off in the direction of the stable yard.

Three days later Christopher rode up to the cottage in Maree.

Thady and Joseph saw him coming and ran yelling in to summon Honnie.

She emerged to find Christopher standing there, a basket over his arm, Barebones cropping the grass behind him.

Christopher held the basket out to her. "Mrs. Smith asked me to bring over these delicacies for your mother," he said.

Honnie was astonished and lost for words. She didn't think it likely that Mrs. Smith would be sending delicacies to her mother, and it was even more unlikely that she would be asking Christopher to bring them.

"Thank you, thank you very much," she said as she took the basket and placed it on the ground. After that she could think of nothing more to say.

Neither, apparently, could Christopher. He was on unfamiliar territory, and he was uneasy, shifting uneasily from foot to foot.

Honnie was embarrassed, especially with Thady and Joseph standing there gawking. She found herself plucking at her apron.

"You two, " she said to the boys sharply. "Go and tend to Mammy while I'm out here."

They reluctantly went inside.

She turned back to Christopher.

"I find it difficult to believe that Mrs. Smith would be sending presents to my mother," she said.

"And I suppose you find it even more difficult to believe that I myself might be thoughtful enough to bring some offerings to help your mother in her recovery?"

"I never said any such thing," said Honnie.

"But you thought it. Well, I have to admit I'm here most of all because I wanted to see you, Honnie. I didn't even know you had left, until Anne told me. And it is true that bringing some small delicacies for your mother was my own idea. I thought it might cheer her up."

He mounted his horse.

"I'll see you soon," he said.

And he rode off.

But a pattern was soon set up. At least once a week, Christopher came, bending his head through the cottage door, with a basket over his arm. He never stayed long. He would put whatever he had brought on the kitchen table, enquire about Mrs. Kane, joke with Joseph, salute the girls if they were around. Honnie would then walk down the lane with him and bid him goodbye. Only the walks got longer, until eventually they were walking on the nearby beach together.

Honnie's sister, Maureen, had been the first to remonstrate with her.

"I'm sure 'tis kind of young Master Christopher to bring good things for Mother. But no doubt he has his own good reasons for doing so," she said acidly.

Bridget came over to visit Honnie at the beginning of December. She sat down at the kitchen table and gratefully accepted a cup of tea and a few slices of the raisin cake which Honnie had made just that morning.

But it was clear that she had something on her mind. And she soon got to the point.

"Honnie, Mrs. Smith is very disturbed about what Christopher is doing. He may say he is bringing gifts over to a sick tenant just to be kind. But he is taking things from the Tyrone kitchens, Mrs. Smith's kitchens. Of course she knows what is happening. He's not coming to see your mother but to see you. And it isn't fair to Mrs. Smith. She doesn't see it is for her to tell Anne what is happening, and she hasn't quite the nerve to say it outright to Christopher – after all he is the eldest son of the house. Do be careful, Honnie. Don't let Christopher St. George lead you astray."

"Have you got feathers in your head?" said Honnie. "First Maureen, now you. Lead me astray indeed! What nonsense! He has been very kind, bringing me nice things for my mother, which she has enjoyed. What do you expect me to do? Throw his gifts back in his face?"

"You know as well as I do why he's bringing all those things for your mother," said Bridget, adding hastily, "not that it isn't good of him. All I'm saying is you should be careful. And I'm not the only one. People are talking. If you ever want to come back to Tyrone to work, you're going the wrong way about it."

"You and I both know I'm never going to be welcome in Tyrone again," said Honnie.

Even Mary Kane began to feel that Mrs. Smith's beneficence was out of the ordinary, and hinted as much to Honnie who tried to reaasure her.

Slowly, as the weeks passed, it seemed to Honnie that her mother was taking a turn for the better. She began to eat a little more. She was able to sit up in bed and talk to neighbours who came to visit her. Some days she was able to come out to the kitchen for an hour or so and sit in the rocking chair close to the turf fire. She was so thin and weak that she felt the cold very much, and the fire had to be kept well built up. As each day passed and her mother seemed that bit stronger, Honnie allowed herself to hope that she might be truly on the mend. She began to look forward to Christmas. It would be the first one she would spend in Maree in six years.

First of all the house had to be cleaned from top to bottom. The chimney was cleaned first, by pulling a prickly gorse bush up and down it with a rope. She sent her Joseph out to clean and tidy the yard and, when he had finished those tasks, she sent him out looking for firewood. There was a plentiful supply of turf in a high stack near the house, but everybody liked to have a wood fire at Christmas, and in particular, a log of bogdeal, a *bloc na Nollag*.

Then the table and stools and chairs in the kitchen had to be scrubbed with sand. The pots and pans had to be thoroughly scoured. The bed linen had to be freshly laundered, and garments washed.

Kathleen, was seventeen years of age now, and for the past two years had been working away in a gentleman's house some miles up the road. Maureen was sixteen, and had been offered a position as well, but she had stayed at home when her mother became ill. Now she and Joseph went out and gathered ivy and holly and any other greenery they could find, to decorate the house. For some months past they had been taking careful note of all the evergreens in and around Maree which might be used for decoration.

Mary Kane was looking forward very much to Bartley's return from Limerick.

He came just two days before Christmas and Honnie was the first person he met as he walked up the pathway to his home.

He waved his stick at her.

"*You!*" he shouted. "*It seems you are the talk of the neighbourhood, you and Christopher St. George!*"

Honnie froze.

Her father glared at her. "I met Mick Murphy on my way and he told me that you and young Christopher seemed to be getting fond of each other's company. I dropped into Moran's at Kilcolgan, for a whiskey to warm me up, and it seemed I was providing great amusement for everybody. One young pup had the cheek to tell me the family would be well away now that Master Christopher looked like setting you up in style. What in heaven's name are you thinking of, Honnie?"

Honnie tried to gather her wits about her.

"I can just imagine what you've been hearing," she said. "But it isn't true. You, of all people, should know better than to believe everything you hear when drink is talking."

Bartley's voice rose further. "*I know enough to know that there is no smoke without fire!*"

Mary Kane's voice could be heard calling in the background.

With an obvious effort, Bartley lowered his voice.

"I'll talk to you later, my girl," he said.

Bartley had been afraid of what he would find when he came home. Maureen had sent him news that Mary was beginning to eat again, and that she hoped this meant her mother was on the road to recovery. He wanted to believe Maureen was right.

As he walked through the door of their bedroom,

Mary Kane's face lit up. "Oh, Bartley dear, I'm so happy to see you," she said, holding out her arms to him. "But what was all the shouting about?"

"Nothing, nothing at all," Bartley said. "Just a misunderstanding between myself and Honnie."

Bartley was shocked by Mary's appearance. She looked thin and frail and ill, and her shoulder blades as he held her were sharp against his hands.

"I can see you are coming along very well," he said gruffly, hoping she hadn't read his thoughts on his face.

"Honnie has me spoilt entirely," said Mary. "I don't know what I would have done without her. But thanks to her I really believe I'm getting a little stronger every day."

"And what's this I hear about Christopher St. George coming to visit?" asked Bartley.

Mary hesitated. "I confess it has me worried," she said. "But he has been very kind, bringing me all kinds of delicacies."

"I can't believe he's doing that from the goodness of his heart," said Bartley dryly.

"I don't think he stays very long," said Mary. "Just bids us all the time of day, and leaves whatever he's brought on the kitchen table. He and Honnie may exchange a few words – I don't think there's any more to it."

"I'm going to have a talk with Honnie later," said Bartley

Mary felt a great sense of relief. They had always shared their worries.

She had accepted that he had to go away to find work, and the money he earned from his painting jobs made a big difference to the family, but she had missed him sorely. He looked tired, she thought.

Bartley kissed her and gave her the warm shawl he

had brought back to her from Limerick, wrapping it round her shoulders.

He had little presents for everybody. There was a hair comb for Honnie, which now he didn't feel like giving her. There were ribbons for Kathleen and Maureen, penknives for the boys. There were bags of biscuits and sweets. He also produced a big joint of corned beef, a present, he said, from Mrs. Jackson, the mistress of the house in which he was painting.

He wanted to know if a pig had been slaughtered?

"Yes," said Mary, "and it was a great day. All the neighbours came to help, and almost all of them brought a handful of salt with them, like they always do. Myles Kelly and Mairtín Breathnach did the slaughtering – I was wondering how we would get it done with you away. Sarah Breathnach and Eileen Kelly helped to prepare the hams and bacon for curing and smoking, and with the making of the black puddings. Afterwards we had tea and cake and great talk, and everyone was given a share of the puddings and the fresh pork to take home with them."

Bartley had also come home with a supply of poteen.

"Not just for myself, mind, but for anyone who comes to visit. If we don't have a decent drop to offer Christmas callers, we'll be badly regarded indeed."

She told him there had been a letter from William, with some money enclosed. William was greatly missed, but the money was welcome.

Later in the evening Bartley found Honnie out in the field alongside the house, with her shawl wrapped round her, looking up at the stars in the frosty sky. His anger had turned to serious worry.

"I have to tell you, Honnie, that these attentions from Christopher St. George are causing me grave concern. Why are you letting him hang around you, why are you letting it happen?"

"Father, nothing has passed between us, nothing, except a few words now and again. I wouldn't have had the time for anything else. I've been working here from morning 'til night, looking after mother, nursing her, cooking for her, and cleaning the house, and trying to get the place ready for Christmas. I can see that Maureen and Thady have been talking to you. If they spent more time helping me, and less time looking for tales to tell you, it would be more to the point."

Honnie knew that Maureen and Thady would have told him that she had gone for walks on the beach with Christopher.

"Yes, Christopher St. George has come over now and again with some delicacies for Mother – he says they're from Mrs. Smith. And I've been civil to him. What would you have me do? Throw them back in his face?"

"All I know is that I come home for Christmas and find half the countryside is talking about my daughter," said Bartley. "Your mother, your sisters and your brother are very worried about you. Nobody wants to see you taking steps you can only regret. We both know what he's after. No good can come of this, Honnie. Master Christopher's place is with a woman of his own kind."

"If half the country is talking about me they must have nothing better to do," said Honnie. "Why do you listen to them?"

"Don't try to pull the wool over my eyes," said Bartley. "Now you listen to me –"

"I think you've said enough," said Honnie.

Bartley's face turned dark red. "I haven't said half enough. You are drawing attention on the whole family, and it's not good attention. Your sisters are upset, your mother is very worried. And you are going lose your reputation, if you haven't lost it already."

Honnie turned towards the house.

"I've got to see to my cake," she said.

Her father's voice bellowed in her wake. "*If I ever see that lad hanging round while I'm here, I'll give him a piece of my mind!*"

The cake was cooking in a round black pot with a lid on it that hung low over the fire, embers built around it. It was very different from the ovens of Tyrone. Honnie lifted the lid apprehensively. But the cake looked perfect, rich and moist.

Bridget came to visit again, and Honnie was glad to see her. "So tell me," she said. "Tell me all the news. How did Miss Matilda's wedding go?"

"It went well," said Bridget. "There wasn't a big crowd in attendance, but there was a deal of work to be done all the same. I can tell you we really missed you."

"Well, I don't miss the work," said Honnie. "But I do miss all the people, the comings and goings, the chat and the joking, the gossip. So what other news is there?

"Well ... Mrs. Hunt and Mrs. Smith aren't speaking. Somebody told Mrs. Smith that Mrs. Hunt thought she was too easy on the kitchenmaids. Mrs. Smith says Mrs. Hunt has got puffed up in herself since the mistress died and thinks she's in charge of the whole house."

"Mrs. Hunt has always been a bit puffed up in herself," said Honnie.

"But Josie is happy," said Bridget. "Robert is being nice to her, throwing her little scraps of attention from time to time. I feel sorry for her."

"Well, it's easier for me to be sorry for her now I'm at a distance from her," said Honnie.

When at last she turned to go, Bridget paused.

"Don't forget what I've said to you before, Honnie. Christopher St. George can only lead you astray. Why can't you take a fancy to a nice lad like Mairtín Breathnach? Maureen says he comes calling at least three times a week."

Honnie's blood boiled. "For the life of me I don't understand why people are always looking for intrigues and entanglements! And Maureen should learn to keep her mouth shut if she has nothing worthwhile to say. Mairtín is a neighbour and I've known him since I was a babe in arms. He's a good man, and I'm fond of him, but that's all. Anyway, what about you? When am I going to hear some good news about you?"

There were times when Bridget would have liked to shake Honnie very hard.

"I care about you, Honnie. And a nicer man than Mairtín Breathnach would be hard to find."

"Well then, maybe you should fancy him yourself," said Honnie, and was surprised to see Bridget's face flush a deep pink.

Mairtín and Bridget, she thought. That was a notion that had never occurred to her. It might be a good match.

Christmas Eve was a busy day, spent in last-minute preparations.

Mary's china, her pride and joy, had to be taken out and washed – the plates were only used for special occasions.

The vegetables were prepared for the next day, the potatoes peeled and left in water, the cabbage cleaned. Creels of hard black turf had to be brought in so that there was no danger of the fire sinking low when the cooking was being done.

The Christmas log, *bloc na Nollag*, had to be placed in a position on the hearth so that it was ready for lighting.

Honnie found jobs for everyone. Christmas Eve was a fast day on which people normally ate only one main meal, and that was a meatless one, eaten in the evening.

In the morning Honnie had cooked three big rounds of soda bread and a big pile of griddle scones, which all quickly disappeared. They would have to wait a long time for the main meal.

By late afternoon everybody had worked up quite an appetite.

"I'm *very* hungry," said Joseph.

"And I'm hungry," said Thady. "When are we going to eat?"

"Soon," said Honnie. "But there's a bit to do yet. Have you forgotten about the candles we put in each window to show Joseph and Mary, who couldn't find any room in the inn in Bethlehem, that they would be welcome here? Why don't you two do that? Joseph is the youngest so he must light the big candle, *Coinneal Mór na Nollag,* and put it in the kitchen window."

At six o'clock in the evening, with the candles all lit, they gathered together to say some prayers before they sat down to eat.

Honnie had cooked a fish stew, with parsley sauce

and onions and carrots and turnips from the vegetable garden at the back of the house, and she had made mounds of fluffy potato cakes.

Mary Kane's eyes shone with the joy of having so many of her family around her. She had got strong enough to sit up for part of each day.

Later that evening Honnie did something she had always done as a child. She went with her father, and her sisters and brothers, up onto the rise of ground behind the house to look at the candles lighting up all the other houses around them.

There was no moon. The sky hung down, overcast and full, in the chill, black darkness of the evening. All around, in the huddles of habitation on the hills and little valleys, as far as they eye could see, candles glowed, in small mud cabins with only one or two openings for windows, in the stouter cottages with glass panes, in the bigger houses of some of the stronger farmers. If Mary and Joseph were looking for somewhere to stay tonight, thought Honnie, they would find no shortage of a welcome.

Bartley had decided that Christmas should not be ruined by argument. He would talk again with Honnie in the New Year.

Looking at the sky, he said he thought it might snow.

"'Twere better so," he said. "It's good to see frost or snow at Christmas, because it's a sign that the spring will be mild. You know what the old proverb says – a green Christmas makes a fat churchyard."

As they walked back to the house, snow started to fall.

"They're plucking geese in heaven," said Honnie, remembering her grandmother telling her this when she was a child.

The rest of the evening was spent quietly, sitting around the turf fire, talking and reminiscing about other Christmases, and the people with whom they had been shared. On the kitchen window the big candle flamed bright and strong, until suddenly, late in the evening, it guttered and flickered out. Honnie felt fear crawl over her. Her mother had nodded off to sleep in her rocking chair, but she saw the look of apprehension on her father's face.

"God between us and all harm," he murmured.

If the Christmas candle went out without any good reason, it was said to be a sign of a death in the family. Honnie quickly lit it again.

At midnight Joseph said they should all go out to the byre to see if the two cows and the horse were really kneeling down.

"People say that cows and donkeys and other animals kneel in adoration of the Baby Jesus at midnight, and that just for a few minutes they can speak like we do," said Joseph.

"And people also say that you must never try to spy on them, much less speak to them," said Honnie. "It brings bad luck. Bad luck is something we don't need."

And she chased them all to bed.

After early Mass the next morning the boys set off for a game of hurling with the other young men around Maree, and Honnie and her sisters returned home to prepare the dinner. Christmas was the biggest feast of the year.

The Kanes enjoyed the corned beef which Bartley had brought, and cabbage, and ham and floury potatoes with buttermilk. They finished Mrs. Smith's pudding, and demolished more than half of Honnie's fruitcake. They drank *poteen* punch and some of the beer from Tyrone, and altogether felt happy and replete.

For the rest of the day they stayed at home. Bartley played some tunes on the tin whistle, Maureen and Thady sang songs in turn. Honnie kept quiet. No matter how hard she tried, she always seemed to sing completely out of tune – to the great merriment of her family.

On St. Stephen's Day, the day after Christmas, when the morning was just brightening, the Wran Boys came. They were a grubby, noisy, boisterous, raggle-taggle band, wearing all sorts of odd clothes, their faces blackened or covered with masks, holding aloft a little dead wren on top of a branch of holly, and singing at the top of their voices.

The wran, the wran, the king of all birds,
On St. Stephen's Day he was caught in the furze,
Although he is little his family is great,
Put yer hand in yer pocket and give us a trate,
Sing holly, sing ivy – sing ivy, sing holly,
A drop just to drink it would drown melancholy …

There were a lot more verses besides.

"It's all just an excuse for drinking and carousing," said Mary Kane. "You'll see. It'll end in rows and ructions come nightfall."

But she didn't demur when Bartley gave them a few pence, as he always did.

Every year Barney said the same thing: "If you don't give them a welcome as they come on their rounds, there is a danger that they might bury the wren opposite the door of your home at the end of the day, and then you would have no luck at all for the whole year. I'm not going to take any chances."

St. Stephen's Day was a much easier day. Only work that was really necessary was done inside or outside the house. There was enough food left over so that no cooking was needed, and the young people in the Kane household were planning some music and dancing for the evening. Ned Breathnach, Mairtín's father, was coming with his fiddle, and Bartley would play his wooden whistle alongside him, and there were half a dozen people who could be depended upon to oblige with a song or two.

People started drifting into the house from about eight o'clock. Honnie made some hot punch with poteen, to make the music flow, and in no time at all the dancing was under way. Soon cheeks were flushed, skirts were flying, and the room was high with the buzz of voices and music and laughter.

Then, just as there was a brief pause in the music, Honnie heard a knock at the door. She had Mairtín Breathnach for a partner, and she shouted "*Tar isteach!*" – Come in! – before the music continued and Mairtín whirled her away in a Galway set.

Suddenly the music stopped and the room fell silent, everyone looking at the door.

Christopher St. George was standing on the threshold.

"I just brought a few things for Mrs. Kane," he said.

He stood there, tall, broad-shouldered and very awkward, not sure quite what to do with himself, under the gaze of a roomful of curious eyes, with a basket in his hand, an uncertain expression on his face.

Honnie was stunned by the sudden force of her feelings. She longed to reach out to him. But all eyes were upon her. It took her a few moments to recover herself and, after what seemed like an eternity, she let go of Mairtín, and crossed the room to Christopher.

"Thank you," she said.

Behind her, Mrs. Kane echoed her thanks.

In his seat beside the fire, a glass of poteen in his hand, Bartley rose as if to say something but when Mary put her hand on his arm, he looked at her, and sat down again.

"It's Christmastime," Mary murmured.

Honnie blurted out the first thing that came into her head.

"Would you like some punch?"

"No ... no, thank you," he said. "I'll be on my way."

And he thrust the basket into Honnie's hands, nodded at Mrs. Kane and the rest of the company, and went quickly out the door.

It took a while for the party to get going again. Honnie saw the inquisitive glances in her direction, heard smothered whispers, the odd giggle, and knew that people were wondering why Christopher St. George should be so attentive.

Mairtín Breathnach was upset. He had thought he was making headway with Honnie that evening. Now it felt like she wasn't with him any more, even as she danced with him.

Later, with one ear alerted, pretending not to be listening, Mary Kane heard him complain to his mother, Sarah.

"I can't believe that Honnie is so foolish as to entertain

the attentions of Christopher St. George. Did you see the way he looked at her – and the way she looked at him when he came in the door. It's the same with all these so-called young gentlemen. They think all they have to do is reach out a hand and take any pretty girl they see. But I would have expected Honnie to have more sense than to fall for fancy words and a handsome face."

In the small hours of the morning, when the last roisterer had finally gone, Mary made her way to bed. She was tired and anxious. She loved all her children, but Honnie was special.

"Honnie has always been so good to me," she said to Bartley. "So many times when I've been sick, Honnie has been there to mind me. There were times when I felt she was *bullying* me to get better. And when I got pneumonia, all those years ago, she gave up her position in the priest's house, and came back and took over the care of everything without a word of complaint. She's always had a willing heart, always a smile on her face, and words of cheer no matter what problem arose. Now I am sorely worried about her. But surely she wouldn't lose her head?"

"Her head wouldn't be the only thing she'd be losing," said Bartley which did nothing to comfort his wife.

Mary had missed Honnie greatly when she went to work in Tyrone, and having her back in the house over the past weeks had lightened her life. She had often heard that Mrs. Smith was very pleased with Honnie, and it had been Mary's hope that Honnie would eventually become a cook in some other house, and perhaps find herself a steady, solid young man with a good position who would appreciate her and look after her and care for her. Honnie hadn't told her mother, or anyone else in the family, about her last days in Tyrone.

When Bartley went out to have one last glass of punch beside the fire, Honnie went in to bid her mother goodnight.

Mary Kane reached out and caught Honnie's hands in her own, her eyes filling with tears. "I don't like all this attention from Christopher St. George, Honnie. I don't like it one bit, and don't try to tell me he isn't after you for I can see full well what his intentions are, and it has me sorely worried. *Please*, Honnie, I don't want to go to my grave seeing you on a rocky road to –"

"*A Mhamaí!* Don't talk like that. You're not going to any grave, not for a long time yet. So don't you speak like that."

Her mother started to cough, and Honnie propped the pillows up behind her back and waited until the painful spasms had passed.

"I can promise you, *a Mhamaí*, that I can look after myself. Have I ever given you cause to worry in the past? That's just *mo dhaidí* talking to you and making a fuss of a small bit of attention."

Mary Kane lay back on her pillows, her voice weak as she began to speak again.

"Attention from a man like Christopher St. George can only lead one way. I can't bear the thought of you being used like that. It breaks my heart even to think about it. And the way I am now, there's so little I can do for you except say a prayer or two."

The tears ran down her cheeks even after her eyes

closed. It had been a long day. With her rosary beads between her fingers she fell asleep.

The 28th of December, the Feast of the Holy Innocents, was always regarded as a day of ill omen.

"Why?" Joseph wanted to know.

"Because it's a feast day in memory of all the little children who were killed by King Herod, long, long ago, back in the times when Jesus was alive," said Honnie.

"There are people who believe that the day on which it falls will be an unlucky day all through the coming year. But I don't believe it for a minute. These are just stories people tell. It doesn't make sense to believe because something bad happened thousands of years ago that the day is unlucky for ever."

In 1833, the feast day of the Holy Innocents fell on a Saturday. And while Honnie kept pushing the thought out of her mind, it did seem an unhappy coincidence that it was on that Saturday morning that her mother suddenly took a turn for the worse.

A chesty cold had been going around the house. Kathleen, who hadn't been able to get home for Christmas, had come on a quick visit. She had arrived with a streaming nose and a sore throat. First Maureen caught it, then Joseph, then Thady. Only Honnie and her father had escaped. The sufferers had been warned not to go near Mary, but it was impossible to contain such an infection in a small house, and she caught it also. With the other members of the family it was a minor ailment, but Mary Kane had no strength left with which to fight it, and it took rapid hold.

Honnie nursed her tirelessly, using some of her

mother's own remedies, and some others she had learned in Tyrone.

For a couple of days Mary Kane appeared to rally and the fever seemed to fall, but then it rose again, until her brow burned under Honnie's hand. Then came another fit of coughing, wracking her body until she fell back exhausted. And with the coughing came blood, and Honnie's heart shrank as she cleaned her mother and settled her down once again.

Father Tom called to the house.

"I will come at any hour of the day or night, whenever you send for me," he said.

Sarah Breathnach came to call, bringing with her Madge Shaughnessy.

"Consumption is a scourge," she whispered to Honnie. "Look at Mary's poor family – her mother, her two brothers, her young lad and his poor little sister. But maybe Madge can help."

Honnie knew that Madge was known for miles around as a woman with knowledge and skill beyond the ordinary. She had been called to many sickbeds and was said to be particularly good with women in childbirth.

"People say she has the healing touch," Sarah whispered.

Madge took Mary's hands in hers and talked to her gently. She felt her pulse and stroked her head. But Honnie knew by the expression on her face that she felt there wasn't much she could do. Before she left she gave Honnie a bottle of one of her own mixtures.

"Give your mother six drops in water three times a day," she said. "The most we can hope for is that the medicine will give her some ease. Truth to tell, I don't think there's much any of us can do now, *mo chuisle*. It's in the hands of God."

Mary Kane visibly faded away, lying quietly in her bed, slipping in and out of consciousness, her rosary beads clutched in her hands. From time to time she asked for William or Seán, but they were far away in Canada.

Father Tom came and gave her the Last Rites and visited each day.

She died on the first Saturday of 1834. It was a bitter, stormy morning, with the wind wailing through every nook and cranny in the house.

Barney knelt on the floor beside his wife, tightly holding one cold hand, his shoulders shaking. Honnie knelt on the other side. Kathleen and Maureen sat silently on either side of the bed. Joseph and Thady stood nearby.

For a few minutes nobody said a word.

"Maybe we should all kneel down and say a few prayers," Honnie said finally.

Since word had gone round that Mary was dying, neighbours and friends had been coming in and out of the house constantly to see what help they could offer, or what comfort they might bring. Eileen Kelly, Sarah Breathnach and Madge Shaughnessy were in the kitchen – one making bread, another reddening the fire, another sweeping the floor. When they heard the prayers being said they fell silent. They waited a little while before they went in and added their prayers to those of the family. Then Sarah led Bartley gently out into the kitchen, and his sons followed.

Madge and Sarah began preparations for the laying out. Madge had laid out many people in the parish, and

Sarah had often helped her, but Mary had been a particular friend, and, as they both said, no matter how often you did it, it was a privilege, but a very painful one, to lay out somebody whom you had known and loved. Just days before she died Mary had told Honnie where to find the shroud she had stored away and given her strict instructions to see that the old linen bedspread, which had belonged to her mother, and her mother before her, should be used to cover her when she was waked. Honnie took them down from the top of the wardrobe where they were carefully wrapped in an old cloth.

"And now, *a stóir*," said Madge to Honnie, "I think you and your sisters should go out to your father and your brothers and have yourselves a bowl of broth, or some potatoes and buttermilk, until we are finished here."

Everyone said that Mary made a beautiful corpse, and certainly in the flickering light of the candles the stress and struggle of her last months seemed to have been wiped away. With her rosary beads in her hands and what looked like a half smile on her face, she looked calm and tranquil.

Bartley broke down when he saw her, crying helplessly.

Honnie stroked her mother's head, smoothing back the hair, touching her cheek.

Mary Kane looked genuinely at peace.

The news that she was dead travelled fast. Two of her sisters came with their husbands, and an older brother. Old friends from Mary's childhood came, and various cousins, and an aged aunt. Everyone who came brought something to contribute to the wake. They had to be welcomed, thanked for coming, and brought in to see the body. Each in turn knelt and said a prayer, then made way for the next mourner. Everybody had to be offered food and drink – tea, or whiskey, or poteen, griddlecakes, or potato cakes, or soda bread. Tobacco was there for anyone who wanted it.

There were many good words said of Mary. Honnie was amazed to hear of all the quiet kindnesses she had done, and for which she was remembered – the sick children she had nursed, the old and lonely she had visited, the people who had a patch of bad luck and had been helped out of meagre resources.

Later that day, the keeners came. One stood at the head of the bed, one at the foot, and one at either side.

"So many wakes I've been at," said Sarah. "So many keeners I've heard. They do help to give voice to all the pain and grief. But the death dirge is still a sound that freezes my heart."

Honnie couldn't believe she was hearing it for her own mother.

At midnight everybody joined in the rosary before some of the mourners went home, while many stayed to wake the corpse all night. Stories were told, poems recited, music was played, and some people played cards.

At her grandmother's wake Honnie remembered asking her mother why everyone seemed to be enjoying themselves when they had all said they were so sad about the person who had died.

She remembered her mother's answer.

"When you lose somebody you love, you need people around you. They help to keep the sorrow at bay. They keep you occupied, they keep you busy, talking to them, looking after them. They talk to you about the person who has died, and you hear stories about them you never knew, good stories, glad stories, stories of kindness. People tell you about a helping hand given in times of need. They tell you funny stories that make you laugh. If people didn't make music and talk and laugh at a time like this, then death would seem very fearful indeed. It helps the mourners through the grim days immediately after the death."

As Honnie made what seemed like the hundredth pot of tea, she thought of what her mother had said. By the time the dawn came, she was so tired she felt ready to drop, but she felt comforted too by the care and kindness of all the people who had come to mourn her mother, and to share their memories of her.

The day of Mary Kane's burial the rain fell down in sharp needles, and a whinging wind chilled the bones of even the most warmly clad. A large crowd of people followed the coffin as it was carried from her house by her husband and Thady, along with some neighbouring men. The women wrapped their shawls tightly around their heads and shoulders, the men pulled their coats close. The keeners' dirge followed the sad procession as it wound its way along the narrow boreen on the two-mile journey from the Kane house. Family, friends, neighbours all took turns at carrying the coffin.

Ballinacourty graveyard was on a windy spit of land overlooking the Atlantic. The wind seemed to grow stronger here with every passing minute, buffeting in from the sea, then battering and boring its way through the mourners as they gathered round the spot where Mary was to be buried.

As chief mourner, it fell to Bartley to take out the first sods. With tears coursing down his face, he drove in the spade, tossing the broken earth up onto the nearby bank. Then Thady took his turn, and eleven-year-old Joseph did his valiant best. All the men in the assembled company, two men at a time, put their hands to digging the grave, Mary's brothers and cousins first, then neighbours and friends. Father Tom also did his share. As the men dug, the women said the rosary: the Joyful Mysteries, the Sorrowful Mysteries, and the Glorious Mysteries. But even though the soil was sandy, and easily dug, it took longer than fifteen decades of the rosary to dig the grave. Honnie's tears mingled with the rain soaking through her clothes as she stood shivering through set teeth.

Finally, Mary's coffin was laid to rest. Father Tom led the last prayers, and people began to make their way back to their own homes.

As she left the graveyard, holding her father's arm on one side, with Kathleen holding his other, Honnie glimpsed Christopher St. George standing some distance away, apart from the mourners.

The house seemed desolate when they got back. The fire was almost out, and the kitchen was dishevelled and disordered after the long wake. There was a great deal of tidying to be done, and Honnie was glad of it. It would keep her mind off things. She set to work with a will, first reddening the fire, and then giving her brothers and sisters tasks to do, until in a few hours everything was clean and neat again – the way her mother would have liked it.

Bartley sat by the fire, looking deep into the red heart of it, talking to Ned Breathnach and Myles Kelly about Mary and the life he had spent with her, and drinking poteen.

"That'll do him no good at all," said Honnie crossly to Kathleen. "He's going to be sick and sorry on the morrow, and who's going to mind him?"

"Leave him be," said Kathleen. "His heart is broke. So what if he's got a sore head tomorrow? I'll mind him."

Over the next few days, the Kane household began to gather up the threads of everyday life. Thady went back fishing with Mairtín Breathnach. Bartley talked about returning to Limerick to finish painting the house for Mr. Jackson. Kathleen went back to work, and only Maureen and Joseph were left at home.

Honnie didn't know what she was going to do. Her family assumed that she would be going back to Tyrone. She knew that was impossible, but her heart quailed at the thought of telling them. Somehow, she would have to find another position, one far away from Christopher.

When Maureen asked her how soon she would be leaving, Honnie played for time.

"Mrs. Smith says I can stay a while longer," she said. "Until things settle down."

Chapter 20

Over in Tyrone, Christopher was missing Honnie more than he could ever have imagined. The more he knew of her, the more his feelings for her had grown. He called over to see her a few days after her mother's funeral. Joseph saw him first and came running in the door.

"Honnie, Christopher St. George is riding up the lane."

Joseph had got quite fond of Christopher, who always gave him a bit of time and attention when he came to visit.

Honnie met him at the door.

"I've just come to say how sorry I am about your mother. I didn't like to intrude at the burial. I know how much you loved her, and I remember what it was like when I lost my own mother. I wish there was something I could say to make you feel better – but – as you said when my mother died, there isn't anything anyone can say."

"Thank you, thank you very much," Honnie said.

"It's good to see you, but now you must go. Quickly, before my father comes. He is angry about the attention you have been giving me. He has gone out fishing with Mairtín Breathnach, but I expect him back any minute."

"I can understand you feel that any confrontation between myself and your father is to be avoided," said Christopher. "I thought he would have gone back to Limerick."

"He goes in two days' time," said Honnie. "Now go, Christopher. Go!"

As he remounted his horse, he leaned down to her.

"I'll see you soon,"he said. "On the beach."

When Bartley came home Joseph told him about Christopher's visit.

Bartley's face grew thunderous. "And I missed him. I'm sorry. There are a few things I'd like to say to that young man."

Before he left for Limerick, Bartley warned Honnie again.

"Honnie, young St. George has no excuse for coming over here any more. So let that be the end of it. I don't want to hear any more stories about yourself and himself."

In the days that followed Honnie walked often on the beach with Bran. She tried to think about what she should do, where she might go. Maureen commented on her fondness for the beach.

"Poor Bran," Honnie said. "Nobody ever takes her for a walk, and she enjoys a walk so much."

"So that's why you're walking on the beach," said Maureen acidly. "I was wondering what it was all about!"

The storms which had railed around the house when her mother was dying were gone. The sky was a clear blue, and the wind coming in off the sea was gentle.

Each day Honnie sat down on the same rock and watched the waves as they sparkled in the sunshine, and broke in froth and foam. The Aran Islands lay pale green and grey on the horizon, and the cliffs of Clare rose in the far distance. The days were more like days in late spring than mid-January.

When she sat on the beach, looking out over the sea, she still found it difficult to believe that her mother was dead. She remembered her calm, still face as she lay in her shroud waiting to be coffined.

She knew that she had been less than honest when she told her mother she had nothing to worry about. She remembered her tears.

She thought about Christopher. The truth was that Christopher St. George had created a lot of trouble in her life, with a lot of people. Her mother had died worrying. She had parted with her father on bad terms. He had returned to Limerick, warning her as he went not to disgrace the family, and to have no more to do with "that young pup".

Kathleen, Maureen and Thady were barely civil to her. She had snapped at Bridget at Christmastide, and only seen her briefly at her mother's funeral. Was she making a fool of herself? Was Christopher making a fool of her?

Each day as she walked on the beach she wondered when he would come, if he would come. After six days she was beginning to despair.

She didn't realise Mairtín Breathnach was near until he came to a standstill beside her on the sandy beach.

"I suppose you're waiting for Christopher St. George," he said.

"I'm doing no such thing," said Honnie. "Where did you come from, Mairtín? Were you spying on me?"

"I wasn't spying on you," said Mairtín. "But I've seen you and St. George over these last weeks. It seems he said he was bringing over some delicacies for your poor mother. A fancy story indeed! I've been out in the boat and seen the pair of you strolling along the beach, in full sight of anybody who might happen to pass by. Have you lost the use of your senses, Honnie? I know I'm a few years older than you, Honnie, but I've always cared for you and at Christmastime I thought, I hoped, you were beginning to care for me – until Christopher St. George appeared at the door on St Stephen's night."

Honnie didn't know what to say. "I'm sorry, Mairtín ... but I never led you to believe that I could or would ... but I'm very fond of you – you're like a brother to me."

"I don't want to be like a brother to you!" said Mairtín furiously. "How can you not see he's only using you? He doesn't care about you, not the way I do!"

"He's not using me," Honnie snapped.

She was sick to death of people telling her what they thought of Christopher.

Mairtín's face darkened. "I can see there's no talking to you," he said. "He has you completely beguiled. I just hope you won't live to rue the day." And he turned on his heel and walked away.

Honnie sat on. Nobody seemed to think that Christopher could possibly have feelings for her. Maybe they were right. She felt confused and depressed. She knew Mairtín was a good man, as good as anyone could hope to meet. If she hadn't met Christopher, she could well have married him. But she had met Christopher, and she had lost her heart before she knew what had happened to her. She hadn't seen him now for almost a week. It felt like six weeks, instead of six days.

Then on the seventh day, as Honnie sat brooding on the rock, she heard a horse's whinny – and turned round to find Christopher riding towards her.

Pulling up nearby, he dismounted and patted Bran's head as she jumped up on him to greet him.

He stood tall beside her, his hair dishevelled from the ride. He took both her hands in his, and the warmth of his smile as he looked down at her made her heart lurch.

He led Barebones by the reins as he walked with her along the strand.

"When are you thinking of coming back to Tyrone?" he asked. "Mrs. Smith must be wondering when you're planning on returning."

"Did your sister not tell you?" said Honnie. "Miss Anne doesn't want me back in Tyrone."

"I did hear her say something of the sort," said Christopher, "but I've been hoping she spoke in the heat of the moment, that she didn't mean it seriously."

"I would take anything Miss Anne says seriously," said Honnie. "You well know she always means what she says. And if Miss Anne doesn't want me, Mrs. Smith can't take me back. She won't want me anyway. If she was worried about the pair of us before I left, she'll be even more worried now. She knows about your visits over here. I can understand that she doesn't want trouble. And for my part I don't like being the subject of gossip and rumour. I think the best thing would be if I looked for a position elsewhere."

Christopher said nothing for a while, just bent to pick a few flat stones from the pebbled strand and skim them over the water. Bran charged after them enthusiastically, never quite managing to catch the stones before they fell down to the sandy bottom, but always coming back for more, shaking herself and showering both of them with water.

"Where would you go?" he asked finally.

"I don't rightly know," said Honnie. "But I've learned a lot in my years in Tyrone. Mrs. Smith is a good teacher. I'm sure I'll be able to get another job in some other house. Father Tom says he thinks he can get me a position with a friend of his, a priest on the other side of Galway, whose housekeeper has fallen ill. If she doesn't get better – and it seems she may not – then he'll tell him about me."

"And you'd be gone out of my life," said Christopher. "I don't think I could bear that, Honnie."

"You'd have to bear it," said Honnie. "So would I. And if we're to be perfectly honest we have to admit that you and I can go nowhere together. It is better that we stop seeing each other now."

They continued to walk along the beach in silence until Christopher stopped and pulled Honnie close to him.

"Honnie, you must know I love you," he said, and wrapped his arms around her.

He kissed her gently at first and then more passionately.

Honnie kissed him back, and then drew away.

"I love you too, Christopher. But there are times when

love just isn't enough," she said sadly.

Christopher mounted Barebones.

"I can't bear the thought of you with another man," Honnie," he said.

Christopher came back three days later and they walked along the beach.

Christopher was unusually silent.

Then he stopped and gathered Honnie into his arms.

"Marry me, Honnie," he said. "Marry me."

Honnie couldn't believe what she'd just heard.

Shaken, she looked up at him.

"You can't be serious," she said.

"I've never been more serious in my life," said Christopher.

"Oh, Christopher, it's a lovely, lovely idea, but you must know it's a completely daft one. More than anything I want to marry you. But we can't get married, for so many different reasons. It's impossible! Christopher, have you thought at all about the fact that I'm a Catholic and you're a Protestant? A marriage between us is *against the law*. I have to marry within my own church, and you in yours. And I have to tell you, Christopher, that I will never change my religion."

"I understand all that, Honnie, my love, but I'm sure we can find somebody to marry us. It might not be legal but we would be married before God."

"But, Christopher, I would only feel married if I was married by a Catholic priest and I can tell you that no Catholic priest is going to marry us. Apart from the fact that it would be a criminal offence for him to do so, it's against our religion."

"Surely we can find some sympathetic priest who would be willing?"

"I don't think we can!" Honnie wailed.

"But what about Father Tom?" said Christopher.

"No! That's out of the question!" said Honnie. "It wouldn't be fair to ask him. He's my dear friend and I could never ask him to break the law and put himself in danger."

"Very well. So we'll find someone else."

"But, Christopher, apart from all that, don't you see that we live in two different worlds? That you don't belong in my world and I could never belong in yours? And my father says that you'll drop me as soon as you get tired of me, and before she died my poor mother was sorely worried about anything going on between the two of us because –"

"What a good opinion your family and friends seem to have of me," he said wryly.

Then he kissed her firmly, and she found herself kissing him back, her head whirling.

"Honnie, I can't stop thinking about you, all day and every day, every waking moment, from the time I get up in the morning to the time I lie down at night. I can't imagine life without you. I don't care what anybody else thinks. It doesn't matter."

Honnie longed to believe him but told herself sternly to be sensible as she tried to pull away.

"But it does matter," she said. "It matters what your father would think and your sisters, and *think* isn't a strong enough word. They'd be horrified. And it matters what my family think, whether I like it or not. My father would be equally horrified. He says that everybody has their station in life, and that those who try to go above their station end up in trouble. That you belong up in the Big House with a woman of your own kind, that I'm a servant girl and should know my place. There's no one who would be pleased to see us marry."

"*We'd* be pleased, *we'd* be happy," said Christopher.

He put both his arms around her and kissed her again.

"Say you'll marry me," he said.

Honnie tried to pull herself together.

"Much as I want to, I can't say I'll marry you," she said, her voice trembling. "It's not possible."

Bran raced up to them with a piece of driftwood, and Christopher threw it for her.

"I don't think you have thought about the consequences," Honnie said fearfully. "Your father would take a seizure at the notion but, more than that, he'd cut you off without a penny! Have you thought of that?"

Christopher shook his head. "He would never do that," he said emphatically. "I'm his eldest son and Arthur is still young. He depends on me. The estate depends on me."

"But there's a risk he might!"

"No. There's not."

"Oh, Chistopher, I'm not so sure. And what about your sisters? I'm sure they would like to have one of their servant girls marrying their brother!" She shivered. "I can just imagine what Miss Anne would say – and what she would do to stop us. And your friends? What would you say to them? 'This is my wife, Honnie, who used to be a kitchenmaid in our house'?"

"I meant what I said, Honnie. I want to go to sleep

with you beside me. I want to feel your arms around me, your body against mine. I want to spend the rest of my life waking up next to you. I'll not take no for an answer."

"Well, I'm giving you no for an answer," said Honnie.

As she walked disconsolately home she wondered if Christopher really did believe it could happen. But the fact that he even talked about marrying her, that he wanted to marry her warmed her heart.

No matter that she couldn't sing even one song in tune, as she prepared the evening supper she sang one song after another.

Maureen looked at her curiously.

"Has Christopher St. George been whispering sweet nothings in your ear again? I saw you on the beach, the two of you. When will you ever learn, Honnie? Is there no way of getting some sense into that head of yours? I'm getting right sick of listening to the neighbours' jokes about you being St. George's fancy woman."

Honnie finished cooking the supper in a more subdued mood and went to bed early. But sleep wouldn't come, and she tossed and turned so many times that Maureen, who slept alongside her, got really exasperated.

"*In ainm Dé*, Honnie, would you rest easy? Whatever about you not sleeping, I want to get some rest. I'd be much obliged if you didn't pull all the bedclothes off me every time you turn around, and I'd be even more obliged if you would decide which way you're going to lie, and then stayed that way for a while."

So Honnie lay on her back and looked at the ceiling and thought about Christopher. She thought about the way his hair curled around the back of his neck. She thought about kissing him. She thought about the way he smiled, and how his arms felt around her. And she thought that she couldn't wait to have his arms around her again. And then she tried to put all thoughts of Christopher out of her head. She wasn't successful.

Over the following days Honnie's mood swung from one extreme to the other. In the morning, she might get up, and tell herself to be sensible, to forget all about Christopher, and to find herself another position far away from him. But as she worked around the house, cleaning and cooking and tidying, thoughts of him would fill her mind, until she felt she couldn't be with him soon enough.

Then she would make herself think of all the reasons why marriage with him was such an impossible idea. She would list them all in her mind, and she would tell herself to be sensible, that marrying Christopher was out of the question, and the pain of the impossibility was so strong she felt sick.

When three and then four days passed without any sign of him, she tormented herself with all kinds of possibilities to explain his absence. Maybe he realised he had made a mistake and was bitterly regretting his offer of marriage. Maybe he was going to keep far away from her in case she took him at his word.

When he didn't come on the fifth day, her thoughts became more frantic. He had made her an offer of marriage to gain her confidence, but he had no intention of going through with it ... he was probably telling his friends how he had fooled her ... his father had heard about his plans and locked him up ... he had been thrown off his horse, and was lying dead on some roadside ... she could even picture the funeral procession as it made its way to the family vaults.

That night she didn't sleep at all, and at the first light of dawn she crept from her bed, and out the front door, into the sharp cold of the winter morning, wrapping her shawl closely around her. The weather had changed again. The sky was a clear, chilled blue, rimmed rosy on the edge of the horizon. The land was frozen. No birds sang, and even Bran seemed disinclined to leave her makeshift bed in the byre to accompany Honnie as she set off to walk up through the fields behind the house.

A flock of pregnant ewes looked miserable and heavy as they huddled together in the lee of a ditch. When they saw her coming, they started hopefully towards her. They thought she might be bringing food. It would be some weeks yet before their lambs were born. When they realised she was empty-handed, they turned away, disappointed. She went on up the rise of ground, towards a small copse of trees standing in pencilled tracery against the sky, and when she reached it she stopped and sat on a granite boulder, looking down at her home below and the countryside around it.

When she glimpsed a man on horseback riding up a lane some distance away, her heart leapt. At first she wasn't sure, but as he drew nearer she became certain it was Christopher.

She watched him approach. He was nearly upon the Kane house before he chanced to look up at the hill on which she sat. His face broke into a smile so wide and warm that she could feel his love flowing towards her.

He kicked Barebones into a gallop, and within moments he was beside her. He dismounted, and held out his arms to her. She ran straight into them, and all at once the day lit up, and she found herself crying with happiness.

"God, I missed you, Honnie. I had to go on an errand for my father. Tell me you missed me too!"

Honnie snuffled into his chest and tried to wipe the tears from her eyes.

"Why are you crying?" said Christopher

"Because I'm happy," said Honnie.

"Well, that's the silliest thing I ever heard," said Christopher. "So ... are you going to marry me?"

"You must know how much I want to," she said. "But, putting all the other difficulties aside, who could we get to marry us?"

"I think we must ask Father Tom?" said Christopher.

"No!" said Honnie. "I couldn't ask him."

With their arms around each other they stood in silence for some minutes.

"I'll seek out Father Tom," said Christopher, "and see what he says."

Honnie shook her head. "No, Christopher, it wouldn't be fair. I would feel I was trading on our friendship."

"He's our best chance," said Christopher. "He may very well say no, and then we'll have to think of somebody else."

"No, I can't put him in such a difficult position," she said resolutely.

But if Tom was their only hope of getting married, said another voice in Honnie's head, wouldn't it make sense to just ask him? He could always refuse.

"If he's such an old friend," said Christopher, "maybe he'll agree to do it. Anyway, it's worth a try. And now I have to leave you, but I'll be over to see you tomorrow, at sundown, at the far end of the beach. Up on this hill half the countryside is probably watching us."

Honnie felt overwhelmed. It was all happening so quickly.

"Honnie?"

She looked up at him.

"And where would we live?" she asked.

Christopher hesitated. "That's the difficult one," he said. "We would have to live here in County Galway. In fact, I would need to be fairly close to Tyrone. As I told you, however my father feels when he finds out about us, he would still need me. And I need him. I've spent all my life here. What would I do anywhere else? I've been thinking ... there's a house over in Drumacoo. It's not in a great state at the moment, but with a bit of work it could be made quite a comfortable –"

"Drumacoo? But that's only a mile or so away. Everyone around will know our business and begin to gossip! I'll be made the laughing-stock of half the country in no time."

"Honnie, I know it won't be easy, and I'm sorry that it will probably be more difficult for you than for me. But if you want to marry me as much as I want to marry you, it's the only way. I'll see you tomorrow."

He gave her one last kiss, mounted his horse and rode off.

Half the countryside hadn't seen them, but Maureen had, and she had told Thady and Joseph. When Honnie arrived back at the house, Maureen was cleaning and tidying the hearth with excessive energy. She looked up at Honnie with an expression of controlled patience. Thady just looked anxious.

"I know exactly what you're thinking, and I don't want to hear any of it," said Honnie.

"You may not want to hear what we have to say, nor care about what we think," said Maureen, "but we care about what you are doing to us. And, though you may not believe it, we care about you."

"I'm not doing anything to you, because it's none of your business," said Honnie.

"You've made it our business," said Maureen. "When men see that one girl in a family is easily got, they soon wonder if the other girls in the family are the same."

"Easily got, is it?" said Honnie furiously. "I haven't been – as you say – 'got'. And that's nonsense about how men think of you."

Maureen's patience was wearing thin. "Ask Kathleen when next you see her and she'll say the same as me. When we go out now men look at us in a different way. And you can see right well what they're thinking. That's what you've done to us, Honnie. I'm sure you didn't mean to, but that's what you've done."

"Since you and Kathleen are obviously so virtuous no doubt the men will soon find out they're wasting their time," said Honnie. "For myself, whether you believe it or not, I haven't done anything of which I need to be ashamed."

"Well, you *should* be ashamed of yourself," said Maureen. "I'm just glad poor mother isn't alive to see the way you're behaving. Everybody we know seems to have seen yourself and Christopher St. George walking up and down that beach, canoodling. The family's reputation is in shreds, and poor Father keeps getting jibes about his daughter 'the fancy woman'. Did you not see how glad he was to be heading back to Limerick, where nobody will know about you, and there'll be nobody to throw your name in his face. You can't behave like that and be surprised when people gossip. The trouble is it's hurting the whole family. I was going to say I'd be sorry to see you hurt, Honnie, but now I'm not so sure. You're just being a selfish cow."

"And you are being a nasty little vixen!" said Honnie, turning to the kitchen door. "And now, if you don't mind, Nóinín is waiting to be milked."

And before her sister could say another word, she grabbed the milk bucket from inside the door and the bit of rope to spancel the cow's legs, and swept out the door.

She headed up the field. She would have dearly liked to tell Maureen and Thady that Christopher had asked her to marry him but, for the present, the fewer people who knew, the better.

The sun was sliding down behind the edge of the sea when Honnie slipped out to meet Christopher next evening. She knew that Maureen had seen her going, but she was beyond caring. He had arrived before her. She ran towards him and he put his arms around her.

"I've talked with Father Tom. You were right. He is less than pleased with the idea," said Christopher. "In fact, he says he won't do it. You don't need me to tell you all the reasons he gave, you know them already. We've just got to make him see that we mean what we say."

"I knew he'd be all against it," said Honnie.

"I'm sure we'll be able to change his mind," said Christopher. "But I should tell you that he is planning to come and see you – soon, he said, probably tomorrow some time. Maybe you can make him understand that we really mean to marry."

Honnie woke up the next morning with a heavy heart. She wasn't looking forward to a visit from Father Tom. They had been friends for so long that she found it strange to be at odds with him. They had always got on so well together. She didn't feel good about asking such a favour of him. She wanted to marry Christopher. It wouldn't be easy, and the idea of living in Drumacoo sent shivers down her spine. But the more she thought about it, the more she was determined to marry Christopher. She would use all her powers of persuasion to get Father Tom to agree to perform the marriage ceremony. Tom was fond of her. Maybe he'd see things differently when he saw how serious they were.

Father Tom arrived at eventide. Thady was away fishing, but she could see the look of satisfaction on Maureen's face.

She's thinking that he'll put a stop to things, thought Honnie.

Tom exchanged a few words with Maureen, but he didn't waste much time before he suggested that he and Honnie take a walk together down the lane alongside the house.

For a time they walked in silence. Father Tom's face was grim.

"I've had Christopher St. George on to me," he said, "with a lot of nonsense about you and he wanting to get married. What on earth's come over you, Honnie? Have you lost leave of your senses altogether?"

"He wants to marry me, and I want to marry him," said Honnie. "I know it might seem mad to a lot of people, but that's the truth of it."

"You cannot be married legally."

"But I can in the eyes of God! And that's all I care about."

"In the name of reason, Honnie, ten seconds' thought must tell you that landlord's sons don't marry servant girls, and even if they did it wouldn't work. There would be one almighty row in Tyrone if Arthur St. George heard anything of this, and I can't believe your own father would be far behind in disapproval. Life is a difficult enough business, without making problems for yourself. Like should marry like. Forget about Christopher St. George, find yourself a new position somewhere away from here – I'm sure I could easily find you one, for there's many a mistress looking for a well-trained girl."

Honnie knew she had to be patient, but she found herself getting cross.

"I'm not *looking* for a new position," she said. "And if Christopher wants to marry me, and he does, and I know I want to marry him, then I don't see why we shouldn't. But I would very much like you to marry us."

"Honnie! Think about it. An alliance with you would mean Christopher being ostracised by his family. Do you honestly think they'd accept someone who had worked in their kitchens into their family?"

"No," said Honnie. "I don't. Nor would I want them to. Christopher and I would be happier without them."

"Honnie, think about your own friends, those who

have always known you. To them you are the daughter of Bartley Kane, the painter, the girl who worked in the kitchens of Tyrone House. They'll think you are setting yourself up to be better than them."

"If friends abandon me that easily, they're not very good friends, are they?" said Honnie. "And I don't think it really matters what anybody thinks about me, except the people about whom I care."

"So do you not care about your father? Your sisters? Your brothers? Are they all in favour of this match?"

Honnie couldn't think of an answer.

They had been walking along in a heavy silence when the noise of hooves drew near and Christopher hailed them. He took in the black expression on both their faces as he dismounted and walked towards them, leading his horse by the reins.

"I take it Father Tom has been telling you he disapproves of our plans?"

"Disapprove?" said Tom. "I think it's a completely insane idea. I have said to Honnie what I've already said to you, Christopher. There can be nobody apart from yourselves who could think this union makes sense."

"Well, we're the people who matter, surely," said Christopher, putting his arm around Honnie.

"And what of your father, and your sisters? And Honnie's family, what about them? And how will Honnie feel, being with a man whose family can only disown the union?"

Christopher stayed silent.

"Will you be content to find yourself cut off – because make no mistake about it that's what will happen?" said Tom. "And how will you survive if your father cuts you off financially? The estate is your livelihood."

"That won't happen," Christopher insisted.

"No?"

Again there was silence.

"So are you saying you won't marry us?" asked Christopher.

"Can you give me any good reason why I should?" asked Tom.

The two men stood facing each other. Although Christopher was tall, Tom was taller and of a broader build. Beside Tom, Christopher looked boyish, but grimly determined.

Honnie's heart tightened as she looked at the two men.

"I can give you several good reasons," Christopher said. "Because I love Honnie, and she loves me. Because we are going to be together one way or another. Would you prefer we were together unmarried?"

Tom's face flushed with temper. "I dislike being bullied," he said.

"I'm just laying the facts before you," said Christopher.

"I've known Honnie all my life," said Tom, glancing at her. "I care very much about her, and what becomes of her. The last thing I want is to see her miserable and unhappy, cut off from her family, with no friends, wondering how she came to make such a mistake."

It was Christopher's turn to get angry. "I can see you regard marriage to me as a fate to be avoided at all costs," he said coldly. "But whether you believe it or not, it's my hope to make Honnie happy, not unhappy, and if that means getting married, that's what we're going to do. If you won't do it, so be it. I'll find somebody from my own church who will."

Honnie spoke for the first time.

"I don't want anybody else to do it, Tom. I always hoped that when I got married, you'd be the one to do it. I don't want to be married by a Protestant clergyman, I wouldn't feel properly married."

She could feel the tears welling up as Christopher put his arms around her.

"Then you should have thought of that before you agreed to marry this young gentleman here," said Tom curtly.

And he turned on his heel and walked off in the direction of the Kane house, and his waiting horse.

By the time Honnie got back home, her eyes were red from weeping. Nothing Christopher had said had succeeded in cheering her up.

Thady had come home while she was out and when they looked at her swollen eyes, she knew that he and Maureen believed that Tom had made her see sense.

Honnie didn't answer any of their questions, just opened up the settle bed, and buried herself beneath the bedclothes. When Maureen came to bed, she pretended to be asleep.

When she got up next day she went about her chores silently, "without a word to throw to anybody, not even the dog," as she heard Maureen remark to Thady when he came back from fishing late in the afternoon.

"She's probably still upset at the lecture Father Tom gave her," said Thady. "Give her time, she'll get over it."

But Honnie had no intention of giving up her dream. She had lain awake for most of the night before trying to think of ways to get Father Tom to agree to their plans. Somehow, she had to get to see him on her own, without

Christopher being there, and make him believe that marrying Christopher was what she truly wanted. But Father Tom lived over in Kinvara, beyond easy walking distance. How could she get to see him?

She was still trying to think of some way to talk to him when she heard Maureen talking to Thady about a funeral they should all go to the next day. A neighbour had died, and Father Tom was coming for the funeral, to the same graveyard in Ballinacourty where her own mother had been buried just a few weeks earlier.

The next day Honnie went with Maureen and Thady to the graveyard, and prayed along with everybody else, and offered her sympathy to the bereaved. Then she went over and stood beside her mother's grave and waited until people had drifted away or were talking together in groups. She shivered. Her mother would not be pleased either.

She caught Father Tom's eye and he came over to her. Before she could open her mouth, he spoke.

"I'm getting very tired of this business between yourself and Christopher," he said. "Trying to make him see reason is like banging my head off a stone wall. I was going to come over to you today, to see if I could make any better headway with you."

"Have you thought about what we said?" she asked.

"Have you thought about what I said, Honnie?" he said. "But this is neither the place nor the occasion for such a discussion. I'll see you back at the house later."

And he walked away.

Honnie was standing at the gate waiting for him, when Tom rode up almost an hour later. His expression was still severe.

He dismounted and they walked together, away from the house, Tom leading his horse.

"Honnie, have you really thought about what I said? You say you love Christopher. Well, have you seriously considered how marriage with you could affect his future and his position in society? You will probably say you love your own family. Do you love them enough to think of them first and foremost and put Christopher aside? Honnie, have you sat down and seriously considered what you are planning to do?"

"Tom, I thought it was a mad idea when he first asked me," said Honnie, "but I do truly love him, and I believe we could be happy together. I know it's unfair of me to ask you, and I feel bad that it could make things difficult for you if it was known that you married us. Tom, I really want to marry him. Please, please, will you marry us?"

Tom groaned with impatience, and neither of them spoke for a few minutes.

"All right, Honnie, you win," he said. "I'll marry you – but against all my wishes, and my better judgement. I'll marry you because I'm afraid of what will happen if I don't marry you. However, the fact that it was I who married you must be kept secret."

"I don't care if no one ever knows – as long as I'm married in the eyes of God," said Honnie, and she threw her arms around his neck. "Thank you, thank you, thank you, Tom!"

He gently disengaged himself. "I'm not finished, Honnie. I would still like you to think some more about it. You're putting yourself into a dreadful situation. There will be ructions in Tyrone House when his family hear about it. If you don't tell them you're married, and they hear that you are living together, they'll just assume that you are Christopher's kept woman. Even if he does eventually tell them you are married, they'll want nothing more to do with the pair of you. How will you feel about that?"

But Honnie was so happy that nothing could dim her joy.

"I don't care, I don't care," she said. "If I can be with Christopher, I know I'll be happy."

"For your sake, I hope that will prove to be the case," said Tom soberly. "Meanwhile, if you want to get married you'll have to find two witnesses, and two who won't broadcast your nuptials abroad to the countryside. Sort it out between the pair of you. The more I think of this whole escapade, the greater my misgivings, so you had better make your arrangements quickly before I change my mind."

Honnie decided not to tell Maureen and her two brothers anything. She just told them that she was returning to Tyrone. What they didn't know about, they couldn't talk about.

Christopher told his family that he was going up to Dublin to visit Thomas St. Lawrence. He had decided that, after the ceremony, he and Honnie would go to stay in Dublin for a while.

And late one dark afternoon, at the end of January, 1834, Honnie and Christopher were married in Father Tom's house in Kinvara, a town about ten miles from Tyrone, to the parish of which he had been appointed as curate just a few months previously.

Bridget was one of the witnesses – she had asked Mrs. Smith for a few hours off to visit her sick grandmother. A friend of Christopher's, Denis Daly, was the other. Denis and Christopher had been born in the same year, grew up together and shared a passion for horses, racing and hunting.

Denis collected Bridget at an agreed meeting place near a grove of trees just beyond Kilcolgan, on the road to Kinvara.

Bridget had found the idea of a secret marriage exciting, and though she felt obliged to raise some doubts, her excitement quickly buried them. Honnie knew that she could rely on her to keep the secret.

Honnie found it hard to contain her own excitement. She wore the soft violet shawl which Olivia had given her over her one good dress, and Olivia's pendant around her neck.

When Father Tom pronounced them man and wife she felt she was the happiest girl in the whole world.

Christopher had brought champagne with him, and after the short ceremony there was a toast to the newly married couple. Then Denis Daly took Bridget back to Tyrone, and Christopher and Honnie set out on their journey to Dublin. They would travel in easy stages, and they set out on the journey under a clear, starry sky.

Chapter 21

"Limerick will be our first big stop," said Christopher. "I don't think that we should go to Dublin through Galway. In Galway there will be too many people who might recognise us, and the news could travel fast. Not that we're going to get to Limerick tonight. It's near enough fifty miles away. But we'll put a bit of the road behind us. We'll look out for a good Posting Inn along the way."

Honnie sat close to Christopher and twisted her new wedding ring round her finger. It was their first time alone together as man and wife.

They travelled in Christopher's phaeton. A phaeton, even a hooded phaeton, was not the best way to travel in mid-winter. Nor was it a very pleasant way to travel at night, when bumps and potholes were hard to see, even with a full moon shining.

Christopher had brought woollen rugs and he wrapped them round Honnie, but they weren't enough to keep out the bitter chill. Honnie grew colder and colder.

"I'm sorry about the phaeton," said Christopher. "But a carriage would have needed a coachman and that was out of the question."

They had very little luggage and what they had belonged to Christopher. Honnie's wardrobe had always been sparse, and she had slipped out of the house with only the clothes in which she stood. With some embarrassment, she said to him that she would shame him up in Dublin because she looked so shabby, but he told her not to be a ninny, and promised her that she would go shopping first in Limerick.

They passed a few inns, but they looked very rough and ready, before they came to one which Christopher thought worth trying.

"It looks well kept outside, so it will properly be well kept inside," he said.

Which indeed it proved to be.

Honnie thought the fresh-faced landlady looked at them rather dubiously, but Christopher had no such apprehensions.

"We would like a warm room, with a good fire burning, and something to eat," he said, giving the landlady one of his particularly warm smiles. "We don't want any fancy food. At this hour of the night, bread and cheese will be fine. I know it's late, but I hope you can help us."

Honnie could see her melting.

"No problem at all, sir," the landlady said. "We'll be happy to accommodate you."

The room she showed them was very simple, but very clean. The sheets on the bed looked crisply ironed, and while they had been having some bread and ham and cheese downstairs she had got the fire roaring merrily.

Honnie still felt the landlady looked at her in a funny way, but Christopher just laughed.

"Nonsense, Honnie, she doesn't care one way or the other. She's just glad of the custom. What you need now is some champagne. It so happens I've brought some along, and glasses as well."

Christopher smiled as he filled her glass. Honnie felt happiness surge up in her like the bubbles which rose through the stem of the champagne glass.

"To us, man and wife!" he said.

For a moment, both their eyes strayed to the large double bed in the centre of the room. Honnie blushed hotly, and Christopher's smile widened. He put his arms tightly around her.

"I've waited such a time to have you all to myself," he said. "I have imagined it, I've longed for it. I can't believe it's really happening."

She could feel the passion in his voice, in his body, and her own body shivering in response.

He undressed her, slowly, kissing her as he did so, on the nape of her neck, on each of her breasts, before running his hands down the long length of her legs, leaving no inch of her body unexplored. Each time, each place he kissed, the pleasure seemed more intense, until the final pleasure, when it came, was almost unendurable. It was near morning before they finally fell asleep.

The day was well advanced when Honnie woke up, and for a few seconds didn't know where she was. She turned to find Christopher, half sitting up in the bed, propped on one elbow, looking down at her, smiling.

Honnie blushed and buried her face in his chest.

He gathered her into his arms and held her, and she wrapped herself around him.

They lay together, and loved each other, until they did indeed feel like one person. Honnie had never been so happy.

But time was marching on.

"We must make haste to get on the road as soon as possible," said Christopher. "These days are very short and night falls early. We need to put as much of the road behind us as we can while we still have daylight. I don't fancy doing any more travelling in the dark. We'll try to make Limerick before night."

The phaeton was definitely not the most comfortable way to travel any distance, and Honnie was relieved when the outskirts of Limerick town eventually came into sight.

"I think you'll like this hotel," Christopher said. "It's small but it's very well run, very comfortable. Mr. and Mrs. Flannery, the proprietors, have high standards. They met when they were both in service in a big house in Limerick, they saved their money, and eventually set up in business in this hotel. They are very discreet. I have stayed here a number of times when I have had occasion to come to Limerick."

The hotel was as Christopher had described it. The other people staying there – one elderly couple, and a younger couple with a small child – were quietly spoken, well dressed, and obviously comfortably off. In her one good gown, which was dusty and tired-looking after the journey from Kinvara, Honnie felt distinctly underdressed. She said as much to Christopher.

"We need to get you some new clothes," said Christopher. "But I am not familiar with ladies' fashions, or where in Limerick you should shop. I think we should consult Mrs. Flannery."

Mrs. Flannery rose admirably to the plea for advice. If she felt curious at the fact that Honnie had clearly arrived in Limerick with little more than the clothes on her back, she didn't show it. She wrote down the names of various emporia and gave them directions as to where they were to be found. And she said that if Honnie found material she liked, she knew of a good seamstress who was a very quick worker and could be relied upon to make up whatever gowns Honnie might want.

"She lives just a few minutes from here," she said. "And I can promise you that you will be happy with her work. You would, of course, have to remain in Limerick for some days."

"We would have no problem staying here for a while," said Christopher.

"Before we visit the shops," said Honnie, "I think I should visit the seamstress first, and ask her advice on what quantity of cloth I should buy, and what trimmings are needed."

"That is a very good idea," said Mrs. Flannery.

Alice Linehan, the seamstress, was a kindly woman, and she got caught up in Honnie's enthusiasm. It would be nice, she thought, to make clothes for somebody who appreciated her efforts, instead of overindulged young ladies who tended to be fussy and fault-finding.

A happy relationship was established, and Honnie and Christopher set off to go shopping.

"The first thing we have to buy is a warm mantle for you," said Christopher. "That shawl is pretty, but it's not near warm enough for this weather."

Honnie had been to Galway town a number of times over the years and had always looked enviously at the fine fashions in the well-known shops. She had gazed longingly at the rich materials, the velvets, the satins, the laces, the ginghams and muslins, and imagined having gowns specially made for her, in colours and materials of her own choosing. She had looked longingly at pretty bonnets and elegant cloaks, and wondered how it would feel to wear kid gloves. But she had never dreamt for a moment that the day would come when any of this would be possible. Yet here she was, being told she could choose whatever she liked, and buy whatever she wanted.

She had imagined what it would be like to be married to Christopher, but she had never really believed it would happen. Now, looking up at him, holding his arm, drinking in the warmth of his smile, she felt there could be no girl in the world as happy as she was.

They visited the English Woollen Warehouse and the Limerick Woollen Mart in Patrick Street. They visited Mrs. FitzGerald's Millinery and Woollen Warehouse in George's Street, and many other shops along the way. Honnie bought a cloak, made of deep, dark-blue wool, with white fur lining, and a furlined hood. She bought the kid gloves she had always wanted. She bought two lengths of wool for dresses, one pale hyacinth blue and the other of silver grey. She bought a length of navy bombazine for an everyday dress. Also, on Alice's instructions, she bought large amounts of white linen for the copious starched petticoats needed under the skirts.

Then, as they walked along Patrick Street on their way back to their hotel, Honnie noticed a little shoe shop down an alley with an array of good-looking shoes and boots on display in the window.

"I know I have bought a lot of things today, Christopher, but do you think I could buy just one pair of good boots? To go with my new clothes?"

"Buy as many of pairs of boots as you want," said Christopher, "and some shoes as well."

The shoemaker measured Honnie's feet, showed her a variety of different boots, and some pretty shoes and promised to have her chosen boots and shoes ready for her within three days or four days.

Suddenly they found they were tired and hungry. They decided to take the materials to Alice, and then have something to eat.

Alice approved of their purchases. She said she had got a niece to come and help her, but it would still take her the best part of a week to make all three dresses. And she would need to see Honnie each day for fittings.

"We can start by measuring you up today," she said.

"Well, I'll leave the pair of you to it," said Christopher. "I feel like a drink. There's a nice-looking inn a little way down the road – you remember, Honnie, we passed it on the way – and hopefully they serve food. You'll find me there when Alice is finished with you."

"And the inn does serve food – very good food too," said Alice.

Honnie and Christopher enjoyed a simple but excellent meal, of roast chicken with beautifully cooked vegetables.

Outside the day was darkening. They walked back to

the hotel, Honnie's hand in Christopher's, her arm held against him.

"I think we both need an early night," said Christopher, and smiled down at her.

Next day they went out to explore Limerick. It seemed a lively and animated town, jostling with gay people. Young officers walked the pavements in their fancy uniforms, tight-waisted, with brass epaulettes. Dragoons clattered by, bright in their red uniforms. Carriages jingled along. Carts rumbled past. But after a few days, when they had strayed off the main streets, Limerick didn't seem quite so splendid a place.

Honnie knew there were poor people to be found in every part of Ireland, but she wasn't prepared for the dismal poverty to be found in the back streets of Limerick. There seemed to be thousands of them, men, women and children, covered in rags and dirt, living in dank cellars, in houses that were half ruined. There was a rank smell of poverty and it was all-pervading. These were people who were wretchedly poor, who would always be poor. They were people without any possible hope of a better life.

Honnie began to feel guilty about feeling so happy, fearful that it might not all be real.

What if it turned out to be just a dream, that one morning she would find herself in her bedroom in Tyrone, with Bridget telling her to wake up quickly, or Mrs. Smith would be calling to know where they were? She pushed such thoughts aside.

Back in the hotel, Christopher laughed at her excitement as each new gown arrived from Alice. On the morning of their last day in Limerick she tried on all three, one after the other, savouring the feel of the rich materials. The skirts were full over her new petticoats and Alice had given the hyacinth and silver-grey dresses fashionable sleeves which were wide over the arm but narrowing to a small cuff at the wrist. As she stood in front of the long mirror, twisting and turning to see how she looked, she could see Christopher lying on the bed behind her. And she thought how handsome he looked, his white linen shirt open at the neck, his hair still tossed from sleep, an amused smile on his face. Her heart turned over and she felt she had to go over and kiss him, and it took even longer to get dressed again.

Then they went out and bought a new portmanteau for Honnie and packed all her new purchases in it, so that they were ready and packed to make an early start the next day.

The journey to Dublin was going to take several days. Christopher left his phaeton and horse in a livery yard where he was well known, and told them he would collect them on their return journey. He hired a carriage with a driver to take them to Dublin.

They would travel first to Nenagh, then to Roscrea, Maryborough and on to Kildare, changing horses as they went. The days were short, so it wouldn't be possible to travel as far in a day as they might have comfortably travelled in the summer months. Christopher decided they would spend their first night in Roscrea, and then make an early start in the morning and hope to get to Maryborough before dark.

Honnie had never been farther from home than Galway town. She was used to a poor landscape, bridled with low stone walls, and trees bent in the path of the winds. She found herself passing through landscape of a very different kind. The land was rich and green, the cattle were fat and content. They passed handsome country houses, and mansions surrounded by parks and plantations. Alongside one estate Christopher pointed out a deerpark and, as they looked, a young doe sprang from the trees.

Yet everywhere, it seemed, there were poor and hungry people. Whenever the carriage stopped in a small village or town, crowds of barefoot and bedraggled men, women and children gathered round, soliciting alms. To give to some was to bring an even greater flurry of appellants. Many of them, clearly, were hungry. Honnie began to dread these stops.

Christopher wanted to show Honnie the Curragh, where, he said, you could find some of the very best horses in Ireland, and see some of the very best races. Honnie had heard much about the Curragh during her time in Tyrone. It was the place where some of the biggest racing names in the country had their establishments. It was near the town of Kildare, not too far from Dublin. This was wide, open, rolling land, with very few trees, and not a sign of a stone wall. In the distance were the rounded hills of County Wicklow.

Christopher pointed out the different race courses to her.

"There have been as many as sixteen courses," he said. "But there are really only three great courses. It's the way they are used, you see. The oldest is the King's Plate Course and it goes back a hundred years and more. You know what a heart looks like? Well, the King's Plate

Course is four miles long in the shape of a heart. Conolly's Mile is the next oldest course. Then there's the Rutland Course, which lies inside the King's Plate Course. All the other courses are made up of bits and pieces of these."

He pointed out Walsh's Hill Gallops, and French Furze Gallops, Jockey Hall Gallops, and the Rath Gallops. He told her about the racing lodges all around the Curragh and the people who lived in them. He pointed out Conolly's stables – everyone had heard of Conolly – and Turf Lodge, Brownstown House, Jockey Hall, Athgarvan Lodge, Lumm Lodge and Whaley's Lodge.

To Christopher, the Curragh was clearly one of the most special places in Ireland.

"I want to have my own lodge here some day, Honnie, with my own horses running. Can you imagine standing at the finishing line and seeing one of your own horses come in first, in your own colours? Thomas St. Lawrence has promised to see that I'm made a member of the Turf Club. I might even get to become a steward! That's a pretty important position. There are only three stewards and they decide what goes."

It was almost a week after they left Limerick before they reached Dublin, late one dark wintry afternoon. As they came towards the centre of the city Honnie was awed by the fine buildings, the big houses, the carriages and coaches, the shops and the streets thronged with people.

They crossed over the River Liffey at Carlisle Bridge which joined the north side of Dublin to the south, and drove up Sackville Street – the widest street in Dublin,

Christopher said. And there, near the very end of it, was their hotel, the Gresham.

As the carriage drew up outside the doors of what seemed to Honnie a particularly grand building she fell silent.

She felt awkward and inelegant and wrong. It would be obvious to everyone who saw her, she thought, that a person like her would never stay in a hotel like this. People would notice how inappropriate she looked and smile at her behind her back. People would wonder what Christopher was doing with somebody like her. Even worse, they would think she was Christopher's fancy woman – for who was going to believe that he would have married her?

She drew back into a corner of the carriage, and frantically started tidying her hair, smoothing down her dress, fixing her bonnet.

"Just give me a few minutes. Just let me get myself together. Just wait a few minutes ..."

"What's come over you?" asked Christopher. "You look fine, you look beautiful. Why on earth are you hiding like that?"

Honnie tried to explain. "I just feel all wrong. I'll stick out like a sore thumb. I know I will!"

"Come on, Honnie," said Christopher. "You look fine, you look beautiful. Now I'll get out first, and hand you down. You'll take my arm, put your chin up, and look happy. We'll go into the hotel, we'll say how do you do to Mr. Gresham, who owns this hotel. "You'll give him your most charming smile, and then we'll go up to the rooms I've engaged, and I'll tell you a fascinating story. I sent a letter up to Mr. Gresham by post, telling him to expect us."

Mr. Gresham was waiting just inside the door, a handsome, imposing man. Looking up at him shyly, Honnie found no hint of disdain in his expression. His face was shrewd, but his eyes were kind. He welcomed Christopher warmly. This was clearly not the first time he had stayed here.

"And this is my wife," Christopher said, with his arm around Honnie.

If a flicker of surprise crossed Mr. Gresham's face, it was hardly noticeable.

"You are most welcome, both of you," he said.

"You know me of old, Mr. Gresham," said Christopher, and for the first time his manner seemed a little less confident. "My family knows nothing as yet about our marriage. I know I can rely on your discretion."

"You can," said Mr. Gresham.

He called a porter and asked him to show them to their rooms.

"Please don't hesitate to ask for anything you need during your stay here," he said. "I hope you have a very pleasant stay in Dublin."

Their rooms, when they reached them, were spacious and elegantly furnished. The bed linen was crisply white, the sheets turned down in preparation for the night. There were comfortable chairs, vases of flowers. In the adjoining sitting room a fire burned brightly in the grate, and the windows looked out over Sackville Street. As Honnie said, it was like a really nice room in a gentleman's house, like a room in Tyrone itself.

She took off her bonnet and cloak, sat at the dressing-table and started to arrange her hair. What she saw in the mirror didn't reassure her. Even with the finest bonnet and gown in the world, she would still be Honnie, Bartley and Mary Kane's daughter who had worked for the past six years in the kitchens of Tyrone House.

"I don't look like a lady," she said finally. "And Mr. Gresham must have known that immediately. And I'm sure those other people in the hall below saw it straight away too."

"Oh, don't be such a ninny, Honnie," said Christopher. "Mr. Gresham was nice to you, wasn't he? He welcomed you, he said he hoped we'd have a good time. So let's have a good time."

Then Honnie remembered what Christopher had said earlier.

"So what is this story you're going to tell me?"

"It's actually about Mr. Gresham, and it's quite a story," said Christopher. "Mr. Gresham was a foundling. He was abandoned on the steps of a building called the Royal Exchange in London, and he was named after the founder of the Royal Exchange, a man called Sir Thomas Gresham, who had been a famous merchant hundreds of years ago."

"But how did he come to Ireland?"

"He came, believe it or not, to work as a servant," said Christopher. "He was employed by a man called William Beauman who lived in Rutland Square not far from here. He must have been a very good servant indeed, because when he was still quite young he became butler to the Beauman family."

"But how did a butler come to own a hotel?"

"He left Mr. Beauman's employment in 1817, and bought two houses here in Sackville Street, and three years later he added a third house. These houses are now Mr. Gresham's Hotel."

"But butlers can't buy houses just like that," said Honnie. "Where did he get the money?"

"That's the big question," said Christopher. "There are plenty of rumours, but it is generally believed that Mr. Beauman advanced him the money. Certainly Mr. Gresham and the Beauman family seem to be still on the most friendly of terms. Nowadays Mr. Gresham is most highly regarded. He is a gentleman of standing in the community. He is the president of a bank, he is much to the fore in charitable works, and he has built some splendid houses out in Kingstown, just beyond Dublin. But he started his life as a foundling, and he worked as a butler. So what do you think of that for a story, Honnie? Does that make you feel better about Mr. Gresham and his hotel?"

Most definitely, Honnie decided.

Honnie looked at Mr. Gresham with new eyes when they met him on their way out of the hotel the following morning, and when he said he hoped she would enjoy seeing the sights, she felt he meant it.

"I'm sure Mrs. St. George would enjoy seeing Grafton Street," he said to Christopher. "All the visitors, and the ladies in particular, who come to Dublin, make a point of taking a turn around Grafton Street. There you will find some of the very best shops and see all the latest fashions – and fashionable people."

Honnie and Christopher set out on a walk of discovery.

In the light of day, Sackville Street was impressive, very wide, with the Nelson Pillar standing tall in the middle and opposite it the imposing General Post Office. A walkway of trees had been planted down the centre of the street and there were handsome buildings on either side. Honnie and Christopher went on up over Carlisle Bridge, crossing the Liffey towards Grafton Street.

Christopher showed her round Trinity College where he had studied for four years. He pointed out the imposing Bank of Ireland nearby which at one time housed the Irish Parliament.

In Grafton Street the shops seemed magnificent, and the goods they were selling were more luxurious than Honnie could have ever dreamed. Outside the doors of these establishments, there were lines of equipages, so many, in fact, that other carriages often had difficulty in getting by.

They looked over the railings into St. Stephen's Green, with its walks and shrubberies. Outside the handsome houses that surrounded the Green were more splendid carriages. But there was also another side of Dublin – sad wretches sitting on steps, standing aimlessly on the side of the road, some of them barely covered with rags, all of them looking hungry. And when they walked up and on into Merrion Square, it was the same: the houses and equipages were splendid, there were liveried servants everywhere, but everywhere also were the tatterdemalions with their gaunt faces and hopeless eyes. Once again, Honnie felt guilty.

"There are more beggars here in Dublin than I have ever seen in Galway," she said. I think it's even worse than Limerick."

Nevertheless, it was hard to resist the bright windows and wonderful clothes in the big emporiums of Grafton

Street. Honnie explored them with enjoyment, and she and Christopher returned there on the following two days. She acquired a number of items of clothing, including shawls, two bonnets, two pairs of gloves, and a pretty reticule. Now she held her head high when she went out walking, her arm through Christopher's.

They had been in Dublin for a week when he told her he would have to meet with his uncle, Thomas St. Lawrence.

"You know about Thomas," said Christopher. "He's my mother's half-brother, but he's only a few years older than I am. We've always been good friends, as you must know. He has first-class stables out in Howth. I told him I was coming up to Dublin . . ." He hesitated. "I didn't tell him about us, Honnie, because close and all as Thomas and I are, I thought the less people who knew about our marriage before it happened, the less likelihood there was of anybody trying to stop us. Now he's sent word that he'll send a carriage for me tomorrow to take me out to Howth Castle to see some new horses he's got. You'll be all right on your own for a few hours, won't you?"

Honnie was silent for some minutes. Common sense told her that Christopher wasn't going to introduce her to Thomas St. Lawrence as his new wife. But she still felt a little upset. She was a part of Christopher's life, and yet not a part of it. Some of the elation of the past few weeks suddenly seemed to disappear. But then she had always known, whenever she had allowed herself to think about it, that it was not going to be easy. After all, she herself had said that it would be difficult – but she had also said that she didn't mind what happened, so long as she was married to Christopher.

She fought back a desire to ask him not to go.

"But did he not wonder why you didn't stay with him?"

"I told him I was coming up to see some old college friends," said Christopher. "I said it was more convenient for me to stay in the centre of Dublin."

"Of course you must go," Honnie said. "And of course I'll be all right."

Thomas St. Lawrence was sending his carriage for Christopher early in the afternoon but Honnie and Christopher had barely finished eating luncheon in their room when a knock at the door brought a porter to say that the carriage had arrived.

Christopher wiped his mouth hurriedly and gave Honnie a quick kiss. He clearly felt a little guilty.

"I'll try not to be too late, Honnie. But don't wait up for me."

The day ahead seemed very long. But Honnie was lucky that their sitting room looked out over Sackville Street, and Dublin was still sufficiently exciting to give her amusement and entertainment just watching the goings-on in the street below. Christopher had told her that many Irish peers and Members of Parliament stayed for short periods in Dublin on their way to Westminster, and there were quite a number of hotels which provided the kind of comforts to which they were accustomed. Mr. Gresham's establishment was one such, and just two doors down there was Jones's Hotel, which was the chief coach stop on the north side of the city.

Honnie watched with interest the variety of vehicles and equipages disgorging all kinds and sorts of people. There were young men who leapt lightly down, evidently in no way fatigued by the journey. There were older men who were stiff and sore, ladies who were pale and exhausted. There were even some grizzling children, with nursemaids who were obviously getting short in temper and sympathy. She watched the beggar boys trying to carry portmanteau for the travellers, only to be roughly pushed aside by the hotel porters. She gave herself over to imagining who these travellers were, and from whence they had come.

But after some hours, looking out the window began to pall.

She took up a ladies' journal which Christopher had got for her and read about the latest fashions. She looked at some of the drawings and tried to dress her hair in some of the styles shown but wasn't very successful. She was feeling quite low when there was a knock at the door, and when she opened it a maidservant in a black dress with a crisp white apron and cap was standing there holding a tray.

"Mr. Gresham's compliments, ma'am. Mr. St. George left word that supper should be brought up to you."

The maid came in, laid a white cloth on the sitting-room table, and laid the table with silver cutlery, and sparkling glasses. She set down a plate of crusty bread, a tureen of rich broth, a chicken-and-ham pie, and some cheese.

At her heels stood a young waiter with a bottle of champagne peeping out from a silver bucket of ice.

"Mr. St. George's instructions, ma'am," he said. He

opened the bottle, poured out a glass, and then replaced the bottle in the ice bucket.

Honnie looked for any evidence in their faces or words that she was in any way a figure of fun to them but found none. They were cheerful young people, who smiled at her, expressed a wish that she should enjoy her meal, and then withdrew.

She discovered that she really was hungry. And the champagne was most pleasant. For a time she felt quite cheerful again. Since two glasses of champagne made her feel so good she had a third. Then for some reason she found she didn't feel so happy any more.

She didn't like spending so many hours in a hotel room on her own. Christopher was ashamed of her, and that was the truth. She had always known it would be so, but somehow it hadn't seemed to matter when they were together. But now he was with his fine relations out in Howth Castle, and she was the wife he was keeping secret. He was ashamed of her. And maybe he was right. There was no way that she could feel on easy terms with lords and ladies, no way she could mix in their company with comfort.

Honnie's spirits sank lower and lower. But she pulled herself together when another knock at the door brought the maidservant to clear away the tray. When the girl asked if she should leave the champagne, Honnie answered her in what she hoped was her firmest manner.

"Please do," she said. "Mr. St. George may like some when he returns."

But it was quite a bit later when Christopher returned, and by that time all the champagne was gone, and Honnie was rather cross.

Christopher himself had imbibed quite a bit. He found it difficult to understand why the Honnie he had left in such good spirits was now so down in the dumps and quite grumpy.

"What's the matter, Honnie, for heaven's sake? I've only been gone a few hours. I left you in fine spirits. Why have I come back to find you in such ill humour?"

"I know I'm being ridiculous," she said. "I shouldn't be in such ill humour. But you seemed to be gone for a long time, and I felt all alone. Then I started thinking. I feel I am going to be a hindrance to you. You're going to end up being ashamed of me."

Christopher took her in his arms and stroked her hair.

"You know I'm not ashamed of you, Honnie. And I'm never going to be. But if I had brought you out to Thomas St. Lawrence's house, you might have ended up much more unhappy. There's no doubt but that the St. Lawrences would have made you feel very unwelcome indeed. Common sense must tell you that to introduce you to them as my wife would have been pure folly – and could have been very unpleasant. And they would have sent word post-haste to my father, you know. I love you, I married you, but I can't control how other people may behave."

"So I'm just being ridiculous?"

"Honnie, you're not being ridiculous, but you are being a bit silly ..."

Honnie punched him in the chest.

Christopher laughed, took hold of her wrists, held her more tightly, and kissed her.

"Maybe I was being a little bit silly," she said.

In Christopher's arms her ill humour was floating away. And as they lay together in the comfort of the big bed, and Honnie felt loved and happy.

There were some realities she would have to face. In the meantime she decided to stop dwelling on problems and to enjoy herself until they went back to Galway.

Next day they went window-shopping again, and this time Christopher bought Honnie a silver-handled manicure set in its own leather case.

That night they went to the theatre to see Mr. Kean, the famous actor. Another evening they watched people going into a grand ball.

Here in Dublin they were just another young couple. There was nobody to look askance at them, nobody to disapprove. But Honnie began to feel very apprehensive at the thought of going back to Galway.

"I wouldn't like to live in Dublin – though I've really enjoyed staying here," she said to Christopher. "But I wish we could go somewhere we could live our lives together without having to worry about your family or mine, or what people think."

"You know we can't," said Christopher. "My father needs me. He has had a lot of blows in recent years. He depends on me and the estate needs me. Besides, Galway is part of me and I am part of Galway."

And Galway is a part of me too, thought Honnie.

Chapter 22

A week later, early on a wet and windy Tuesday morning, they set off on their return. Again the journey had to be made in stages, and the nearer they got to Galway, the more apprehensive Honnie became. It would be all right for Christopher. He would have his horses, his hunting and his hunting friends. He could still go out and about in society. But what would life be like for her?

Christopher had told her that, as planned, they would live in the house on the St. George lands at Drumacoo, just a short distance from Tyrone. It was a house which had been home at one time to an agent on the St. George estates. It had been idle for some time, but Christopher said he had arranged for it to be cleaned and readied for their arrival.

"I asked my old nurse, Molly Flaherty, to look after it for me and I know she will have done a good job. I told her I had an old college friend coming who wanted to stay in Galway for a while."

Honnie knew the house well, but the idea of living there with Christopher seemed very strange.

It was a dismal night. The rain hammered against the carriage, and the horses strained against the gusting wind.

"People know we have gone off together by now," she said to Christopher. "I know, I know, we've been through all this before. But I wouldn't be surprised if they try to run me out of the parish."

"They'll do nothing of the sort," said Christopher. "These are St. George lands, that is a St. George house, they are St. George tenants. If they attempt to make trouble in any way, I can promise you they'll be sorry."

When the carriage drew up outside the gates, there were a quite a number of people waiting. Somehow word had got out. They must have been seen on the road from Galway. No doubt the work done on the house had provoked widespread curiosity, and a wealth of rumours.

Suddenly Honnie felt her back stiffen with determination. They could do nothing to her. She knew she was married to Christopher. What did she care what people thought?

She still had to steel her nerves to step out of the carriage. But with Christopher holding her arm and her head held high, she walked to the gateway, knowing there was a sea of faces gaping all around her. She looked straight ahead, trying not to focus on any which might be familiar.

"Look at that for style!" said one voice.

"Them's fine feathers indeed," said another.

"Ah, but fine feathers don't make fine birds, now do they?" said a third voice.

Christopher and Honnie walked up the short path to the front door.

"You can dress a girl up as much as you like, but that won't make her a lady. She'll stay as she started, St. George's kept woman. For that's all she'll ever be."

That was surely Ellen Connors, thought Honnie.

Christopher turned on the crowd in fury.

"Away with the lot of you! Away I say! Do you want to keep the roofs you have over your heads?"

At that, they dispersed. Whispered remarks and answering low laughter faded into the distance.

The house was two-storeyed, and a woman stood waiting with a lamp at the open door.

Molly Flaherty's face, when she saw the "old college friend", was a study in horrified disapproval. She must have heard the rumours but obviously had persuaded herself that they weren't true. Somehow, she pulled herself together. She clearly doted on Christopher.

She led the way into a large, roomy kitchen, where a blazing fire sent out waves of warmth. A stout wooden table was covered with a crisp white cloth and laid for two people. There was wine, and freshly baked soda bread. There was a platter of potato cakes keeping warm by the hearth, and a rich smell of lamb stew coming from the black iron pot nearby. It was all very welcoming after the long cold journey.

Molly pointed out a wicker basket crammed with food. "Ye won't go hungry anyway."

Then she took them upstairs.

"I've done the best I could, Master Christopher, but I can't work miracles," she said, as she showed them the two bedrooms which had been readied for Christopher and his "college friend".

There was a broad iron bed with brass knobs in each, with stiffly starched sheets turned back, and the humps of stone hot-water bottles tucked in beneath them.

Honnie cringed as they surveyed the beds while Molly talked on about her preparations. Her manner was as starched as the sheets on the beds, and not once did she look Honnie in the eye.

It's as though I'm invisible, thought Honnie.

She felt very tired and ill at ease. She knew Molly Flaherty and Molly knew her, since their paths had inevitably crossed from time to time in Tyrone. Now she was clearly made aware that Molly regarded her as a very big mistake, a loose woman who had led Master Christopher disastrously astray.

Molly had a cottage on the estate, and while there were no longer any young St. George children to care for, she was devoted to the family, and still came to visit regularly. Christopher, as the eldest son, and one of only two boys among eight girls, had always been her particular pet. No matter what escapades he had been involved in over the years, in Molly's eyes there were always mitigating circumstances, and the fault, when there was one, had to lie with somebody other than Christopher. Seeing him setting up house with a girl who had been a servant in the St. George kitchens was very difficult for Molly to accept. She had done as she was asked because, despite the rumours, she had believed Master Christopher would not lie to her. In any case, she had never been able to say no to Christopher.

They returned to the kitchen where Christopher led Honnie to a chair by the blazing fire.

"Warm yourself there, Honnie," he said, "while I have a word with Molly."

She gratefully sat down and held her hands out to the flames.

Christopher ushered Molly from the room and Honnie was too tired to worry about what he might be saying to his old nurse.

At length they came back into the kitchen where Molly continued to address all her remarks to Christopher.

"As I've said, I've done the best I could," she repeated. "If the house feels cold and damp, it's because it hasn't been lived in this long while. I lit fires in the rooms to try to dry the place out a bit. There's firing out the back – wood and turf, enough to keep you going for a while anyway."

"Thank you, Molly," said Christopher.

"Of course I don't know how long you're thinking of staying here, but there's a lot that needs doing. There's a leak in the roof over that back room. You'd want to get that seen to. The back door doesn't close properly, but maybe it will close easier when the house dries out a bit. And there's a broken window in that sitting room beyond."

Having said all she had to say, Molly left, wrapping her shawl around her with the air of somebody who is relieved to have finished a distasteful chore. Honnie could feel the fumes of disapproval still heavy in the room.

"Well, what do you think, Honnie?" said Christopher. "Molly didn't do too badly by us, did she? I had to tell her we were married, but that it was to be a secret for a while. I knew she would never be able to swallow the idea of us just setting up house together otherwise. I know she doesn't approve, but she will stand by us."

"You mean she will stand by you," she said. "She just thinks I'm a hussy."

Honnie felt miserable. Why should she feel so bad? She had wanted to marry Christopher, and she had married him. Getting married secretly had been exciting. Travelling, getting new clothes, staying in the big hotel in Dublin had all been fun. And she loved Christopher more every day. She had always known that they would have to return to Tyrone, and she had always said that as long as she was with Christopher, nothing else mattered. But back in Galway on this cold dark night, the world seemed suddenly a difficult and harsh place. Would she have any friends here any more? What were her family going to say to her?

"Will I ever be able to go out of the house at all, without everybody pointing a finger at me?" she asked.

"Yes, you will," said Christopher. "It will just take courage, and you've plenty of that. They'll get tired of their gibing – especially if you hold your head high and take no notice of them."

"Easier said than done."

"I know it's been a long cold journey and this isn't exactly a palace," said Christopher, "but I know when you get going on it, it will be greatly improved.You'll feel much better when you've had something to eat. Here, take off your cloak. What you need now is a good glass of hot punch. Did you know that I'm a very good punch-maker?"

Slowly, Honnie began to feel better. It was her life, her life and Christopher's. Together they would make it work. But, later, as she drifted off to sleep, deep in the big feather bed, warm in Christopher's arms, she found herself wondering what she was going do tomorrow, when Christopher had gone about his business? And what about the next day, and all the days after?

Chapter 23

The rain beating hard in from the Atlantic woke Honnie up next morning, hammering at the windows, running down the panes of glass. She put her hand out to reach for Christopher, but he was already up and dressed.

He bent to kiss her.

"I must go to my father. He will have heard I'm back and be anxious to see me. You'll be all right, Honnie? I haven't time to get the fire going before I leave. But there's plenty of food."

"Of course I'll be all right. I'm no doubt better at lighting fires than you are anyway – do you even know how?"

"Of course I do," he said with a grin. "The well is in the far corner, to the right. Everything's very overgrown now, so it might take you some minutes to find it. It's near a big sycamore tree. While you're out there, have a look at the old buildings. I plan to get them converted into stables."

"Right." So she would be the one to draw the water. "When do you think you'll be back?"

"Father will expect me to spend time with him, and then there will be the horses to see to. It could be evening. But I'll get back as soon as I can."

And, with a quick kiss and a hug, he was gone.

I'd hazard he wants to see the horses even more than he wants to see his father, thought Honnie. She stretched out in the big bed, looked out at the rain-filled sky, and considered the day stretching ahead of her. There was nobody to tell her what to do, nobody to order her around. She was mistress of herself, mistress of this house, to do with as she wished.

Will I get up now? Or in half an hour? Maybe not for an hour, she thought happily.

She wriggled deep down into the comfort and warmth of the bed and thought about all the changes in her life. She dozed for a while. And finally got up.

There was a jug full of water standing in a basin on the dressing-table. Honnie washed her face and hands. The water was icy, but it stung her awake.

There was so much silence. All her life she had been used to people around her. Being alone in an empty house felt quite strange.

The night before, she had hung up her new clothes in the tall mahogany wardrobe that took up one side of the room, putting her new shawls and underwear in the chest of drawers. She opened the wardrobe door and looked at her new dresses again. Alice Linehan had certainly proved to be a clever needlewoman with a fine eye for fashion. The dresses she had made were simple, but looked fashionable and elegant. She held the hyacinth one up against her face and knew that the colour suited her. The silver-grey one was also very flattering. The dark bombazine dress she saw as tough and hardwearing.

Hanging at one end of the wardrobe, like a poor relation, was the gown she had worn when she left her home to get married. She took it off its hanger and began to dress herself slowly. Then she sat down and brushed her hair. A hundred strokes, that's what you were supposed to do every day. And when her hair hung long and shiny and smooth, Honnie braided it around her head.

The kitchen was cold. She suspected Christopher never had any intention of lighting a fire. She soon had the flames soaring up the chimney. Keeping the fire going had been one of her chores in Maree, and years of battling with the range in Tyrone made lighting a fire an easy task. She set the kettle on to boil for tea. She found some soda bread and a jar of blackberry jam in the wicker basket left by Molly. She drank two cups of tea and ate several slices of bread and jam and looked out at the grey day, at the clouds glowering down on the sodden landscape. Holding her second cup of tea in both hands, she drew closer to the fire. The fears that had besieged her the previous night began to close in around her again.

Honnie took a deep breath and shook herself.

She finished her cup of tea and considered the kitchen. In size and shape, it was not all that different from the kitchen of her childhood – but it was nothing like as clean, nor as well equipped. There was the solid wooden table, but only three chairs. There was a battered dresser, and some chipped cups and saucers, along with a few chipped plates, and a teapot which Honnie had washed very thoroughly before using though Molly had no doubt already washed it. There was an ancient-looking black kettle. There were a couple of iron pots, and a griddle, and that seemed to be the sum of all the cooking utensils. Honnie began to suspect that in the years in which it had been unoccupied, the house had seen a number of visitors, and quite a few of the kitchen contents had walked.

There were holes low down along the edges of the room, two near the fireplace and a couple more near the dresser. Too large for mice, thought Honnie. When she sat quietly for a few minutes she could hear scuttling. She wasn't afraid of mice, though she didn't want them in her kitchen. Rats, however, were another matter. She must ask Christopher if he would get her a cat.

Now in the light of day she could see that Molly Flaherty hadn't done such a great job after all. Spiders lurked in the corners of the ceiling. Silver fish darted around in the drawers of the dresser, and Honnie was sure she had seen at least two cockroaches. Over everything was a fine dust. Honnie knew as well as anybody that turf fires always spread a coating of dust all around, but the dust she found in some parts of the kitchen looked as if it had been there for years. The first thing to do was to give the place a good clean.

Two pails for carrying water stood at the back door. The rain had eased off a little and, wrapping a shawl around her shoulders, she took up the pails and started for the well.

There was an acre of land at the back of the house, surrounded by a rough stone wall, with some derelict buildings on one side.

At the time and again now, it rankled somewhat that he assumed she would be the one drawing the water and hauling it into the house.

A wild waste of brambles, neglected apple trees, rampant fruit bushes and a height of weeds filled the garden. Honnie knew there had to be at least the remains of a path down to the well, and she found it fairly quickly. As she walked, the branches of the old fruit bushes brushed wet against her skirt.

The well when she reached it was a little pool, overhung with thorn bushes. She dipped her fingers into the pool and tasted the water. It was cold and sweet, and clearly came from a good spring, deep below. Carrying back the full pails reminded her of the many pails of water she had fetched every day for her mother, from the well near her own home in Maree.

Back at the house, Honnie set two pots of water to boil. She found an old pail, some dirty cloths, and a scrubbing brush near the kitchen window, and beside them was a container of washing soda.

Honnie looked down at the dress she was wearing. It might be old, but she didn't want to ruin it completely. She went upstairs and in an old chest of drawers she found a worn sheet which she could use as an apron. She pinned it over her skirt, rolled up her sleeves and got to work.

It took three more trips to the well, many pots of water, and much scrubbing before Honnie was half-satisfied with the cleanliness of the kitchen. She stopped briefly to eat some of the food left by Molly and drink some tea. Then she laboured on. By the time she rinsed out the cloths and emptied the last pail of dirty water, the winter evening was already darkening.

She put on the kettle to make some tea and, as she sat in front of the fire sipping a cup, she realised she was exhausted – and that she couldn't remember ever spending so much time in her own company, without exchanging a word with another human being.

She felt dusty and grubby and very tired. She filled a big bowl with hot water from the pot boiling over the fire, added some cold water, found a clean piece of towelling, and some soap. She took off the old dress she had been wearing and scrubbed herself in front of the fire. Then she went upstairs to change into one of her new dresses.

She looked at her new finery. Two lovely dresses, she thought, but not to wear every day for doing housework.

She took the bombazine dress out of the wardrobe and laid it at the end of the bed. Before putting it on, she decided she would lie down and rest a while.

When Christopher came back some hours later, she was fast asleep.

"I came up to change my clothes, and I just lay down for a few minutes," she said when he woke her.

"So what are we having for dinner?" asked Christopher.

"Dinner!" said Honnie. "Dinner! I spent the day trying to get the kitchen clean. I can't cook in a dirty kitchen. It didn't look so bad last night, but in the broad light of day it looked filthy. Besides, Molly left enough food to last for three days. I put it in the scullery behind the kitchen. There's a joint of lamb, there's a chicken-and-bacon pie. There's soda bread. There are pickles, eggs, potatoes. There's cheese, a Madeira cake, and six bottles of wine. And much more besides. Why don't you go down and see what you fancy?"

"I fancy some food. I'm not fussy, I'm just very hungry."

He turned to go downstairs.

"You didn't even ask me what kind of a day I've had," said Honnie crossly.

"I'll be delighted to ask you about your day when I've had something to eat," he said over his shoulder.

When Honnie went down a little while later Christopher had laid the table. There were two big plates of thinly sliced cold lamb, potato salad, pickles, hardboiled eggs. There was cheese. He had also put out the rich-looking Madeira cake. There was an opened bottle of claret, and two glasses waiting to be filled.

"It's been a long day," said Christopher, "for both of us. Now let's sit down and have some food and wine."

"Do you not notice anything?" said Honnie.

"I notice that you are looking particularly pretty this evening," said Christopher, coming over and putting his arm around her. "And the nearer I get to you, the prettier you get."

"Christopher, for heaven's sake, do you not notice the kitchen?"

"Of course I notice the kitchen. I'm standing in it."

"Did I not tell you that I spent the whole day cleaning it, from the time you left, until an hour or so before you came home?" said Honnie. "Do you not see any difference in it?"

"Now that you mention it, I suppose it does look cleaner." He looked around him. "A *lot cleaner*," he added quickly, as he caught the glint in Honnie's eyes. "Honnie, when you're in the kitchen I don't notice anything else."

Honnie couldn't help laughing. "What you are,

Christopher, is a terrible chancer," she said. But she didn't put up any struggle when he took her into his arms and kissed her firmly on the mouth.

Later, as they sat by the fire, Honnie found the courage to ask the difficult questions.

"What about your father?" she asked. "How was he? What did he have to say?"

Christopher's face darkened. "He's worried about money, but then he always is. He gave me a lecture about duties and responsibilities."

"Has he heard about us?"

"No, no."

"Well, he'll surely be delighted when he does," Honnie said dryly. "I'm surprised it hasn't reached his ears already." Her spirits sank at the thought. "Maybe you should tell him yourself, Christopher? At least then he'll hear it from you."

"I'll choose my own time to tell him," said Christopher shortly.

For a few minutes neither of them spoke.

"He finds things much harder since Mother died," he said then. "And recently, I don't know, he just seems different. Dr. Veitch thinks he may have suffered a slight stroke, and I'm inclined to agree with him."

"And where does he think you are tonight?" asked Honnie.

"It doesn't concern him," said Christopher. "I'm a grown man. He knows I come and go as I wish. Stop worrying, Honnie. Come to bed."

Honnie woke very early next morning, her mind buzzing with plans for the day. She tried to interest Christopher.

"I want to plan my day. There's so much to be done. First of all, I need provisions – I need –"

"It's far too early for plans and provisions." Christopher's eyes remained closed. "I need another hour's sleep."

Then his eyes slowly opened and he looked at her speculatively.

"Or . . ." he said and reached out for her.

"Not now," said Honnie unconvincingly.

Later in the morning, after a good breakfast of scrambled eggs, bacon, soda bread and good strong tea, Honnie tackled Christopher again.

"I need provisions for the house, and I've no way of getting them," she said. "I've written out a list of what I need. I don't expect you to go and get them yourself, but could you get somebody to get them for you? I have to have the basic necessities with which to cook."

It was clear from Christopher's expression that he had no idea how to go about getting household necessities.

"I've been thinking, maybe if you showed the list to Bridget she might be able to advise you or help you?" said Honnie.

He looked relieved. "That seems a very good idea. Give me the list."

"And I was wondering if Johnny O'Connor in the gardens might give us some vegetables," said Honnie. "Do you think he would?"

"I'll ask him," said Christopher. "I'm sure that will be no problem."

When Christopher came home later that day he looked quite pleased with himself.

"I showed the list to Bridget. She wrote down the names of the different shops in Galway where your requirements would be met, and I gave Mick Murphy some money and asked him to go shopping."

Honnie was taken aback. "He must have found that a bit odd."

"Possibly," said Christopher, "but anyway he went. I often send him to Galway to get things for me. And I talked to Johnny O'Connor. He'll give us as much vegetables and fruit as we need, and he'll have a word with Paddy Scully and ask him to bring us some fish. I had to take the pony and trap from Tyrone to bring all the stuff over. Wait 'til you see!"

Christopher went out into the yard and came back with three full bags of household goods from Galway. He went out again and came back with a basket of vegetables from Johnny O'Connor, two rabbits, unskinned, and a fat chicken. "With Mrs. Smith's compliments," he said.

"Mrs Smith's compliments?" said Honnie, astounded.

"Well, not exactly her compliments," said Christopher. "I just told her I needed them, for a friend, and I was sure she would understand. What could she say? Now, Honnie, say I did a good day's work."

"I'll tell you what I'll say. I'll clean and pluck the chicken. Tomorrow we'll have rabbit stew." She smiled. "And you can skin the rabbits."

"You think I can't skin a rabbit," said Christopher, grinning back at her. "I can, you know, and in jig time. It wasn't for nothing I spent quite a bit of my youth with Billy the poacher."

"You and your childhood companions! I can just

imagine what Johnny O'Connor must be thinking now."

"Well, whatever he thought, he said nothing," said Christopher.

"If Johnny has nothing to say, I'm sure there are plenty who have," said Honnie. "Josie must be loving every minute of it. The men in the yards will be making a meal of us."

"Oh, for God's sake, Honnie! Do you really care what Josie or the men in the yards think?"

"No," said Honnie thoughtfully. "I don't suppose I really do."

But what her family thought of her would be a different matter.

Later, after Christopher made love to her and then quickly fell asleep, Honnie lay awake and decided that, instead of worrying about what people might think of her, she would think of all the things she wanted to do with the house, and what she would need to buy. Living in Tyrone had given her a taste for nice things. Good china, white maybe, with a silver edge, say six big and small plates, six cups and saucers, plain water glasses for everyday use, some cutglass wineglasses for special occasions. And a teapot, a white china teapot, maybe with a floral design. She would need cutlery, pie dishes, some linen tablecloths, pots, pans, cooking utensils, cutlery . . . soap and beeswax polish . . . The list was getting rather long.

She would need to make curtains, not only to keep out the cold, but to stop prying eyes looking in. It wasn't so bad up here in the bedroom, at the back of the house, but downstairs in the kitchen she hated the feeling that people could be looking in.

A watery moon came out from behind the clouds and shone across the bare boards of the bedroom. It wasn't going to be easy, this new life, but then she had never thought it would be. But she had made her choice, and now she would have to live with it, and she would, to the very best of her ability.

Chapter 24

Honnie worked hard over the next few weeks, cleaning the house from top to bottom, washing windows, whitewashing walls, gathering the rubbish of years into a pile for burning. But a lot was still needed to turn it into a real home. A shopping expedition, Honnie decided, was what she needed, and it would be good to get out of the house for a while. Christopher was frequently gone during daylight hours, looking after the affairs of Tyrone, busy with his horses, out hunting, meeting up with his friends. Honnie found it increasingly strange, after a life spent with people all around her, to be totally on her own, with nobody with whom she could exchange a word. Definitely, a shopping expedition would be something to enjoy.

She put the idea to Christopher.

"I want you to take me on a shopping expedition," she said.

"Shopping! For what?"

"For all sorts of things. Some china, to begin with, cups and saucers and plates. There are only two plates here, in case you haven't noticed, and they're cracked and chipped. We need jugs, and glasses, pots and pans, pie dishes, a sugar crock and a butter dish. We need cutlery. We need tablecloths and towels. And we definitely need curtains. I can make them myself, but I need to buy the material ..."

Christopher looked less than enthusiastic. "Tell you what – shopping isn't really my thing. I'll take you to Galway. We have accounts in most of the good shops in town. Andersons should have most of the things you want – I'll tell them to give you what you want. When you're finished you'll find me in Mr. Kilroy's Hotel, and we can have lunch. How about that for a good idea?"

On the morning of their excursion Honnie woke up bubbling with excitement. She brushed her hair and braided it carefully. She put on her new grey dress, and her new cloak, and her new shoes. It was a crisp spring day with a clear blue sky.

As she stepped up into the trap beside Christopher, her first time travelling in to Galway with him as his wife, Honnie's heart felt overflowing with happiness.

The journey to Galway passed easily enough. The only people who showed any interest in them, just after they left Drumacoo, were three women with a gaggle of children hanging out of their skirts, who exchanged knowing glances and whispered comments. Later travellers merely glanced at them.

The nearer they got to Galway, the more people they met on the road, people travelling in gigs, in traps, in jaunting cars, quite a few in an ass and cart, an occasional carriage, many just walking, people bringing produce to sell, people going in to shop, people on other errands of their own.

The fields and hills were turning gold with gorse, and as they got nearer to Galway town the smell of the sea came in on the western breeze.

In Galway, Christopher drew the trap up outside Andersons in Abbeygate Street.

"I'll go in with you and tell them to give you whatever you want," he said as he handed her down from the trap. "I'll see you later in Kilroy's Hotel."

Honnie put her hand on his arm. "Christopher, I would prefer if you stayed with me. I have never been shopping like this before. Suppose they question what I want to buy? Suppose they say they have to be sure that you will agree to what I have spent? They will recognize me for what I am, what I have been. Please stay with me."

Christopher reached out and tucked her arm through his. "Of course I'll stay with you," he said. "But you know there is no need for you to feel so anxious."

Inside the shop, Honnie gazed at all the goods on display.

"Like a child in a sweet shop," said Christopher, smiling.

Andersons seemed to have everything she might possibly want or need. There were tables of fine china, delicately decorated tea services, elegant dinner services, shelves of glittering glass, stands of pots and pans and ovenware. They had snowy tablecloths and table napkins. They had bed linen and blankets – she would look at those another day when she had sorted through the bedding stored in the big press at home.

Years of working with Mrs. Smith in Tyrone had given Honnie definite opinions on the basic necessities of a good kitchen, but faced with such a wide choice her biggest difficulty was making up her mind. She saw quite a few things she hadn't known she needed until they were put in front of her.

The night before, sitting beside the fire, she had made a list of her needs. In Andersons, she found she wanted considerably more than she had intended to buy and the list had gradually become longer.

After an hour and a half had passed, Christopher had had enough.

"I don't know about you," he said, "but I'm getting hungry."

He arranged for their purchases to be delivered to the house in Drumacoo and steered Honnie in the direction of Kilroy's Hotel.

After lunch, they strolled around the streets of Galway and Honnie was surprised anew by the number of beggars they met, many of them young children, barefooted, in ragged clothes, who crowded around them, beseeching alms.

"Long life to Your Honour, long life to Your Honour!"

"Oh Christopher, can't we give them something?" said Honnie.

"Honnie, if we give to one lot of them, we'll have all the others after us, following us down the street. We'll give them something on the way back."

"All right," she sighed. "Christopher, I want to go by the Claddagh. Whenever I'm in Galway I always like to visit the Claddagh."

"They're a fierce wild breed, the people who live there. Why would you want to go there?" asked Christopher.

"They're wild, but they're different," said Honnie, as they headed towards the harbour and the network of streets and lanes that made up the Claddagh. "I think they are very interesting. They live the way they want to live, they make their own laws. And their cottages are so neat and clean and well-furnished."

"And they don't answer to anybody except their own king," said Christopher. "The king settles all their quarrels and disagreements. And they have a special ring, passed on by the mother to her first married daughter, and then on to her descendants."

Honnie looked surprised.

"You thought I knew nothing about them, didn't you?" said Christopher, laughing.

Sometimes she wondered if she really knew him. She loved him but did she know him?

Next morning Honnie surveyed her kitchen. There was no range. She would miss not having one. But then she had grown up with an open fire, so it wouldn't be any great hardship to go back to one again. She remembered all the good food her mother had contrived to cook with just an open hearth – succulent rabbit stew, warming chicken broths, Hallowe'en colcannon, potato cakes dripping with butter, soda bread eaten almost as soon it was cooked, smothered with butter and blackberry jam.

The kitchen was certainly cleaner, after all her hard work. But it had a bleak, bare look about it. The couple of coats of whitewash had helped, but curtains would make it warmer and more cheerful. Making them would be another matter. Despite all the hours Honnie had spent under her mother's tutelage, she had never succeeded in achieving the neat rows of stitching her mother had produced so effortlessly. But making curtains should be reasonably straightforward, although it would be much easier, she realised, if she had remembered to buy some needles and thread.

The dresser still needed a good scrub with sand, and so did the table. That would mean a trip to the seashore.

Honnie looked down at the floor. It had been one of the nice surprises in the kitchen. Instead of the usual earthen floor, Honnie had found tiles like the ones in the kitchens of Tyrone, a kind of slate which she knew came from Liscannor, in nearby County Clare.

Their purchases from Galway were not to arrive until the afternoon. Christopher had gone over to Tyrone, saying he would be back before dark. Outside the sky was bright. It seemed as good a time as any to fetch some sand. Honnie wrapped her shawl around her and, taking one of the pails she had used to carry water, she headed towards Killeenaran and the inlet known as Brandy Cove.

She couldn't stay inside forever, nor could she expect Christopher always to accompany her. She needed air and space. But her heart tightened at the thought of meeting people. Going out with Christopher in Galway, where few people would recognise her, was one thing. Going out around Drumacoo, where many people knew her, was another. Honnie closed the door behind her with a sinking feeling. Christopher had said she shouldn't care what people thought. That was easy for him to say. For the hundredth time she reminded herself that she had nothing to be ashamed of: she was a properly married woman in the eyes of God. But not in the eyes of those around her, said another small voice.

The first person she encountered on the road was Finny Joyce, a local fisherman, who occasionally brought fish to Tyrone. Mrs. Smith didn't like him. She said his tongue was too sharp, and his fish often stale. She preferred to buy all her fish from Paddy Scully.

"If it isn't Honnie!" he said as her drew abreast of her. "Back from her travels in Dublin. Isn't it lucky for some!"

Honnie drew herself up straight and went on walking. Don't look at him, don't answer him, she told herself. His words followed her.

"What I want to know is what Christopher St. George has that I haven't got – apart from money, that is!" And he laughed heartily at his own wit and went on his way.

Her next encounter was with three women, on their way to the village of Drumacoo. They whispered among themselves as they saw her approach.

"Now isn't that a bit of a come-down from cooking for the gentry," said one of them as they passed her by. "From kitchen-maid to kept maid!"

"Only she isn't a maid any more, is she?" said another voice.

And they went giggling on their way.

As Honnie drew nearer to Killeenaran and its huddle of cabins, she wrapped her shawl around her and hurried past them towards the sandy shore beyond the quay. She walked quite a distance until she was alone with herself and the sea, the wind, and the gulls wheeling in the blue and white of the scudding sky.

Gathering the sand could be quickly done. She sat on a rock and savoured the solitude. This was the kind of ease she would have envied when she was working in the Tyrone kitchens and even a few minutes to herself had to be stolen. Now she found it strange to know that she had all the time she could want to be on her own. She drew in deep breaths of the salty air and played with the sand, letting it run between her fingers.

She looked across Ballinacourty Bay. There were boats out fishing – for mackerel, she guessed, or maybe herring. She had heard the mackerel fishing was good this year. One of those boats would surely be Martín Breathnach's, and Thady would be on it. Honnie strained her eyes to see if she could make out the *Lon Dubh* – the *Blackbird* – but she couldn't be sure.

She didn't find the journey home as bad as the journey out, but she felt safer when she had closed the door behind her. She took off her shawl and hung it up on a nail on the back of the door. Then she picked a handful of thick sticks, and some lumps of black turf out of the basket alongside the hearth, and set the fire to redden. She hung a big pot of water over it and waited for it to boil. She wanted to have the dresser ready to receive her new china.

The house felt very quiet. There was very little sound, just the whistle of the wind in the chimney, the lonely cry of a curlew outside, and an occasional creak from old timbers.

When the water was hot enough, Honnie began scrubbing the dresser. It was well made, but sadly neglected. The dirt of ages seemed to be worn into the grain. But after three assaults with the scrubbing brush and sand Honnie was pleased with the result. Now she would let it dry completely, and then she could feed it with some beeswax polish and bring it to warm life again.

Meanwhile she started on the table. It wasn't as dirty as the dresser – probably because it had been washed more often when people were living in the house, but it still looked the better for a good scrub. Honnie was standing back admiring it when she heard men's voices and the sound of carriage wheels outside.

A tall, grey-haired man had just alighted and was making his way up the path.

He nodded at Honnie as she opened the door and stood uncertainly waiting.

"Good morning, ma'am. We're from Andersons. Would you be expecting a delivery for Mr. Christopher St. George?"

"Yes," said Honnie. "That's for here."

The man turned and spoke briefly to another man still in the carriage. Together they unloaded a number of boxes and carried them in one by one. The delivery only took a matter of minutes, but even in that time people had gathered, mostly women and children. They said nothing and, while Honnie was happy to see her shopping arrive, she was very aware of all the watching eyes. She could feel her face reddening with embarrassment.

When the last parcel had been handed in, the men bid her goodbye. Honnie went quickly into the house, glad to close the door behind her.

She began opening the boxes. The china with the silver rim looked plain but elegant, and would look well on the dresser. The cutlery could be put in the dresser drawers, but the drawers would need some kind of lining. Very little could be put into the dresser or onto it until it was polished. But the new brass candlesticks could be lit and stood at either end of it without doing any harm.

The pots and pans would hang from hooks beside the hearth. And the new glass vase, gleaming in the sunshine coming through the window, could be filled with flowers. Honnie remembered seeing some daffodils in the back garden, staunchly pushing themselves upward through a welter of weeds. She went out, picked a bunch, put them in the vase and placed them proudly on the newly cleaned table. There was something special about daffodils. They came up, year after year, demanding no care and attention. They were among Honnie's favourite flowers. Glowing brightly in the dark kitchen, they made her feel happy and hopeful. She remembered them in her own garden at home, and how cheered her mother always was when Honnie brought her in the first bunch of the year.

"Winter is really on its way out," she would say. "Spring is coming and the days are getting longer."

Meanwhile, Christopher had spent most of the day in the Tyrone stable yards with Mick Murphy, examining Waterwitch – a black filly sired by the famous Sir Hercules. It looked like the horse had done herself an injury, when she had been taken out for a run earlier that morning.

The sound of his father's voice made Christopher jump. Arthur St. George was rarely to be seen in the yards these days, after a fall off a horse two years before.

"You seem surprisingly hard to find these days," he said to Christopher. "Could it be that you are trying to avoid me?"

"Nonsense, father," said Christopher. "Why on earth should I want to do that?"

"Why, indeed?" said his father. "I would like to see you in the library tomorrow morning at ten o'clock sharp."

Christopher was conscious of Mick Murphy's eyes upon him, and that Rory, another groom, had also heard the exchange.

"That would be good," said Christopher. "We don't seem to have seen much of each other recently. Until tomorrow, then."

When Christopher returned home later his mood was black. He glanced around the kitchen and, after some prompting from Honnie, he agreed that it looked more cheerful. But he didn't seem disposed to talk. Then he ate his supper in silence, drank a few glasses of wine, and sank into a chair beside the fire.

"What's wrong?" Honnie asked.

Christopher shrugged. "Waterwitch is lame. You know what high hopes I had for that horse. I can't get the truth from any of the men. Even Mick Murphy doesn't seem to have found out what actually happened. Everyone's telling me a different story."

"But that isn't the only thing that's upsetting you," said Honnie.

For a few moments Christopher said nothing, and then he turned towards her.

"My father wants to see me, tomorrow," he said. "I fear he's heard about us."

Honnie put her arms around him. "Maybe 'tis better to get it over with. Until you've had it out with him, you'll never rest easy."

Christopher pulled away from her.

"*Easy, is it?*" he said, furiously. "Nothing is ever easy with my father. He'll sit behind his desk, and have me standing up in front of him, and he'll lecture me as if I were still a growing boy. He'll tell me all the ways in which I have disappointed him, all the ways in which I have failed. Well, it's my life, and I am going to live it the way I want to live it, and I'll tell him so."

Over the next half-hour Christopher angrily recalled his many confrontations with his father, the arguments, the lectures, the criticisms. Honnie didn't try to stop him. It would, she thought, probably do him good to talk. Finally he cooled down.

"Why don't we go to bed and get some sleep?" she said. "It's late and you're tired. In the morning, in the daylight, after a night's rest, you'll feel better able to face him."

But they were newly married and had made love every night before they went to sleep. This night was no different.

As they lay together afterwards Christopher gathered Honnie fiercely close to him.

When Christopher set off for Tyrone next morning, it was dark and dismal, with heavy rain streaming across a water-logged countryside. He arrived promptly at ten and knocked at the library door. His father was standing by the big window that looked out over the gardens. He turned, tall, grey-faced, and moved over to sit behind his desk. The thrust of his jaw, his grim expression, seemed to bode the worst.

"You know, when you were born after six girls, your mother and I were so happy. I welcomed all my daughters, but we did long for a son. You came, and we had a big party to celebrate your arrival, not just for the family, but for all the tenants as well. We watched you growing up, healthy and strong, and we felt that you would become a very able master of Tyrone. When you came down from Trinity, I was pleased to see how well you got on with the people here, and at the way you involved yourself in local activities. But now it seems you get on so well with the local people that you actually want to be one of them. You need to keep a certain distance, Christopher. They'll respect you the more for it. Christopher, I've said this to you before and now I am saying it again. The estate is in serious financial trouble. There are charges on it going back to your grandfather's time. What we now owe goes into six figures. We need you to make a good match, take a wife who comes with a good dowry."

Christopher's heart jumped and he felt his face flush.

"Yes, Father, you have said all that before," he said, trying to control his voice, "and I have also told you before that I was never going to marry any girl just because she had money. In any case she would need to be quite an heiress to get this estate out of trouble. Most heiresses know their worth and, if they don't, their families certainly do. Why would any right-minded girl want to come to the rain and winds of the West of

Ireland, to an estate that is obviously heavily in debt, just to marry me?"

"If you made yourself pleasant I'm sure the right girl might think it worthwhile. You are a good-looking fellow. I'm told you can make yourself very popular with the ladies when you are of a mind to do so. A girl with a dowry, a sizeable dowry, could make a huge difference to Tyrone, to you, to me, to all of us."

"Father, the world and his wife know the estate is in debt. If you had a daughter with a handsome dowry, would you honestly feel happy about her marrying somebody who clearly just wanted her money?"

Christopher could see the colour rising in his father's face, his shoulders stiffening.

"I don't think you fully appreciate the situation, Christopher. The only way Tyrone can go is down, unless we find some way of solving our financial problems. There is such a thing as a sense of duty. If your mother were alive today she would expect you to do whatever is required to help."

Christopher could feel his own temper rising.

"Father, Tyrone is already irredeemable. And it isn't just Tyrone. Other houses like ours are going down too. Even if I could delay things by making what you like to call an advantageous marriage, I'm sorry but I don't see it as my duty to be miserable with someone for the rest of my life."

"I'm not saying you should marry anybody just for their money," said his father. "I'm just saying that there must be a nice girl, a girl of your own kind, with an adequate dowry, with whom you could be happy."

"Well, I'm sorry," said Christopher. "That's not going to happen."

"It's certainly not going to happen while you are running around the country with a kitchenmaid!" said his father. "I've been hearing stories lately which have deeply distressed me. It seems you brought that Kane girl up to Dublin, to stay in the Gresham Hotel, no less. And you have been strolling around the Claddagh together, and lunching in Kilroys. Flaunting your cheap liaison for all to see. What in God's name are you thinking of? Have you lost your wits completely?" He struggled for breath before continuing. "Have you no thought for the family name and reputation? And now I hear that you've set her up over at Drumacoo, just a few miles away from Tyrone itself. You are making the family the object of ridicule in the whole of Galway."

"Clearly, your spies have been very busy," said Christopher.

"It so happened that Thomas St. Lawrence wrote to me on another matter, and mentioned in passing that he had seen you, and you were staying at the Gresham," said his father. "I take it he didn't know you were not on your own?"

"I saw no reason to mention it," said Christopher.

"Well, I'm glad to see you have some shame left in you," said his father.

Christopher raised his voice. "I'm not ashamed of anything. And I'm sick and tired of hearing about the St. George name and the St. George reputation. Can you think of nothing else but respectability? Maybe if you had thought more about your daughters and less about their reputations, two of them wouldn't have run off the way they did!"

Arthur St. George's face reddened further and he spluttered with rage.

"How dare you speak to me like that, you young pup!

I am simply trying to find a way of salvaging something out of this sorry mess. Have you thought about your sisters? Do you realise they're going to be tarnished by your behaviour. What about Arthur, your young brother – what kind of example is it going to be to him?"

"I'm sorry about my sisters," said Christopher, "but I can't live my life just thinking of them. As for Arthur, he's still very young. I don't believe what I do can affect him."

For a few minutes his father said nothing. When he spoke again he sounded almost bewildered.

"I just don't understand you. Your mother spoilt you, and now look at you. You'll never amount to anything."

"Because I refuse to marry a so-called respectable girl and redeem the family fortunes?" said Christopher. "I love Honnie and I mean to spend the rest of my life with her."

"*Love!*" said his father. "You don't know what the word means. And with a chit of a kitchenmaid. A kitchenmaid! Have your fun if you must, but don't flaunt it in front of the whole countryside. When I think of your poor mother, a lady to her fingertips. And now her son has set up house with a servant girl. Thank heaven she isn't here to see it."

Christopher felt rage boiling up inside him. "Can I remind you that your own father lived happily with his Rebecca in Kilcolgan Castle, and that didn't seem to bother the family too much. Were they even married?"

Arthur St. George controlled his temper enough to reply. "Your grandfather and Rebecca came together after your grandmother died – *long* after your grandmother died. And of course they were married. It was a small private ceremony."

"Well then," said Christopher, throwing all caution to

the winds, "you'll be glad to know that I too have been married, in a small private ceremony, to Honnie."

Arthur St. George crumpled back into his chair, grey-faced and speechless.

Suddenly he looked older, smaller, beaten. Christopher couldn't help but feel some compassion for him. He tried to think of something to say.

"Father, I'm sorry, really sorry that this has all fallen so heavily on you –"

"Just go, Christopher, just go."

So Christopher bid him goodbye and left, quickly.

After Christopher left, Arthur sat, unmoving, for a long time. The rain had stopped and pale sunlight crept into the room, onto the tumbled papers piled on his desk. Outside the birds started to sing, and lingering raindrops pattered down from the budding trees. But Arthur saw and heard nothing, as he sat there, motionless, staring into a blank, black distance.

He wished, as he had done many times, that Harriet was still alive. She was a wise woman. Whenever he had been upset or worried, she had always been able to calm him down, make him see things in perspective. But even Harriet, he felt, would have found it difficult to see something positive in the present situation.

He *had* to talk to somebody. Then, with a great swell of relief, he remembered that Thomas St. Lawrence was due to visit in the next couple of days. He wasn't much older than Christopher but he was much more grounded, more sane, and more sensible. He mightn't be able to do much to help, but he was a good listener.

When Christopher got back to Drumacoo he was more

sombre that Honnie had ever seen him.

"Tell me what happened," she said.

"I hate this place," he said bitterly. "Everybody knows everybody else's business. There's always someone to carry the latest piece of gossip."

Honnie froze. "What did he say?" she asked, her lips dry with fear.

"That I was a disappointment to him, that I was irresponsible ... that I've disgraced him."

He was clearly much shaken and very angry as he went on to tell Honnie of the exchanges between his father and himself.

"Did he know about us?" asked Honnie

"Of course he did. I told him we were married."

"And what did he say to that?" asked Honnie faintly.

"Well, what do you think?" asked Christopher. "He was horrified. He told me to go. So I just left."

In his mind's eye Christopher saw his father again, sitting ashen-faced at his desk.

Most of the people in Tyrone House had heard the raised voices, and knew that there had been a serious argument between Christopher and his father.

Anne and Louisa had been in the drawing-room when they saw Christopher arrive. With the rain pouring down outside there was no question of any outdoor pursuits. Anne was doing her needlework, and Louisa was leafing through the pages of a novel.

"Well, he certainly doesn't look in a very good humour," observed Louisa.

"Maybe Father is finally calling him to order," said Anne. "He's been let away with far too much."

"The question is *can* Christopher be called to order," said Louisa. "Father has tried before, but in the end Christopher has usually gone his own way."

It was almost an hour before they saw him storming out of the house.

"And looking even crosser than when he arrived," said Louisa.

"I wonder what happened."

Josie could have told them what had happened. She had been passing the library door a few minutes after Christopher's arrival. She had no hesitation about listening from behind the curtain of a nearby window, where she pretended to be cleaning the glass.

When Anne and Louisa eventually went looking for their father, he was nowhere to be found. It was Robert, the footman, who finally told them he had seen him go outside, in the direction of the gardens.

The rain had stopped and a dull, pallid sun was creeping from behind the clouds. The ground was squelching wet, and every leaf dripped. They found Arthur St. George in Lady Harriet's herb garden. He seemed to have aged ten years.

Anne stepped forward.

"What's happened, Father? Are you all right?" she asked.

Arthur looked up at them, grim-faced.

"Your brother has disgraced us all. He has set that Kane girl up in a house over at Drumacoo. He says he loves her and intends to spend the rest of his life with her. He says he has married her."

"Married!" cried Anne. "How could he be married? Where was he married? Who married them?"

"I don't know the answers to any of your questions," said Arthur. "And really at this point it doesn't seem to matter any more. The damage is done. Now I don't want to talk about it. There's nothing more to be said."

The two sisters were on their way up the stairs to Anne's bedroom when they met Harriet.

"I know by looking at your faces that something has happened," she said. "What's wrong? Tell me?"

"It's Christopher," said Louisa. "This time he's excelled himself. He's gone off with the Kane girl, and set her up over in Drumacoo. He says he's married her."

"He's done *what*?" Harriet's voice rose to a shriek.

"I've just told you," said Louisa. "He's married the Kane girl and set up house with her."

Harriet started to sob.

"Oh, for heaven's sake, Harriet, stop blubbering," said Louisa. "That will do no good at all. Do you want the servants to think the whole house is falling apart?"

The sisters didn't talk again until they were in the privacy of Anne's bedroom. But enough had been heard by at least two or three servants, who had been drawn into the hall at the sound of raised voices and overheard the news as delivered by Anne and Louisa.

In Anne's bedroom the three sisters stood staring at each other.

"He has been going from bad to worse," said Harriet, starting to cry again. "But this is the very worst. What was he thinking of?"

"He was thinking of himself, as always," said Anne.

"It's that Kane girl," said Louisa. "He's been hankering after her for years."

"And now he's got her," said Anne.

"Oh lord, everyone will be laughing at us," said Harriet.

"Laughing?" said Anne. "They'll do worse than that. They'll drop us. And as for being invited out, and inviting people here, this puts an end to all that. Christopher has not only put himself outside society, he has put us outside as well."

Josie, who had managed to eavesdrop on the conversation in the bedroom, was very excited.

Wait 'til I tell them all about this downstairs, she thought gleefully.

Chapter 25

Honnie and Christopher lay awake.

"So what do you think will happen now?" asked Honnie.

"My father needs me, Honnie. He is less and lesss able to handle affairs himself. I feel duty bound to help him in any way I can. But he is a very difficult man, and not easy to work with. There are times when I feel I am biting my tongue half a dozen times a day, that nothing I do is right. He is never going to accept our marriage, I know that. I suppose I couldn't expect him to. It's all very unpleasant. And now I'm tired of talking about it. I'm going to go to sleep, and I advise you to do the same."

He rolled over and was soon snoring gently.

But Honnie lay awake long hours after that.

Next day when Christopher went over to Tyrone the atmosphere was unpleasant. He and his father didn't speak to each other unless it was absolutely unavoidable.

"But there were no more confrontations," he told Honnie when he came home in the evening. "Which was a mercy. It hurts me just to look at him. He suddenly looks much older. It has helped him to hear that Thomas St. Lawrence is coming to stay. Father is very fond of Thomas and Thomas would be a sympathetic listener when my father unburdens himself of all his troubles, as he undoubtedly will. And I have to admit that it takes some of the heat off me."

Arthur St. George gave Thomas a very warm welcome when he arrived at Tyrone on a chilly spring evening.

"You can have no idea how very glad I am to see you," he said. "I trust everyone is well up in Howth? I'm afraid things are not so good down here, but we'll leave our problems aside until later in the evening. Now you must have a good glass of punch to warm you after your journey, and you must be hungry after all your travelling. Dinner will be ready in an hour or so."

It was some hours later, as they sat together in the library with a decanter of port on the table beside them, that Arthur told Thomas of Christopher's new living arrangements.

"Setting us up for ridicule in front of the whole county," said Arthur. "You know that Christopher has always been wayward and wilful, but this is my worst nightmare."

"I suspected something was afoot when I saw him in Dublin," said Thomas. "And yes, I know Christopher's always been a bit of a wild one, but he has a good heart, Arthur. Hot-blooded young men can be impulsive, rash. You have to hope this is just a passing escapade."

"It's more than just a passing escapade," said Arthur.

"He says they're married. Married! He says he loves her and wants to spend the rest of his life with her … I still can't believe it."

For a few moments Thomas was stunned into silence.

"But where were they married, and by whom?" he said finally.

"I didn't ask," said Arthur.

He poured himself another glass of port and passed the decanter to Thomas.

"You must know that I had always hoped Christopher would marry some suitable girl, who would come to Tyrone with a good dowry. And Christopher's behaviour is not going to enhance his sisters' marriage chances – in fact it may destroy them. It is incredibly selfish of him to do what he has done. Raising a family, especially a large family, Thomas, is a demanding, heavy task. Things were different when I married your sister back in 1801. Of course, even then there were some £36,000 of charges on the estate. In the last years of the last century it cost a great deal of money to build Tyrone. My father wanted it built with the best materials, to the highest specifications. The times seemed good. It seemed reasonable to borrow. The future looked bright. But it all proved to be an illusion, as you know. Times got worse rather than better, and instead of debt being reduced, more mounted up. My father gave me Tyrone, but then he went on to build Kilcolgan Castle, which cost more money. He married for a second time, and had a second family, and since he died in 1826 his widow and their children have had to be maintained. The debts kept mounting. Now, every which way I turn, I owe money."

"It's true that the country doesn't seem in a great state now," said Thomas. "And, of course, you are very distressed about Christopher. I find it hard to believe myself. But who married them? Can the marriage be binding?"

"Christopher says they are married, how or by whom he didn't say. And they have set up house in Drumacoo, a stone's throw from here. He'll make no advantageous marriage now. Who'd have him? The world is a harsh place. What is going to happen after I'm gone? Will Christopher want to bring that Kane girl to live in Tyrone? The idea of Anne and Harriet and Louisa all living in the same house with her doesn't bear thinking about. I worry about Anne most of all. She has been so good to me since her mother died. She has done her best, against severe odds, to keep Tyrone running smoothly. She has always said she wanted to travel. Somehow I have to find a way of giving her a reasonable competence."

Thomas looked at the broken man before him with great sympathy. He wanted to offer some comfort and help. "Perhaps, Arthur, I could try to talk to him?"

"I thank you, Thomas, and there is no-one he respects more than you. Indeed, my first thought when I remembered you were coming here was to beg you to do just that. But, in these past few days I have come to admit that not even you can change his mind – now that he has set himself on this course."

"I'm afraid that is so. He was ever wilful." Thomas sighed. "But, Arthur, this clandestine marriage – perhaps it is not legal? You need to find out who married them and in what circumstances."

Arthur looked bleakly at him. "What difference would that make, Thomas? Married legally or not, he is determined to spend his life with her."

Chapter 26

In Drumacoo Honnie gradually began to relax, but she wasn't finding it easy to get used to her new life. Christopher was away a lot, caught up again in all the activities of Tyrone. But he remembered to bring Honnie the cat he had promised her, along with two of her kittens.

"Johnny O'Connor says they'll have to be kept inside for a few days to get used to the house, or else they could run away," he said. "And – I'm sure you know this – he says that if you rub the pads of their paws with butter it helps. Apparently when they lick the butter off their paws they smell the scent of the house, and this makes them less inclined to wander away."

"Oh, yes, we always used to do that at home – whether it made any difference I don't know!"

"Oh, he gave me something else for you too." Christopher produced an old tin tray filled with a mixture of sand and soil. "He said to put it in some quiet corner. Cats apparently like privacy when they're doing their business. And be sure to empty it at least twice a day."

"Christopher, I do know how to deal with cats!"

Honnie decided to call the cat Báinín after the white homespun cloth, even though she was not completely white. For two small creatures, the kittens produced an amazing amount of dirt. Báinín was good, and dutifully used the tray. The kittens had yet to learn. Honnie hoped they would follow their mother's example. One kitten was black and white, the other was a tabby. She gave them a little ball of wool and spent an amount of time watching them as they played, and disentangling them from the wool.

When Bridget came to visit some days later, Honnie was delighted to see her. Christopher had gone off hunting, leaving Honnie struggling to make curtains, and wishing she had paid more attention when her mother was teaching her how to sew. Her heart leapt when she saw Bridget walking up the path to the house. She knew that it had taken some courage to be seen calling on her and said so.

"I was afraid you were never going to come. I would have understood. But oh, Bridget, I do miss being able to talk to you."

"Get along with you," said Bridget. "Haven't we stuck together through thick and thin? And wasn't I a witness at your wedding? You didn't think I'd desert you now, did you? I'd have been here before, but Mrs. Smith had the influenza and I was run off my feet."

She looked round the kitchen in admiration.

"I love the china. I much prefer plain white china to

decorated china, don't you? It looks so elegant."

"Well, I only bought a few pieces, enough for ourselves, but I will be able to add to it as time goes on," said Honnie.

"And look at those new pots and pans. Wouldn't they make you want to go cooking straight away!" said Bridget. "And the candlesticks!"

Bridget looked at everything in turn and then around the kitchen again.

"It's a lovely kitchen, Honnie, not too big, not too small, but with plenty of space for anything you might need. I can see you've put a deal of work into it."

"There's still a lot to do," said Honnie. "But it certainly looks much better than it did the first day I walked in here. I'm still struggling to make curtains, which will take a bit of time. Needlework isn't my strong point, as you well know."

Bridget settled herself comfortably in a chair near the fire.

"Well, tell me," she said, "how is married life agreeing with you? Did you have a great time in Dublin? Did you stay in a big hotel? Did you buy lots of new clothes? It must be wonderful to be mistress of your own time, and not be always at somebody else's beck and call."

"It is," said Honnie. "We had such a time in Dublin and, yes, we stayed in a big hotel, the Gresham Hotel."

She told Bridget the story of the Gresham Hotel, and its owner Mr. Gresham.

"He was so nice to me, Bridget, he made me feel completely at home, and not at all out of place, because I can tell you I felt very shy and awkward going into it the first evening we arrived."

"So you saw a lot of Dublin?" said Bridget.

"Yes, we did," said Honnie. "One day we hired a carriage and drove around to see the sights, but mostly we just walked. We watched lords and ladies going into a grand dress ball in Morrison's Rooms in Dawson Street, all dressed up in their fine clothes. Some of them looked very elegant, but not all. If you are expecting to see women in the height of fashion, there is nothing worse than seeing a woman well past her prime, all decked out in frills and furbelows and ribbons and lace – just mutton dressed as lamb."

Bridget laughed. "I'm sure!"

"We went to the theatre, to see Mr. Kean, a famous actor. And we went up Grafton Street, where all the fashionable people parade. It's the very best street in Dublin, with some of the very best shops."

"So you really enjoyed yourself," said Bridget.

"Yes, I enjoyed Dublin, but I wouldn't like to live there. Too many people, too many carriages, too many cabs and coaches, too many *crushes*."

It was a long time since Honnie had enjoyed another woman's company, and she found herself talking compulsively.

Bridget wanted to see the clothes she had bought, so Honnie took her up to her bedroom. As she showed her the gowns she had made for her in Limerick she could see the longing in Bridget's eyes. Bridget had her working clothes, and one good dress, and one old, not-so-good dress.

"And look, Bridget, I bought something specially for you," Honnie said.

From a chest of drawers she took out a large parcel,

carefully wrapped in fine paper, and tied with a blue ribbon. She had spent quite a while choosing this present.

"I remembered how much you admired the shawl Miss Olivia gave me and I thought you might like one too. I found it very hard to decide which one to buy. I hope you like it."

She watched Bridget carefully untie the ribbon and saw her eyes light up as she took out the shawl.

"Oh Honnie, it's lovely, really lovely!! It's the colour of that flower you see everywhere in summertime, the cornflower, such a delicate colour. Thank you very, very much!" And she threw her arms around Honnie and gave her a warm embrace.

"I thought the blue would bring out the blue in your eyes and suit your fair hair and your fair complexion," said Honnie. "It may seem very light, but it's made from the very best of wool, so it's very warm."

Bridget watched as Honnie put away all her new finery.

"It must be wonderful to get up in the morning and spend time deciding which gown you're going to wear," she said.

"To tell you the truth, Bridget, it's not exactly like that," said Honnie. "The gowns are beautiful but where am I going to wear them? I can hardly walk around the highways and byways of Drumacoo in fine clothes, can I? And I'm not likely to be asked up to dinner in Tyrone House."

Together they burst into peals of laughter.

Back down in the kitchen Honnie made tea. There was fresh soda bread which she had baked that morning, and butter and honey for spreading on it.

"So what do you do all day?" asked Bridget.

"I know you think you would like nothing better than to have time to yourself," said Honnie, "but – don't laugh, Bridget – I miss all the hustle and bustle of Tyrone. During the daytime I'm here on my own. In fact, Bridget, you are my first real visitor." Honnie straightened her shoulders and smiled. "But I don't regret marrying Christopher for one second. Now, tell me the news of Tyrone. Is Robert still leading Josie on?"

"Of course he is, and poor old Josie is getting more besotted with every passing day. It's right cruel of him. He has no feelings for her. He's just doing it to amuse himself."

"And how are Mrs. Smith and Mr. Scott getting on?"

"They have finally agreed on one thing – that Tyrone House is going downhill with every passing day. And it is. But then there is no real mistress in the house, no one to devote time and thought to it, the way Lady Harriet did, God rest her. She seemed to know everything that was happening – didn't you often say the same thing yourself? Then Christopher's sisters are a bit featherbrained, aren't they? I suppose they've never had to run a house. Lady Harriet took charge of everything. Now, even when they try to do things, they never seem to agree among themselves. Miss Anne, being the eldest in the house, feels people should do what she says. Then Miss Matilda comes along and says something different. And of course Mrs. Hunt believes that as housekeeper she is holding the whole place together."

"And what are people saying about us?" Honnie wanted to know.

"Well, there are all sorts of rumours flying around –

you know the way stories grow and grow. There are some who say Christopher is using you. There are others who feel it is a great come-down for you and are happy to see you come down. There are those who say you are ruined. Then, two days ago, Christopher and his father had a huge row. You could hear them shouting way down the hall. I didn't hear it myself, but Josie did – surprise, surprise! She just happened to be passing when the argument was going on. And strangely enough she happened to be nearby when Christopher's sisters heard the news as well. She says she heard Christopher telling his father he had married you. So I'm afraid your secret is out, Honnie. I wish I could tell them you were properly married by a priest, that I was there to see it done."

"No. That would just cause more trouble, especially for you. And I heard about the row. Christopher told me. He came home very upset, very angry." Honnie sighed. "And I suppose everybody knows by now that we are living in Drumacoo."

"It would have been difficult not to know," said Bridget. "I don't know how you ever thought it wouldn't be common knowledge. The word was out on that before you ever came back from Dublin, what with the two of you vanishing at the same time, and the house here being readied."

Honnie said nothing for a few minutes. Then she spoke.

"So things are going downhill in Tyrone. That's sad."

"Well, it's certainly not like it used to be. You could see that happening yourself before you left."

"So Miss Anne isn't coping?"

"She's doing her best. She goes to her father almost

every day with problems of one kind or another, and pleas that he should intervene in some domestic crisis. But you know what Mr. St. George is like. I think he forgets what she's told him as soon as she's left the room. Anne's latest story was about the disappearance of some of the best wine. Mr. Scott is very upset. He says at least ten bottles of the good claret have disappeared. He insists all the wines are under lock and key and he can't understand how it's happening. And it seems Miss Anne thinks Master Christopher has been taking it."

"Well, you can tell them that any wine Christopher has taken he's made no secret of taking it," said Honnie tartly. "And it seems to me that as the eldest son of the house, he is fully entitled to take any wine he wants! What did Mr. St. George say?"

"Not much. He didn't do anything about it."

The truth was that Arthur St. George felt utterly defeated. Christopher's marriage to Honnie had been a cruel blow. He knew vaguely that the house was not running as smoothly as it used to run. When his wife was alive it used to run like clockwork. He had never had to involve himself with household matters before, and he wasn't going to start now. So he made a show of listening to Anne when she came to him to voice some concern or other, then made some placatory noises, and quickly put whatever she had told him out of his mind.

But even Arthur St. George had taken aback when Anne said she believed Christopher had taken the wine.

"I didn't say anything to Mr. Scott, Father – but it's my belief that Christopher has taken it, for the delectation of himself and that girl over in Drumacoo."

"I know that you are grievously displeased with Christopher, Anne, but to be fair to him I don't think he is going to go around stealing our wines. Have you asked him directly?"

"No," said Anne. "I hoped you might do that."

"Since you are the one making the charge, I think it should be you," said her father.

The next time Anne saw Christopher she confronted him about the wine.

He told Honnie about the encounter when he came home.

"I lost my temper. I asked her was she seriously suggesting that I was thieving wine from my own family? I told her that she had a nasty suspicious mind, and that she was getting worse with every passing year. I told her I didn't steal any wine, that I had asked Mr. Scott for some and he gave it to me, and why shouldn't he? It is mine as much as any other members of the family. He did tell me that wine was disappearing. Since he guards it so carefully, I cannot understand how this can be happening. God, Anne can be so obnoxious."

Anne wasn't one of Honnie's favourite people either. She undoubtedly had good qualities – and some really disagreeable ones. It was hard to warm to her.

Chapter 27

The weeks sped by and Honnie worked on at getting the house in order. Christopher got some more furniture from Galway – more chairs for the kitchen, including a rocking chair which gave Honnie much pleasure, and a nice small armchair for their bedroom. She finished making the curtains, with considerable effort and much irritation.

But, once she had got everything to her liking, she found time lying heavy on her hands. Tidying and cooking and cleaning for two people didn't take long, and by early afternoon she often found herself wondering what she would do next.

She occasionally went out for a walk, but she kept to the nearby fields and smaller laneways. She had steeled herself to the knowledge that she was an object of interest to the local people, but it took the pleasure out of her wanderings.

As spring arrived, she turned her attention to the

garden. It was a long time since it had known cultivation. She found some old garden tools in the buildings outside and got to work. Trying to clear the ground was slow and backbreaking effort and, after a week of trying, all she had was sore hands, a pain in her back, and a few yards of heavy, lumpy soil. She knew that even with the best tools it would take a long time on her own to clear away the matted tangles of many years of weeds. It was already March, and more than time for planting. When she told Christopher how much she would like to plant some vegetables and flowers, he said he would ask Johnny O'Connor to come over from Tyrone to see what could be done.

Honnie wasn't sure how she felt about this offer. One half of her wanted so much to see the garden cleared and planted. The other half flinched at the prospect of meeting Johnny eye to eye.

But Christopher was insistent that Johnny wasn't one of the people who disapproved of them.

"Truly, Honnie, whenever I meet him he asks after you. I promise, he'll be only too happy to help."

Two days later Johnny knocked at the door. He was a big, burly, slowmoving man, who had spent his life in the gardens of Tyrone. He had come there at the age of twelve, and now, a man in his mid-fifties, he was head gardener. His knowledge of plants and vegetables and flowers was unequalled, his love for them obvious to anybody who watched how gently his huge hands worked with the smallest of seedlings.

He greeted Honnie with a smile and asked her how she was as if it was the most natural thing in the world for her to be living in this rundown house with the son of the master of Tyrone. Honnie felt her fears melting away. She knew he would look at the whole garden slowly and carefully and discuss all the possibilities before deciding on the best course of action, and there would be no point in trying to hurry him, because he simply wouldn't be hurried.

"It's a lot of land to manage," he said thoughtfully as they walked round the neglected acre of brambles, rushes, ragwort, furze and nettles. "And it's land that hasn't had any kindness or care over many a long year."

"I've been trying to clear it," said Honnie, "but even a small bit seems to take forever."

"Most of those weeds will be hard got rid of," said Johnny. "They are dug in deep, and they won't give up easily. It's far too much for a lass to tackle on her own. The thing is to do it bit by bit, not try to do too much too soon. Look at those rushes. You really have to get them out by the roots. That's heavy work, and if you don't watch them they come up again as soon as your back is turned. Scutch grass or couch grass – I knew it as *broimfhéar* when I was a lad – is another bad one. You can see it everywhere you look here. It beds itself down in the soil, and it has very tough roots, and they spread out and throttle everything in their way. Nettles aren't all that bad. They make great soup, which is said to be good for the blood in springtime. There are butterflies who love them. So leave that bunch in the far corner where you have them already. Just keep an eye on them. *Buachalán Buí*, the little yellow fellow, is called ragwort in English. It can be poisonous to some animals. Get rid of it."

Having walked the land a number of times, Johnny

finally chose a plot of ground near the kitchen door.

"We'll clear that first," he said, "and start with some potatoes, maybe some turnips. It would be good to be able to plant carrots and onions, though the soil is a bit heavy for them. We will have to bring some sand and a load of fine soil over and see if we can lighten it."

The ground around the apple trees would have to be cleared.

"The trees are old, but they might still be made productive. It's a bit late for pruning them, because they are about to blossom, but that can be done later in the year. In the meantime they need feeding, with some manure around the bottom of the trees, and maybe some seaweed. And ash from the fire is good too."

Later, as they sat drinking a cup of tea in the kitchen, Johnny explained that as head gardener he wouldn't be able to do the work himself, but he would send somebody over to give Honnie a hand. He saw the look on her face.

"I was thinking of a nephew of my own," he said. "He's very young but he's a big, strong lad, and he knows a bit about gardening. And I'll be over from time to time to keep an eye on him. He doesn't talk much but keep him well fed and he'll work as hard as the day is long."

Honnie had one more request to make of Johnny. She had grown up with the sound of hens scuffling in the yard outside, squawking to each other, fluffing themselves in a dust bath, murmuring sleepily in the evening time – and producing lovely fresh eggs. The taste of a newlaid egg was very special.

"I've been thinking, Johnny, that I'd love to keep some hens. Could you get me some baby chickens?"

"No bother at all," said Johnny. "I've a sister who has reared a fairsized clutch of them. How many do you want?"

"Maybe six or seven to begin with, until I see how I get on."

Christopher was away in the Curragh for a few days, but when he came back Honnie told him about her plans to keep hens.

"Could we use one of the outbuildings in the yard to house them? Maybe that one nearest the house."

"Of course you can," said Christopher. "It's just lying empty as it is. But it will need to be cleaned out. I've heard Johnny's nephew, young Dónal, is coming over to help – I'm sure he'll do the job for you. And I'll get somebody to come over from Tyrone to put up a few perches for them."

In bed at night Honnie lay awake and thought about her garden, and saw it full of good vegetables, of fruit trees and bushes, and flowers as well, with the hens clucking and grubbing happily in the afternoon sunshine. It was a good picture on which to go to sleep.

She was hanging out clothes on a makeshift line some days later when she saw Father Tom coming up the pathway. She hadn't seen him since he married her.

"So, Honnie, how are you finding your new life? I know I tried to dissuade you from the idea, but I would not like to see you unhappy. You look pale. Are you all right?"

"Why wouldn't I be?" said Honnie. "It's just a bit strange to have so much time on my hands, and I'm unaccustomed to being in a house with so few people.

But of course I'm happy. I wanted to marry Christopher, and I'm married to him."

Tom looked a little surprised at Honnie's defensive tone. She suddenly felt ashamed of her sharp answer.

"Truly, I am pleased to see you, Tom. Tell me all the news."

"First I want to thank you, Honnie. I know how much you would like to have told them that it was I who married you. But if Arthur St. George knew about the part I played, he could make it very difficult for me to minister and help my own people."

"I know it was difficult for you, Tom, and it's I who should thank you," said Honnie. "Tell me, how are my family?"

"Well enough. They've had another letter from William. Things are good in Canada. Seán is hoping to go over soon, and they're talking about sending for Thady later, but I think he's happy enough fishing with Martín Breathnach. There was word from your father in Limerick. He won't be home for some time. He's got another painting job, in another big house."

"Meaning he doesn't want to be round here listening to all the gossip about me," said Honnie.

"Your family, they're all upset, Honnie. They think people are laughing at them. They think everybody is talking about them – and that wouldn't be too far from the truth. And they're worried about you."

"They don't need to worry. Now come inside. I'll make a pot of tea and we'll have some of the shortbread biscuits I made this morning."

As Honnie busied herself around the kitchen, neither of them spoke for a few minutes.

"Maureen always thought the worst of me anyway," she said then. "And she's not so much worried about me, I'll warrant, as about herself and her precious reputation. Oh, I wish I could tell her that you had married us good and proper."

"Be patient, Honnie," said Tom.

"As for Christopher's family!"

"Honnie, remember it hasn't been easy for Arthur St. George either. He had two daughters who went off and married people of whom he didn't approve. His wife died. Olivia died. And then he hears his eldest son has set up house with his kitchenmaid. How do you expect him to feel? I'm amazed he hasn't cut Christopher off without a penny. You should be grateful for having been spared that at least."

They went on to talk of other things, of the spring weather, and Honnie's garden, and fish catches, and how well Mairtín Breathnach and Thady were doing. He told her about the problems he met in his daily life, about all the people who came to him looking for help.

"And I can do so little," he said. "There are people with hungry children and not enough food to feed them, people whose crops have failed, people who can't pay their rent. People who can't get work, so many people who see no hope in the world around them. I do my best, but what help I can give is so little in the face of so much need."

After Tom left, mounting his horse and raising a hand in farewell as he turned down the lane, Honnie felt guilty about feeling so happy. But nothing could take away the joy of being married to Christopher, of lying beside him at night, and waking up beside him every morning.

In daylight hours Christopher spent, as he always had, a

great deal of time with his horses and dogs. In the evenings he would tell her about the horses, which ones were doing well, or badly, and how a certain few looked particularly promising.

"At least Waterwitch seems to have recovered. I was really worried about her."

"Oh, I really miss seeing the horses," said Honnie. "Apart from Barebones, of course, when you bring him over."

Christopher had already fixed up a makeshift stable for Barebones where he sometimes stayed overnight. But Christopher often just walked home, feeling that Barebones didn't like to be stabled alone – he missed the company of the other Tyrone horses. Rua, too, he had not uprooted from his lifelong home, Tyrone.

"I tell you what," said Christopher. "As soon as we have decent stabling, I'll ride the others over occasionally and let them spend the night here. How would you like that?"

"I would like that very much," said Honnie,

There were other days when Christopher brought over the phaeton, and they went out for a drive, and he let her take the reins. It was good to get beyond the environs of Tyrone and go walking on pale sandy beaches where there were few people to see them and gossip.

Bridget paid her another visit, full of the story of how the wine thief had been caught.

"It was Robert! Mr. Scott worked out that he was the most likely person. He often helped in the cellar when wine was being bottled. He knew that Mr. Scott sometimes left the keys on a shelf near the cellar door.

Last Thursday they were working together, and Mr. Scott couldn't find the keys when he went back to the shelf. Robert made a show of helping him to find them, saying he might have left them in the kitchen, or in his sitting room by mistake, and when Mr. Scott went to look Robert must have taken out some bottles and hidden them. When Mr. Scott came back Robert was able to tell him that he had found his keys, on the floor, behind a barrel. But it all made Mr. Scott suspicious, and he watched Robert, until the day before yesterday he saw him going out in the evening with a heavy coat on and what he called a funny bulge where the pocket was. So he followed him. And he found him, way down in the turf yard, and he was there along with Josie, and they both drinking wine. So now he's gone."

"And what about Josie?" asked Honnie.

"Oh, Mrs. Smith gave her a right telling-off, and Josie sobbed and sobbed and in the end Mrs. Smith said she was a very silly and foolish girl, who had been led astray by a rogue who could turn on the charm, but had no heart and no conscience. She told Josie she was well rid of him, and that she'd give her one more chance."

As the March days lengthened Honnie worked in the garden and rejoiced to see it taking shape.

Johnny O'Connor's nephew Dónal was as Johnny had described him, a quiet, taciturn lad, but a good worker. Methodically, he cleared away all the rough growth, making a big heap of anything he would burn, and put the rest in a heap in a corner of the garden to rot away. When he had cleared a patch down to bare earth, he started digging and turning it, carefully pulling out any roots that remained. Next he came with a cartload of horse manure, spread it all over the surface, and began to dig it in, then brought more manure, and dug the soil over again. It was the work of weeks, not just days.

The garden had been a scratching wilderness of briars and weeds. By the end of March, at least half of it had turned into a crumbling spread of rich brown soil, in deep beds, and long straight drills, waiting to be planted. In her mind's eye Honnie imagined how it would look in a few months' time, with the green spears of onions alongside the feathery leaves of carrots, with peas and beans scrambling up stakes from hawthorn bushes, with cabbages and lettuces, and cauliflowers growing tall, with parsley and thyme and sage smelling sweet. She remembered how much her mother had loved this time of year, and as a little girl how she had always begged to be allowed put the seeds into the soil. At first she had only been allowed to sow the bigger ones, like peas and beans, but later on her mother had trusted her with all the seeds, even the tiny carrot seeds, which could blow off your fingers, and which had to be planted mixed with sand to spread them out, so that the carrots could grown evenly in rows, not in clusters.

Johnny O'Connor came over from time to time, and he never came empty-handed. He brought seed potatoes "which need to go in soon or it will be too late". He brought baby cabbage plants, and onion sets. He brought carrot seeds. Honnie spent happy hours planting, often coming indoors only when the light failed, to fall asleep in the rocking chair in front of the fire.

On one such evening, Christopher woke her up with a broad smile on his face.

"I've got a surprise for you," he said. "I've brought

you somebody to keep you company."

"Somebody to keep me company?" Honnie looked at him warily

"Come and I'll introduce you."

Under the hedge inside the gate was a large wicker basket, and nestled within it was a small, black, furry puppy.

"One of the dogs in the stable yard had a litter a couple of months ago. This little chap is the liveliest and smartest of the lot."

The puppy scrambled out of the basket and heading for the gate onto the laneway. Honnie picked him up and leant her face into his soft coat. He was warm and wriggly, and he smelt of other dogs and his mother's milk. He looked up at her with bright eyes and proceeded to lick her enthusiastically. It would be very hard not to love him.

"He looks just the colour of a sod of good black turf," she said. "I'll call him Fóidín."

"Now what kind of a name is that?" asked Christopher.

"It's the Irish for a little sod of turf," said Honnie.

Fóidín turned out to be very good company. But he also required time and attention. Whenever Honnie opened the door, he was off on a journey of exploration. He kept escaping out the gate into the laneway. Honnie tied the gate shut. Then he went through a gap in the wall around the garden – part of it had collapsed and needed to be rebuilt. Another job for Dónal, thought Honnie,who was finding Dónal a young man of many talents. Foidin chewed everything that was chewable and tried to chew quite a few things that weren't. He attacked one of Christopher's boots, and one of Honnie's new shoes. He made splinters of a wooden spoon that had fallen on the floor. He gnawed the rocking chair. When he was chastised he would roll himself into a ball and retire whimpering into a corner, looking at Honnie with sad, accusing eyes, until she picked him up and talked nicely to him again.

Christopher worried about his father. He had not had any real conversations with him since the day of the argument, just a cursory greeting, a murmured nod in passing. But he grew more and more aware of how badly his father looked.

"He looks shrunken, so much smaller," he said to Honnie as they lay in bed one evening. "I can't help feeling guilty about him. You must admit he has been tolerant – in effect, letting me go my way. Maybe the old boy has a heart after all – or maybe he hasn't got the strength. I'm certainly not the most popular person in Tyrone at the moment. My sisters don't speak to me. The servants are barely civil."

Honnie tried to think of something to say. She gathered the bed quilt close around her. It smelled of lavender. The St. George linen and bedding always smelled of lavender. Every year Lady Harriet had made little silk bags, and filled them with the lavender from her garden, and tied them with ribbons. Every bedroom in Tyrone, all the linen cupboards, smelt of lavender.

"I think that as time passes people won't stay so angry," Honnie said. "I'm sorry that you feel cut off."

"I never expected my family to be pleased about our marriage," said Christopher. "And I am not sorry in any way – just a little saddened."

"I wish I could think of something to say to make you feel better now."

"I can think of one way in which you can make me feel better," said Christopher, and reached out and took her into his arms.

Chapter 28

March had gone and the green fingers of spring were shooting to life in fields and hedgerows, on trees and bushes, in cottage gardens, when Christopher told Honnie that he had been thinking about the two of them going up to County Kildare for a big race meeting in the Curragh at the end of the month.

Honnie was thrilled at the thought but, as the time grew nearer, she found she was apprehensive. She had begun to feel safe in her house, and she was enjoying her garden. She wasn't sure she wanted to go out into the whole new world where she would spend her time wondering how she was supposed to behave, and how people were going to behave towards her. Besides, she didn't feel that well.

"It will be different on the Curragh," Christopher assured her. "Everybody talks to everybody else, and people will accept us together much more easily. You'll enjoy it, I promise."

Just a week before they were due to leave, Bridget called again, this time with the news that Josie had disappeared.

"Mrs. Smith is furious. She's certain she's has gone off after Robert – there was talk around she'd found another place in one of the hotels in Galway city. Mrs. Smith says she's washed her hands of Josie, and it's good riddance to bad rubbish."

The morning Honnie and Christopher set off for Kildare was dull and overcast. This time they were travelling in the St. George coach, driven by one of the men in the stable yard. They were to spend their first night in Ballinasloe. There had been heavy rain the night before and the road was bad. The carriage jolted them from side to side. It wasn't long before Honnie began to feel quite ill. She closed her eyes and tried to sleep. Christopher was shocked to see how pale she looked as he handed her down from the carriage. But she assured him that she would recover quickly if she could just get out of the coach for a while.

They continued their journey next day. In all it took them almost four days to get to Kildare, by which time Honnie was wishing they had never left home. She was confirmed in what had only been a suspicion up to now.

The mornings were the worst. Honnie lay in bed at the inn, feeling sick and weak, and refused any of the food that Christopher offered her.

"Just leave me some water," she said "Or maybe a dish of tea."

She told him to be off, because she knew he was anxious to meet up with all his friends in the racing community. They would many happy hours discussing the merits and form of the horses which had come from many parts of the country to participate in the six-day event.

"You won't do me any good by staying here, because I'm going to go to sleep. There's no point in the two of us being miserable. I'm sure I'll feel better later in the day."

Honnie began to feel better as the days passed. The weather had improved, and she was able to see some of the sights and watch some races. These were the best of April days. The fields around the course were new green, the distant Wicklow Hills a blaze of glowing gorse, and everywhere the banks were studded with primroses. There was nobody who knew her to point and stare. But it wasn't until their last evening that she felt she could face a dinner table and strange faces, and conversation.

Christopher had told her about the informality of the racing fraternity in the Curragh, and she discovered at the dinner that, for the most part, this was true. It was a very male gathering. There were some women, though not ones who would customarily be described as ladies. A great deal of wine was drunk, and many bottles of port. Stories were told of other meetings, and famous horses, races which were won, races which were nearly won, and races which were badly lost, and there was much talk of plans for improving the course.

Honnie felt out of place. And by the end of the evening she was the only person who could be said to be still sober. She had been very careful to drink only two small glasses of wine, and a modicum of food. There was no point in tempting providence.

They arrived back to Galway on a shower-struck afternoon.

As they approached Clarinbridge they heard a commotion of raised voices. The carriage drew to a standstill. There was no way it could get passage through the coaches and carts and horses and the many people who all seemed to be looking over the bridge into the Clarin river.

Honnie and Christopher got out to see what had happened. Yet another heavy shower was shafting down. It was the kind of rain that drenches people in minutes, cold, hard rain that stung faces and chilled hands. But the gathered crowd didn't seem to notice. They were too concerned with what they saw in the river below them.

Christopher asked a woman standing near them what had happened. She told him that there was a dead body floating in the water.

Despite herself, and with a strange feeling in her stomach, Honnie pushed her way through the crowds to look. The body floating in front of her horrified eyes was that of Josie, blue, bloated – and very definitely with child.

Honnie was glad to be home, as happy to see Fóidín as he was to see her, and as pleased to see Báinín and her kittens when they came and rubbed themselves around her ankles and purred loudly.

Dónal was working away in the garden and came to greet them.

"I can tell you that cat is a great one for catching mice," he said. "And she's tackled a rat or two as well. I reckon there are a lot of mice and rats around this place, there's been nobody living here for so long. But that cat will have the place cleared in jig time."

Honnie said that was good news. She congratulated him on all the work he had done as she looked around. But the image of Josie's body floating in the river would not leave her mind. She recalled all the times when she had been sharp with her and felt guilty. Poor infatuated Josie. She thought she had found somebody who loved her, only to find she had been used. Honnie wondered if she had found Robert when she went in pursuit of him, if she had found him and been turned away, or not found him at all. Whatever happened she must have been feeling very alone and helpless to end up in the Clarin river.

To quieten her thoughts, she walked around the garden. Even in the short while she had been away, there had been a leap of growth. The potato plants were showing dark on the tops of drills, the turnip seeds had sprouted, the onions were sending green fingers up towards the sun and the two old apple trees at the bottom of the garden were about to blossom.

Later that evening she told Christopher that they were going to have a child.

She had to laugh at his expression. He looked so startled.

"For heaven's sake, Christopher, what did you expect?"

"I suppose I hadn't thought of being a family man so soon," said Christopher. "But that's wonderful news, wonderful!"

And he wrapped his arms around her, and held her close, and kissed her, and told her he loved her.

"When do you think it will be born?"

"I'm not sure," said Honnie. "But probably around Halloween."

"I must talk to Molly Flaherty about getting somebody to help you in the house," he said.

"Don't be silly," said Honnie. "I can manage perfectly well on my own. It's not exactly hard work looking after a house for two people. And being with child is not an illness."

But Christopher wasn't listening

"You may find you will be glad to have help," he said.

Three days later he arrived home with a young girl of about fifteen years of age.

"This is Lizzie, Molly's niece," he said.

Honnie was reminded of herself on her first day in Tyrone, but this girl was much more nervous than Honnie had been. Lizzie was tall and bony, with a pale complexion, and light brown hair pulled severely back from her face. She didn't say anything when Honnie told her she was welcome, just nodded shyly, clenched and unclenched her hands and looked anxiously from one of them to the other.

Are we that intimidating, Honnie wondered. Or is it that my reputation has frightened her?

"There's a very cold wind blowing today, isn't there, Lizzie?" she said. "You must be frozen. Come and sit down here beside the fire, and we'll have a cup of tea, and you can tell me all about yourself."

"I'll leave you two together, then," said Christopher, pleased with himself.

Lizzie sat up very straight, wrapped her cold hands around the cup of tea, and looked down at the ground.

"Now tell me all about yourself," said Honnie. "Do you have brothers and sisters?"

"Yes," said Lizzie.

"And how many of you are there?" asked Honnie.

"There's Julia, she's the eldest. She has a position in a house in Galway town. Then there's Patricia, and then me. I'm the middle one. Johanna's my younger sister, then there's my brother. My mother died when he was born."

"And Molly's your aunt?" said Honnie. "Your father's sister?"

"Yes," said Lizzie.

"And how did your father feel about you coming to work here?"

Lizzie hesitated.

"Well ... Aunt Molly told him that it would be all right."

Having parted with this much information, Lizzie's conversation dried up, and she gulped down her tea as she began looking uneasily around her once more.

"Come on upstairs, and I'll show you where you're going to sleep," said Honnie. "And then we'll come down and get supper ready."

It was a small room, overlooking the garden at the back of the house. There was a plain iron bed, a chair, and a small chest of drawers. Honnie had started getting the room ready in anticipation of Lizzie's arrival, but she hadn't expected her quite so soon. So there were no curtains on the window, and the bed was not made up. But Lizzie seemed very pleased with it. At home, Honnie guessed, she would have had to share a room, and probably a bed, with her sisters – as Honnie herself had done. This was a room of her own, something Honnie had never had, in Maree, or in Tyrone.

"You can help me make up the bed," she told her, as she gathered bedding from the big press on the landing at the top of the stairs, where she had stored all the new linen.

Lizzie was awkward but willing, and Honnie got pleasure from the way her hands stroked the crisp sheets and soft blankets with obvious delight.

Next day, as Lizzie watched Honnie working round the kitchen, it became clear that cooking was something of which she had done very little.

"Julia and Patricia always did it together," she said. "And when Julia left, then Patricia did it on her own. She said I was better at taking care of my brother and sister and looking after the cow and the hens. Something always seemed to go wrong when I was cooking. I'd forget about the potatoes and water would dry off them, or I wouldn't remember the bread that was baking, and it would get burned. And then they'd get mad at me."

Well, that would certainly be worth remembering, thought Honnie, if she ever got round to teaching Lizzie to cook.

They soon settled down well together. Lizzie was very willing. True, at times she was awkward, and would stand looking out the window with a dreamy expression on her face and forget to stir the stew which was meant to be cooking gently over the fire. Sometimes she let soup cook so fast that there were only a few cupfuls left. But she was always so sorry when she let things go wrong that Honnie never had the heart to be cross with her.

She told Honnie that what she really enjoyed was working in the little vegetable garden they had at home.

"Much nicer than a dark smoky kitchen," she said. "I

was good at weeding. Now my brother, he was no good at all. It wasn't that he couldn't do it well, it was more that he wouldn't. He never had the patience, you see. He'd be off with the other lads, and what he used to do was go along the drills, and just pull off the top of the weeds, so that it would all look good when he had just done it, but the roots would be still there and up they'd come again after a matter of days. My father would get right mad at him. I *always* got all the roots out, even though it takes much longer."

Lizzie was good company, and Honnie was happy to have it, but she still found herself thinking often about life in Tyrone, of all the people who came and went, the joking, the laughter, the stories told. Then she would remember all the hard work. She could never wish to be back in those steamy kitchens again at the beck and call of Mrs. Smith.

Honnie thought often about Maree and her family. Before her child was born, she deeply wished to make her peace with them. Clearly, they were not going to come to see her, so she would have to go to see them. Would they still be angry?

Christopher said he would take her over himself in the pony and trap. But he would not go in with her. He would wait for her at the end on the lane.

She agreed but had mixed feelings about his presence on the trip. She was fearful of meeting people on the way. It was bad enough around Drumacoo and it would be much worse to encounter the familiar people around Maree. Easier, of course, in the pony and trap. She would be glad of Christopher's company and yet it might prove more embarrassing to be seen with him.

They set out early one morning at the end of May, in some trepidation, and they met only a few people on the roads. She held her head high as they drove smartly past them.

When her old home came into sight, she found she was shaking. It seemed a lifetime since she had lived there.

Christopher helped her down from the trap and she set off up the lane. Nóinín, the cow, grazing in the nearby field, looked up and made her way to the fence. Did Nóinín remember her? She couldn't be sure. The hens were clucking quietly around the little shed Bartley had made to keep them safe from foxes.

Bran was the first to see her. She barked, stopped, and slowly her tail began to wag, then she raced towards Honnie and pranced about in an ecstacy of greeting.

Honnie's old home looked poor and small. She could hear voices in the kitchen. As she drew nearer, the door opened, and Maureen and Thady came out, to see why Bran had been barking.

When Maureen caught sight of Honnie, her face grew dark and angry. She wrapped her shawl around herself.

"What do you want here?" she asked, her voice sharp.

Honnie froze. "I don't want anything," she said. "Except to see all of you ... to tell you that we are married ... I thought ... you might be glad to know. "

"Married, is it?" said Maureen. "And by whom, may I ask? It wasn't one of our own priests, for sure."

"You know right well I wouldn't be married by any but a Catholic priest," said Honnie.

"And what kind of a priest would marry the pair of you, a Protestant and a Catholic, knowing that the marriage is no marriage in the eyes of the law?"

"What does it matter who married us," said Honnie, "so long as we are wed in the eyes of God?"

"Why should we believe you?" asked Maureen. "Do you believe her, Thady?"

Thady, who had been standing nervously in the background, mumbled something unintelligible.

Honnie held out her left hand, biting back the sharp retort that sprang to her lips.

"It's easy enough to put a ring on your finger," said Maureen. "Anybody could do that."

Joseph had been standing in the background, just inside the door, looking and listening.

"I think you look like a very fine lady, Honnie," he said.

"Handsome is as handsome does," said Maureen. "Off you go now, Joseph, and feed the hens."

But Joseph stayed where he was, staring wide-eyed at Honnie.

"Where did you get all those clothes?" he asked.

"The wages of sin," said Maureen tartly.

Honnie pushed past Maureen and into the house. She gave Joseph the little wooden boat she had brought as a present for him.

"Look, Joseph," she said. "You can sail this along the stream below, and pretend it's going all the way to Canada, to see William."

She took the fine shawl she had bought for Maureen and the shirt she had bought for Thady out of the basket she carried and held them out.

"And these are for you, Maureen, and for Thady."

Maureen brushed them aside.

"We want none of your presents," she snapped.

"Presents won't stop us being the talk of the countryside."

But Joseph held firmly on to his boat.

Honnie turned to go, leaving the shawl and the shirt on the kitchen table.

Maureen's parting words followed her down the laneway.

"And you're with child as well. You certainly didn't waste much time!"

The journey home seemed very long and Christopher, sensing her mood, stayed silent. In her head she went over and over her visit. Somehow in her head she had believed that once she told her family that she was married, they would believe her, and be happy for her. Which was very stupid of me, she thought.

Back home, Christopher tried to coax her into better humour.

"They'll come round, you'll see," he said

"And pigs will fly," said Honnie. "And I won't see. Because I won't go next nor near them again. That Maureen is a right harridan. Her tongue is so sharp it's a wonder she doesn't cut herself with it. All she thinks about is respectability. And as for Thady! What kind of lad is he that just stands there, muttering and mumbling, and afraid to open his mouth for fear of her. Better to have no sister at all than one like her."

As the garden grew, so did Honnie, and by high summer it was getting harder to bend over the drills and beds and pull out the weeds. She was glad of Lizzie's help. It was also getting difficult to conceal her pregnancy.

As the days passed and the time of the baby's birth drew nearer and nearer, she found herself longing for the advice and experience of an older woman, like Sarah Breathnach or Madge Shaughnessy.

So when Peig Breathnach arrived to visit her one evening, Honnie welcomed her with open arms.

At first it felt as if they had only just met, thought Honnie. Peig clearly felt the same way, bending down to pat Fóidín when she felt particularly ill at ease. But after Honnie had shown her the house, and they had walked around the garden together, they began to be more comfortable.

"I miss you, Honnie," said Peig, "I truly do. But you must forgive me if I say what I think, what I've been thinking ever since I heard about you and Christopher St. George. I do so hope this won't all turn out to have been a terrible mistake. You were always so independent, so sure of yourself, and now ... I do want you to be happy, Honnie, but it all seems very strange to me."

"I won't pretend it is always easy," said Honnie, "but I promise you I'm happy, and I don't regret any of it."

"I always thought you and Mairtín would be a match," said Peig. "You seemed so right for each other. Mairtín was right sore when he heard."

Honnie thought for a moment and decided to tell Peig that she and Christopher were married.

"I can't tell you who married us, or where it took place," she said. "But we were married by a Catholic priest."

When she saw that Peig didn't look too surprised, Honnie realised that Maureen or Thady had wasted no time in spreading the word.

"So I've been told," said Peig. "But is it lawful?"

"It's lawful in the eyes of God," said Honnie.

They were both silent for a moment.

She knew that Peig must have noticed that she was with child – it would have been difficult to avoid noticing. But she said nothing until just before she left.

"When is it to be born?" she said.

"I think about the end of October, or the beginning of November," said Honnie, "but I'm not rightly sure." She paused for a moment. "Peig, I'm in real need of advice. There are so many questions spinning round in my head. Does the pain in my back mean anything? Is the child moving enough? Suppose there's something wrong with it? Who is going to be with me when my time comes?"

"Well, I did hear my mother once say that when a woman with child gets a lot of heartburn, it's a sign that the baby has a big head of hair!" said Peig.

They laughed for a moment, and then Honnie grew serious again.

"Oh Peig, I would dearly like to talk to your mother. Do you think you could persuade her to come and see me, for my mother's sake if not for mine?"

Peig hesitated. "I'll ask her," she said. "But I don't know what she'll say. Why can't you come over to Maree yourself? Don't you want to see your family?"

"They have made it very clear that they don't want to see me," said Honnie. "And after the reception I got when I paid them a visit a while back, I certainly don't want to see them. That apart, I don't feel like facing the neighbours, the friends, the people I grew up with, the thought of them all looking me up and down. But I would dearly like to talk to your mother. And maybe she could bring Madge Shaughnessy with her?"

As time went by, Honnie found she was remembering all

kinds of pishogues about pregnant women, half-forgotten memories of women talking together in the kitchen at home. It was said that if an expectant mother saw a hare, the child could be born with a hare lip, that a woman in her condition shouldn't go near a graveyard, because if she did and stumbled, the child could be affected – neither should she go near a corpse or a coffin.

At night Honnie lay uncomfortable and restless. What if she died in childbirth, and her baby was left without a mother? Who would take care of it? Her sisters wouldn't want it. Christopher's family would want nothing to do with it. One such night she voiced her fears to Christopher.

"Honnie, you are young and strong. We just have to see that you get proper care and attention."

"What to do you mean?" asked Honnie, suspiciously. "Proper care and attention? From whom?"

"Bridget told me she has talked to Molly Flaherty," said Christopher, "and she has agreed to help you. She's widely respected for her knowledge and skills in such matters."

"You mean you and Bridget discussed me with Molly Flaherty?" said Honnie furiously. "Without asking me what *I* thought? I'm the one who's having the baby. *I* will decide who I want to have with me. And Molly Flaherty, of all people, who thinks I'm the worst thing that ever happened to you! What were you thinking of, Christopher? Well, you can tell Bridget that she should have asked me before she made any such arrangements. And she can unmake her arrangements."

"She was only trying to help," said Christopher. "She worries about you."

"I'm sure you and Bridget meant well," said Honnie crossly. "But that's not what I want. I want somebody with me with whom I feel easy, somebody like Madge Shaughnessy, who was so good to my mother when she was dying. Madge has brought many babies into the world. I'm hoping Peig Breathnach's mother, Sarah, will come, and I'm hoping that she'll bring Madge with her."

"We can talk about it again tomorrow," said Christopher. "Stop worrying. I'm sure everything will be fine. Now I think we should both get some sleep. At any rate that's what I'm going to do."

And he rolled over and closed his eyes.

Beside him, Honnie lay awake and watched a pale moon slithering across a wet sky, while fear crouched at the bottom of her stomach, and the baby kicked inside her.

Chapter 29

It was a silken September evening. The sun was hung low in a clear sky, the birds were murmuring of sleep, and the countryside around had a still peace about it. Christopher was over at Tyrone and Honnie was out in her garden, picking stray weeds from between her carrots and wondering if she should gather up the rest of the onions. She spotted a few pods of peas still on their stalks, and pulled them, running her finger inside their crisp shells. The peas were tough – they should have been gathered some time ago. She considered the turnips, and wondered how much bigger they might grow, and rubbed some leaves of sage and thyme between her fingers and held them up to sniff. She didn't know she had visitors until she turned round to look under the apple trees for windfalls, and found Sarah Breathnach and Madge Shaughnessy standing a few yards away from her.

Sarah was a woman of stature, big, brown-eyed and fresh-faced. Her hair had been blue-black when she was a girl, but she had started going grey early, and now the hair coiled neatly round her head was almost white. Madge Shaughnessy was almost as tall as Sarah, but of a leaner, more sinewy build. Her hair had been red but had faded to a pale ginger as she grew older.

The two women looked awkward, and Honnie was suddenly very conscious of her swelling belly. She searched for words of welcome.

"It's truly good of you to come," she said.

For a few moments nothing more was said.

Honnie felt she had to be direct.

"I know you disapprove of me," she said, "but I really need your help. If you could tell me what ... if you could just ..."

"I've come for the sake of your mother, who was one of my best friends," said Sarah, rather severely, "and because Peig asked me to come."

Her tone softened a little when she saw the tears gathering in Honnie's eyes.

"Oh Honnie," she said, "what madness got into you? Yes, yes, I know you say you were married, but you know right well that it isn't a marriage according to the law of the land. And now there's a babe to be born. It isn't that I disapprove, it's that I worry about you. I've known you since the day you were born. Your mother loved you so much. She said you never gave her a moment's worry. She was so proud of you, so pleased at how well you were getting on in Tyrone. What would she say if she could see you now?"

"I hope she would understand, and be pleased for me," said Honnie. "I'm married in the eyes of God. Isn't that all that matters?"

"Eileen Kelly thinks that Tom had a part in all this, and I'm beginning to think she may well be right," said Madge, looking shrewdly at Honnie.

Honnie looked at the ground, and scuffed her feet in the brown, crumbling earth.

"We are married, and I regret nothing. But I'd welcome your advice, Sarah, and yours, Madge." She struggled to hold back tears.

Sarah's severe expression melted. She held out her arms. Honnie hesitated, then went into Sarah's embrace.

After a moment, she drew back.

"I want you to know that I'm very happy about this baby," she said. "And I don't regret for one minute marrying Christopher." Her tender smile was a witness to the truth of what she said. "But forgive me, I'm forgetting my manners. Come into the kitchen now and I'll make us some tea."

As they went into the house Madge Shaughnessy put her arm round Honnie's shoulders.

"You'll be fine, *a chuisle,*" she said. "You're not the first woman to give birth, and you certainly won't be the last."

In the kitchen Sarah and Madge sat down by the fire while Honnie readied the tea. She was glad she had baked that morning. She laid out a round wheel of soda bread on the table, still warm from the baking, and a pot of her own apple jelly.

"Every bit as good as your mother's," said Sarah, after a second slice.

They talked about Maree, of how well Thady and Mairtín were getting on at the fishing, and how tall Joseph had grown, and a letter that had just come from

William and Seán, saying how well they were doing in Canada.

"They're still hoping Thady will go out to them," said Sarah. "But I know Kathleen and Maureen are hoping he won't. He seems happy enough fishing with Mairtín, at any rate."

Honnie made no mention of her own visit to Maree, but she felt it hanging in the air.

"Do you have any news of my father?" she asked.

"Very little," said Sarah. "It seems he is likely to be in Limerick for some time."

There was a lull in the conversation.

"So, how do you feel?" Madge said finally.

"Huge," said Honnie, "and uncomfortable. And my back hurts."

"Most women who are with child have backache," said Sarah. "It usually doesn't mean anything serious – though it isn't going to do your back any good to go weeding, especially if you have to bend down to do it."

Honnie told Madge that she sometimes got pains in the middle of the night.

"Not bad pains," said Honnie. "But they make me worry that I'm going to have the baby before its time, with no kith or kin near me."

"That's just the baby practising to be born," said Madge, smiling. "Most women have those pains in the last few months. Sure now that I'm here, maybe I'll take a look at you. Let's go upstairs to your room."

Honnie lay on the big double bed and looked at the long rays of the afternoon sun pouring through the window while Madge gently felt her stomach.

"You'll get pains when your time comes, probably

every half hour or so and then more often. You will probably think you've started a few times before you really do." said Madge. "This feels like a fine child and a big one. But you have a while to go yet, *a chuisle*. When this child is really coming, you'll know all about it, and you'll have plenty of time to send somebody for Sarah and myself."

Honnie's heart lifted.

"You mean you will come? You and Sarah?"

The two women looked at each other.

"We'll come," said Madge reassuringly. "And now stop asking me questions for a few minutes and let me see how this child of yours is doing."

For a few minutes all three were silent, as Madge concentrated on what she was learning through her hands.

"Everything seems fine," she said finally. "I don't think you have anything to worry about."

She looked at her ankles.

"No swelling there," she said. "That's good."

"Can you tell if it will be a boy or a girl," said Honnie. "Though in truth I don't mind, so long as everything is all right."

"Well, you're carrying it high," said Madge. "And they do say if you are carrying it high, it's likely to be a boy."

"I'll need a cradle," said Honnie.

"Don't worry about a cradle," said Sarah. "I'm sure I can get one somewhere."

"I've made a list of clothes," said Honnie. "But I'm not sure I remember everything. It's so long since Joseph was born. I thought if somebody lent me some baby clothes, I could copy them. I know I've not got the best hands with a needle, but it would give me something to do these last weeks."

"We'll find some clothes," said Madge. "But yes, it's probably a good idea to make some yourself. You should buy some material – and a good scissors."

While they discussed what Honnie would need, Sarah and Madge had a last cup of tea before they left for the long walk home, with promises to visit soon again.

"Don't you be worrying yourself," said Sarah. "There's no better woman than Madge to advise you. She's been bringing babies into the world for twenty years or more. She's as good, if not better, than any medical man. Anyone who has been lucky enough to have her beside them at their time of need will tell you so."

Honnie hugged them both goodbye.

"Thank you," she said. "Thank you both. It's made me feel so much better to know you'll both be there for me when the baby is coming."

"We'll be here," said Madge. "Now rest easy."

The baby gave a kick, as though it had heard what she said and agreed.

Honnie remembered that Christopher had said he would ask Molly Flaherty to help at the birth. Should she tell them now, or should she say nothing until the time came? But then if Molly turned up and found Madge and Sarah there, how would she react? And how would Madge and Sarah feel about Molly being there? Honnie had a vivid mental picture of three formidable women eyeing each other around her bed, and disagreeing about what should be done, while she struggled in labour. It would be best, she decided, to give them some hint of

Molly's possible presence.

"Listen ... before you go ... I have to tell you that Christopher was speaking with his old nurse, Molly Flaherty, and she said she would come and help. I hardly know Molly, though to be sure she saw that this house was readied before we came back from Dublin. When you're having a baby, you need people you know around you. But I can't tell Molly I don't want her now.

For a minute, Sarah and Madge looked a little put out. Then Madge spoke.

"Master Christopher has known Molly all his life, so you can understand why he might want her to be there when his child is being born. Of course you can't tell her you don't want her. So just tell Master Christopher that we're going to be here and let him take care of Molly."

But as they were leaving Christopher rode up on Barebones.

He was clearly happy to see Honnie getting some help, happy to see Sarah and Madge.

"Hold on a while," he said. "I'll ride back to Tyrone and harness the pony and trap – and take you home. You were very good to come over."

A couple of days later Christopher drove Honnie in to Galway. She bought lengths of flannel, and white lawn. She bought blanketing and material for small sheets, and yards of white ribbon. Peig came over one evening with some old baby clothes. Over the following days Honnie ripped them apart, ironed the pieces flat and laid them on pages of an old copy of the *Connacht Tribune* to make a pattern for each garment.

At her third attempt she produced what seemed to her

a creditable little nightgown. Delighted, she went on to sew more. Sewing was proving more enjoyable than she had ever imagined. The pile of baby clothes mounted. Looking at them, Honnie wondered how one small person could need so many clothes. And it was hard to believe that any infant would be small enough to fit into them.

When Honnie got tired of sewing, she wandered around the garden. She picked buckets of the blackberries hanging heavy on the brambles around the edges of the field behind the house, and made pots of dark, lustrous jelly. She remembered the time, just a year ago, when she had picked blackberries with Christopher. Things had changed so much in one short year.

She gave Lizzie some intensive lessons in cooking. Lizzie had got more confident in the months she had been with Honnie. From being afraid to prepare anything on her own, she had grown into an enthusiastic cook. One evening she made an apple pie by herself and, after sampling a piece, Honnie announced it was perfect. Lizzie's pride and pleasure lit up her face.

Meanwhile, Tyrone was not a happy place, according to Bridget who came to visit every week or so.

"There seems to be a lot of bickering going on," she said.

Mrs. Smith wasn't on speaking terms with Mrs. Hunt the housekeeper.

"Well, to say they don't speak to each other isn't quite true," said Bridget. "They speak to each other all right, but only when they absolutely have to, and you'll remember how friendly they were. Mrs. Smith would go to Mrs. Hunt's room in the afternoon, and Mrs. Hunt would visit Mrs. Smith's room in the evening."

"Does anybody know what happened between them?" asked Honnie.

"Nobody knows for sure," said Bridget. "There's some say that Mrs. Hunt told Mrs. Smith that she was too fond of the drink, and that Mrs. Smith asked Mrs. Hunt who did she think she was, to tell her what she could and couldn't drink, that she only took it for her nerves. And there are others who say that Mrs. Smith criticised Mrs. Hunt's housekeeping, that she said the house was not as well kept as it used to be in the mistress's time. Which it isn't, of course. But that's not really Mrs. Hunt's fault. The fact is there's no real mistress."

According to Bridget, Mrs. Smith's temper had definitely disimproved.

"It was always a bit short, but now the smallest thing sets her off. The other day she told Maria, the new scullery maid, to get out of the house and never show her face again, and all because she dropped a bucket of cleaned vegetables when she was bringing them in from the scullery to the kitchen. We all go in fear of her tongue these days. I think Josie's death, and the way she died, has upset Mrs. Smith far more than she'll admit. Josie made her mad, but she was fond of her in a funny kind of way. Josie's death has upset everyone. Maybe you most of all, after seeing her in the river at Clarinbridge?"

"I can't get her out of my mind," said Honnie. "How did it happen that we came along at that very point? Bad enough to hear about it – but to see it! I'll never get it out of my head. She annoyed me too, but now I feel guilty about her, guilty that I wasn't nicer to her. She'd had very little to be happy about in her life. Has there been any word at all of Robert?"

"Neither seen nor heard of, and won't be either, I should think," said Bridget.

"So what are they saying now about myself and Christopher?" asked Honnie.

Bridget looked uncomfortable.

"Well, truth to tell, there's many who still see it as a terrible scandal," she said. "Mr. Scott says it's far worse than Isabella and Emilia running off, because at least they ran off, but Master Christopher has brought the scandal to the family's doorstep. Mrs. Smith is furious with you. You were one of her pets. She says it's more your fault than Master Christopher's, but that both of you have behaved disgracefully. Mrs. Hunt says that the Master has failed greatly, and it's all because of you and Christopher. The other servants –"

"I think I've heard enough," said Honnie.

Horses were still a big part of Christopher's life, and he was often away at various race meetings around the country. Honnie didn't mind so much early in her pregnancy. He had been up at the Curragh in June, at Howth Park Races at the beginning of July, at Ennis Races at the end of the month. In August he was at Castlebar Races and at the Curragh for a big five-day meeting in September. He was talking about going to another two meetings in October. His travels around the countryside with Daniel Murray had become rare.

In the summer months the days were long and Honnie had been happy tending to her garden. But as the days grew shorter, and her time drew nearer, she became more and more unhappy when Christopher was away.

She was feeling awkward and cumbersome. Sleeping became more difficult. It didn't matter which way she turned. Her back hurt, or she had a cramp in her leg, or her arm fell asleep. But she was also getting more and more excited at the thought of the baby she hoped she would soon hold in her arms.

She began to worry about what would happen if the baby decided to come early.

"I need you here, Christopher. What's going to happen if the baby decides to be born, and I'm just here with Lizzie? How will I send for Sarah and Madge? Who will fetch them?"

"But the baby is not to be born for another month, or so you told me."

"Babies can come early."

"When the time comes it's women's help you'll need," said Christopher.

"If you're not here to get the women, there won't be much help," said Honnie tartly.

"I'll tell you what," said Christopher. "I'll go to the first meeting, early in the month, but I won't go to the later one."

And with that Honnie had to be satisfied.

It was in the small hours of the morning that she felt most anxious. The muscles in her stomach seemed to pulsate. She was sure the baby was going to be born sooner than Madge thought. Sometimes the baby didn't seem to move at all and Honnie would wonder in panic if it could have died inside her. But then it would give an energetic thrust of an arm or a leg, that rippled across her stomach, and she would heave a sigh of relief, only to find something else to worry about.

There were nights when she woke Christopher up, and told him he should go and get Madge straight away. Then they would wait a while, and she would decide no, it wasn't necessary, not just yet. After Christopher had been woken up for the fourth time in a week, he refused to take her seriously.

"Wake me up when you really decide to have this baby," he said, turning around and going back to sleep.

When Honnie thumped him furiously, and told him he was a callous, unfeeling brute, he laughed, turned his head and gave her a warm kiss.

"Try to get some sleep," he said.

After his trip to the Curragh at the beginning of October, Christopher spent more time at home. He still went out quite a bit during the day -- he wasn't the kind of man to sit still in one place for any length of time. He had to be up and doing something. But when he went it was usually only for a few hours, over to Tyrone, or into Galway. He promised Honnie he would be there when she needed him.

It was on a day at the end of October when Christopher had left to pay a fleeting visit to Tyrone, and Honnie and Lizzie were out picking up the last few windfalls of apples from the old trees at the bottom of the garden, that Honnie realised her time had come. It was a lovely autumn day. Fóidín was frisking around beside them and the half-grown kittens were skittering among the bushes, chasing some late-surviving butterflies. The sun's rays were still warm, gold and russet leaves were fluttering from the trees, and the earth smelled richly of growth dying down for the winter ahead.

Honnie paid no attention to the cramping pains in her stomach at first – they felt just like the ones she had been having on and off for weeks, which had never amounted to anything. But gradually the pains came more and more frequently, and there was no denying their force. As she doubled over with one particularly strong pain, Lizzie looked at her with frightened eyes.

"Are you all right? Do you want me to go and fetch somebody? What should I do?"

Honnie could see that Lizzie thought the baby might be in imminent danger of arrival, and the thought of being on her own, with Honnie about to give birth, terrified her.

"Don't worry, Lizzie," said Honnie. "Babies don't get born that quickly. Master Christopher has just gone to pay a quick visit to Tyrone. He'll be back soon, you'll see."

But the pains were coming faster, and the time was passing. It seemed an eternity before Christopher came back.

When he saw her he went pale. He actually looks *frightened*, thought Honnie

"It's time to get Madge and Sarah, isn't it?" he said. "Take it easy, Honnie. I'll fetch the pony and trap and they'll be here before you know it."

The next hour was one of the longest hours of Honnie's life. She made her way up to her bedroom and lay down, but it didn't seem to make things any easier. She tried walking round. She tried sitting down, bent over double. She didn't want to show her fear to Lizzie who was clearly, if possible, more frightened than she was. Each fresh pain gathered itself up to a peak, until Honnie felt herself caught up in an iron grasp, and then the pain died slowly away again. But they were still quite far apart.

"There's nothing to worry about, Lizzie," Honnie said, praying she was right. "I don't think the baby will be born for a long time yet."

When she finally heard the pony and trap drawing up, and the sound of voices, and the steps on the stairs, and saw Madge and Sarah walking into the room, relief flooded through her.

"*Buíochas le Dia!*" she said. "Thanks be to God! I was afraid the baby was going to come and you wouldn't be here."

"Honnie, *a stór*, you'd be very lucky indeed if it came that quickly," said Madge. "Now let's have a look at you."

Honnie's stomach rose hard again with pain.

Madge took hold of her hands and Honnie held them tightly, until the pain died down.

"Now lie back and try to take some ease," said Madge. "If you take a rest between the pains, you'll be better able for the next one. Birthing is hard work, and you'll need all your strength."

"How long do you think it will all take?" asked Honnie.

"A good while yet," said Madge. "There still seems to be a good gap between your pains. But we'll know more in a few hours' time. When the pains do come, try not to fight them. Tightening up your tummy will only make them more painful."

"That's easy for you to say," gasped Honnie as

another pain rose up and clutched her. "But not easy for me to do."

"I've had six children myself," said Madge, "so I know what I'm talking about."

The pain robbed Honnie of a suitable retort.

So it went on all night. And each pain spread not only over her stomach, but into the small of her back, and right down one of her legs.

Sarah tried rubbing her back. But Honnie fought her off. Gentle as Sarah's hands were, being touched at all seemed to make everything worse. However, she was glad to grip her hands when the pains came.

Every so often, when the pain seemed to be filling her whole world, Honnie asked Madge how much longer it was going to be.

Madge's replies were evasive.

"It may take a bit longer than I thought it would," she said finally.

There was an early frost outside, but the room was warm. Sarah had lit a fire in the little fireplace a few hours earlier when the chill of the night started to make itself felt.

Honnie could hear Lizzie moving around in the kitchen, and Christopher talking. She heard a door shutting, and the sound of the pony and trap leaving.

It seemed a long time before she heard it returning.

Minutes later Christopher came into the room, leading Molly Flaherty, his old nurse.

The three women eyed each other warily as Christopher went to kneel by the bed.

"You seem to be having a very hard time," he said, taking Honnie's hand.

She smiled weakly at him as he squeezed her hand.

He pulled a chair over and sat beside her. He didn't know what to say. He took her hand again.

"I think these lovely ladies will be able to help you much more than I can," he said finally. "But I'll be just downstairs. Call me if there is anything I can do, any way I can help."

Madge beckoned Molly over to the far side of the room, near the window, where they whispered at length.

Honnie watched and didn't like their expressions and demeanour.

When they came back to her bedside Molly took her hand.

"I'm here to give whatever help I can," she said gently.

"Good help is always welcome," said Madge.

So Honnie let Molly examine her, and when the pains came she was glad to hold tight to her hand. She asked Molly if she thought everything was all right. And Molly said that as far as she could judge, there was nothing seriously wrong.

"It is just going to be a bit longer before the baby is born," she said.

"But how much longer?" gasped Honnie as another pain hit her. "Please God let it not be too much longer."

As the pain died down, Molly and Madge moved away from the bed again and spoke in low voices. But this time Honoria managed to hear them as urgency made their voices rise slightly.

"No, it's not a breech," Molly said. "The head is down as it should be but it's facing the wrong way – the spine is against Honnie's instead of being against her belly."

"That's exactly what I thought," said Madge. "I've seen births like this before, and each time the woman had a pain in her back, and down her leg."

Madge and Molly eyed each other.

"It should be alright, God willing, but it will be slow," said Molly. "Poor girl. She's exhausted already. But I think it could well be nightfall before the babe is born."

She was not far wrong. The sun was sinking in the evening sky before the baby was finally born, a big blue-eyed boy. He cried indignantly as he emerged, his little face crumpled and furious after his long journey into the world.

Madge wrapped him in a towel and handed him to Honnie.

"There now, wasn't he worth all the trouble?" she said.

Honnie found she was laughing and crying as she held him in her arms. She stroked the dark hair on his head. She examined his hands, and each of the tiny fingers. She counted his toes, kissed his soft cheek, and smiled through her tears at the three women around her bed.

"Could you ever imagine that any body so small could be so perfect?" she said. "Look at his nails, his eyelashes. Look at all that hair!"

"I always think every new baby is a little miracle," said Madge. "No matter how many I have delivered."

"He's a fine fellow indeed," said Sarah. "And big for a newborn. But that's enough praise now. They do say that praising a new baby too much can be unlucky."

"Give him back to us for a minute or two," said Madge. "We must clean him up and dress him before his father sees him. Sarah, get Lizzie to bring up some warm water."

Opening the door, Sarah called out, "Lizzie! Lizzie! Some warm water and towels for the baby boy!"

At that Christopher came bounding up the stairs. He wrapped his arms around Honnie and the baby.

"Poor Honnie. You've had a very hard time of it. The night seemed very long indeed. You must be exhausted."

He hugged her and kissed her, then stroked the baby's head with tentative fingers.

"He's a lovely little fellow, isn't he?" he said.

"He's not that little," Honnie said indignantly. "Sarah says he's very big. Who do you think he looks like? I think he's the very spit of you. He has the same ears, and the same eyes, and he looks very like you do when you're cross." She kissed the downy head again. "I would like to call him William, after my brother in Canada. Do you mind? It's just that William was always my favourite brother, and he's so far away. I'll probably never see him again. So it would be a kind of connection."

Honnie had written to William in Canada to tell him about her marriage to Christopher. She had been surprised and pleased to get a letter back, not of condemnation or congratulation, just saying he hoped she would be happy, and that things would work out for her. Ever since she had written to him every couple of months. Now she would have something special to tell him.

"No, Honnie, I have no objection. Call him whatever makes you happy."

"And now he needs to be cleaned up and have some clothes put on him," said Sarah. "Where is that girl?" She went out onto the landing. "*Lizzie! Lizzie!*"

"Coming!" Lizzie came quickly up the stairs, handed

the towels and the basin of warm water to Sarah, and turned excitedly to examine William.

"Isn't he just perfect!" she said. "And look at the head of hair on him – did you ever see the like? I've seen babies six months old who didn't have as much."

Sarah and Madge washed him and dressed him. Lying back on her pillows, Honnie watched almost jealously. When they handed him back to her, all sweet and clean, she kissed him again, his eyes, his nose, his fingers one by one. The long painful labour began to recede from her mind and she felt a huge surge of exhilaration – followed by a stab of hunger.

Sarah brought her a bowl of broth, and a couple of slices of soda bread, and Honnie ate ravenously.

Molly had been standing by, watching all the goings-on.

"That was a long birth, but a good birth," she said. "And now I think it's time for me to go. I hope I was of some help."

"Of course you were," said Madge. "It was a great comfort to know a woman of your knowledge and experience was here beside us, I can tell you."

Molly's face softened. "I'll visit again," she said. "But now I'll go downstairs and have a cup of tea, and then, Master Christopher, maybe you'd take me home."

Sarah turned to Madge when Molly had left the room. "She's a decent woman, and wise as well," she said.

"'Tis true you had a bad enough time of it," said Madge. "The pain is always hard. But you were able to have your baby in a warm house and a fine bed. I've seen women having their babies on a cold floor, with very little bedding, and nothing to cover them but an old coat, and a house empty of creature comforts. Some of those births I will never, ever, forget."

William was a big, handsome baby and, like most new mothers, Honnie thought he was a wonder. His ears were definitely like Christopher's, she decided, and his blue eyes. He had her mother's mouth, she thought. But when she asked Christopher whether he could see these resemblances, he said he just looked like himself – a baby.

Christopher was proud of him, but he was very caught up with his horses, and plans for his new stables on the Curragh in County Kildare. He talked about horses and races and the Curragh until Honnie, even though she shared his interest, felt she had heard enough, particularly as she couldn't share any of the fun.

Her days revolved around William, feeding him, changing him, bathing him, or just holding him, warm in her arms, against her breast, looking down at him. He grew fast and strong and was remarkably good-humoured. Within weeks he was smiling, a big sunny grin. He fed, he slept, he gurgled happily, and Honnie and Lizzie vied for one of his smiles.

Madge and Sarah came to visit, and expressed themselves suitably impressed with his progress. Molly Flaherty came and agreed that he was indeed a fine baby. Father Tom came to call, but no one came from Honnie's family.

Honnie told Father Tom that she wanted him to christen William.

"I'm going to ask Bridget to be his godmother, and I was hoping you could be his godfather – but I don't know if you can christen him and be his godfather as well," she said.

Father Tom looked somewhat surprised but also pleased.

"Well, it would certainly be somewhat unconventional," he said. "I'm not sure if it is possible, but I don't see why not. And yes, I would be very happy to be William's godfather and have a place in his life."

Bridget came to visit and, when Honnie asked her, she said she would very much like to be a godmother.

Some two weeks later, just three weeks before Christmas, Christopher and Honnie and Bridget together with a very well-wrapped baby drove over in the trap to Father Tom in Kinvara, and William was duly christened.

Chapter 30

Bridget came over to Drumacoo often to see her new godchild, but one day when she came, early in March, she seemed distracted, uneasy, as though she had something on her mind.

"Come on, Bridget," said Honnie. "Tell me. I can see that something is bothering you."

Bridget hesitated. "The way it is," she began nervously, "myself and Mairtín Breathnach are walking out. I was afraid to tell you, because you and he –"

"Were never anything to each other except good friends," said Honnie firmly, "no matter what Mairtín might have hoped for."

She wasn't really surprised. She remembered how Bridget had always praised Mairtín and said what a nice man he was. And she remembered thinking once that Bridget and himself would make a good pair. Still, at the back of her mind, there was a twinge of jealousy. After all, it was less than a year before that he had said he cared for her.

She gave Bridget a warm hug. "I hope you'll be very happy," she said.

"Oh, nothing is settled yet," said Bridget. "It's still early days. But we get along well together and I thought I should tell you before somebody else mentioned it."

As she walked home, Bridget thought about Honnie and Mairtín. Honnie, she knew, had been very fond of Mairtín, though she didn't think her affections had ever been completely engaged. Yet if Christopher hadn't happened, the chances are they might have been married by now. She felt a surge of gladness.

Bridget had watched Mairtín's pursuit of Honnie with an ache in her heart. He was a handsome man, strong, tall, broad-shouldered, his face burnished from days out fishing, with warm brown eyes which looked unusual under a head of blond hair. She knew he was also a good and kind man, always ready to lend a hand to a friend or neighbour in time of trouble. She knew he felt greatly for the hardships which many people endured in the battles of everyday living and had strong opinions on what could be done to help them. She hoped that, in time, Mairtín would learn to love her as much as she loved him.

Bridget felt that Honnie had been just a little piqued that Mairtín had taken up with her so soon, but that was as it should be.

In the summer Bridget called to tell Honnie of her approaching marriage.

"I would like you to be there, Honnie, but it is very difficult. You must know that there are people, even my own mother and father ... who see you as ..." She struggled to find the right word.

"Disreputable, to put it politely," said Honnie. She gave Bridget a hug. "I do understand and, to tell you the truth, while it would be nice to see you getting married, I wouldn't feel at all comfortable being there. I don't want to go back and feel people are looking down their noses at me, seeing me as Christopher's kept woman. So, I'll be thinking of you, and wishing you the very best of luck."

But after Bridget had gone home, Honnie had to admit to herself that she felt a bit cross, and she felt sad. She knew she had said the right thing to Bridget, and she knew that to go to the wedding would have been a mistake. But she had always been a part of the life of Maree, her family, the people who lived there, the people with whom she had grown up. Not any more. It felt quite lonely, like being outside a warm circle.

Bridget came to see Honnie some months after she got married, when Honnie was wondering if she was ever going to see her again.

"We had great sport at the wedding," she said. "The singing and the dancing went on until the small hours of the morning. Everybody had a great time. People said it was one of the best weddings they'd ever been at. So much has happened in the last few months, Honnie! And now I'm very happy living with Mairtín in Maree, though sometimes I worry when he's out in the boat and the weather's turned bad. And guess what, Honnie, I'm going to have a baby! I'm so happy. I'll be looking to you for advice."

She promised to come again soon. But that was the

last Honnie saw of her for many months. Sometimes when Fóidín barked she would look out the window and expect to see Bridget walking up the pathway. But she never came.

Finally, Honnie got a letter from Bridget. She had lost the baby.

"*I so much wanted this baby,*" she wrote. "*I thought about it all the time. I could feel it growing in my stomach. And just before it all went wrong I was sure I could feel it moving inside me. And then, suddenly, there was a lot of blood, such a lot of blood, and no baby any more. Eileen Kelly and Madge Shaughnessy were good to me. They did their best to help me and console me. They told me it happened to other women too. Well, I knew that, I know that. It doesn't make it any easier. They said there would be other children, but I wanted the baby I had lost. In all the long winter days everything seemed very black. I didn't write to you because I just couldn't face putting pen to paper. But now I'm pregnant again. Pray God things will go better this time.*"

And Honnie was again with child. Her second child, a girl, was born in the late summer of 1836.

"We'll call her Anne," said Christopher.

Honnie couldn't believe her ears.

"*Anne!*" she said incredulously. "Of all the names to choose, why Anne?"

"Because it's my sister's name," said Christopher. "After all, William was called after your brother."

"We're talking about Anne, your sister, with whom you have been quarrelling for as long as I can remember!"

"Yes, my sister Anne, who is rising thirty-five years of age, and unlikely ever to get married. Anne, who was once my mother's right hand. Anne, who thinks Tyrone is in a state of disorder, but isn't the kind of person who can command a household the way my mother did. What has she got to look forward to? Being a useful aunt to her sisters' children and growing old on charity?"

Honnie said nothing.

"She's always said she would like to travel," he said. "My father is trying to raise some money, but it's not easy. We already owe so much. But maybe he will be able to give her some sort of a competence. She could probably live quite cheaply in France or Italy."

"Why can't you sell some land?" asked Honnie.

"The land is entailed," said Christopher. "It's entailed to me, and what's entailed theoretically can't be sold."

"Your family owns a lot of land," said Honnie. "If you really need the money, there must be a way you can sell a part of it."

"There are ways," said Christopher, "but it's all very complicated. "Whenever I meet with Father now, it's usually in his study, where his desk is piled high with papers and documents. He is desperately hoping he can sort things out in some way or other. There are many charges on the estate. He wants to raise enough money to meet the most pressing charges, and have something left to give to Anne and his other children."

Meanwhile Christopher was throwing himself into the racing activities at the Curragh. 1836 was a good year for him. Thomas St. Lawrence had proved to be as good as his word. By the time Christopher was twenty-six years old he was not only a member of the Turf Club, but had been appointed one of its three stewards. And his horses were winning all before them.

Barebones had done well in various meetings throughout the season and, at the October meet at the Curragh, Waterwitch was the first winner of the newly initiated Mulgrave Course.

Christopher came back from the October meeting in high good humour.

"It's been so exciting, Honnie. To see two of my horses racing first past the post, with the jockey wearing my colours, the sea-green jacket, the black cap. I had hoped, but I couldn't really believe it was happening. I felt sure Waterwitch could do it, but horses can have good days and bad days. To see her there on the Curragh, racing first past the post, was one of the most exciting experiences of my life!"

"I so wish I had been there!" said Honnie.

After William was born, and then Anne, Honnie found there was always something to be done. Even with Lizzie's help she spent every day changing nappies, soothing, washing and cleaning the babies, cooking – and waiting for Christopher to come home. Lizzie was good company, but there were times when she longed for a bit of *craic* and conversation with a woman friend of her own age.

She had neighbours, but no contact with them. Nóra Burke, who lived down the road, had young children not much older than Honnie's. She was a widow woman. Her husband had died of consumption two years earlier. She made her living now hawking fish. Life could not be easy for her, yet her children were well-behaved and well cared-for. Honnie would have liked to be able to visit her and talk with her, but Nóra had made it very clear that she wanted no dealings with the likes of Honnie. And Honnie was aware that other women in the neighbourhood felt the same way. There were times when she felt very lonely, and thought often of Bridget.

It was Father Tom who was the next to bring news of her.

"I'm sorry that I haven't been to see you sooner, but the days never seem long enough for the needs and demands of so many people. There's a great deal of poverty in Galway these days, Honnie. There are so many people with no work. There are people starving. Whatever your circumstances you are very lucky indeed to have a good roof over your head, and not want for food and sustenance. Luckier a great deal than poor Bridget. She hasn't been to see you because she doesn't want to see anyone. She was very unwell expecting her second child, and then it was stillborn. The world seems very black indeed to her just now, and there are some who fear for her reason. She has taken to walking the beach, day and night. Mairtín is sore afraid she'll do herself an injury. He's worn out from watching her."

"That's sad news indeed you bring," said Honnie. "Poor, poor Bridget! I wish I could help her, be with her. But I don't think my appearance in the middle of Maree would do her much good. Yet I want to do something for her. What I can do?"

"Pray for her," said Tom.

"Of course I'll pray for her," said Honnie. "But I want to *do* something. Tom, if I can gather good things for her to eat – you know, cakes, fruit, pies, bread, a cooked chicken, some ham, maybe a bottle of nice wine from

Tyrone – and put them all in a basket, could you get it sent over to her? I could send a letter with it as well."

And so it was agreed that Tom would call again in three or four days, by which time Honnie would have the basket ready.

In Galway poverty seemed to increase with every passing year.

"I know I don't see much of what's going on," said Honnie to Christopher one day, "but when I do get out I seem to see more and more poor people every time. Tom says the poverty is great."

"The poverty is indeed great," said Christopher. "And the numbers of poor are increasing all the time. A special Commission was formed some years ago to try to find out how many people in Ireland needed help. They spent over three years trying to gather all the information they could. They have said that the number of persons out of work and in need of assistance for six months of the year is well over two million. That's a huge number of people, a huge problem. Can it be solved? I can see no easy answer."

"But surely they must have made some suggestions?" said Honnie.

"The Commissioners agreed that state intervention was necessary, but they rejected a Poor Law modelled on the English Poor Law system, which is based on relief inside a workhouse. Instead they recommended that the government should introduce a number of schemes to promote the economic development of the country. They also suggested the large-scale emigration to the colonies should be introduced to reduce the population. Are you still with me, Honnie?"

"I think so," said Honnie. "So this is what's going to happen?"

"No, it's not what's going to happen," said Christopher, "because the government in London didn't like the suggestions made by the Commissioner. They decided they wanted a fresh investigation. They sent a special English Poor Law Commissioner over to Ireland. He spent nine weeks here and submitted his findings within three months. He said the English Poor Law system *would* be suitable for Ireland. The government has decided that drastic measures are needed to deal with Irish poverty and Irish paupers. So, under the Irish Poor Law Bill, Ireland is going to be divided into 130 different divisions or areas, and these will be known as Unions. Each Union will have its own workhouse and be administered by a Board of Guardians drawn from the local community. A new tax, known as poor rates, is to be imposed, which is an attempt to make local landlords responsible for the local poor. Which may sound like a fine idea, but the landlords are almost all deeply in debt themselves. They are not getting any rents. They have no other source of income. Many are virtually bankrupt. As you well know. Have you heard enough, Honnie?

"For the moment, yes," said Honnie.

Later that afternoon she sat down to write to William about this latest news before she had forgotten all the details. She was on her third page when she heard a knock at the door. She went to open it.

Joseph was standing there, looking uncomfortable. A taller, broader, older, fourteen-year-old Joseph, the first member of her family to visit her.

She threw her arms around him and hugged him tight, and tight again.

"Joseph, Joseph, it's so very good to see you! Come in, come on in!"

After a few awkward minutes, they spent a happy couple of hours catching up on all the news from Maree, admiring William and Anne, drinking tea with bread and apple jelly, and enjoying being together.

"I've just been writing to William," said Honnie, "to tell him about this Irish Poor Law Bill, and the new workhouses that are being built. Have you heard about them, Joseph?"

"I've heard too much about them," said Joseph, "and none of it good. Relief will only be given in the workhouse. There will be no outdoor relief. So unless you go into the workhouse there will be no help at all. And these workhouses will be very strict, very severe, the kind of place you'd only go into if you were desperate. Families will be separated, husbands from wives, parents from their children. They'll be fed, but only enough to keep them alive. And everybody will have to work, and work hard. I can tell you no self-respecting man or woman will cross the door of one of those places, unless they see death staring them in the face. No man, no woman, is going to leave his home, his cabin, no matter how poor it is, to be castigated and humiliated and bullied in a place like that."

Thinking about it later that evening, Honnie began to wonder what was going to happen to all the people who needed outdoor relief, who didn't want to go into the workhouses.

"So many must be starving. Who is going to feed them?" Honnie asked Christopher.

"That," said Christopher, "is the big question."

Chapter 31

By the end of 1838 Honnie was heavy with her third child, and there were days when her patience wore thin.

William was more trouble than Anne.

"Isn't he an absolute demon?" she said to Lizzie, one afternoon when he had been particularly bad. "You can't take our eyes off him. Anne will play with that old rag doll I made her, or with a ball, or the wooden blocks Christopher brought over from Tyrone. But William! He never sits still for a moment. You turn your back and he's gone – out the back door into the garden, over the wall into the next field, or out into the front garden and down the lane, and Fóidín with him. Ten minutes ago I made sure all the doors were closed fast and now I find him climbing out the window. And he's not yet four."

That evening, with both children finally in bed, she found herself still working, making bread for the the next day, feeling exhausted, and very pregnant, and very tired and very cross.

She thought of Christopher out on the hunting field with his friends, enjoying himself.

He came home, as she had expected, in high good humour, fresh-faced, and exuberant about the thrills of his day hunting, about which he told her in detail. He put his arms around her and gave her a slapping big kiss.

"What's for dinner?" he said. "Where are the children?"

"The children are in bed, finally," Honnie said. "And they've just gone to sleep. *Please* don't wake them up –"

But she wasn't quick enough. He was up the stairs before she finished. Within minutes he was back down, swinging them up in the air, chasing them round the kitchen, tickling them, lying on the floor and letting them crawl all over him, until they were so excited that Honnie knew they wouldn't go to sleep again for hours.

"It's all very well for you," she snapped. "You're not with them all day. It's fine for you to come back and be the father of all the fun but, while I love them dearly, I like to see them asleep of an evening. I'm glad for you that you have had such a good day out, and I know the enjoyment you get from hunting. But do you not think that I'd like a good day too, that I might enjoy some diversion?"

Christopher looked taken aback.

"I thought you were happy?" he said.

"I never said I wasn't happy," said Honnie crossly. "I just get tired of cooking and cleaning and minding children sometimes. I would like to see a bit of life outside Drumacoo. It isn't as if people are beating a path to my door. I never said I wasn't happy. I'd just like a bit of diversion sometimes."

"You're tired," said Christopher. "The children have been getting you down. You'll feel better when you've had a night's sleep. Come on, now. Don't be cross."

He put his arm around her, but Honnie shook him off. She couldn't help herself.

"You've had a long day doing what you wanted to do, with your horses, with your friends!" She could hear her voice rising. "You didn't have to do anything you didn't want to do! And you'll be off again tomorrow, to the next hunt, the next race meeting!"

"Yes, I will," said Christopher, and his voice began to rise too. "That's my life. You knew that when you married me."

"It seems to me you care more for your horses than you do for your wife and children!"

"What on earth's got into you? I don't need to come home to this. I want a wife who greets me with a welcome smile, not this –" he searched for words, "this *termagant*!"

"*Termagant!*" said Honnie. "*Termagant, is it? I'll termagant you!*"

She picked up a large lump of dough from the table and threw it at him. But he caught it before it hit him, and laughed heartily, which infuriated her even more.

"Fine," she said. "As you said, I'm tired, and I'm going to go to bed. You woke the children up, you can settle them down again."

When Christopher came in some time later, she pretended to be asleep. When he put an exploratory arm around her, she shook him off.

"Come, Honnie," he said. "What about a goodnight kiss?"

She turned her back to him.

"Well, if that's the way you want it," he said, and quickly fell fast asleep.

Honnie spent an uncomfortable night, near the edge of the bed, trying to make sure she kept her back firmly turned.

By the following night she was back in Christopher's arms again.

Chapter 32

There had been a heavy snowfall the night before, but the morning of the 6th of January 1839 was very calm. The feast of the Epiphany was known to everyone as *Nollaig na mBan*, or the Women's Christmas. On this day the women of the house were supposed to take it easy after all the cooking and baking of the festive season, while the men looked after them for a change.

"Not that this happens very often," Honnie said dryly to Lizzie.

She was heavily pregnant and tired, but like women all over the country she was planning a special meal.

"Maybe you could take the children outside," she said to Christopher. "It would be much easier for me to cook without two small children under my feet. They've been begging me to take them out all morning – they've never seen so much snow before. You can all make a snowman together."

"That will be a real treat," said Christopher wryly.

"But I can tell you that I'm quite a good snowman-maker – it's one of my many talents."

Honnie wrapped the children up warmly, gave them old socks to keep their hands warm, "for a little while at least, until they get wet from the snow", and off they went with their father.

Outside it was an incredibly calm day – almost eerily calm, Christopher thought. Nothing stirred, not a blade of grass, not the rushes in the field. So quiet and calm was it that he could clearly hear the voices of people speaking in cottages down the road.

He helped William and Anne make a snowman. He found small stones for eyes, some holly berries for a mouth, and even gave them the cap he was wearing to put on the snowman's head.

They threw sticks for Fóidín, but he didn't seem to be in a playful mood. The clouds loured low in the dark stillness of the day. The children's feet got wet. They complained of the cold but then the weather suddenly turned warm. Unnaturally warm, thought Christopher.

Honnie had prepared a chicken which Christopher had brought over from Tyrone. There could never be a question of killing one of their own birds to eat, because the children were very fond of them, fed them every day, and had pet names for their favourites. She had rubbed some butter over the chicken, sprinkled it with salt and pepper and a scattering of parsley and thyme, put some carrots and onions around it and nestled it in the bastable oven – the big iron pot with three legs, handles at either side and a close-fitting lid. She had then stood the pot in the middle of the fire, raked the red turf sods up all around it and put more sods on top of the lid so that it was getting heat from all sides at once.

Honnie had boiled potatoes earlier – now she peeled them, then mashed them with butter.

"The children will be hungry when they come back," she said to Lizzie. "When you come in from the cold, on a winter's evening, hot fluffy potato cakes covered with melting butter taste really good. The potato cakes will keep us all going until the chicken is ready later this evening."

She added some salt and a beaten egg, then gathered the mixture into a ball and gently floured it, so that she could roll it out flat. She cut it into squares, and cooked them, three or four at a time, on the flat round iron plate with a handle on it that hung over the fire. When Christopher and the children came back, there was a pile of potato cakes on a platter near the fire, steaming, buttered, asking to be eaten.

It was eight in the evening by the time Honnie brought the chicken to the table. Everyone's appetite was hearty. Within half an hour only the bones were left.

"And that will make good soup tomorrow," said Honnie as she cleared the dinner plates away.

Christopher had also brought over a cake from Tyrone. Honnie cut it and gave everybody a slice, along with some apples and nuts.

Christopher poured a glass of wine for Honnie and himself.

"It's like Christmas all over again," said William. "A real feast."

At nine o'clock in the evening they were all sitting around the fire, warm, full and a bit sleepy, when Honnie remarked on the wind.

"It seems to be rising," she said. "I hope we don't get more snow."

By half-past ten the wind had become a gale, rising in force with every passing minute, rumbling and roaring around the house.

"Like a great big monster," said William, who was getting quite frightened.

Christopher put two sacks of potatoes against the front door, and a bag of corn, then pushed the table over against it. He barricaded the back door in a similar way. He was thanking God he had decided to leave Barebones in Tyrone the night before, and walk home. If he had ridden him home, the poor animal would now be in the makeshift stable outside, alone and terrified by the big wind and more than likely to do himself an injury.

He proceeded to block the windows as best he could.

"If they go the roof will follow," he said grimly to Honnie. "And no more turf or wood on that fire," he said. "In fact, I'm going to put some water on it. The last thing we need is for the house to go up in flames."

"There's a bit of a lull now," said Honnie. "I'll put some bread and jam in that big old chest, along with the cake that's left, and some milk. We'll be glad of it when this is all over. And that chest is so heavy I don't think any wind would be able to move it."

She had just closed the lid of the chest when the storm blew up again. With every gust of wind, the house trembled as though it was about to break into a thousand pieces. The plates on the dresser shivered precipitously, then smashed into smithereens against the opposite wall. Stools and chairs did a dizzy dance around the rocking kitchen floor. The rafters in the roof creaked ominously. It seemed as if some huge giant outside was flinging rocks at the house.

Lizzie put her apron over her head and face, and curled up in a corner, crying and calling on God, the Blessed Virgin, and all the saints in Heaven to come to their aid.

William clung to his father, howling in terror. Anne whimpered with fear, Honnie's arms tight around her. Outside they could hear the big boom of the wind, as it wreaked destruction and havoc on everything in its path.

As the night went on, they all huddled closer and closer together, Christopher with one arm around William and the other around Honnie, who was holding Anne, and Lizzie holding Honnie's other arm in an iron grip.

By two o'clock the storm seemed to reach its full force and they hoped that it was on the turn, but it still went on and on. Every time it quietened down a little, they prayed that it was easing off, but then it would come back again with its dreadful, awful roar. And the ground would shake more than ever.

"In some ways the lulls are almost as bad," said Honnie, "because now I know that a lull doesn't mean it's going to end, and I keep waiting for it to start up again."

Honnie prayed for Christopher and herself and their children and Lizzie. She prayed for her family over in Maree.

"I can't stop thinking about them," she said to Christopher. "Do you think it's as bad, or maybe even worse over in Maree? If I survive this night in one piece,

I'm going to go over there as soon as I can, no matter that Maureen mightn't want to see me."

It was five o'clock in the morning before the storm finally began to die down. It was nine before Christopher suggested they should venture out. Honnie was not so sure.

"I don't think I want to go out – I'm afraid of what I'm going to see," she said. "I can only imagine it, and I don't want to see it. Besides, how can we be sure that it has really stopped? It could start again at any minute."

"We can't stay here for ever," said Christopher. "We have to go out and face whatever has happened."

He took away the sacks from the back door first.

"Come on, Honnie. Give me your hand."

So Honnie told Lizzie to stay behind and mind the children. Taking Christopher's hand, she walked through the opened door. The sight that met her eyes was worse than anything she could have imagined.

They both stood, silent.

Honnie's vegetable garden which she had carefully readied in neat beds for spring planting was now a flattened spread of sodden clay. The apple trees were gone, the fruit bushes as well. The hedges had been ripped apart.

The roof of the makeshift stable seemed to have collapsed into the building.

"Thank God I left Barebones in Tyrone, Honnie," Christopher said, his voice almost a whisper. "He will have been safe over there. The stables are very solidly built. We could have lost him if he was here. I have been promising myself for too long to make a better stable. And now I certainly will."

The roof was gone off the henhouse, and there were no hens to be seen. The only sign that they had ever been was the body of Blackie, William's favourite hen, hanging on an old hawthorn bush, bereft of almost all her feathers. Honnie recognized her because of the three black feathers she still had.

She heard William's voice in the background, and clutched Christopher's arm.

"Quick!" she said. "That's William's favourite hen. Get it and throw it as far away as you can to the end of the garden, where he won't see it."

Christopher grabbed the hen and flung it away.

William darted out, followed by Lizzie and Anne.

"He wanted to see where you had gone," said Lizzie. "I tried to stop him, but he pushed his way out."

"What happened the roof of the henhouse?" he asked. "And where are the hens?"

"I'm afraid the hens have all gone away, *a stór,*" said Honnie. "They decided they didn't like all the wind and the noise, and they've gone away to find a nicer place."

"But where's *mo chircín dubh* – my little black hen?" asked William.

"I'm afraid she went with the other hens," said Honnie. "But we'll get more hens, I promise you."

William burst into tears. From the day he had first seen her, he had decided that she was the hen in the rhyme his mother used to sing to him.

Gugalaí gug, mo chircín dubh,
Suíonn sí síos is beireann sí ubh,
Ubh inné, is ubh inniu,
Gugalaí gug, mo chircín dubh!

Gugalaí-gug, my little black hen,
She sits down and lays an egg,
An egg yesterday, an egg today,
Gugalaí-gug, my little black hen.

"I don't *want* more hens," he wept. "I just want my own *circín* back. You have to find her!"

But worse awaited them when they went out the front door. The landscape that met their eyes was naked, flattened, devastated, unreal.

"The cottages, Christopher, their walls are on the ground, their roofs gone," said Honnie.

"We have been fortunate indeed," said Christopher quietly. "Our walls are made of stone and our roof is slated and, while we have lost many slates, the roof held fast. Most of the dwellings around us were made of sods and mud. The roofs were thatched and were only anchored on the cottages by their own weight. The wind just lifted them off."

"Where are the people?" asked Honnie.

"Probably cowering in any place of shelter they can find, in the corners of buildings which fell down around them," said Christopher. "Or else they were afraid they would be buried beneath them, so they left. They're probably sheltering in any hedges or ditches left, even out in the fields. But, look, not all the houses have fallen – I'll bet the ones still standing are full of people. "

They tried to make their way around the village, but the ground was covered with debris of all kinds, and it was also very wet and slippy. Their progress was very slow.

They could see the contents of the cabins strewn

across the countryside. They could hear voices from the ruins. Clearly, the people who had lived in them were still around.

Some of the people they saw were half-dressed, cold and shivering, in whatever rags they had been wearing when the storm struck, keening to themselves. Some were sitting dazed, with their rosary beads in their hands. Some were calling out to each other.

"We can only hope that nobody has been killed," said Christopher.

Ricks of turf had taken wings and flown. Stacks of hay and oats had come to land in places where there had been no hay or oats before. Hedges had been wrenched out of the ground.

"And the trees, Christopher," said Honnie. "There's not a tree been left standing. That big stand of trees up the road is gone. The trees we planted in the garden three years ago have vanished. There's not a tree to be seen."

"And there are dead birds and animals everywhere," said Christopher.

"It's like the end of the world," said Honnie.

"But it isn't the end of the world," said Christopher. "We are all here safe and sound. And we have a roof over our heads. We have been very lucky."

Honnie and Christopher had indeed been lucky, but their neighbours had not.

Nóra Burke and her three children were the first people they met. The children were blue with the cold, barely covered with the clothes in which they had been put to bed. Nóra was shaking, her face grey with exhaustion, and didn't seem able to grasp what had happened, or where she was. Only the walls of her cabin were standing.

"I see your roof is gone," said Honnie gently. "Why don't you come with us and we'll see if we can get the fire going again, and warm you up. You're all frozen."

Nóra looked at Honnie, then nodded numbly, and let Honnie lead her back to the house, with her children clinging to her skirts. Warily, the Burke children eyed the St. George children, and were met with equally wary eyes in return.

Honnie and Christopher cleared away as much as they could of the debris. They salvaged some unbroken dishes and some mugs, and Honnie piled plates high with bread and jam.

But Nóra and her children were too shattered to be hungry, though they drank the milk greedily. Christopher went out to bring in turf and came back with the news that it was snowing again.

"Thick heavy snow. You can hardly see beyond the end of the garden path. God help those poor unfortunates out there and grant they have found shelter of some sort or other. Tomorrow we'll have to see what we can do to help them."

Later, Honnie made space on the kitchen floor and laid down blankets for the Burkes to sleep on, and she and Christopher went upstairs with William and Anne.

They got little sleep that night. Instead they lay there, listening, waiting for the storm to start again.

Over the following days everyone had their own story to tell about the storm. What had been bad for some people, had been good for others.

Nóra Burke, who made her living from selling fish, had no takers for her fish in the days after the storm.

"There was a risen tide, and the beaches are squirming with herring and cod, and all sorts of fish," she said. "I'll be getting no money from selling fish for another little while."

"The country is strewn with dead and half-dead animals," said Christopher, "and there are cattle who were maimed or injured in their byres. A quick mercy killing is the only solution."

"Many people," Honnie said wryly, "seem to be eating better now than they have ever eaten before. But what I think is quite extraordinary is the way people are helping each other, the way they are reaching out to one another. Neighbours are helping neighbours, people are sharing whatever small thing they have left with those who have nothing at all."

Two days after the storm Christopher made his way over to Tyrone. Everybody was alive and well. Most of them had spent the night down in the cellars and "drunk quite a quantity of wine," according to Mrs. Smith.

There had been damage, but nothing too serious. Two chimneys had been blown away, a number of slates had fallen, a new plantation had been flattened. But nobody had been injured. The stables and horses had survived.

"The Martins were not so fortunate," said Christopher, when he came back to Drumacoo. "When they came up from the cellars of their mansion, they could see nothing but the sky."

It was a bitter January, and a great deal of work went into rebuilding cabins or repairing them where possible, or at the very least fashioning some form of sturdy shelter, all made more difficult because of the many tools and implements that had vanished, tossed up and fired in mighty gusts across the fields, and hedges and ditches.

"But aren't people still amazingly cheerful and good-humoured," said Honnie to Lizzie "as though some good spirit has welled up inside them. They are laughing together, talking together."

Honnie found it hard to be good-humoured as she viewed the flattened wasteland that had been her garden. The stone walls surrounding it had been scattered. Fruit bushes had been torn out of the ground, and two stumps were all that remained of the venerable apple trees. Honnie's neat beds were gone, the soil strewn far and wide. The ground was littered with slates and branches, broken garden tools, and dead birds. Two dead sheep had been hurled in from a nearby field, and already they smelt of decay.

When the spring comes, thought Honnie, I'll have to start all over again. But spring was a long way off yet. In the meanwhile there was much to be done.

The roof of the house had to take priority. It had lost a number of slates, and there were leaks which had to be repaired immediately. Christopher brought over a man called Hugh Cassidy, who worked in Tyrone from time to time. When he had finished replacing the slates, Christopher asked him to have a look at Nóra's house, and at some of the other houses which had been badly damaged.

Nóra's house, Hugh said, would need a new roof – "and the makings of a new roof are harder to find now, what with the storm tossing everything hither and thither. But I'll see what I can do."

Meanwhile Nóra and her children remained with Honnie and Christopher.

Nóra was a very quiet woman, and her children were very well behaved. In a shy way she tried to be of whatever help she could be in what was a very crowded house, while the children, unaware of any possible tension between the adults, played easily together after the first day or so. William and Anne liked having older children to play with, and Niall, Seamus and Siobhán liked having the advantage of age, so everyone was happy.

It took some weeks to fix Nóra's roof, but Honnie knew that she was delighted when she could finally move back into her own house. By the time they left, Honnie would feel that she had found a good friend.

It would take months, not weeks, for things to return to some semblance of normality, while the countryside around them, barren of growth, would take much longer.

All through the awful night of the storm, Honnie had worried about her family in Maree. She had to get over to see them.

"Well, one thing's for sure, Honnie, you can't go walking over to Maree in your present condition," said Christopher. "Tell you what, I have to go over to see how our oyster beds in Ballinacourty have suffered in the storm. Suppose we go together in a horse and trap, and I drop you off on my way over, and collect you on the way back?"

"That sounds like a very good idea," said Honnie, "but how will I know when to expect you?"

"I won't be too long," said Christopher. "An hour, maybe an hour and a half. When you hear Bran barking you'll know I'm outside."

Later, as Honnie made her way out to a waiting Christopher, she found she was filled with trepidation. But she had a lovely surprise in store for her.

Drawn up outside the front door was a brand new trap harnessed to the loveliest little pony Honnie had ever seen, with a smiling Christopher holding the reins.

"I thought you'd like this," he said. "Now you'll able to make your own way out and about. The pony's name is Maggie."

Honnie threw her arms about him and kissed and kissed him.

"Can I take the reins over to Maree?"

Maureen met Honnie at the door. Her hair was, as always, combed smoothly into a knot at the back of her neck, her dress was neat. She looked older, she looked tired, and she looked *prim,* thought Honnie.

"So you've come to see if we are still alive," she said.

She opened the door a little wider.

"I suppose you'd better come in."

Joseph appeared behind Maureen. Honnie felt warmed by the beam of welcome on his face.

"There's only the two of us here now," he said. "Thady is out fishing with Mairtín. Well, they're looking to see if there are any fish left in the sea, and Kathleen is back working for the priest in Oranmore."

They had survived the storm remarkably well. The vegetable patch had been devastated, trees had fallen, and the walls around the garden had crumbled, but miracuously the roof of the house itself was still intact.

"We think the roof held on because of the way Dad had roped it down so well," said Maureen. "He hung big stones over the thatch to keep it well weighted."

"I believe Mam was minding us," said Joseph. "I could feel her near."

Inside, the house seemed remarkably tidy.

"There was china thrown down and broken, and Father's favourite chair, and pots were tumbled about the place," said Maureen.

Honnie held out the homemade bread she had brought with her, along with a pot of last year's blackberry jam, one of the three pots to have survived the storm. She had also brought a pretty china teapot, which she had bought two years ago, but forgotten about and never used. She had found it in the wooden chest when she was putting the bread and milk away. She didn't like parting with it, but she knew it was the kind of thing that Maureen would like.

Maureen accepted the offerings, though not very graciously.

But imperceptibly, as Honnie asked about friends and neighbours, where they were, what they were doing, the atmosphere began to thaw.

Maureen offered Honnie a cup of tea, and as they shared the bread and jam, Honnie was surprised when Maureen had the grace to say that Honnie's soda bread had always been the best she'd ever eaten.

She looked at Honnie's swollen belly. "This will be your third, won't it?" she said.

"It will and it's due in about eight weeks' time," said Honnie. "William is the eldest, and then there is Anne. But tell me, what is the news of Bridget? I was so very sorry to hear of all her troubles, but Sarah Breathnach told me some months ago that she finally had a healthy baby boy at the end of last summer."

"She had a very hard time of it," said Maureen. "We were all very worried about her. There were times when we thought she would lose her reason entirely. It's great to see her now with a big, bonnie baby, and a smile always on her face. She and Mairtín are truly happy. The baby is the light of their lives, as you can imagine. And now that they've got going, it seems they can't stop. The word is that she is going to have another in about six months' time."

By the time Honnie left Maree she felt the rift might eventually be healed. She couldn't say that she and Maureen parted on really amicable terms. But they were sisters, and she and Kathleen and Thady and Joseph were all the one family, her family.

"I'm so glad I visited," she told Christopher on the way home. "I feel a great ease in my heart. I'll visit again soon, and next time I'll bring young William with me, and maybe Anne as well. They should know the house and home in which their mother grew up."

Chapter 33

In February a very bright spot appeared on Honnie's horizon. Christopher told her that, for £20 a year, he had taken out a lease on 20 acres of land at Rathbride, on the edge of the Curragh, in County Kildare.

"With it comes a house," he told Honnie. "It's not very big, but it's big enough. It's called Rathbride House. You and the children will be able to travel up and stay there from time to time."

Honnie's spirits soared. Since William was born she had never been far from Drumacoo. With a third child due soon, she had begun to feel hemmed in, with no prospect of any diversion in sight. Hearing about life on the Curragh from Christopher, remembering their visit there when she was first pregnant with William, she longed to see it again. Now she would have the chance. But this baby would need to be born first.

Mary made her appearance in the middle of March 1839. From the day she was born her blue eyes spun one way and another, taking in every detail of the people and places around her. Like her brother William, she was a good-humoured, smiling baby. New life was good life, and Mary was a ray of sunshine in the grim weeks and months after the night of the Big Wind. The flattened countryside was trying to recover. What trees were left were struggling to survive. There was no blossom, there was no birdsong.

The prospect of going up to the Curragh for a few days lifted Honnie's heart.

"I should be well able to go up to Kildare for that big race meeting at the end of April," she said to Christopher. "And you have no idea how much I am looking forward to it."

She would be able to wear the gowns she had purchased in Limerick over four years ago. That was if they still fitted her.

"I wish they weren't so tight," she said, as Lizzie strove to button up each dress.

"They aren't really *that t*ight," said Lizzie diplomatically."If you lost a small bit of weight over the next few weeks, you'd be fine."

"I've promised myself that's exactly what I'll do," said Honnie.

Lizzie was even more excited than Honnie. She had never been outside County Galway in her life.

Christopher was occupied with concerns about his father.

"Colonel Bingham has been paying court to Louisa and it looks as if they will marry in the autumn. The wedding will be costly. My father still has many pressing debts. He's raised some money by mortgaging more of our lands. But he's very downhearted. He sees no end to the estate's problems."

As the date of their departure drew closer, Christopher went up to the Curragh ahead of his family, saying he wanted to make sure everything was ready for their arrival.

Honnie and Lizzie and the children set out some days later.

Honnie couldn't help remembering her first journey up to Dublin with Christopher. In Limerick she had been so impressed with the bustling shops in the city centre, and then so horrified by the awful poverty behind the facades of fine buildings. When she thought of that journey, she remembered the barefoot, ragged people, begging for money and food, and thinking that whatever you gave them would never be enough. They might spend it on drink, or on food, but tomorrow they would be hungry and thirsty again.

Nothing had changed. The needy still crowded around the door of the carriage every time it stopped. Lizzie, who had been looking out, round-eyed, and listening with fascination to Honnie as she pointed out all the different sights along the way, grew silent as the journey progressed.

For the children, the first day of the journey was all a novelty. William and Anne enjoyed looking out at the passing towns and countryside, but the novelty wore off. By the second day, they were asking how soon they would arrive.

"Are we nearly there?" they would chorus. "Are we there now?" they would ask every time the carriage stopped for one reason or another.

Rathbride House was a long low building with a thatched roof, set back behind a pretty garden of gravelled paths and a small green lawn, dancing with daffodils and other spring flowers. Creepers clambered up the whitewashed walls.

A plump, smiling woman stood in front of the porch, with a younger woman beside her.

"This is Mrs. Rosie Byrne, our housekeeper, and her daughter Meg," said Christopher. "I've been telling them all about you."

"You're more than welcome," said Mrs. Byrne. "Come in, come in. You must be very tired after your long journey. Let me take the little one."

She reached out and took the grizzling Mary from Honnie and held her in her arms, cooing to her and rocking her gently.

"My mother loves small babies," said Meg, as she led William and Anne into the kitchen. "We made some special biscuits when she heard you were coming," she told them. "And when you've drunk some nice hot milk and eaten some biscuits we can go and visit the cat and her kittens out in the stables. Wouldn't you like that?"

William and Anne drank their milk and went off with her quite happily.

Honnie was soon ensconced in a comfortable armchair beside a glowing fire, feeding Mary. And Lizzie was trying to sort out clothes for the children.

"Just take out what they will need for tonight," said Honnie. "Tomorrow we'll go through them together."

They were all tired, and they were all hungry. The steaming pot of lamb stew and dish of fluffy mashed potatoes that Mrs Bryrne brought in and set on the big kitchen table were very welcome indeed.

Christopher didn't partake. "I have a lot to do to

make sure that everything is properly organised for the races tomorrow," he said. "And I have to have dinner with the other members of the Turf Club tonight."

He gripped Honnie's shoulder on his way out, and smiled down at her.

"It's good have you here. I'll see you later tonight."

The night had gone and it was about three o'clock in the morning when he returned, in high good humour.

"Well, you've certainly had a skinful," said Honnie.

"And why not?" said Christopher. "There are few things better than an evening in the company of good friends, with the drink flowing."

He smiled at her happily, and planted a warm kiss, redolent of the previous evening's libations on her cheek.

"Exactly how well did the drink flow?" asked Honnie.

"We have rules in the Club. No matter how much champagne you drink – and I must say we did drink quite a lot – you still have to drink three bottles of Sneyd's claret before you rise from the table. Otherwise you must pay a guinea a bottle for each bottle you don't consume. Well now, I was never going to lose any guineas for not drinking claret, was I?"

He fell silent for a moment, and a worried expression crossed his face.

"Although I think I may have lost some money later, at French hazard. I seem to remember giving somebody an I.O.U. – damned if I know who it was, though."

He put his arm round Honnie, drew her towards him, told her how much he loved her – and fell asleep.

Mrs Byrne said she and Meg would mind the children if

Honnie wanted to take Lizzie to see the sights. But Honnie knew she couldn't stay away from Mary very long. Mary was a hungry feeder. The journey to and from Rathbride House to the course, though short, would take a little while. If she got to pay a visit to the course three times during the trip she would be lucky.

Their first visit next morning was to the stables where the St. George horses were kept. Mick Murphy nodded in a friendly fashion to Honnie – he was spending most of his time now up in Kildare. The other groom from Tyrone, Rory Costello, smiled at her.

"It's good to see you here, ma'am," said Mick. "You're a sight for sore eyes."

To be called 'ma'am' by Mick seemed strange, and she knew from the twinkle in his eye that he said it deliberately.

"And it is very good to be here and see you too, Mick," Honnie said with a straight face.

They both smiled at each other.

"I trust you like it up here in Kildare?" said Honnie.

"I do, very much," said Mick. "Now, would you like to see Master Christopher's latest purchase?"

Honnie took a deep breath and gave herself to the warm pungent smells of horses and stables, the noises of horses moving and whickering, the feel of a horse's soft mouth under her hand. This was a world she had missed even more than she had imagined. She spent a very happy few hours, getting to know the horses, talking to Mick and Rory, listening to Christopher discussing the merits of each animal and giving her own opinion of them.

In the afternoon they set out for the race course. Lizzie

was very excited, having never been to the races before.

Not long after they arrived Denis Daly, Christopher's oldest and closest friend and witness at his wedding, hailed them and greeted them warmly.

"It's good to see you, Honnie," he said, shaking her hand. "I fancy you don't get to a racecourse very often nowadays, so you must enjoy yourself."

"I intend to," said Honnie. "And now that Christopher has a house and stables here I hope to come more often."

"And this is?" said Denis, smiling down at a tongue-tied Lizzie.

"Lizzie," said Honnie. "And this is her very first time at a race meeting."

"Why don't I walk around with you and Lizzie, and we can talk about some of the sights?"

He waved his hand around the span of the racecourse and explained there were a number of different courses within the main course, some long, some short. He told them about the lodges and stables around the course, and the people who owned them. Of course Honnie knew all this from her previous visits. He showed them horses lining up for a race which was about to start and he and Honnie discussed the merits of the different animals. He chose one horse, she chose a different one. He stayed with them to watch the race. Honnie's choice won. Altogether it was an enjoyable experience. Then he had to go to meet some friends.

After he left Lizzie spoke for the first time. "Now there's a real gentleman," she said

They didn't see much of Christopher. From time to time he would snatch a few minutes and come and ask them if they were all right, if they were enjoying themselves? And he would be gone again.

On their second visit to the course Honnie looked around for Christopher and saw him in animated conversation with two men. She started walking towards them.

"Christopher!" she called. "Christopher!"

He turned round and looked somewhat embarrassed.

She reached the group and stood waiting to be introduced.

"This is Honnie," Christopher said lamely.

One man gave a perfunctory nod, the other averted his head and looked into the distance.

Honnie drew herself up. "I can see I'm intruding," she said, and turned on her heel. "Come, Lizzie. The next race is due to start."

Later in the afternoon they were standing at the edge of the course, waiting for the last race to start, when they overheard the same two men talking.

"He's certainly very knowledgeable about horses, St. George, but in many ways I think he's an arrogant young pup," said one.

"Mind you, he can be entertaining company," said the other, "but yes, I'm inclined to agree with you. And as for his domestic arrangements!"

"Scandalous," said his companion, as they walked up the course.

Honnie could barely contain herself with rage.

"Talk of *arrogance!*" she said. "Of all the arrogant, overbearing ill-bred people! They may talk like gentlemen, but gentlemen they are not! They are just ignorant *bostoons*. Oh, how I would like to give them a piece of my mind! "

She continued to fulminate for quite a few minutes until Lizzie managed to distract her by telling her that the race had started.

"It would seem that I am not a respectable person," she said to Christopher later in the evening, back in Rathbride House. "Or maybe I'm just invisible."

Christopher hesitated. "People see things differently," he said. "There will always be those who see our relationship as unorthodox – you know that."

"Because they don't know we are married," said Honnie. "And you won't tell them."

"They wouldn't believe it," said Christopher. "If I told them that we were married by a Catholic priest, they'd say it's an illegal union, and look even more scornfully at you."

Later, in bed that night, Christopher put his arm around Honnie.

"I'm sorry you've been so much upset. I wish I could change things, but I can't. We love each other. We both know we are married. These people don't matter. If they choose to look at us awry, that's their problem, not ours, and I'm not going to worry about them, and you shouldn't either. Our domestic affairs are none of their concern."

And with that Honnie had to be satisfied.

Despite everything, Honnie and Lizzie managed to enjoy the rest of their stay. Lizzie found the whole scene exciting, and Honnie found Lizzie's enthusiasm infectious.

Chapter 34

Christopher's first visit when he got back to Galway was to his father.

"He was as I left him," Christopher told Honnie later that evening. "Sitting at his desk, worrying about money. We're fending off the the bailiffs all the time."

"I feel very sorry for him," said Honnie, "but what can be done?"

"An idea has been running through my mind," said Christopher. "You'll probably think it's a mad idea, but I can see no other solution. I think we should have an auction ... of some of the contents of the house, the furniture, our stock of animals."

Honnie looked at him in consternation. "Yes, I do think it's a mad idea," she said. "And I don't believe that your father will entertain it for a minute."

"Drastic problems need drastic solutions, "said Christopher. "Yes, Honnie, I know you think I'm being cruel. But I can't think of any other answer. There is no question but that something has to go."

He came back from Tyrone next evening pale-faced and shattered.

"Before you ask, Honnie, of course he didn't like the idea. He said I was raving mad. I tried to make him see the facts. I reminded him that our creditors are pressing hard for payment."

He saw his father in his mind's eye, the horrified expression on his face. For a moment he had seemed to lose his breath altogether. Then he roared. "I have never heard such utter nonsense in my life. It would take you to come up with an idea like that. Sell the household furniture, sell the stock that I've spent a lifetime rearing? Sell the furniture! And how, may I ask, are we to live here in an empty house? Sleeping on the floor? Eating with the servants in the kitchen?"

"Something has to be done," said Christopher to Honnie. "I am not suggesting that we sell everything. But there is much that could be sold. Mother, God bless her, could never resist an auction. The place is cluttered with furniture. We could afford to sell some of it. We also have a great number of animals on our lands, and father's skills as a stockbreeder are well known all over the county. People will come for the stock alone. We can always breed more."

Honnie thought of the tall, proud, reserved man of whom she had been in awe when she worked in Tyrone.

"Your poor father, Christopher. He always gave his animals so much time and attention, so much love. It would kill him to lose them."

"It will hurt him deeply, but if we don't find some way of pacifying our creditors, we could soon be in really serious trouble Will he agree to the auction? Eventually, I hope."

But his father's last words hadn't been very encouraging.

"And I am supposed to stand there and see everything I've worked so hard on over the years being offered up for the delectation of the gentry of County Galway, who will only have come to gloat over our situation? *Never!*" His voice was quivering with indignation and outrage. "Now get out. And let me hear no more of such lunatic ideas."

But, as the demands on the estate became more and more importunate through the early months of 1840, Christopher continued to push the idea of an auction.

In May of 1840 Honnie had another baby, a girl. She was to be called Elizabeth.

William was not impressed.

"*Another* girl! Where are all the boy babies?"

Over the summer it seemed that Arthur was becoming more willing to at least consider the idea of an auction.

"Finally he's agreed." Christopher told Honnie one November day. "The demands have grown more and more vociferous, and over the last month a bailiff has found his way to the front door four times. But Father has also said he wants no hand, act or part in it. I just hope he doesn't change his mind."

On the 9th of November 1840, Christopher brought home the latest edition of the *Tuam Herald*.

"Read it for yourself," he said to Honnie. "It's really going to happen."

Honnie read it out: "'*Joseph & James Marshall, the*

Limerick auctioneers, are advising the public of an Important and Extensive Auction to be held in Tyrone House, the residence of Arthur F. St. George, Esq., in Co. Galway, on Wednesday, November 27th, and the days following ...' Why, Christopher, that's not much more two weeks away – how can you possibly have everything ready by then? '*It is to be an auction of Sheep, in calf Cows, Heifers, Fat Cows, Bulls, Household Furniture, Wine, Silver Plate, House Linen, Horses, Carriages, Wheat, Oats, Hay, Implements et cetera, et cetera ...*'"

At first it seemed that Arthur St. George had decided to ignore the forthcoming event. Tyrone buzzed with activity. Furniture was moved around, silver was laid out for viewing, wines were brought up from the cellars. Horses were groomed. Bulls, cows and sheep were brought into fields and paddocks close to the house where they could be easily inspected.

As the 27th of November grew nearer and preparation for the auction gathered momentum, Arthur grew more and more agitated.

Christopher came home in a black mood some days before the auction was due to be held.

"He says he can't let it happen, that he would be betraying my mother, his own father, the whole family, and everything that the St. George name once stood for in Galway, the respect in which it was held. He said he cannot allow our name to be held up to ridicule. He told me to call the whole business off." He buried his head in his hands and groaned. "I told him we can't *not* go through with it. The arrangements have all been made. The announcements have appeared in the papers. It must go ahead. And he said that it cannot go through without his permission, that he is still the owner of Tyrone, and the landlord of the Tyrone estates. He says he isn't going to change his mind."

The argument continued for a number of distressing days. Finally it was agreed that the auction would be postponed for the time being. Eventually, however, Arthur Sr. George was persuaded, not just by Christopher, but by close friends whose opinion he respected, that the auction was his only possible course. It opened almost a fortnight or so after the original date and lasted some weeks.

This time it was the *Limerick Chronicle* that Christopher brought home.

"This will break Mr. St George's heart," said Honnie to Lizzie in the kitchen. She read aloud: "'*The high repute in which Mr. St. George had been held for years as a stockbreeder, attracted large attendances each day . . . Top ewes in lamb, which were really superior, sold at an average of 67s. each; the two-year-olds 58s. each; the year and a half olds 34s. each; the lambs 31s. each. Among the horned stock were some fine specimens of the old country Limerick longhorns, beside many experimental crosses . . . People came from the counties of Galway and Mayo, including all the celebrated sheep breeders of these districts. Among those who attended were many well-known Galway names – Thomas Redington of Kilcornan, John Martin of Tulira, the Dalys* of *Dunsandle, as well as the Blakes, Lynches, Lahiffs, Lamberts, Persses and many others.*'"

One person who was not seen at the auction was Arthur St. George.

Christopher met his father on the stairs, the day after

the auction was finally completed.

"Well, Father, we've have raised enough to quieten our creditors, for a while at least," said Christopher. "And we are not sitting in an empty house. Most of the old familiar things are still around us. We have most of our silver. We can enjoy a glass of wine and the unsold lots can be put up for auction again in the springtime."

"You've had your way," said his father. "I hope you're happy."

And he went into his study and closed the door.

"But Tyrone hasn't been emptied?" Honnie asked Christopher that evening.

"Quite a lot remains, enough for my father and the family to live still in relative comfort. And I've kept back some of my father's stock. He can start breeding again."

"At his age, Christopher, I can't imagine he will have the heart," said Honnie.

In November Louisa St. George married Colonel Bingham of the 60th Rifles. And all around the country the building of workhouses went ahead apace.

Chapter 35

On the morning of March 6th, 1841, Honnie was once more pregnant and feeling distinctly out of sorts. She waved goodbye to Christopher, who was setting off in high good humour to meet some friends in Galway City. But when he came home in the evening, he was white-faced and clearly distressed. When Honnie asked him what was the matter, his answers were evasive.

"There's been a bit of trouble over in Tyrone," he said.

"Trouble," said Honnie. "What kind of trouble?"

"Nothing that need concern you," he said.

"Of course it concerns me," said Honnie, "if it concerns you."

As Christopher's account of the happenings in Tyrone unfolded, Honnie's stomach churned. It didn't sound like a bit of trouble, it sounded like a lot of trouble. It seemed that earlier that day a man had been attacked on the St. George lands by five men. They had threatened him with a gun, beaten him badly and left him for dead.

"But he was found and taken into a nearby house where he was cleaned up and cared for," said Christopher. "His name is Heathers, and he works for the Ordnance Survey Office in Dublin."

"How badly hurt is he?" asked Honnie.

"Mr. Hynes, the medical attendant, doesn't think he has any broken bones," said Christopher. "But he was badly beaten and some of his injuries are quite severe. Mr. Hynes thinks he is in a fair way to recovery. I certainly hope so."

"And the men who attacked him – dare I ask – were they some of your bullyboys?" asked Honnie. Like most landlords, Christopher hired people to protect the estate and its people.

Christopher bristled. "Those men are there for the protection of Tyrone House and the people who live in it, and the lands around it. If we didn't have them we would have thieves and vagabonds robbing us left, right and centre, and bailiffs knocking at our doors day in, day out. How would you like that? How do you think my father would cope with it?"

"And their idea of protection is for five men to beat up one man and leave him lying there senseless, a man who wasn't attacking anybody, who meant no harm, who was only doing his job?" said Honnie.

"They didn't know he was from the Ordnance Survey Office," said Christopher, his voice rising.

"Well, they should have found out who he was before they beat him up," said Honnie. "Who did they *think* he was? There is no reason on earth why it would be necessary to beat him! May I ask the names of the men who were doing the protecting?"

"*That is more than enough!*" said Christopher furiously. "And no, you may not ask the names of the men. You don't need to know."

"But I could make a good guess," said Honnie.

"*Guess away!*" said Christopher savagely. "I've told you, Honnie, I had nothing to do with this attack. Not for the world would I have wished any harm on Heathers. I only wish the young fool had come to me before he started doing his survey, and I could have told my men to watch out for him. I hope to God he doesn't die."

Honnie's words followed him as he turned to go out the door.

"Because then it would be murder, wouldn't it?"

The following morning, when the police called Christopher and his three friends in for questioning, Honnie could feel the blood chilling in her veins.

"Christopher, I'm frightened. Where are they going to take you? What are they going to do to you?"

"Honnie, you need not worry about me. I can assure you they are not going to clap me in gaol," Christopher said coldly. "As I told you already, I had nothing to do with the attack on Heathers. I was with Denis Daly and Edward Staunton in Galway town. I only heard about it when I called into Tyrone on my way home. The police are simply looking for information and, understandably, since the men carrying out the attack were in my hire, they want to talk to me."

He was only gone for a few hours, but it seemed a very long time to Honnie.

"So, what happened?" she demanded when he returned.

"As I thought, they wanted information about the men who work with me, and who generally accompany me through our demesnes, and who are armed for my protection. The police wanted their names and addresses They are being summoned to appear in Kinvara before local magistrates, on Tuesday next."

"And how is Mr. Heathers?"

"Well enough, it seems, to describe the circumstances of his attack. He said that being a stranger, and only four or five days in the county, he was ignorant of whose land he was on at the time, but he believes he would know the faces of the men who assaulted him if he could see them."

"So what happens now?" asked Honnie

"There was circumstantial evidence against one man in particular and he was brought to Mr. Heathers' bedside so that he might identify him, which he did, saying that this was the man who assaulted him, and the man who carried the gun. That man is now in Galway gaol."

"Who is he?" asked Honnie. "What's his name?"

"His name would mean nothing to you," said Christopher. 'He's not from these parts. I only hired him a few months ago."

The next day, Sunday, was a brisk, bright day and Honnie decided she needed to get away from Drumacoo for a while. She would pay a visit to Maree. It was a beautiful spring day. Leaving Mary with Lizzie, she packed an excited William and Anne into the pony and trap and set out for Maree.

She was met with a gathering of people sitting all around the big kitchen. Maureen and Thady were there, and Joseph. Bridget had come visiting with her two boys. Tom had come home to visit his family and called in to see how Maureen and her brothers were getting on. It seemed the fine weather had brought everyone out.

It was the first time Honnie had brought William and Anne with her. Very young children are unaware of divisions between their elders. Anne, in Honnie's arms, looked at Maureen with mild curiosity. William looked trustingly up at her, all blue eyes and tumbling dark hair, and smiled. Honnie could see Maureen melting.

For her part, Honnie admired Bridget's baby boys and Bridget said William and Anne were a really handsome pair. They were exchanging their experiences of motherhood and childrearing when, from the far side of the kitchen, Honnie could see Father Tom approaching her.

"Poor Heathers," he said without preamble. "A sorry business."

"Very sad indeed," Honnie agreed. "We are all very distressed about it."

Maureen, moving about the kitchen with tea and scones, overheard their conversation. "Not half as distressed as that man's mother, I should imagine," she said. "I hear she's a widow woman. Was Christopher St. George about when it happened?"

"Of course not," said Honnie indignantly. "He's the most upset of all about it. Apparently Heathers was from the Ordnance Survey Office, but nobody seems to have known he was coming. He just appeared."

"But it was some of Christopher's bullyboys who carried out the attack, wasn't it?" said Maureen.

"It was some of his men, yes," said Honnie, remembering that she had used the words 'bullyboys' herself to Christopher. "But he never said they were to go about beating up people. They were hired only to stop people straying onto St. George lands."

"People like bailiffs and process-servers," said Maureen.

"He wouldn't be the first landlord and he certainly won't be the last to chase off bailiffs and process-servers!" Honnie snapped. "And anyway we've been told that Heathers is in a fair way to recovery."

"We must hope that he will be fit and well soon," said Father Tom. And he turned the conversation to enquire about their father. "Is your father still working in Limerick, Maureen?"

"Yes, he seems to have taken a great fancy to the place and is getting plenty of work. But I think part of it is that he can't bear coming home and my mother gone. And, of course, in Limerick he doesn't have to listen to jokes about Honnie and Christopher. Then he's not really a letter writer. It's five or six months now since we had a letter from him."

"I might be in Limerick myself soon," said Father Tom. "I could see if I can find him. Do you have any address for him?"

"The last time he wrote he was working on a house belonging to people called Holahan, just this side of Limerick," said Maureen. "I'm sure he's gone from them now, but they might know where he is to be found. I have that letter somewhere, if I can find it."

She was still searching for it when Honnie was leaving, but she stopped to bid them goodbye, giving the children a kiss and a hug each – and a biscuit.

When Tuesday came a number of the men who had been summoned to appear before the magistrates in Kinvara could not be found.

Each day Honnie asked Christopher if there was any news about Heathers. His replies were usually quite terse.

"He seems to be doing all right," he would say.

But by Wednesday, when she asked him she saw that Christopher was seriously worried.

"He seemed to be doing well enough some days ago, but now the news doesn't sound so good. It seems he has contracted an infection."

By Thursday it was clear that Mr. Heathers was sinking fast.

"I'm afraid his condition took a turn for the worse last night," Christopher told Honnie on Friday evening. "He died this morning, in Kinvara. It's a sad business. He was very young and had just started his career with the Ordnance Survey Office."

"But he *shouldn't* have died, he *needn't* have died," said Honnie. "It just makes me mad – the sheer heartlessness of it all! What must it be like to see your son leave you full of health and vigour, and then to hear a few weeks later that he is dead? And what's going to happen to his mother now?"

"She has one other son," said Christopher. "As I said, it's a sad business. But I can assure you that I will try in any way I can to make it up to Mrs. Heathers."

"You can't bring back her son," said Honnie.

"Oh for God's sake, Honnie!" said Christopher, and left the room.

Honnie heard the front door slam.

An inquisition was held the following Saturday morning, before Thomas Walsh, one of the coroners for Kinvara, and twelve jurors.

"And on the basis of information gathered, two more men were committed to Galway Gaol, to join the man already identified by Heathers," Christopher told Honnie. "Their trial was postponed, but they are to stay in gaol until they appear before the next Assizes. The other men involved haven't been found but the investigations are still ongoing."

No charges were ever brought against Christopher. He offered Mrs. Heathers money by some way of compensation, but she wouldn't hear of it. She said she wouldn't accept any money that came from where her son was so brutally murdered.

She did, however, consent to having his body buried in the churchyard nearby.

Christopher refused to talk about Heathers' death.

"It happened, and it shouldn't have happened. All the talking in the world won't bring him back."

He left the house early most days and had little to say when he came home.

Honnie lay awake night after night, going over all the events of the past couple of weeks, thinking of Heathers' mother, saying a prayer for her, and trying to imagine how she herself would feel if she lost William in some such way in the years to come.

She was very happy to see Father Tom walking up the

lane to the house one sunny April afternoon.

He told her that he had indeed gone to Limerick and managed to find her father.

"He was recovering from a cold, and he certainly had a bit of a cough He looked a little tired, I thought. But he is getting plenty of work and seems to be reasonably content."

It was Honnie who brought up the subject of Heathers' death.

"I can't get him out of my mind," she said. "It should never have happened. And Christopher and I are at odds about it. Imagine saying goodbye to your son as he goes off on his first job, and then hearing just a few weeks later that he is dead! When I try to talk to Christopher about it, he says he doesn't want to discuss it any further."

"Christopher may not want to talk about it, but I think you should know that many other people are talking about it and as gossip whirls round the county the stories grow and grow. There are some who say that Christopher had a part in the actual attack himself."

"Christopher attack somebody brutally like that! No! He can be hot-tempered and he can let fly, but beat somebody up like that? Never!"

"Honnie, I don't believe that Christopher is capable of such brutality. And I also happen to know that he was in Galway the whole day that Heathers was attacked, because I've spoken to people who saw him there. But idle gossip spreads its wings and pays no heed to the truth. I'm sorry to have to say this, Honnie, but Christopher doesn't come well out of this episode. He was not personally involved in the attack, but his men were."

As Tom was leaving, he turned back.

"Christopher should be more careful about the men he chooses to hire," he said.

After Father Tom's visit, Honnie found herself looking at people and wondering if they had heard the rumours. When Lizzie came back from an Easter visit to her family, Honnie thought she was more subdued than usual. Heathers had died in Kinvara, and Lizzie's family lived near Kinvara. She must surely have heard any stories that were going around. She decided to take the bull by the horns.

In the kitchen Lizzie was cleaning up after breakfast.

"Are the people in Kinvara saying that Master Christopher killed Mr. Heathers?"

Lizzie was taken by surprise and for a few moments she was shocked into silence.

"I told them it wasn't true," she said then. "I told them I'd seen Master Christopher with my own eyes going off to Galway early that morning. I told them ..."

She seemed about to cry.

"Don't, Lizzie, I didn't mean to upset you," said Honnie. "I just wanted to find out if it is true that these awful rumours are being passed around."

Over the next months it was clear that the rumours were spreading far and wide. In Tyrone Arthur St. George saw them as yet another blow to his crumbling world. Christopher's sisters and younger brother were predictably appalled, and deeply worried about the effect on their father.

Finally, after a night's drinking with Denis Daly and Edward Staunton in Galway, Christopher came home and began to talk. Honnie suspected that Denis had told him he should do so.

"Poor Heathers," he said, as he sat at the kitchen table, looking down into the full wineglass in his hand, twirling it idly round. "Of course it was a terrible thing to happen. Of course everybody is very upset. I am upset. And apparently it is largely my fault, or so my sisters seem to think. Anne has assured me that she doesn't believe that I was involved in the attack. She just thinks trouble always follows in my wake, whatever that means. And you too seem to hold me responsible. I repeat, I wouldn't for the world have wished any injury on the poor man."

"Christopher, I don't for a moment believe that you were involved in the attack," said Honnie. "But ..."

"But what?" said Christopher. "The men behaved atrociously, misled I believe by one of their number whom I only hired recently. But they never intended to murder Heathers, just give him a good fright. It wasn't the beating that killed him. At first it seemed that he was going to recover. He died from an infection that got into his wounds."

"Christopher, they didn't just give him a beating to frighten him, they gave him a bad beating and left him there for dead," she said gently, reaching out across the table to take hold of his hand. But he pulled away angrily. "Your men didn't care whether he lived or died. And – I don't like saying this – the fact is that while you may not have been part of the attack, people are going to feel that you are responsible because you hired the men who carried it out."

"Honnie, do you think I don't know that?" Christopher

snapped. "When I wake up in the morning, it's the first thing I think about. When I meet a group of friends on the street, or at a race meeting, or in Kilroy's Hotel, they fall silent when they see me coming. I wish to God it had never happened. But nothing I can say or do can bring the young lad back."

She reached out to put her arms around him, but he shook himself free.

"I'm going to bed," he said.

And he seemed to sleep soundly, with his back firmly turned against her.

Then, early one morning at the end of June, there was a knock on the door of the house in Drumacoo. When Christopher opened it, he found the caller was Denis Daly, newly down from Dublin.

"Denis! I'm not used to seeing you at this hour of the morning," said Christopher. "What brings you here?"

"I think you should see this," said Denis, without stepping inside.

He was holding a copy of a London paper, the *Morning Chronicle.*

He started to read. "'*Mr. St. George of Tyrone House, in the County of Galway, was arrested on a charge of inciting persons in his employment to an outrage that ended in the death of the late Mr. Heathers, an officer engaged in the ordinance survey of Ireland …*' The story has since been copied by the *Tuam Herald* and the *Dublin Monitor*. I can't tell you how sorry I am to bring you such news, but I felt you had to be told."

Christopher grabbed the paper from Denis's hands. As he read his face grew thunderous.

"They are accusing my *father* of causing Heathers' death!" he said furiously. "They are saying he's been *arrested*! Where do these people get hold of such stories? How *dare* they print such rubbish! I must go to my father straight away."

In Tyrone someone else had brought them a copy of the *Morning Chronicle*, and the house was in an uproar. Arthur had already heard the news, and was incensed, fulminating at length about newspapers and newspaper men, talking about legal action against the papers in question.

At the beginning of July, Arthur sent a letter to the *Chronicle*, decrying a "*most foul, malignant, and unfounded attempt to injure my character, and that of my family* ..." He said he was inclined to believe the paragraph in question was furnished by conspirators.

At the end of July the *Morning Chronicle* published a lengthy apology. Christopher brought home a copy of the paper.

The article read:

"In the *Morning Chronicle* of the 28th of June last, appeared an article in which it was falsely stated that Mr. St. George, of Tyrone House, in the County of Galway, was arrested on a charge of inciting persons in his employment to an outrage that ended in the death of the late Mr. Heathers, an officer engaged in the ordnance survey of Ireland ... an article in which other injurious and unjustifiable imputations were thrown out against that gentleman. Mr Heathers was no doubt murdered on the demesne of Mr. St. George, but the statement that Mr. St. George himself was arrested for inciting the

perpetration of the murder, is utterly without foundation. In the *Chronicle* of the 2nd of July we inserted a communication from the correspondent who furnished us with the original statement, in which it was admitted that the statement was unfounded, and he added that it was his impression that every member of Mr. St. George's family was clear of the most remote participation in the outrages.

We owe to Mr. St. George all the atonement we can offer for the wrong he has sustained at our hands, and we can only express our sincere regret that a statement so unfounded with regard to him, and at the same time so much calculated to wound his feelings, should ever have found its way into the *Morning Chronicle.* It cannot be supposed for a moment that, in inserting the statement, we were actuated by any malice towards Mr. St. George – indeed we never heard of that gentleman till we saw his name in the communication of our Irish correspondent."

Meanwhile, the three men accused of the crime had remained in gaol until they appeared before the Assizes in July, when their trial was postponed, and they were granted bail.

In August Honnie gave birth to another daughter, to be called Olivia.

William was disgusted. "Can nobody tell the person who brings these babies that we want a *boy baby*?" he said.

In Tyrone House, Arthur St. George was still writing letters of complaint to the *Morning Chronicle*.

"He just won't let go of it," said Christopher. "He can

think of nothing else, nor talk of anything else. He is not satisfied with the apology published in the paper. He wants to know who wrote this libellous story And he looks terrible. He won't leave Tyrone. He can't go anywhere, he says, because he would see his disgrace in the eyes of everyone he met."

Finally, in the middle of September, the Irish correspondent of the *Morning Chronicle,* who had been responsible for the original story, sent a long and grovelling apology to the paper:

"As the writer of the article in question, I can truly vouch that I am personally unacquainted with Mr. St. George, and free from any influence which might bias me against him. My letter was written in a hasty moment, after hearing the rumours that were afloat, and sent to the post before there was time for revision or reflection. It was one of those heedless faults, to which persons, even the most wary, who are engaged in this desultory kind of writing, are so liable. I have never since ceased to regret it, nor omitted an opportunity of repairing it, as far as it lay within my power to do so.

I have also to state, in the most solemn manner, that as it was written and sent forward without premeditation, it was not done with the privity of, or in concert with, any other person.

I freely acknowledge that I have been guilty of great and culpable precipitation: but anything like a feeling of personal ill-will I utterly disclaim ..."

His apologies, he went on to say, were voluntary and "not extorted by a threat of prosecution, or by the apprehensions that such a measure might be resorted to; or by any dread of personal consequences to myself, but

solely prompted by what I considered to be due to truth and to the feelings of a gentleman whom I felt that my rashness had wronged."

It was unfortunate that this apology was published in the *Chronicle* four days after Arthur St. George suffered a severe stroke. He was told about the apology, but nobody was ever sure that he understood.

The three men who had been gaoled in connection with Mr. Heathers' death and had been given bail in July, could not be found when they were due to appear in court in September. They had vanished.

"I have heard it said that they managed to escape to America," said Honnie. "I can't imagine that they managed to do that all on their own. They must have had help. I wonder who could have helped them ..." And she looked Christopher straight in the eye.

He looked back at her blank-faced.

Chapter 36

Just before the Christmas of 1841 came the news that Bartley Kane had died as a result of an accident. He had been up high on scaffolding, painting a wall in a house that was almost completed, when he had some kind of a turn and had fallen thirty feet onto a stone floor. He never recovered consciousness. His body was brought back to Maree for burial. It was just over six years since his wife, Mary, had been lowered into the grave where he now joined her.

Honnie went over to his burial in Ballinacourty. Christopher came with her. Honnie hadn't seen her father since he left Maree some days after her mother's funeral.

She and Christopher stood together on the edge of the crowd but apart from them. Like the day on which her mother was buried, it was a raw, cruel day.

Her last memory of her father was his anger. She had always been much closer to her mother, but she had loved him, and she knew that despite all their differences he had loved her.

She knew that he had loved her mother dearly, and had worked hard to provide for his family, even when work took him away from home for so many long periods. She knew that he sent money to Maureen from time to time. She could even understand that, after her mother's death, he preferred to be away from home where everything reminded him of her. And. as Maureen had said, he also wanted to be away in an anonymous place, where he wouldn't have to listen to remarks and ridicule about herself and Christopher.

She wept for him, and for herself.

In 1842 Honnie and Christopher had a second son, to be called James. They now had two sons and four daughters.

"I told the person who brings the babies that you wanted a brother," said Honnie to William. "So now are you happy?"

"Well, it doesn't matter any more, Mama," said William, "because myself and Niall Burke are best friends now and we can go exploring together. It will be a long time before James is big enough to play with me, and by then I'll be too big to play with him."

That year also saw the founding of *The Nation,* by Charles Gavan Duffy, Thomas Davis and John Blake Dillon. Joseph came over to see his new nephew and brought Honnie a copy. He was getting somewhat disenchanted with Daniel O'Connell, who had been his hero.

"O'Connell may have got us Catholic Emancipation," said Joseph, "but his speeches aren't going to get us Repeal of the Union."

Christopher came into the kitchen, where Honnie and Joseph were enjoying a cup of tea. He was fond of Joseph and smiled at him warmly.

He asked him how he was getting on working in the oyster beds. Some months earlier Honnie had told Christopher that Joseph needed to find work. Christopher had arranged for Joseph to work on the St. George oyster beds in Ballinacourty.

Joseph told him that he found the work interesting, and he was happy to have it.

"I much prefer working on the oyster beds than going out in a boat fishing," he said.

Christopher joined them at the table and Honie poured him a cup of tea.

"I heard what you said about Dan O'Connell," he said to Joseph. "And no, I don't think he can get the Union repealed. But then few politicians ever get us what we want. Myself, I find horses and horse-racing far more rewarding than politics."

Christopher was more concerned about a new law that was passed by the English Government.

"It makes landlords responsible for paying the poor rates on land valued at under £4 per annum. This is going to fall heavily on landlords like us," he said, "and indeed on most of the landlords here in the west of Ireland, where property is highly subdivided. I don't know how we are going to meet these demands."

Honnie had her hands full with five young children and a small baby. William grew hardy and more adventurous with every passing day. He often went off exploring the countryside with Niall Burke, and sometimes as the day drew to a close she or Nóra would have to search the fields and lanes before they found them. Nóra worried, and Honnie worried also, but she had some sympathy for the boys. She had wandered the countryside herself as a child, and she knew how easy it was to forget time, finding something new or interesting in a hedge or a pond or a running stream, a rock pool, a fox thicket, until suddenly you noticed that night was falling and everything was getting dark. But she worried about William running wild, without learning, or discipline.

Anne was very different from William, a serious, thoughtful girl. She liked to be with Honnie in the kitchen and she loved it when she allowed her to help in the cooking. She had a special stool she stood up on so that she could see what Honnie was doing. She had turned into a real little mother, helping to mind the smaller ones, and sometimes Honnie felt guilty about what she expected of her.

Arthur St. George got frailer by the day, cared for by his daughters, Anne and Harriet, and by a faithful servant, Mattie, who had been with him since he was a boy. Christopher had got the estate carpenter to fashion a kind of wheelchair so that he could be taken out into the gardens on good days.

"But he can't talk to us any more," said Christopher. "He can make sounds, but he can't make sense. And we can see that he finds this very frustrating. He gets very angry."

This seemed a far cry from the man Honnie remembered – a tall, upstanding man, a man of dignity, proud of his standing in society.

"You wouldn't recognise him if you saw him now,

Honnie," said Christopher. "It breaks my heart to seem him so failed. He seems to be disappearing before my eyes. He doesn't go out much, but if he does go out, even to the gardens, he has to have somebody with him. He needs help with washing and dressing. He has to be persuaded to eat. He spends most of his days in his study, messing with old papers."

When he finally died, in the early days of January, 1844, it was a relief not only for him but for everyone in Tyrone, but the family was nevertheless shaken and sad.

"But of one thing I'm glad," said Christopher to Honnie, when he returned to Drumacoo after a visit to Tyrone some weeks after his father died. "That my father wasn't alive to hear about Arthur. It would have upset him. It seems my young brother, my only brother, has turned Catholic and married a woman called Maria Smith. Do you know her, Honnie?"

"I know of her," said Honnie. "Her mother was a Connor. The St. George men seem to fancy the Connor women. You will remember you once had a fancy for a Connor woman yourself?"

Chapter 37

By early March Christopher was talking about moving his family to Tyrone.

"I am master of Tyrone now. It's my house, my home, and I think that you and I should live there with our children."

Honnie's heart sank. She had often wondered what it would be like to be mistress of Tyrone, but now that it seemed a possibility she was filled with fear. She had grown to love her home in Drumacoo. She loved the house. She loved her garden. The more she thought about moving into Tyrone House, the more fearful she became. And she was six months pregnant. She told Christopher she didn't want to move.

"I don't think moving to Tyrone is a good idea, not just yet anyhow," she said. "Taking me and the children to live in Tyrone would be seen as totally unacceptable to most people. You must know that. I think most of the servants working there now would just look for other positions and leave. And whatever about servants, do you think for a minute that Anne and Harriet would welcome me there? Of course they wouldn't, nor could I blame them."

"You won't have to worry about Anne or Harriet," said Christopher. "Anne and Harriet are going to Italy."

"To Italy!" said Honnie. "Why on earth are they going to *Italy?*"

"Yes, well, I was flabbergasted, too, when Anne first told me. Of course it's something she has always wanted to do – she's always wanted to travel. But I was astonished to find that she's been planning this for some time. She says she wants to get away from Ireland. She's got the two thousand pounds that Father left her, and she believes this will support her for several years in Rome. And if it runs out she says she can always give English classes. It seems she has been in regular contact with some distant St. Lawrence cousins who live in Rome. I dimly remember them coming to visit many years ago. They were cousins of my mother. There was Caroline, and Jonathan, I seem to remember. Anne has been corresponding with Caroline for some time. She has said that Anne and Harriet can stay in their family house in Rome until they find accommodation."

"Anne had it all worked out!" said Honnie. "Who would ever have guessed?"

"She says she has had plenty of time to think about it," said Christopher. "And now *you* must think about moving to Tyrone, sooner rather than later."

He brought up the subject again some days later.

"Honnie, what is the matter with you? I thought you'd be pleased at the idea of moving to Tyrone. What's bothering you? It can't be Mrs. Smith because she's gone to live with her sister in Scotland. Mrs. Hunt has gone. It can't be Mr. Scott, because he's found a position in Dublin. He said he'd had enough of country life, and he felt a spell in the city would be more congenial to him."

"What about all the other servants?" said Honnie

"Truth to tell, many of the servants have already left to take up other positions," said Christopher. "With my father gone, and Anne and Harriet going, they felt the house was not the same."

"And I'd say the possibility that you might install me in Tyrone hastened their steps," said Honnie.

"That may be the case," said Christopher, "but I am master of Tyrone now. It is my home, and I have decided that you and I should live there and to hell with what people think. Drumacoo is simply not big enough for us. And Tyrone has gone sadly downhill in recent years. With nobody in charge the house is wide open to theft. The sooner we move in the better."

But Honnie found she still felt very anxious about the idea and as the weeks passed she produced various excuses for postponing the move, and Christopher got increasingly exasperated.

"Honnie, I'm listening to no more excuses. We will move in a week's time."

So on a bright May day, the family set out on the short journey from Drumacoo to Tyrone. They had intended to leave early in the morning but it was late afternoon before they eventually left. It wasn't just about gathering themselves together, it was about gathering all their belongings, all their bits and pieces together as well. The children were overexcited and ran around getting in the way of everything. Honnie had to say goodbye to

Nóra Burke and tell her that she would come and visit her soon. William promised Nóra's son, Niall, that they would still see each other often.

The children and Honnie and Lizzie travelled in one carriage. Behind them came another packed with the children's belongings, and the special keepsakes Honnie hadn't wanted to leave behind. There was the china she had chosen on her shopping trip to Galway, the brass candlesticks that always stood on her dresser in Drumacoo, the glass vase she had kept filled with daffodils that first spring.

As their carriage rumbled off Honnie looked back with sadness at the home she was leaving behind. She had been very happy there. Her children had been born there. Her eyes filled with tears, and her stomach churned. She was still fearful at the prospect of living in Tyrone. But this wasn't the time for dwelling on things.

Anne had the cat and three kittens in a basket at her feet. Lizzie had Olivia on her knee while Honnie held James. Mary and Elizabeth clutched their favourite dolls, having explained that the dolls couldn't travel on their own in the other carriage because they would be frightened and cry. There were blankets and coats and all sorts of oddments the children had picked up at the last minute, insisting they couldn't possibly be left behind. Altogether it was a very crowded carriage, and it was a very excited carriage, full of chatter and life.

Christopher rode along beside them, Fóidín running at the horse's side.

The children had only ever seen Tyrone House from outside – they had never been inside. They kept asking questions.

"Where are we going to sleep?" asked Anne.

"I don't know yet," said Honnie.

"Will we have a room of our own?" asked William.

"The rooms are so very big that the older five of you could sleep in one room."

"Will we be sleeping upstairs?"

"Probably."

"Can Fóidín sleep in our room too?"

"I don't think that's a good idea."

And on, and on.

As they drew nearer to Tyrone, Honnie remembered the girl who had walked up the driveway seventeen years ago. So much had happened since then. When the carriage rolled up outside the front door, she still felt like a nervous young girl.

People stood at the edge of the driveway. Christopher had dismounted from his horse ahead of them. He held his hand out to Honnie to help her from the carriage. As she stepped down, he stood tall, put his arm firmly around her, and faced the crowd.

"This is my wife," he said, "and these are my children. I expect you to give them a warm welcome."

Honnie held his hand tightly, stood straight and smiled up at him, and bubbles of joy and love soared up in her heart – and courage.

Her eyes scanned the assembled company. There were a lot of new faces and now she saw a few old ones. She saw Hannah, the housemaid who had shown her over Tyrone when she first came to work there, Seamus the kitchen boy who had so irritated her, now a married man with two children. There was Rory, the groom, whom she was accustomed to seeing in Kildare, and Mick

Murphy the head groom who now bade her welcome. She smiled at each of them in turn, and then turned her attention to the children who were clamouring to be allowed out of the carriage to see their new home.

Carrying James in her arms, with Lizzie following close behind, Honnie started up the steps towards the house. Christopher followed with the older children.

In the hall the children stood quietly. With so many strange faces, such grand surroundings, they were for once bereft of speech.

"Would you like some tea?" Hannah asked. "And I'm sure these young people wouldn't say no to a glass of milk, and maybe a bit of cake or some biscuits?"

"Thank you, Hannah, but no. It would spoil their supper. They can have some after."

Honnie looked around the hall and was gripped by a wave of sadness. This was not Tyrone as she had known it. This house seemed disordered, and down-at-heel. There were muddy footprints on the floors, and smears of mud on the walls – where passing dogs had brushed against them, Honnie decided, as Fóidín brushed past her, covered in the filth and detritus he had collected running alongside Christopher's horse on the journey from Drumacoo. Lady Harriet had never permitted dogs to come into the front of the house.

Correspondence was thrown in a random pile on the big mahogany table in the hall. In Honnie's time in Tyrone that table was always polished 'til it glowed and there was always a bunch of fresh flowers standing on it. The lovely oval mirror hanging above the table obviously hadn't been cleaned for months.

She looked around for Christopher and saw him

disappearing out the door again.

"I need to see to something in the stables," he said. "I'll be back shortly."

And he was gone.

The drawing-room spoke equally of neglect. The loose covers on the sofas needed to be washed. On two curtains the hems hung loose, on others the hooks holding them onto the rail had come adrift or fallen off. The ashes of an old fire were still in the grate. On a small table beside a corner sofa two glasses spoke of late-night drinks. The walls needed painting. The pictures were hanging crooked, and there were pale patches where pictures had obviously once hung.

Honnie turned to Hannah and smiled. She had always liked Hannah. She remembered her as a girl, but now she was a middle-aged woman, her dark hair turning grey, and plumper than she used to be.

"Things are very different to what they were when you were here," said Hannah, "but that's a long time ago. I've done my best. I spent most of the day trying to ready rooms for yourself and Master Christopher and the children, and there are not as many servants as there used to be. Mr. Scott is gone, and Mrs. Smith too. Mrs. Hunt went over a month ago."

"I suppose she told you all that under no circumstances would she be told what to do by an upstart like me?" said Honnie. "Never mind – you don't have to answer that question. As you can imagine, Hannah, this all seems very strange to me. I never really believed I'd end up living here. And I was so very glad to see your smiling face amongst the crowd. Now let's feed these children."

Two hours later, the smaller children were fast asleep on sofas in the drawing room while the older ones were getting restive, begging to be allowed explore the house, and pleading to be allowed stay up.

"Time to get them settled," said Honnie.

"We could only find one cot," said Hannah, "and that's a bit the worse for wear. It's a long time since we have had a baby or a small child in this house. And I didn't know if the others were in cots or beds."

"That's all right," said Honnie. "William will need a bed of his own but Anne and Mary can share a bed. And Elizabeth and Olivia too. We'll keep James in with us in our room. We only need a cot for him, and luckily I've brought one with me. So lead the way."

Carrying Olivia, Lizzie shepherded the older children in front of her, and Honnie followed with James in her arms.

Hannah brought them to a large square room on the second floor with decorative coving around the high ceilings, and evening sun streaming through two tall windows. Even with three beds, it didn't look crowded.

"I hope this is all right," said Hannah anxiously. "The bedding is a bit worn, but everything is newly washed and clean."

"It's perfect, thank you, Hannah," said Honnie. "Now we'll just have to hope they will go to sleep quickly."

They didn't. They jumped up and down on their beds, chased each other round the room, and tried to peer out the windows. William wanted Fóidín to sleep in the room. Anne wanted the cat and kittens. With each new demand, Honnie got more and more exasperated.

"Fóidín is sleeping in a special house out in the yard," she said. "The cat and her kittens are sleeping in a basket in the stables. Now go to sleep."

The children still hadn't settled down by the time Christopher returned. He threatened dire punishments if he heard another word and they took heed.

But when at last Honnie and Christopher retired exhausted to their bedroom, they heard a small voice.

"It's very dark. I'm frightened."

"Can you please leave the door open?" said another little voice.

"All right," said Christopher. "There, the door's open, but just a little. There is a lamp out on the landing. Now go to sleep. We'll be in the bedroom next door. And I don't want to hear another word from any of you."

Later, as they lay in bed with their arms wrapped round each other, Honnie thought that the day of which she had been so fearful had turned out to be one of the happiest days of her life. Christopher had acknowledged her as his wife, in his own house, in front of all his people. When he reached out for her she responded with all her heart.

The night passed quickly. With the first light of day came the sound of the children's voices next door, Anne's first as she woke up William. He was a heavy sleeper, and Anne probably had to prod him before he grumbled awake. Honnie soon heard Mary and Elizabeth chattering excitedly. It was only a matter of minutes before the four of them tumbled into Honnie and Christopher's bedroom, all talking at the same time, all asking questions. Olivia had come into her parents' bed during the night.

"Can we get dressed and explore the house?"

"Not on your own. Maybe later when you've had your breakfast."

"Where are we going to have breakfast?"

"Probably in the kitchen for today."

"Can we go out in the garden?"

"Not if it's raining the way it is now."

"Can we see the stables?" This from William.

"I'm sure your father will take you later."

"Can we ride the horses?"

"Ask your father."

"But he won't wake up," said Anne.

Under the blankets Christopher murmured something unintellligible.

"He's tired," said Honnie. "He'll show you everything when he wakes up. Now go back to your room and play for a while."

After they had gone Honnie shook Christopher by the shoulder.

"Come on, Christopher," she said. "This is all very strange for the children. It is very strange for me. I would feel very uncomfortable trying to find my way around things on my own. I need you with me. *Wake up!*"

Another shake.

Christopher rolled over and pulled himself up in the bed and gave her a hug.

"See! I'm awake, Honnie. I'll see you downstairs in two shakes of a ram's elder."

"What an inelegant expression!" said Honnie. "And a ram doesn't have an elder."

"That's the whole point, Honnie. It's a joke. But I

promise I'm getting up now and I'll be down straight after you. Oh, and by the way, Honnie, we have a new cook. Mrs Smith recommended her before she left. I knew you wouldn't want to arrive and find no cook in the kitchen. Her name is Mrs.Dunne."

"Without even consulting me? How could you?"

Children's voices drifted up from a distance. It was clear that they had decided to go exploring by themselves.

Quickly Honnie finished dressing herself, picked up a crying James, and went down to see what the others were up to. She met Hannah coming up the stairs.

"I was just coming to tell you that they're fine," said Hannah. "They're downstairs with Lizzie in the drawing room. Lizzie says she'll keep a close eye on them – and see they do no damage. Is that all right?"

"Of course it's all right," said Honnie. "Hannah, I realise that six children coming all at the one time is enough to daunt anyone, even somebody as kind as you. Things are very *trína chéile,* upside down, at the moment. It will take a bit of time, but I'm sure that with your help we will get everything sorted. You'll find Lizzie a tower of strength. Now I'm going to mind the children while Lizzie sees if she can find clothes for them. We put a lot of their clothes in one big bag so that we'd have them handy. When Master Christopher comes down he is going to introduce me to the new cook. Mrs. Dunne, isn't that her name? Then we'll see about breakfast for the children. Later, Hannah, when you have a bit of time to spare, maybe you and I could have a little talk, and you could tell me more about how things are in Tyrone, how many servants still work here, who does what, and which are the most pressing problems."

Down in the kitchen, Christopher introduced Honnie and Mrs. Dunne to each other.

"I'm afraid the kitchen isn't my area of expertise," he said. "But I'm sure you'll deal with it very well together, so I'll leave you to it."

And he was gone.

Mrs Smith was not very welcoming. She wasn't positively uncivil, but she certainly wasn't very civil. Honnie found some oatmeal and some milk, made a big pot of porridge, and sat the children down at the servants' table.

"Mrs. Dunne, I'm sorry we're taking over your space a little," she said. "I hope you don't mind. It just seems the easiest way to feed them this morning."

"Not at all," said Mrs. Dunne sourly.

While the children were eating, Honnie considered the kitchen. Mrs. Smith would have been appalled at the disorder Mrs. Dunne presumably had achieved in just a few weeks.

By the time the children had finished their breakfast the heavy rain of the early morning had turned into a warm clear day. Hannah took charge of Olivia, and Lizzie took the other four children out for a walk around the grounds.

Honnie carried a sleepy James and a mug of tea up to the drawing room and settled him down on a sofa. She pondered all the things that needed to be done. It might be a good idea, she decided, to write down some of her thoughts.

After some searching she found an old journal stuffed into the top drawer of a cabinet. Somebody had started writing a diary in the journal four years earlier, but quickly tired of it. Apart from the first four pages it was empty. She also found two corkscrews, pages from an old newspaper, a single glove, and various other odds and ends.

There was a small desk at one of the windows, equipped with a small bottle of ink and a pen. She sat down at the desk, dipped the pen in the ink and gazed out the window at the children playing a chasing game. She doodled a flower on the top of the first page.

She looked around the room and felt sad at its decrepitude.

She wrote "*Cleaning*" at the top the page. It felt so strange to be sitting in the drawing room of Tyrone House drinking tea and making lists. She looked out the window again. At least the gardens seemed to be in good order. Johnny O'Connor was clearly in command.

She thought about her recent encounter with Mrs. Dunne. Even if Mrs. Smith had recommended her, she didn't seem an ideal choice. It remained to be seen what her cooking was like.

She wrote "*Kitchen*" beside "*Cleaning*".

She began to make notes under each heading, pausing for long periods as her thoughts strayed.

Eventually she heard the children coming back from their walk, running up and down the big stairs, shrieking and laughing, delighting in all the space that Tyrone offered compared to their house in Drumacoo.

But they couldn't be let run riot. Some shape would have to be put on their days. She would need someone to help Lizzie.

She added "*Children*" to "*Cleaning*" and "*Kitchen*".

She wrote on until Hannah came in to ask if this would be a good time for their talk.

"Yes, of course. Sit down, Hannah." Seeing Hannah hesitate, she pointed to a chair near hers. "There."

"I'm not sure that would be appropriate," said Hannah.

"Oh, for heaven's sake," said Honnie. "We've know each other for nearly twenty years. Next you'll be calling me Mrs. St. George."

When Hannah said nothing, Honnie looked at her in disbelief.

"You're not serious, Hannah."

"The way it is," said Hannah, "since you are now the mistress of Tyrone, you have to be seen to be treated as the mistress. Servants never call their mistress by their first name. So I must call you Mrs. St. George."

For a few minutes Honnie was struck into silence.

"You know, Hannah, such thoughts never occurred to me. I suppose you are right, but not completely. You may call me Mrs. St. George when other people are around, but when we are alone together I must be Honnie to you as you will always be Hannah to me." And, standing, she gave Hannah a warm hug.

Hannah flushed, then hugged her warmly back.

"Now sit down and let's have a chat."

Hannah sat.

"It's been a long time, hasn't it, Hannah, since you and Bridget showed me over this house?"

"Almost eighteen years ago," said Hannah.

"You've been here longer than almost anyone else," said Honnie. "I'm looking to you to fill me in. But first of all I want to hear what you have been doing all these years. Is it true that you were Mrs. Hunt's second in command? I can't imagine her being an easy taskmistress."

"No, that she certainly wasn't," said Hannah. "It's been difficult these past few years. The master was poorly for so long and needed a lot of care and attention. Servants came and went. We were never quite sure from whom we should take orders. Mrs. Smith and Mrs. Hunt seemed to be always at odds with each other. Mr. Scott seemed to lose interest. Then he left. Mrs. Hunt fought with everyone. I had difficulty keeping a civil tongue in my mouth. I was so glad when she decided to leave. She said she 'deserved a decent, respectable house, and a mistress who appreciated a housekeeper with proper standards'."

"Poor Hannah," said Honnie. "You've had a very bad time. Mrs. Hunt was always difficult, but difficult and contrary as she was, she had standards. You must have learned a lot from her. In fact, I've been thinking that it would be an excellent idea for you to take on her duties here in Tyrone."

Hannah's eyes widened in surprise. "Really?"

"You've been here a long time. You are very familiar with the house, and you know all its ways. I would consider myself very lucky to have you as housekeeper to help me."

"Then I would like that very much," said Hannah. "But things are in such a bad way here nowadays that it won't be housekeeping the way Mrs. Hunt understood housekeeping."

"That's settled then," said Honnie. "I don't know what your wages are now, but I imagine they haven't been increased for quite a while. I'll be happy to pay you more, especially since you are taking on more responsibility. But we won't talk about that today. Now, tell me about the servants. How many have we got, and what do they do? Who do you have to help you in your work?"

"Well, I had two girls. Sally is willing enough. She's still with us. The other girl, Elinor, was just plain lazy. And when she heard Mrs. Hunt was going and that you might be coming with all the children, she left. She said her mother told her it wouldn't be good to work in such a place."

"I see," said Honnie. "Now tell me about Mrs. Dunne."

"I'd like to be able to say that she's a good woman," said Hannah, "but I don't think she is. And she isn't much of a cook either. Nor does she get on very well with the two girls who are working in the kitchen, Nelly and Abby. There's also a little scullery maid called Treasa. They're very young, and they haven't been here that long, but she seems to bring out the worst in them. Most of the servants who were any good have left."

"It won't be easy to get new servants," said Honnie. "But there must be people who need work. We should be able to find a few girls. But they'll probably be untrained and inexperienced. Would you be willing to train a girl or girls like that?"

"I'd have to feel they were willing to work hard and wanted to learn," said Hannah.

"And men servants?" asked Honnie.

"We have two footmen. George, who has been with us a long time, and a young man called Simon. We haven't had a butler since Mr. Scott left. Would Mr. St. George be in the way of hearing of someone?"

"I'll ask him," said Honnnie. "About the children, Hannah. I'd like to turn one room into a nursery, a room in which they can play and keep their toys, where somebody can mind them all in one place – it would make life a lot easier for everyone. Later on, it could also be used for tutoring. So far I've taught William and Anne the rudiments of reading and writing myself, and I've worked a little with Mary but they need someone who can teach them properly. Is there any particular room which you think might be suitable?"

"Well, there is the room which used to be a nursery when Master Christopher and his sisters and brother were growing up," said Hannah. "It's a big room, quite near their bedroom, a nice bright room. I haven't looked around it for a long time, but I remember there were quite a lot of toys, almost all for little girls, because Master Christopher had so many sisters, and only one brother."

"That sounds quite exciting," said Honnie. "Shall we go on a grand tour, then? And we'll start with the nursery."

The room, at first sight, was disapointing. It had been used as a dumping ground for the unwanted furniture and fittings accumulated in Tyrone House over many years. There were four tables, some chairs, a sofa, an old wardrobe, two clotheshorses, travelling trunks, a fire fender, fire irons, a hip bath, and much more. Every so often a sad, dejected doll appeared, usually missing an arm or a leg. But there were two exciting finds: a big, wooden rocking horse, which still worked, and a dolls' house, shabby and broken in places but not beyond repair.

The rest of the rooms, as Honnie had expected, were

disordered and untidy and grubby, especially the servants' quarters at the top of the house. She remembered her first night in Tyrone when she had felt so terribly lonely, and Kate Rooney had comforted her. She sat on the bed that was hers, and looked out the window, as she had looked all those years ago, at the lawns and flowerbeds of the Tyrone gardens, at the grey waters of Galway Bay, and the Aran Islands beyond.

She remembered Mrs. Hunt coming to look at the rooms and expecting everything to be in first-class order.

"Do you remember, Hannah, how fearful we used to be when we heard her footsteps on the stairs?" she said.

"As if I could ever forget," said Hannah. "Her footsteps and the sound of her voice struck terror into my heart."

The main bedrooms on the middle floor were not so bad, but then nobody had been using them for quite a while. Arthur St. George's bedroom had been left as it was when he died. It still smelt of death, a sickly sweet smell.

"The house is in a sad way, isn't it, Hannah?" said Honnie. "It feels unloved, uncared-for."

"It must look very different from when you last saw it," said Hannah. "But it's been going downhill for a number of years."

"We'll have to improve it, bit by bit," said Honnie. "But three adults and six children are quite an addition to any household. It will take some time for all of us to settle down. But we'll work together, take it one room at a time and do things slowly. There's no rush. But the one room on which I would like to make a start as soon as possible is the nursery. How would you feel about yourself and myself tackling it tomorrow morning?"

"The sooner, the better," said Hannah.

"And now I must talk with Mrs. Dunne," said Honnie.

Honnie could hear voices as she made her way down to the kitchen.

"A new mistress, is it?" said a male voice. "As I understand it she's been a mistress for a good many years now."

There was a burst of laughter,

As Honnie opened the kitchen door, she glimpsed a red-haired young man disappear up the back steps.

She looked at the disordered kitchen, took a deep breath, and smiled at Mrs. Dunne, and at Abby and Nelly standing nervously behind her. A very young little maid, all dark curls and big blue eyes, peeked out from the scullery. She looked as if she expected Honnie to gobble her up.

"As you probably know, Mrs. Dunne, I worked in this kitchen many years ago, and I have many memories of it."

Mrs. Dunne muttered some unintelligible response.

"I know that things have been difficult here in recent years. The kitchen has seen better days ..."

There was a decided sniff.

Honnie pretended not to notice, and ploughed on.

"So when did you come to work here, Mrs. Dunne?"

"About three months ago, when Mrs. Smith left."

"And where did you work before that?" asked Honnie pleasantly.

"In a gentleman's house in Limerick," said Mrs. Dunne. "I was with him for nigh on ten years. Then his wife died, and after a while he married again. Myself and the new mistress didn't see eye to eye. A friend of mine knew Mrs. Smith and heard about the position here."

"So you've really only been here a matter of weeks," said Honnie diplomatically and not very acciurately. "It takes time to settle into a new place. "You wouldn't have seen this kitchen looking as I remember it. I'm afraid it has gone down quite a bit over the years. I hope, Mrs. Dunne, that together we can bring it back to the way it once was."

Mrs. Dunne murmured something.

"First I want to talk to you about the meals," said Honnie. "Having nine more people to feed, two adults, three counting Lizzie, and six children, must seem a lot of extra work. But I don't expect you to cook anything fancy, just good plain food, for the present. The children will need to eat something soon. Hannah thought of giving them eggs and mashed potatoes. Would that be possible, do you think? Then there's dinner tonight. What were you thinking of cooking?"

Mrs. Dunne, it emerged, planned to cook leek and potato soup, roast lamb with whatever vegetables Johnny O'Connor could offer her from the garden, and apple pie.

"That sounds good," said Honnie. "I'll be looking forward to it. Tomorrow we'll try to plan things a little further in advance."

As she made to leave, she turned around.

"Tomorrow morning in the drawing room," she said, "I'm hoping to talk to everyone working in the house here, so that we can all get to know each other. So please let the rest of the staff know."

And she went out to find Lizzie and the children.

The girls were playing out on the lawn, and James was doing his best to join in. When they saw Honnie they raced towards her, all trying to tell her what a great day they were having. They had been in the stables and had seen a new foal. Their father had put each of them up on a pony called Sorrel and walked them in turn round the stable yard. They had been to see the ducks in the pond, and thrown food to them, and a stable boy had told them to be very careful of one duck who was very cross. She was called Jezebel, and if you went near her when she had ducklings she'd fly straight at you. They'd seen geese too, and they were even crosser than Jezebel. They'd talked to Johnny O'Connor, and he had given them some of the very first strawberries from the glasshouse. They'd been in the hayshed and jumped up and down on the hay, though Rory, one of the grooms said they wouldn't want to let Mick Murphy see them doing it, because he didn't like anybody messing with his hay.

When they stopped for breath, Honnie looked around,

"Where's William?" she asked.

"We left him in the stables with Mick Murphy," said Lizzie. "Hanging on Mick's every word. I didn't think you'd mind."

Honnie told Lizzie to take the other children inside and get them washed and cleaned up, while she fetched William. She found him still in the stable yard. He was a handsome little boy, straight-limbed and tall for his eight years. His dark hair needed a trim, and his blue eyes were fixated on Mick, as he listened intently to him discoursing on the merits of a bay filly that Rory was walking up and down.

"He has a sure eye for a good horse, this lad," said

Mick. "He's his mother's son. But he tells me he has never had a horse of his own. We'll have to remedy that. Master Christopher has asked me to look out for a suitable mount for him."

All the way back to the house William talked non-stop about horses, and the mount that would one day be his.

Honnie brought the children into the kitchen for their eggs and mashed potato. Mrs. Dunne clearly regarded it as an invasion of her space and quite obviously disapproved. The sooner the nursery was ready the better, Honnie thought.

The children played outside again all afternoon, but by half past five they were tired. By six o'clock they were washed and clean and all sitting around the dining-room table. It was to be a very special dinner, their first as a family together in Tyrone house.

But there was no sign of food. Honnie had not really expected it to appear on time, but as the hands on the clock on the wall went from ten minutes past six, to fifteen minutes past six, then twenty minutes past six, the children got more and more restive.

"I'm really hungry," said William.

"When are we going to eat?" asked Anne.

Christopher became quite irascible. "What is the wretched woman doing?" he asked.

"Don't be too hard on her," said Honnie. "She came to this house where she has been cooking for fewer and fewer people, and now, suddenly, she finds she has to cook for all of us. It will take her a bit of time to get used to it."

But ten minutes later even Honnie was getting

anxious.

"I'd better go and see what's happening," she said.

Downstairs she found a kitchen full of steam, and a flustered Mrs. Dunne, her voice raised in a torrent of recriminations, loudly cursing the range.

When she saw Honnie she wiped her hands on her apron, and drew herself up, her ample bosom quivering with exasperation, wisps of grey hair hanging down the sides of her face.

"I'm sorry, I'm sure, ma'am," she said. "Dinner will be a little late, through no fault of mine. I don't know what's wrong with the range, but whatever we do it just won't get hot. So the leg of lamb isn't cooked yet. It will take another good half hour. And I asked Abbey to peel some apples for me because I wanted to make the apple pie, and while I was making the pastry at the other end of the kitchen she peeled the apples and left them bare, even though I'm sure I told her to put them in some water with a drop or two of lemon juice. Now they're all brown. Then I asked Nelly to keep an eye on the potatoes – I always boil them before I roast them. But of course she forgot about them, and now they're overcooked, and I'll have to mash them. They let the soup boil over. The parsnips should have gone into the oven alongside the lamb. They have my heart broke, those two girls."

At this point Mrs Dunne ran out of breath.

"You tell us to do too many things at the one time!" Nelly burst out indignantly. "You sent us up to ready the dining room too, because there was nobody else to do it. You told us to set the table. We couldn't be down here if we were up there, could we?"

Mrs. Dunne glared at Nelly and cast her hands up in the air.

"Do you see what I have to put up with, ma'am? Common impudence!"

"I think you should all calm down a little, and I'll see what I can do to help," said Honnie.

She turned first to the range.

"I worked with this range for many years," she said. "It has good days and bad days, and this seems to be be a bad day. But usually I was able to get it to work."

She knelt down and riddled the ash grate, emptied the contents into nearby bucket where the ash was collected every day and riddled the grate again. She raked out more ash from the floor of the cooker under the pan. She put back the ash pan and opened the draught control. And the cooker began to light up.

"It has to be as clean as possible," said Honnie. "The air has to go round. That's what makes it work. Do you understand what I'm saying, Nelly? Abby?"

She eyed the pot of potatoes.

"If you mash them, with plenty of butter and pepper and salt, and a little milk, and put them in a pie dish in the oven they'll brown nicely. About the parsnips. Cut them in sticks, and put them around the meat."

"What about my apple pie?" asked Mrs. Dunne.

"The pie will be fine," said Honnie. "When it's cooked and sweetened and covered with pastry, nobody will know whether the apples were brown or not. Now what about the soup?"

"The soup is ready," said Mrs. Dunne.

"Then let's serve it," said Honnie. "Everybody is getting very hungry upstairs. I'll go up and tell them that the soup is on the way, and the lamb will be following soon."

In bed that night Honnie told Christopher about her plan to talk to all the indoor staff in Tyrone the following morning.

"And I will need you with me, Christopher. For a little while at least. I want them to see that you see me as mistress of Tyrone, that we are in this together, that we hope to make life here better for everybody."

The following morning Honnie was in the drawing-room long before 11 o'clock. She had made a note of what she wanted to say, had pen and paper handy in order to write down any special information. She felt very nervous indeed. But having Christopher beside her gave her courage.

The servants came in twos and threes. Mrs. Dunne was the last to arrive, with Abby and Nelly beside her. They gathered just inside the door, until Honnie told them to come into the room, so that she could see them properly, and they could hear what she had to say.

Christopher spoke first.

"This is Mrs. St George, the new mistress of Tyrone, and I want you to treat her accordingly." He smiled down at Honnie. "And I think she is possibly the very best mistress you could have, because she is familiar with Tyrone in all its aspects. If you have a problem, she will be able to see it from your point of view, not just her own. If you ever need help, I know she will be there for you. She will expect you to work hard, but she'll value your contribution and work even harder herself. Now, I think I will let her speak for herself."

Christopher moved sideways and Honnie moved forward. She let her eyes travel across all the people looking up at her. And she began speak.

"When I came here nearly twenty years ago this was a well-run house. I want to bring back some of the standards I learned to respect in my years here – standards of good housekeeping, good cooking, and good management. I want people who will help me to do this, people who are conscientious and diligent, hard-working and good-humoured. If people give me of their best, I will do my best to look after them." She smiled. "Just remember that because I was once a servant I am familiar with all the tricks servants can get up to. I worked hard here. I know how this house should be kept. Now it is rundown and shabby. It is never going to be as grand as it once was but I hope that, together, we can make it a great deal better than it is today."

She paused and surveyed them all again.

"I have met Mrs. Dunne our cook, Nelly and Abby the kitchen maids, and Nancy who works in the scullery. I know Hannah of old, and she is going to be our housekeeper. I've met Sally, who helps Hannah, and also John-Jo, the houseboy. Maybe the rest of you can introduce yourselves to me?"

George came forward first. He was middle-aged, of sturdy frame, with grizzled, greying hair, and a direct expression. Christopher had described him to Honnie as a reliable, solid man, who had come to Tyrone shortly after she had left. Then there was Simon, a very young footman, clearly nervous, and "as yet untrained", according to Christopher. Daisy was a housemaid who didn't look at all like a daisy, for she was well into middle age, with fuzzy greying hair, and a soft, shapeless billowy figure beneath her apron.

None of them had very much to say for themselves, beyond giving their name and position.

Honnie looked around the assembled company and asked if they had any questions. They were silent.

Then she spoke again.

"There is just one other thing I want to say before we go our separate ways. As most of you know, I once worked here, first as a scullery maid, and then as a kitchenmaid. There may well be some of you who feel uncomfortable working for me, unhappy working for me. If this is the way you feel I would prefer you to leave without further ado. I know quite a number of the servants have already left."

They all looked uneasy but stayed silent.

"Very well. You may go," she said. "I expect the very best from you."

That afternoon Honnie and Hannah made a start on the nursery. The sun was shining outside and Lizzie had taken the children into the gardens. Daisy came up to help Honnie and Hannah. She was very willing and good-humoured. Hannah got John-Jo, the young houseboy, to come up and help as well.

"He's young and strong," said Honnie. "He'll be able to lift things and move things much more easily than we could."

Together they cleared the big room, moving all the unwanted pieces into a smaller unused room nearby, but keeping the sofa, some chairs, a table, the small desk, and of course the rocking horse and the dolls' house. It was hard dusty work, and at the end of the afternoon they were all tired, but the room was beginning to show promise.

"And that's enough for today," said Honnie.

Over the following weeks the floor was scrubbed, the walls were washed, and John-Jo was given the task of cleaning the windows, which was quite a task because they were very big and very dirty. George was roped in to hold the ladder and keep it steady while John-Jo cleaned the windows outside.

But after weeks of work the room still looked a little grim.

"The walls need to be painted," said Honnie.

She remembered a young man called Eoghan O'Reagan who had worked with her father for a number of years, before her father had moved to Limerick.

"Mick Murphy will know where to find him," she said to Hannah.

Not only did Mick know where to find him, he brought him up to Tyrone to talk to Honnie.

She took him upstairs and showed him the nursery.

"Could you make up a distemper wash for the walls in a nice yellow," she said. "A yellow that is not too yellow, if you know what I mean – but cheerful."

Eoghan considered the room. "I think I know what you mean," he said. "I think it may be the colour you want, but I'll mix up a small bucket of the wash and you can see what it looks like on the walls."

It was exactly what Honnie wanted, and before a week had passed the walls had been painted a lovely golden yellow. The ceiling, in contrast, had been painted a creamy white. The windows, too, had been painted white.

The children were brought up to see their new room

and they danced around in excitement. Within minutes they had collected their toys and books from their bedroom, and got busy arranging them in their own special places.

"It's a transformation, isn't it, Hannah?" Honnie said. "And thank you, Eoghan."

Eoghan smiled down at the children, and turned to Honnie.

"You do know that distemper can't be washed?" he said. "It could be hard to keep it clean with this lot."

"I know," said Honnie, "but it's cheap and it is quick and easy to put on. If we have to paint it every couple of years, that's not the end of the world."

Gradually, over the following months, the house began to look better. The drawing room was thoroughly cleaned, curtains mended, covers washed. Furniture was cleaned and repaired. The big mahogany dining-room table and the dining-room chairs were cleaned right down to bare wood, and then a special man was brought in to build up a new coat of polish layer after layer.

"It's called French polishing," Honnie told the children. "It takes a lot of work and a lot of time to do. But doesn't the wood look absolutely wonderful? It really glows with life. So if you are ever sitting at the dining-room table you have to be very careful not to spill anything on it, or mark it in any way, do you understand?"

The kitchen was a different matter. Mrs. Dunne still complained bitterly about Abby and Nelly, and blamed them for any mishaps, of which there were many. She continued to be late with meals, and her cooking got worse rather than better.

Honnie ended up spending more and more time in the kitchen. When Christopher told her she should stay out of the kitchen and let Mrs. Dunne "get on with it", she said she couldn't.

"I hate to see good ingredients being murdered. If I'm there with her, at least I can try to make sure that the food isn't too bad. And I thought she might learn."

"Mrs. Dunne probably thinks she doesn't need to learn," said Christopher dryly, "and I can't imagine she appreciates your presence in her kitchen. If she's that bad, maybe you should get rid of her."

Honnie and Mrs. Dunne trundled on together for another three months. But Honnie didn't have to get rid of her. One wet Wednesday Mrs. Dunne announced she was leaving anyway.

"In the other houses in which I worked my cooking was appreciated," she said. "I don't see why I should have to put up with your criticism, your high-handed ways, and your fancy ideas."

So, for some weeks, until they found a new cook, Honnie was queen of her own kitchen.

On the bright side, the nursery was a great success. The children ate there. The little girls were happy to spend time there, particularly when the weather was wet and cold. Honnie had got the estate carpenter to mend the dolls' house, and she herself had repaired some of the rag dolls.

William, however, spent most of his time out in the stable yard.

Honnie was in the kitchen making blackberry jam one September afternoon, when he came running in, tears streaming down his face.

"Jerry O'Grady says I'm a bastard, Mama! He says you and Father aren't married. He says that makes me a bastard. And I told him that when I grow up I'm going to be master of Tyrone, and he said I could never be. Because I'm a bastard. Am I a bastard, Mama?"

"Of course you're not," said Honnie furiously, "and you are *not* to use that word. What was Jerry O'Grady doing in the stable yard? He has no business there. And what were you doing playing with him? That lad is trouble. Wait 'til your father hears of this!"

"But are you married?" asked William.

"Of course we are," said Honnie firmly.

"But properly married?" asked William. "Jerry says you're not properly married if you're a Catholic and Father is a Protestant. I told him you had been married by Father Tom, and he said that meant nothing. That it wasn't a marriage under the law of the land. And that makes me a bastard."

"*You are not a bastard!*" said Honnie, her voice rising. "And who told you that we were married by Father Tom?"

"Everybody knows that," said William. "And if the law says that isn't a real marriage, then I'm a bastard."

"*Stop* using that word!" said Honnie.

But William had run out of the room.

Honnie tried to run after him, but she knew she was not going to catch him. All she saw as she reached the front door was the blur of his blue woollen gansey hurtling round the corner of the house down towards the woods at the back, and probably to the harbour beyond. Which was, she remembered, where she used to go when she wanted to get away from everyone. Tears of fury rose in her eyes, fury at Jerry O'Grady, fury at stupid laws made by stupid people, fury at her inability to do anything about it or help William feel better.

She was still furious when she saw Christopher riding up the driveway. She didn't even wait for him to dismount before she launched into an account of the day's events.

"Oh Lord," said Christopher, his face darkening. "I suppose something like that was bound to happen sooner or later. But Jerry O'Grady has no business in the stable yards, and by the time I'm finished with him he won't want to see them ever again."

When Christopher went looking for him, Jerry of course had long fled. It was almost a week before he spotted him one morning walking along the road to Clarinbridge. Christopher pulled up his horse. Jerry looked round for a way of escape and could see none. He stood there, white-faced, looking very frightened indeed.

"And what did you do to him?" asked Honnie later, afraid that he might have really lost his temper, and harmed the boy.

"I didn't lay a finger on him," said Christopher. I just described in detail what I *might* do to him if he ever crossed my path again. I think I put the fear of God into him. I don't think we'll see him around here any more."

Christopher and Honnie's seventh child, another girl, was born on a bright October morning, the first child to be born in Tyrone House. She was to be called Honoria, or Nóra for short.

Chapter 38

The newspapers in the summer and early autumn of 1845 were full of plans for a new railway network. There were hopes for a Dublin to Galway railway, and one from Galway to Ennis. Engineers were already laying the Wexford and Waterford lines. But the newspapers were fast abandoning stories about the proposed railways and turning to the growing stories about a blight which was destroying the potato crops.

In July it had been just a noxious whisper, but it soon made its presence felt. It was described as an airborne fungus which killed the potatoes. By September the blight had been reported from many parts of the country. Potatoes were inedible in Wexford, and in Mayo people digging potatoes reported an intolerable stench. And it was now appearing in Galway.

Honnie, confined to Tyrone with a family of young children, and frequently pregnant, had become an avid reader of newspapers. Christopher brought home the

Tuam Herald whenever he went to Galway, and occasionally he brought the *Dublin Monitor* and the odd time he brought the London paper, the *Morning Chronicle*.

Joseph, who had become a regular visit in Tyrone, came to visit Honnie and her new daughter a few days later. Having duly admired his latest niece, he sat at the kitchen table, accepted the tea and soda bread Honnie offered him and went on to talk about the blight.

"You've never seen anything like it," he said. "People planted them, watched them grow and green all through all the hungry months, and looked forward to eating the early crop in August, and overnight they were dead."

"I've read about it," said Honnie, "but I've been hoping the stories were exaggerated. Is it really that bad then?"

"It's worse than anything you could possibly imagine," said Joseph. "Plants that were strong and vigorous a month ago are just a spread of filthy slime. Potatoes, which looked perfect when they were were dug and pitted, have collapsed into a rotting mass of decay. And the smell, Honnie, is horrible, the smell is almost evil, as if the blight is stretching out long fingers of death and destruction, trying to claw us into the grave. There are many fathers out there, looking at their children and wondering how they are going to feed them during the coming months. Thank God I don't have a wife and family."

"Has it reached Maree?" asked Honnie.

"Not yet," said Joseph, "but we can't hope to escape it."

Honnie had never seen Joseph so distressed.

"There must be something that can be done," she said. "They'll have to eat other food instead of potatoes. The Government will have to help."

"What other food?" said Joseph furiously. "It's easy for you to talk like that and you set up here with full and plenty. There's no fear of your children going hungry. Where do you think people are going to get other food? And even if they could, how are would they pay for it? They have nothing. If we had our own government, things would be different. We're just an English colony, an out-farm. And Thomas Davis is gone, dead at only thirty years of age. I had great hopes of him. I tell you, Honnie, it's famine we're facing."

"What about Daniel O'Connell?" said Honnie.

"Daniel O'Connell is all talk," said Joseph.

"Didn't he say that there could be employment on railway construction, that people could get work, and people could keep their self-respect?"

"And where is the work? Where is the construction going on around here? Didn't the House of Lords say no to a railway between Dublin and Galway? People need work now, not at some time in the dim and distant future. It's as useless as the idea of taxing absentee landlords at 50 per cent of their income, and resident landowners at 10 per cent. As the *Nation* says, '*a parliament composed of absentees will never tax themselves to one-half nor even one tenth of their income*'."

"How are things at home?" asked Honnie, trying to steer the subject to less heated ground.

"Our potatoes haven't been affected – yet," said Joseph. "But it could happen overnight. And we're better off than a lot of people. We can still fish, we have a few hens still laying, just about. We sowed other crops. We have some oats stored, and carrots and turnips. There's only Kathleen and Thady and myself. Even so things are going fast. But we're luckier than most of our neighbours."

If Honnie had felt worried and weary before Joseph came, by the time he left she felt utterly disheartened. Each day brought stories of the potato blight blasting its black way across the countryside, reducing green fields to foul slush. Honnie had seen the fear in the faces of people working in and around Tyrone. She had heard the prophecies of famine, disease, and death. Tired and anxious, unable to sleep at night, she'd tried to shut out the stories, hoping they were untrue. Now fear coiled a knot in her stomach, for her children and their future, fear for her family over in Maree. She had always prayed, and in recent months she found herself doing so more fervently. At night she groped for the rosary beads on the table beside her bed and prayed once more for help. But she didn't feel anyone was listening.

Throughout October the blight spread to the counties of Kilkenny and Carlow, to Tyrone, Roscommon and Cork.

Honnie, who had been writing regularly to William in Canada, filled pages with news of the unyielding horror.

"The newspapers are hoping that the reports of the blight are exaggerated, even saying that some of the potatoes in a damaged crop might be saved, but whoever wrote that can't have seen the effects of the blight. Christopher took me out in the trap some days ago, and showed me places, just a few miles from here, where the

blight has struck. It was truly horrible, William. Everywhere patches of healthy potatoes had turned into a stinking sludge, smelling of death and decay.

They say a Temporary Relief Commission has been formed. But when they tried to talk to the Lord Lieutenant or Sir Robert Peel, neither of them would listen. The Poor Law will give people relief, but only in the workhouses. Nobody, only the most truly destitute, will go into a workhouse. There's to be no outdoor relief."

Christopher had become quite irascible. His father's debts hung heavily over the estates. Creditors seemed to be gathering on all sides, and bailiffs and process servers were never very far away. Nothing Honnie said could cheer him up.

She tried food, and went to some trouble to cook him a special Sunday dinner.

"We're very lucky," she said. "We may not have potatoes, but we have vegetables from our own garden. We have beef from our own herd. And we still have wine in our cellars."

Christopher ate heartily, but wasn't to be sweetened.

"I've inherited Tyrone, and a half century of debt along with it," he said. "I'm getting very little rent money. With the widespread failure of the potato crop, the tenant farmers are using any money they have to buy food for their families, and who can blame them? Farmers with holdings above a £4 rateable valuation are exasperated because they are now liable for Poor Law rates as well. On holdings of less than a £4 rateable valuation, the landlords have to pay the rates. What am I supposed to do? I'm buried in debts and mortgages, with bailiffs on all sides of me. I have virtually no money coming in, but I will still be liable for those rates. What is the Relief Commission doing? Nothing as far as I can see. Making up a report, I've been told. Will that feed people? Will that help the situation?"

His mood grew blacker by the day. Things were getting worse and worse.

"I want to help my tenants, but how can I help my tenants when I can't help myself?"

Honnie listened to him raging against the government.

"What use are they, sitting in their ivory tower in London?" he asked.

And against the Irish land tenure system.

"A father has eight or nine children and divides up his land so that they each have a place. Then they have children, and try to divide up their small piece, and it goes on and on until people are trying to feed a family on a piece of land the size of a pocket handkerchief. It doesn't make any kind of sense! I can understand why Father felt he had to make provision for my sisters, but it was done at a price. You remember those auctions? They raised only part of what he needed. He borrowed money as well. The estate is mired in debt. How am I ever going to repay even part of it? The devil take those damned bailiffs!"

The year wore on, and the blight spread across the land, and Christopher's mood grew blacker with each passing day. When he was in the house Honnie found him difficult to cope with, when he was out of the house she worried for his safety, and she began to dread his return each evening.

One night early in the New Year of 1846, Christopher returned home in a particularly angry mood. He threw a copy of the *Dublin Monitor* on the kitchen table.

"The Relief Commission Report says that not less than £500,000 is needed to deal with the emergency. But of course Mr. Charles Trevelyan, in the Treasury Office in London, didn't like being told this. The Government plan to spend no more than £50,000 on famine relief. Fifty thousand pounds! A drop in the ocean! All over Ireland people are starving, and talking about 'famine'. A *famine* is when there's no food in the country. But there's an abundance of food in the country. Daniel O'Connell has told the House of Commons that more than two million quarters of grain and nearly two-and-a-half million cwt. of meal were exported to Britain last year. So while people are starving here, food is going out of the country. Rather than feed the Irish their own produce instead of exporting it, the Government has decided that Indian meal would be imported as a cheap substitute. The first supplies of the meal, I've been told, have already arrived secretly in Cork."

What Christopher had heard turned out to be true.

By the end of March the meal was going on sale in food depots in Cork, Clonmel and Longford. There were, as always, people who saw an opportunity for profit.

Those who had the money to buy it found they were being charged almost double the cost price.

"It's known as Peel's Brimstone," Joseph told Honnie, "after the Prime Minister. Irish people have never seen this corn before. They don't know how to cook it, but the Relief Commission has kindly provided cooking instructions – in English, to many people who don't speak English, and can't read anyway. The meal has to be ground twice to make an edible meal. It is hard to digest and causes stomach cramps. But Charles Trevelyan told the Chairman of the Relief Commission, Sir Randolph Routh, that he didn't believe it was necessary to grind Indian corn twice!"

By the end of April Honnie had to accept that she was pregnant once more. Christopher's attentions may have been only occasional lately, she thought wryly, but they were still productive. She continued to write regularly to William.

"*I was very sad to see you go to Canada, and I miss you very much,*" she wrote, "*but I think you are so much better off there than we are here. People are desperately looking for work to get some money to feed their families. Christopher says that the £50,000 to be spent on public works will go nowhere – applications for works to cost £800,000 have been received. Things are getting worse. This was always a bad time of the year, the gap between the last of the old potatoes and the first of the new. The old potatoes have long festered into the dirt, and I can't see how we can expect any new potatoes this year because people have had no seed potatoes to plant. It's a nightmare. All we seem to hear are stories of hunger, destitution, disease, of spectral figures walking the roads in search of any food, of death stalking the land. I don't go out much. I don't want to leave the house. Not that it would be easy with seven small children and another to be born later this year. Truth to tell, William, I feel bone-tired. I just feel I want to stay here until it's all gone away. Our tenants come knocking at our door, more and more of them, looking for food, for help. I do my best, but my best is not enough."*

Honnie read what she had written. She crossed the bit about being bone-tired – why give William cause for worry?

"*Tomorrow I will go over to Maree to see how they are over there, and to Nóra in Drumacoo."*

These were dangerous times. Mick Murphy now went with Honnie whenever she went out in the pony and trap. And they made many trips over those awful months. Honnie loaded the trap with all she could gather together – vegetables, tea, sugar, eggs, the occasional chicken, a cake, flour, and anything else she thought might be useful, and Mick did the driving. In Maree they weren't too badly off. Thady was still bringing in fish, and the hens were still laying. Nóra was much more badly off.

In Tyrone the younger children were unaware of all that was going on in the world outside, but William and Anne knew things were not right. They felt the fearfulness in the house. Anne wanted to know why people were so sad.

Honnie found herself shouting at William one day when he didn't finish his dinner.

"There are children near here who are not just hungry, they are starving! They have nothing to eat. And here are you turning away food!"

William burst into tears. And Honnie gathered him into her arms, and covered him with kisses, and said she was sorry.

"But why are people so hungry, Mama?" he asked. "Why haven't they got food?"

"For many people in Ireland the potato is their most

important food," said Honnie. "You'll have seen the potato plots alongside many a cottage. Whole families live on potatoes all the year round. But remember that last year the potatoes were attacked by a very nasty disease called the blight, and almost all the potatoes were turned into a black mush."

"But can't the people eat something else instead of potatoes?" asked William.

"It costs money to buy food," said Honnie. "And the trouble is they don't have the money to buy other food."

By June the supplies of Indian corn were beginning to run low, and as July was expected to be the month of most distress, the government purchased a further supply. Some 3,000 tons was bought from Mediterranean countries.

"But Mr. Trevelyan says that the government will not purchase a third quantity," Honnie wrote to William in July. *"And they say that the spread of the blight is more widespread than last year, that the new potato crop is already almost wiped out. What are people going to do?"*

By the middle of August the operation of the Relief Commission was being wound up.

Joseph brought Honnie a copy of *The Nation.*

"Just listen to this," he said, and started reading.

"'This day ends the commission of one set of government relief commissioners. Today they close their office, balance their books, and retire from their labours. The distress arising from last year's deficient crop is passed by: the state alms-givers shut their doors – because it is the 15th of August, and the new crop ought to be crowned with abundance.'"

"Can you believe it?" said Joseph. "They've closed their doors. No more aid because it is August and the new crop of potatoes should be able to feed the masses. But there is no new crop, just a black, slimy, rotting mess, in every county in the land."

He read on.

"'*And on this very day a cry of Famine, wilder and more fearful than ever, is rising from every parish and county in the land. Where the new crop ought to be, there is a loathsome mass of putrefaction: the sole food on which millions of men, women and children are to be fed, is stricken by a deadly blight before our eyes, and probably within one month those millions will be hungry and have nothing to eat. Yes, there have been, by this time, accounts received from every county in Ireland: and they all concur in representing the blight's being even at this early period of the season, almost universal; for one family which needed relief during the past season there will now be three. Last year the government had to bethink themselves how to provide against a general deficiency – this year they will have to consider how a starving nation is to be fed.*'"

"Can I cut this piece out?" Honnie asked Joseph. "I'd like to send it to William."

She continued to read any newspapers that Christopher brought home.

"Though sometimes I wonder why," she said to Christopher, "because they so often upset me."

She got particularly cross with the *London Times*.

"It says: '*Lord John Russell has said he has no intention of allowing the government to supply food, as*

Sir Robert Peel did last year.' He said: *'It must be thoroughly understood that we cannot feed the people. It was a cruel delusion to pretend to do so. Repeated state intervention would not only paralyse private enterprise, but increase Irish dependence on Britain ... And Sir Charles Wood, the Chancellor, believes in what he calls a retributive yet beneficent providence. A want of food and employment, apparently, is a calamity sent by providence. Except through a purgatory of misery and starvation he can't see how Ireland is to emerge into a state of anything approaching quiet prosperity...'*

Honnie got more and more angry.

"Can you believe," she said to Christopher, "that any man with any decency, any human feeling could come out with statements like that? And I suppose they call themselves Christians! They are mad, bad, wicked people. I wish I could transport them over here and drop them down in the midst of all our misery and see how they get on."

"You are just getting upset," said Christopher. "I agree with what you're saying. But you can't do anything about it. Don't read the papers."

Honnie snapped. "What do you mean, *don't read the papers*? Of course I'm going to read the papers! How else will I know what's happening?"

She poured it all out in a letter to William in Canada and went on to tell him about the road works which were replacing food depots as the principal means of famine relief.

"The road building has just started. The trouble is that it is very hard work. The men who do it need to be strong and healthy and well-fed. The men who come to

work on the roads are often weak, ill, and starving. Many of them have walked miles each day to get to work. As they get weaker, they are less able to work. And even if they do manage to earn eight pence, or sometimes only seven pence a day, and want to buy meal for their families, they are at the mercy of the men selling the meal. They can charge what they like."

She told William she was sorry for sending him such a tale of misery.

"But I feel better now that I have written it all down. In some sort of way it gets it out of my head."

The desperate poor were finally going to the workhouses. Western unions sent urgent requests to the Poor Law Commission for money to keep their workhouses open. It was almost impossible to collect any rate or tax in the Connacht Unions. But Sir George Grey, the Home Secretary, wouldn't budge. Adequate rates had to be struck and collected.

In Tyrone Honnie found her eighth pregnancy difficult. For most of the time she was nauseous, and for all of the time, it seemed, she was tired. Accustomed to having the energy and inclination to be busy most of every day. she found that small chores left her looking for a chair to sit down. Even the garden didn't offer its usual solace. She only went out to visit Drumacoo and Maree, and was feeling less and less able for even these short journeys.

A chest infection in October kept her sitting up at night, coughing and wheezing into the early hours. None of the homely remedies, remembered from her mother, or given to her by Madge Shaughnessy, seemed to make any difference.

The coughing kept her awake. And she knew it must also be keeping Christopher awake. But apart from the suggestion that she should do something "about that awful cough", he didn't complain. He just lay there with his back firmly turned, twitching and muttering in his sleep.

Honnie decided to move to a spare room, where she could cough if she needed to cough. She could also arrange the bedclothes and pillows as and when she liked, and best of all she could light a lamp and try to read. But each day brought stories of death and desolation, and each night the stories walked around in her head.

By November it was clear that the public works relief scheme had failed to provide the destitute poor with adequate means of subsistence. In fact, it was a disaster.

Those employed were paid, irregularly, from 6d. to 8d. a day – with the price of Indian meal rising to 2d a lb. The labourers were not paid because there were no pay clerks to pay them; the works were not started because there were no engineers to lay them out; work was not measured because there were no stewards who could be entrusted with the calculation.

But Trevelyan still saw a bright light shining through the dark cloud hanging over Ireland.

"*The morbid habits are gradually giving way to a more healthy action. The deep and inveterate root of social evil remains, and I hope I am not guilty of irreverence in thinking that, this being altogether beyond the power of man, the cure has been applied by the direct stroke of an all-wise providence ...*"

He saw the blight as a heaven-sent opportunity to convert the land from a potato economy to grain cultivation.

Whatever light was shining over Ireland was to come from the Quakers, who held a meeting in Dublin, in the middle of November, which was to lead to the formation of the Central Relief Committee of the Society of Friends.

Chapter 39

In the middle of November Christopher told Honnie he had to go to Connemara to meet some of his tenants. His agent, John Linnane, had already told the tenants that they would be required to give up their holdings so that they could be re-applotted. But Linnane had also told them that after the land was re-apportioned in a more productive way they would immediately be put back into their holdings which would be set so that, when the allotments were made, they would still have the benefit of whatever crops they had sowed.

Honnie's heart sank. She knew Christopher would come home in an even worse mood than usual.

Christopher set out early from Tyrone. To get to Connemara he had to travel through Galway City, and quite a distance beyond it. Even early in the day there were many hungry people walking the roads, some of them barely clothed, most of them barefooted, many of them with small children holding onto their mothers' skirts.

Connemara was Christopher's least favourite place. On a dark November day it seemed more than ever uninviting.

A north wind flailed across the bleak, looming mountains and the sodden bogs, driving a mixture of sleet and rain before it. Clumps of miserable sheep huddled in any spot they could find shelter. Wisps of smoke purling up from low-crouched cabins told him that most people were indoors, gathered around their turf fires.

Martin Cosgrave's farm was the second one to which he called. Martin Cosgrave held twenty-four acres of land from Christopher at an annual rent of £24 a year. He had lived on the farm all his life, as had his father before him. He had a comfortable house, a wife and ten children. He worked long hard hours to provide for his family. He was at the end of his tether.

Early in October a man called Linnane had called on him. Linnane, it seemed, had been employed by Christopher to survey his estates. Among other things Linnane said that Martin's holding would be re-applotted, and that his house, his home, would be taken down in the spring of the next year.

Martin and Mary Cosgrave were in the little vegetable garden beside the house, scrabbling for any root that might have been overlooked in previous gleanings, when they saw Christopher and Linnane approaching. Since Martin had been told by Linnane that his house was to be levelled, a dark rage had grown inside him. The past few years had been very difficult. He hadn't enough food for his children. He was finding it hard to warm his house. After a long, wet, summer the sods of turf were damp. They sent up sulky, wet tendrils of smoke rather than the bright leaping flames produced by good turf.

Martin's father had built the house, and Martin had added to it and improved it. It had been the home of his childhood and was now the home of his children. He didn't want to be re-applotted. He wanted to live in the house in which his father had lived, in the house in which he had hoped one of his sons would live. And now it was to be levelled at the whim of an uncaring landlord.

At the sight of Christopher and his agent, Martin's molten rage boiled up inside him. When Mary plucked at his coat sleeve and begged him not to lose his temper, he shook her off. He found he didn't care any more about the consequences.

"So, you've come yourself," he said to Christopher, as he watched him dismount. "To tell me you are going to throw me and my family out of the only home we've ever known."

"Yes, your house is to be levelled," said Christopher, "though not until next spring. But you can still cultivate the land and have the benefit of the crops for a year after."

"And what about my wife and family? What about our children? Where are we supposed to live? *On the roadside?*"

Martin's voice rose above the whining wind.

And suddenly people began to appear, as if from nowhere, and gather round him. Any argument between a tenant and a landlord was entertainment on a winter's day.

Martin's natural language was Irish, but he had acquired a good command of English. Throwing caution to the winds, he prepared to tell Christopher St. George exactly what he thought of him.

"What kind of man are you? I'll tell you what kind of man you are. You're inhuman. Selfish. Greedy. You're a grasping, godless monster. But worst of all you're a landlord, and it's landlords who have this country ruined!"

A murmur of agreement rippled through the crowd.

The veins on Christopher's neck swelled with temper.

"How *dare* you speak to me like that?"

But Martin had gone too far to stop.

"Are my wife and children, my babes, to live in the ditches, under trees, with nothing to cover them from the ravages of the weather? I hear tell you have your own family of bastards over in Tyrone. How would you feel about them living on the side of the road?"

A hushed titter came from the back of the crowd.

Christopher shook his whip in the air.

"*Damn you!*" he bellowed. "*Damn the lot of you!*"

The assembled listeners fell into frozen silence.

"As for you, Martin Cosgrove, upon my oath I'll see you whipped for your insolence, whipped to within an inch of your life. Or maybe I'll just have you gaoled. A good long sentence will give you plenty of time to cool down. Either way, you'll live to rue this day, I tell you. Upon my oath I'll see you out of here."

And he mounted his horse and rode off, a wave of pure hatred following him on his way.

Night had long fallen by the time Christopher got back to Tyrone. A few whiskeys in Moran's hadn't helped. His world looked dark and it was getting darker every day.

Honnie took one look at him as he came through the

door and decided to ask no questions. She gave him his supper, a beef stew, and put an open bottle of claret by his side. He ate fast, and drank even faster, thanked Honnie in a perfunctory way, got up from the table and, opening another bottle of claret, he left saying he had papers to attend to in his study.

In the spare room Honnie lay awake waiting to hear him coming up to bed. She finally fell asleep some time after the big clock in the hall truck two. Much later she awoke to hear him stumbling around their bedroom. Clearly more claret had been drunk. Even from the spare room she could later hear him snoring.

He was up early the next morning and had finished breakfast before Honnie came downstairs. He said he had business in Galway town and wouldn't be home until the following day. He made no mention of his visit to Connemara, and Honnie didn't ask.

She had other things on her mind. She had wakened up knowing that her eighth child was soon to be born, and she had sent for Madge Shaughnessy and Sarah Breathnach who had been with her at all the other births.

This would be the second child of the family to be born in Tyrone House. It was a long and difficult labour and it was late the following evening before the child was born.

When Christopher came home he found her sitting up in bed, tired and tearful, holding their new daughter in her arms.

Guilt smote him.

"Oh Honnie! I didn't think this baby was due for another while. Did you have a hard time?"

"A *very* hard time," said Honnie, and felt tears spilling. "A hard labour, a day and a half long. I wanted you here."

Christopher wrapped his arms around her, kissed her and with his fingers gently wiped away her tears.

"I'm sorry, Honnie," he said again. "I know I've been difficult and grouchy lately. Things haven't been easy these last years. These are very bad times, and things just seem to get worse and worse. But that is no excuse for my behaviour. I shouldn't have gone off when you were so near your time." He kissed her again. "Now you must rest, and we must look after you,"

He ran his fingers over the baby's downy head.

"Another girl," he said. "What shall we call her?"

"Matilda," said Honnie. "I think she's a really lovely baby. I think she looks like your sister Anne. What do you think?"

"You know I think they all look the same at that age," said Christopher.

"Here, you take her and hold her and really look at her," said Honnie.

Christopher took her, and held her, rather awkwardly, and looked down at the crumpled little face.

"You know I like them better when they are a bit older, Honnie." And he handed her back.

That night back in her own bedroom again, lying close to Christopher, Honnie felt happier than she had been for quite a while.

"It's good to be together again," she said.

"It's good to have you in my arms again," said Christopher.

"Tell me how you got on in Connemara?" asked Honnie.

"What I want to tell you about are the Quakers," said

Christopher. "They're sometimes called the Society of Friends. I met one of them in Galway, an Englishman, called William Forster – he seemed to me a man of fine character. He has travelled all over the west and the north of Ireland. He says the reports in the public newspapers are by no means exaggerated."

"Well, it's good to hear that there are people out there who are are actually going around Ireland, and seeing the awful things that are happening all over the country," said Honnie. "But what can they do to help?"

"The Society is forming a Central Relief Committee," said Christopher, "and they have made it one of their objects to obtain trustworthy information respecting the real state of affairs. It won't be easy. The weather is bitter, with constant snow falling and a savage northeast wind tearing across the land. They seem to me an admirable group of men and are most anxious to help us. They're talking about what they call soup kitchens, to be set up especially in the more remote districts. They see soup as the best way of feeding large numbers of people."

"Any bit of good news is welcome," said Honnie.

"We can only hope they can help us, in some kind of way. But hope is very hard to find in times like these."

For some minutes neither of them spoke.

Christopher stroked Honnie's shoulder gently, tenderly, told her he loved her, and told her once again that he was sorry.

Then Honnie again remembered his visit to Connemara.

"But how did you get on in Connemara?" she asked.

Did she feel him stiffen, or was she imagining it?

"I don't want to talk about it," said Christopher. "It's nothing to bother you. Now I think we should both try to get some sleep. I need to sleep, and you most certainly need to sleep."

The following morning Christopher handed a newspaper to Honnie.

"Since you like reading all the bad news, you can add this one to your collection. It is written by one of the Quakers who visited Donegal."

It read:

"In Dunfanaghy, where the sea is teeming with fish, the people starve because they have no one to teach them how to build seaworthy boats. In Dungloe, the crowds are crying with hunger and cold. In the Glenties workhouse the inmates are half-starved and half naked. The day before they had but one meal of oatmeal and water, and at the time of our visit had not sufficient food in the house for the day's supply. Their bedding consisted of dirty straw, in which they were laid in rows on the floor; even as many as six persons being crowded under one rug; and we did not see a blanket at all. The rooms were hardly bearable for filth. The living and the dying were stretched side by side beneath the same miserable covering. No wonder that disease and pestilence were filling the infirmary, and that the pale, haggard countenance of the poor boys and girls told of their sufferings which it was impossible to contemplate without pity."

On the Christmas Eve of 1846 the Ennis poorhouse was full. Captain Edmond Wynne, inspecting officer for West Clare, reported that that **"police are stationed at the**

doors to keep the numerous applicants out".

The relief committees were broke.

In Tyrone Honnie was stressed and struggling to cope with seven children and a new baby. Into what kind of world had her children been born? She was glad to see the end of 1846, but full of fear as to what the New Year might bring.

Chapter 40

With the New Year came more severe weather. Christopher's moods became black again and got blacker with every passing day. John Mitchell, writer for *The Nation*, visited Galway, and recorded what he saw. Joseph brought a copy over to Honnie.

"In the depth of winter we travelled to Galway, through the very centre of our fertile island, and saw sights that will never wholly leave the eyes that beheld them: cowering wretches, almost naked in the savage weather, prowling in turnip-fields, and endeavouring to grub up the roots that had been left behind, but running to hide as the mailcoach rolled by; very large fields, where small farms had been 'consolidated', showing dark bars of fresh mould where the ditches had been levelled; groups and families sitting or wandering on the highroad, with failing steps and dim, patient eyes, gazing helplessly into infinite darkness; before them, around them, above them, nothing but darkness and despair; parties of tall,

brawny men, once the flower of Galway, stalking by with a fierce but vacant scowl; as if they knew that all this ought not to be, but knew not who to blame, saw none whom they could rend with their wrath; for Lord John Russell sat safe in Chesham Place; and the grand commissioner of the pauper system wove his webs of red tape around them from afar.

Around the farmhouses which were still inhabited were to be seen hardly any stacks of grain; it was all gone; the poor rate collector, the rent agent, the county cess collector, had carried it off. Sometimes I could see in front of the cottages, little children leaning against the fence when the sun shone out – for they could not stand – their limbs fleshless, their bodies half naked, their faces bloated yet wrinkled, and of pale greenish hue – children who would never, it was plain, grow up to be men and women."

Honnie enclosed the piece in her next letter to William.

"Each day seems to bring more and more dreadful stories. At night I cannot sleep because my mind is filled with horrors."

Meanwhile, a vast number of ratepayers were reduced to pauperism, and landlords said that they could not pay rates when they were getting no rents.

The public works had been a costly failure and a humanitarian disaster. They were to be replaced by soup kitchens.

"And now even Mr. Trevelyan is admitting *'The tide of Irish distress appears now to have completely overflowed the barriers we opposed to it. This is a real famine, in which thousands and thousands of people are likely to die',"* said Christopher, reading it out to Honnie from the *The Times* of London. "But he doesn't propose to do anything about it. '*I believe if the Irish once find out there are any circumstance in which they can get free government grants... we shall have a system of mendicancy such as the world never saw.'"*

In February, Daniel O'Connell told the House of Commons that Westminster appeared ignorant of the real state of horror in which Ireland was plunged. He looked close to death himself, and could barely stand for trembling. He threw his country on the mercy of England. He said that 25% of the whole population would perish unless the House offered effective relief. He said he was not exaggerating.

By the middle of February churchyards were being enlarged throughout the country.

Father Tom, who came to visit Honnie, told her about a man he had met walking the road with a donkey and cart.

"On the cart there were three coffins, containing the bodies of his wife and two children. He was alone. When he got to the churchyard he was so weakened by starvation that he couldn't bury his dead. I went the next day, and a man along with me, to help dig the graves. We found ravenous dogs eating the remains – and I mean the remains – not only of the man's wife and children, but of the man himself."

Honnie's stomach churned over. She looked at Tom in horror, and then suddenly got very angry. She took hold of Tom by the lapels if his coat and shook him.

"How could a good God allow something like that to happen? And happen not just to that poor family, but to families all over the country? How can He? People are starving, they are diseased, they are dying in their thousands. How can you believe in a God who allows all this to happen?"

Gently Tom removed her hands from his coat.

"Honnie, I can't answer your questions, any of them. I only know I still believe in God. I still believe in prayer. I believe that I must do my best to help as many people as I can."

And he left, telling her he'd come to see her again soon.

Conditions in the workhouses were horrendous. One hundred of them had an excess number of inmates. In Gort, in County Galway, one quarter of the paupers were suffering from fever or dysentery. The Cork workhouse, built for 2,000 was housing 4,400 paupers. In one day 100 bodies were buried in a mass grave.

Soup had come to be considered the cheapest means of keeping the Irish alive until harvest time. The Quakers had pioneered soup-kitchen relief. Now the government recommended that soup kitchens, organised by local relief committees, be established in areas of intense distress.

Trevelyan didn't intend to address the financial difficulties which Irish unions, particularly in the south and west, were experiencing.

"The owners and holders of land in these districts had permitted or encouraged the growth of the excessive population which depended upon the precarious potato and they alone had it in their power restore society to a safe and healthy state."

"That man," said Honnie. "That horrible, horrible man. With each passing month I hate him more."

In March there was a fever epidemic sweeping the country, and scenes of unbelievable suffering abounded. Ireland seems about to turn into a Golgotha, John Mitchel predicted in *The Nation*.

In Galway, the Sisters of Mercy – with Quaker support – fed up to 600 children daily; the Presentation convent provided about 500 breakfasts.

In Tyrone Honnie felt a deep, creeping sense of despair. She had known tough times in her younger years, but never anything like this. Each day seemed darker than the last. Each day seem to offer less hope. It didn't help that her children were constantly getting colds, with dripping noses and hacking coughs. And always at the back of her mind was the fear that the fevers raging across the countryside would reach Tyrone. But she knew that her problems were nothing compared to those in the world outside.

She had seen people walking the roads when she went to visit Nóra Burke in Drumacoo, or when she had gone to visit Joseph and Maureen and Kathleen in Maree. She now had difficulty in recognising the grey, gaunt shadows of people she had once known, and the worst of all were the children. The air was filled with cries for help, and she felt utterly helpless. She knew that to give to some would bring more and more people in hope. She knew that the provisions hidden in the bottom of the trap for Nóra and her own family would give sustenance to a few to the rage of many.

People came knocking on the door of Tyrone looking for food.

"As they did in my mother's time," said Christopher. "And in my father's time."

Now people began to come again, people who had lived and worked around Tyrone all their lives.

"And by all means we must help them," said Christopher, "but we can't feed all those in need. There is only so much we can do. I have given my men instructions that only those people we know, our own people, are to be allowed to come up to the house."

Honnie had been much taken with the idea of the soup kitchens.

"I thought I could do one here," she said – adding hastily, "in a small way."

"You can make soup to give to the people who come to the house," said Christopher. "But if you're thinking of a soup kitchen to feed more people, forget it. The country is rife with disease and pestilence and fevers. Word gets round, and if the word got out that you were running anything like a soup kitchen, people would try to come here from much farther afield. They would bring with them disease and death. We have six young children and a baby here in Tyrone, and you yourself are still recovering from a difficult pregnancy. We must try to protect ourselves, and our own people, and try keep ourselves safe."

So Honnie started making bread each day, and soup, and putting aside any other food that she could spare, so that she had something to offer when people came. She got Anne to help her make soda bread. Anne still loved to work the kitchen beside her mother. William was sent out to Johnny O'Connor in the garden to bring whatever vegetables were available for soup, and herbs for flavouring – parsley, rosemary, thyme, sage, whichever herbs Honnie felt would improve the soup of the day.

She found herself thinking and worrying about Christopher's November visit to Connemara. She had learned about it in bits and pieces, from various people. In Tyrone House itself she overheard people discussing it, voices hushing as she came near. It was from Hannah that she got most of the story, and then only because she insisted that Hannah told her what people were saying, and because she knew Hannah would not exaggerate, would have sieved out the known facts from anecdotes that simply gathered momentum as they travelled round. Clearly what happened between Christopher and Martin Cosgrave on that November day was known across the country.

Hannah's account burnt pictures into her brain, and she found herself awake at night looking at the ceiling, thinking of the potato crops destroyed across the land, of the sick and starving people. She thought often of the Cosgraves, until one morning, as they were sitting at the kitchen table after breakfast, she decided to challenge Christopher.

"I heard what you did over in Connemara to the Cosgraves," she began.

Christopher bristled. "Honnie, it's none of your business. You mind your own affairs, the children and the house."

"It's the children and the house that keep reminding me of what you've done to another woman and her children," said Honnie. "What has come over you? I hardly recognise you."

"Honnie, there are farms, holdings, plots all over the

country which are not paying their way. Land is being poorly used, smaller and smaller plots trying to feed more and more people. It couldn't go on, and now with the failure of the potato crop, it is not going to. I don't know what the answer is."

"Well, your answer seems to be to put people out on the side of the road to make your land more productive," said Honnie.

"The only person I am going to put out on the side of the road is Martin Cosgrave," said Christopher, "and he put himself out by talking to me the way he did. And by making that land more productive there will be more work for people, not less."

"It isn't just Martin who will suffer," said Honnie, "but his wife and young children as well."

"So maybe you would do well to remind yourself how lucky you are," said Christopher sharply. "Your children are safe and well with a roof over their heads, and enough food to eat."

That stung.

"Lucky? With everybody I meet pointing a finger at me?" said Honnie furiously. "Calling me St. George's woman, and saying my children are being well fed while other children are starving. I'm afraid to put my face outside the door. And our children are getting their share of abuse as well. I'm fed up telling William he is not a bastard. The truth is, all this row with Martin Cosgrave is about your pride, and your pride will be the death of you. What you have done is *wrong*. But you have never been able to admit you are in the wrong. *I'm ashamed of you.*"

They'd had disagreements in the past. Most had

blown over quickly. A few had taken longer to heal. But this one, Honnie felt, was different, deep-seated.

Now Honnie found she didn't want to talk to Christopher, and he didn't seem eager to talk to her either. He had withdrawn into some dark place of his own. There was very little conversation between them except about matters concerning the household. There was no banter, no jokes, no fun, and very little loving.

Always, it seemed, he had somewhere to go, something to do. He left the house early and came home late, falling into bed full of claret and brandy, tossing and turning restlessly. He had nightmares, talking angrily in his sleep.

And if any man deserved to have nightmares, Christopher did, thought Honnie.

On the evenings when he came home early he left the table as soon as he had finished eating, and retreated to his study, closing the door behind him with a firm thud.

If he wasn't out and about round Galway, he was up in Rathbride House with his horses on the Curragh in County Kildare.

Over the years Christopher had built up quite a name for himself as a breeder of good horses. Honnie hadn't been on a horse's back for years, but her love of horses had never died down. She still paid regular visits to the stable yard, which is where she met Mick Murphy one bright spring morning. He was watching a young stablehand trying to walk a big, powerful, grey horse around the yard, and having a hard time of it.

"Ah, Chanticleer," said Honnie. "I never liked him. He's a truly bad-tempered horse."

"I absolutely agree with you," said Mick. "I think he is he most ill-tempered horse I have come across in all my years working with horses, even worse than Necromancer. He's a great, big nasty brute. Just look at him!"

Honnie had known and watched Chanticleer since he was a young foal – she knew his dam, Whim, was a fine mare, and that his sire, Birdcatcher, had a big reputation.

"Master Christopher is convinced that he can put manners on him," said Mick. "He thinks he has a great future ahead of him."

"I could never really like him," said Honnie, "or trust him either."

They talked of Christopher.

"He seems to think of nothing but horses," said Honnie. "Sometimes I think that horses are more important to Christopher than anything else in the world."

"He certainly spends a lot of time with them," said Mick, "and a lot of time thinking about them and talking about them and planning for them. And he rides very hard, as if the hounds of hell are after him. He needs to take more care."

Which wasn't exactly what Honnie wanted to hear, and added to her worries.

She hated the feeling that he was shutting her out, but she didn't feel like making overtures. She felt isolated and miserable. So miserable that she eventually decided that she had to try to break the ice because he wouldn't.

When she asked how things were going, he gave a clipped reply.

"These are very difficult times," he said and walked

away.

When she tried to tell him some story about the children, he merely nodded.

In the middle of March Father Tom came to visit Honnie again. His mien was serious. Almost formal. He clearly had something particular on his mind, but he seemed hesitant about discussing it. He drank tea and ate some biscuits almost absent-mindedly. He played with the children for whom he was a favourite visitor. Finally he suggested that he and Honnie take a turn around the garden.

Honnie agreed and went to get a shawl. Though the sun was shining the wind was cold. But the trees were greening, the daffodils spreading golden across the lawn and the birds were still nest-building. A chaffinch flew past them, looking as if he was wearing a big moustache.

"Fóidín's fur," said Honnie. "He always sheds his coat at this time of the year, and the birds love it. It makes a nice warm lining for their nests."

She reached down and patted the dog on his head.

"Poor Fóidín," she said. "He's quite an elderly gentleman now. I'll be very sad when he dies."

Still Father Tom said nothing.

Finally, Honnie taxed him.

"Tom, what is it? What's on your mind?"

Father Tom began to speak.

"Honnie, you will know that things are bad for a great many people. Crops have failed, they have no food to give their children, no money to buy food, they have no money to pay the rent. These are desperate, desperate times. Connemara can be beautiful when the sun is shining, and things are going well. But times are very, very bad indeed right now. People see hunger, starvation, destitution, disease and death staring them in the face. You know that Christopher has land over there and many tenants. I wonder if he told you about the altercation he had with one of them last November?"

Honnie's heart sank. "Christopher always hates going to Connemara, and when he does he usually comes back in black humour," she said. "He says it's wild, inhospitable country, and very hard to get around. I remember him coming home that day last November. He didn't seem inclined to talk, and I didn't ask any questions. Maybe I felt I would hear something unpleasant I didn't want to hear. It was the day before Matilda was born. I did hear about it later, though, but all I know I know from Hannah."

"Martin Cosgrave is a tenant of Christopher's, and he rents twenty-four acres for £24 a year," said Father Tom. "He has lived there all his life, and his father before him. He's a decent man, a hard worker, who, as far as I know, has always paid his rent on time. Christopher wanted to alter the allotments of the different farms. He hired a man called Linnane to survey his estates and give him advice. Linnane's advice was that Cosgrave's house, which had been built by his father, should be knocked down, and he had already told the Cosgraves that they would be required to give up possession. Christopher's agent, John Linnane, said that having done so they would immediately be put back into their holdings, which would be set to them for a year certain."

"Yes," said Honnie, "Hannah told me that."

Father Tom went on. "The Cosgraves, like many

people in Galway, have had a very rough couple of years of it. When Christopher told Martin that day in November that his house was going to be taken down, it was the last straw for Martin. I've heard the story from quite a few people. Apparently Martin let fly, telling Christopher exactly what he thought of landlords. He spared no words and by the time he had finished quite a crowd had gathered. As far as the crowd was concerned Martin was simply saying what most of them thought anyway. Christopher responded with threats and anger – telling him he'd have him whipped or gaoled – swearing that he'd see him out of there."

Honnie was incredulous. Hannah hadn't told her that. "Surely not! Surely the story has gained in the telling? I mean you weren't there yourself – you have only heard what happened?"

"I can assure you that is *exactly* what happened, because a very old friend of mine was there – Father Horan, the parish priest in Garumna, and he described it to me in detail. He said things got very nasty. And he said Christopher lost his head completely."

"But, Tom, words said in the heat of the moment! Christopher won't have meant those threats!"

"I am sorry to say, Honnie, but he did. Martin owes Christopher less than six months' rent, but just a few weeks ago Christopher proceeded for the rent on two civil bills, and got two decrees against Martin, one against his goods for £15, and another against his person for £20. What has got into Christopher, Honnie? Has he lost all sense of *reason,* of *compassion*? How can he destroy a man's life, a good man and a good tenant, for such a paltry sum of money? Even when Martin's own brother, Edward, offered to pay the monies owed, he refused the offer."

"I don't think it's about the money," said Honnie. "It's about whatever was said that day. It's a matter of pride."

"Pride! But in a few weeks' time, he intends to level Martin's house! A man's life, his family, destroyed, put out on the roadside, because one man has so much power, power not earned, but inherited. I simply cannot believe that he is going to go ahead with it. Christopher and I have not always seen eye to eye. But I never thought of him as cruel."

Honnie fell silent as they took another turn around the gardens.

Finally she spoke. "It's a very distressing story and I can think of nothing to say to excuse Christopher. I can tell you that he worries all the time about money. There is so much owed on the estate, debts that have built up over many years, very little of them of Christopher's making. They go right back to Christopher's grandfather. Even when Christopher's father and mother were married nearly fifty years ago, there was a big debt on the estate. Then just six years ago his father borrowed money to make provision for all Christopher's sisters. Since his father died many of those borrowings have come home to roost. There is hardly any money coming in. People simply haven't got it. Christopher is besieged by people dunning him for money, bailiffs trying to deliver demands, letters from creditors reminding him of how much is owed. He is at the end of his tether. But none of that is any excuse for behaving the way you describe."

"As you said – it's Christopher's pride that is causing

this misery. And his selfish pride is going to destroy a good family. Put children on the road to starve."

For a few moments neither of them spoke.

"Anyway, Honnie, we are not going to fall out over this. We have been good friends for far too long. I came over here to see you in the hope that you might persuade Christopher to change his mind. You have children yourself. Can you imagine what it must be like to have your home knocked down, and your family exposed to the elements? I know that Christopher is headstrong. But if anyone can persuade him to think again I am hoping it is you."

"I can try," said Honnie finally. "But to tell you the truth, right now I find Christopher difficult enough myself. He doesn't seem to listen when I speak to him. He never sits down in one place for any length of time. He's always coming from somewhere or going somewhere. And with a new baby and seven other children my hands are full. It all makes me very sad. But ... I will do my best."

"That's all I ask," said Father Tom.

Honnie spent that evening and night thinking about the best way to approach Christopher. Finally, after two days of waiting and watching she decided to take the bull by the horns. She found him, in the early evening, sitting at his desk in his study, the study that had been his father's. There was a pile of papers in front of him. Suddenly the likeness became eerie, but where his father used to look depressed, Christopher looked in the humour to pick a quarrel with anybody who came near him.

"I need to talk to you," she said.

"This isn't a good time," he said.

Honnie hesitated. "Tomorrow, then," she said.

"Oh, for God's sake! If you have something bad to say, say it now," said Christopher. "Get it over with."

"Father Tom came to call the other day..."

"And what did he have to say for himself?" said Christopher. "He doesn't turn up too often nowadays, does he? Now he comes twice in a couple of months."

"He's travelling the county from morning 'til night trying to help the people of Galway who are hungry and in want."

"Isn't that what priests are meant to do?" said Christopher. "Tend to their flock?"

Honnie could feel her anger rising. "He wanted me to ask a favour of you." She was getting a sinking feeling that no good was going to come out of this conversation.

"And what would that be?" asked Christopher.

"It's about the Cosgraves," said Honnie. "He said that you swore an oath, Christopher, that you would see Mairtín Cosgrave in gaol, and off your land. Is that true?"

"Yes, I did swear an oath," said Christopher.

"Well, Father Tom was hoping that you might be persuaded to change your mind," said Honnie nervously.

"And he hadn't got the guts to come and ask me himself," said Christopher.

"No, no, that wasn't the way of it," said Honnie. "He just thought you might listen to me."

"Well, he's wrong," said Christopher. "My mind is made up. I swore an oath. I intend to keep it."

"Couldn't you unswear it?" said Honnie. "Tom says they are a decent, hardworking family. They have ten children. According to Tom, they've almost always been good about paying their rent. They've had a hard time of it. I'd hate to think of me and mine being thrown out to suffer the elements. How could you *think* of taking down their house, and leaving them without a roof over their heads at the mercy of wind and weather? In a time of famine?"

Christopher stood up suddenly and, slapping both his hands down hard on the desk in front of him, he leaned towards her.

"Maybe Martin Cosgrave should have thought of all that before he tried to make a fool of me *in front of my other tenants!*" he said, his voice rising. "You weren't there, Honnie! He said I was inhuman. He said I was greedy and selfish, and that landlords are the scum of the earth. He said I had a family of bastards here in Tyrone!"

"He wouldn't be the first person to say all that," said Honnie dryly. "Just not in your hearing. And if I was living as a tenant farmer's wife with ten children, and a landlord came and told me that my home was to be pulled down, I might well have thought as Martin did – but I probably wouldn't have said so. You are doing this because your pride is hurt, and that's not a good enough reason. I think what you are doing is wrong –"

"I don't want to know what you think!" snapped Christopher. "He ridiculed me in front of my other tenants. And I could see that the crowd around him were agreeing with him and laughing at me. He held me up to obloquy and now, apparently, he has become a local hero. No, I will not change my plans for Martin Cosgrave. I'll be damned before I budge an inch on the matter. I made an oath and I'll stick to it. I'll see him in gaol yet. And next time you see Tom Kelly tell him to mind his own bloody business."

Chapter 41

In the weeks following, Honnie went on trying to bring provisions to her family, to Nóra, and to the Kellys.

On one nippy March morning she and Mick Murphy set out once more on their rounds.

Things went badly from the start. They always did but now it was as if a tide of anger beat against them all the way.

Mick's face was grim as he whipped the pony to a brisk trot. "If we stop at all we're undone," he said.

Honnie tried to ignore the taunts, but she couldn't.

"*There she is, St. George's kept woman, living off the fat of the land while the rest of us starve!*"

"*It isn't her children who are starving!*"

"*Far from it she was reared over in Maree!*"

Honnie wrapped her shawl around her, sat straight up in her seat and kept her eyes on the road ahead.

Finally Mick suggested that the next time she wanted to send provisions to Nóra or her own family and friends in Maree, it might be better if he took them by himself.

Honnie knew that Mick was right. She was just an aggravation to the people she passed.

When Christopher told her a few weeks later that he was going over to Connemara and would be gone a couple of days, she asked him if was still going to take possession of Martin Cosgrave's house.

"That's what I said I'd do, and that's what I'm going to do," said Christopher curtly.

"But he owes you barely a half-year's rent," said Honnie. "How can you do it?"

"As I've already told you," said Christopher, "it's not just about the rent."

When Christopher and his men arrived with the sheriff at Martin Cosgrave's holding on the 9th of April, 1847, they found a crowd had gathered around the Cosgrave house, watching, waiting. It was a bright spring day, but there was a wind that snaked through Christopher's bones.

There was no sign of Martin, but his wife Mary stood at the door, with the younger children clinging to her skirts, and a babe not much more than a year old in her arms. They had moved all their furniture and household goods into a nearby barn. But they found it hard to believe that it was really going to happen, that their house was going to come down.

The men told them roughly to get out of the way. The children were crying, and the babe in arms was howling.

It was all over very quickly. The roof was gone, only the crumbling walls stood. Christopher took possession of the land, which had been cropped by Martin under an express agreement with Christopher's agent. He left with the keening cries of Mary and her children ringing in his ears, and the cold chill of hatred reaching out from the assembled crowd.

When he came home he went straight to his study, where Honnie found him sitting at his desk, looking gloomily out the window.

He looked up when she came entered. His face did not invite questions.

"So," said Honnie. "Did you have Cosgrave's house knocked down?"

"I did what I said I'd do. Now I don't want to discuss the matter any further, with you or anyone else."

"So you threw a whole family out on the side of the road, exposed them to all the elements, in these bitter winds," said Honnie. "How could you do it? I just don't understand!"

"You don't have to understand," said Christopher. "It's none of your business. It doesn't concern you."

"Of course it concerns me!"

"I have work to do," said Christopher. "I'm sure you must have things to do as well."

Honnie turned to leave.

"Christopher," she said. "What have you become? I feel I don't know you any more."

In the weeks that followed they hardly spoke to one another, but Honnie lived in fear of what Christopher was going to do next. When he told her he might have to go to Connemara again, she was seriously worried.

"There is trouble brewing in Connemara," he said.

"What kind of trouble? Explain it to me, please."

Christopher hesitated. "It's quite complicated," he said, but for once he seemed more inclined to talk. "Some ten, eleven, years ago, in 1836, my father leased out lands we owned in Connemara, the districts of Lettermore and Garumna, to two women, known as the Mesdames E. O'Shaughnessy and O'Flaherty, at a yearly rent. They in turn rented out the lands to various tenants, more than six hundred of them. Between the two women and the tenants there has long been conflict. The two women say they haven't been paid any rents by the tenants. The tenants are saying that they are not going to pay any rent while there are squatters all over their lands, stealing sheep, killing their cattle. The end result is that I am now owed a year-and-a-half's rent and various other monies as well. And I have small hope of getting any of it. But one thing is certain. The two old dames will have to go – but getting rid of them is likely to cost money. And the squatters will certainly have to go."

And there the matter stood, until five days later when Christopher announced that he wouldn't be going to Connemara after all.

"Well, I'm happy to hear that," said Honnie.

"John Linnane, my agent in Connemara, thinks that issuing ejectment orders will help bring things to a head."

Now Honnie was horrified.

"So everybody living on or at all interested in those lands is being served with an ejectment order," said Christopher.

"Are you seriously saying that you are going to eject 600 tenants?" said Honnie.

"No, I'm not saying that I'm going to evict all those people," said Christopher. "All I'm saying is that this whole business needs resolution and the threat of ejectment may bring resolution."

"Are you even sure of the facts?" she said. "You need to go over there and find out the true facts for yourself."

"I was going to go myself. But I've changed my mind. I have great trust in John Linnane. He will handle this business better than I can. Besides, I'm going up to Rathbride –"

"Rathbride, at a time like this!" said Honnie in disbelief. "When there is death and devastation all around you? You know your friend, George Moore, has given up racing altogether because of the state of the country."

"Good for George," said Christopher. "But horses and racing are the only things that are keeping me sane right now. Besides, I don't believe that putting my horses out to grass and eschewing racing would make the slightest difference to the appalling state of this country. I am not an absentee landlord. I have reduced all my rents but I know I can't have an expectation of any rents at all. The people haven't got any money. I wish I could wave a magic wand and change the world around me. But I have no magic wand. I wish I could perform miracles because miracles are much needed. But I'm no miracle worker. So I'm going to Rathbride. I am hoping that I might be able to make a bit of much-needed money out of Chanticleer. He is showing very good form at the moment. If he does well in the Queen's plates in June I may be able to sell him for a pretty penny."

"*Chanticleer?*" said Honnie. "The most bad-tempered horse in the whole country? He's a savage. You'll be well rid of him."

"Especially if I get a good price for him," said Christopher.

On the 15th of May Daniel O'Connell died in Genoa.

Honnie wrote to William.

"*Poor man. I think he was a true Irish patriot. He killed himself working for Ireland. I think he really believed that he would get us repeal of the Union. But when the Government banned his big Monster Rally in Clontarf in Dublin, just a few years ago, in October 1843, it was the beginning of the end. They banned it the night before it was due to take place, and sent two warships and 3,000 troops to make sure it didn't happen. Apparently O'Connell was horrified. He hated bloodshed, and he had always insisted that the Repeal Association was non-violent. He called off the rally. And people who used to believe in him didn't believe in him any more.*

I have heard that his last request was that his heart should go to Rome, the rest of his body to Ireland, and his soul to Heaven."

She didn't tell William about Christopher's confrontation with Martin Cosgrave, but she did tell him about his hopes for Chanticleer.

Ireland suffered on. The Poor Law Amendment Act was passed in June and placed the burden of relief exclusively on Irish taxpayers. A Poor Law designed to help 100,000 people was expected to provide relief to one-and-a-half million people.

"*It just can't work*," Honnie wrote to William. "*People are desperate and those who have enough money are emigrating. But after they have paid for their passage – £2 to British North America – they have hardly any money left to pay for food on the journey. Those who can't emigrate are going to the workhouses. There are empty villages, with locked-up houses. Nobody is working on the land. But the saddest news I've had this week is about my friend, Nóra and her children, in Drumacoo. Mick told me that when he went to visit them the house was empty, and a neighbour told him that they had gone to Gort workhouse, where it is said, the fever is rife. The word is that all of them are dead.*

"But one piece of good news is that Chanticleer won three Queen's Plates at the Curragh. Then Christopher sent him over to Liverpool, where he ran very well and a trainer called William I'Anson saw him, and gave Christopher 1000 guineas for him. I never liked Chanticleer. He was a truly mad horse. He was always savage. One time we had to get a stable lad out of his box through the window. There were times when he would roar like a bull. Mr I'Anson is welcome to him."

By July famine mortality was dropping. The soup kitchens were working. They were to remain open until September 30th. But the government decided to begin closing them in August.

The year's potato yield was good, but very small. Only about one-sixth of the normal acreage was planted. The seed potatoes had long been eaten.

One morning at the beginning of August, Honnie came down the stairs to see Christopher heading out the door. She had been sleeping in a separate bedroom with Matilda, who was teething, and kept waking up crying during the night.

"Electioneering again?" she asked.

She knew that Christopher was heavily involved in campaigning for his friend Denis Daly, who was hoping to get a seat in the British Parliament in the elections which were due to be held on August 11th.

"Yes," he said. "But first I must go to Connemara. I'll be staying with Denis when I get back. It's more convenient for these last few days."

And he was gone out the door.

It was from Joseph that Honnie learned what happened when Christopher went to Connemara. Joseph had been following the election campaign with great interest and heard many speeches – and gossip – at the hustings around the county. He had listened to various accounts of Christopher's visit to the Cosgraves.

"It seems that when Christopher went over earlier in the year the Cosgraves were told that they would have the benefit of whatever crops they had sowed," said Joseph. "They had sowed two acres of potatoes, which had failed, and then they sowed wheat in the same ground. They had cut about half the wheat when Christopher came. He brought men with him, men with firearms, and they prevented any more wheat being cut. They put keepers on the wheat which had been cut, and then Christopher's men reaped the rest of the wheat and carted it away. The Cosgraves had been living in the barn, and he told them to take themselves and their furniture out of the barn. He put Martin into his vehicle and took him away, the bailiff sitting before, and he himself behind with a double-barrelled pistol. And that is the story as I have heard it from a number of people, at least two of whom were there and saw it happen."

As Joseph's story unfolded Honnie began to feel sick to the pit of her stomach, sick and furious. She had never ever been so angry. There was not one redeeming feature in his behaviour, not one excuse which could be made.

But she found few opportunities to challenge him. He was campaigning across the county for Denis Daly. The one brief encounter with him brought her little solace. She caught him one morning hurrying out the door.

"I have heard what you did to the Cosgraves," she said. "Where did you take Martin?"

"I did what I always said I'd do," said Christopher. "I took him to gaol."

"You put him in *goal*!" said Honnie, her voice rising.

But he was gone before the words were out of her mouth

Four days before the elections were due to be held, on August 7th, Denis Daly's father, the Earl of Dunsandle, died. Denis withdrew from the election, and Christopher was persuaded to go forward in his place. A speech Christopher made in the hours before the election was reported in the *Tuam Herald.*

"Electors of Galway, no individual that has ever stood before you as a candidate for your suffrages, feels more thoroughly impressed than the humble individual who now addresses you how high the honour is to be permitted to aspire to be one of the representatives in Parliament of this important country ..."

In Tyrone, William, picked up a copy of the *Tribune* on a table in the drawing-room, and was excited to see his father's speech.

"Look, Mama! Please read it out for me." At nearly twelve years old, he now had a tutor and was making excellent progress but the article was too difficult for him to read.

She began: "'*I am appearing as an anxious aspirant to enter political life as the representative of this my native county – where I have resided all my life. I am happy to boast of an intimate acquaintance with all the inhabitants of it, and I trust I reciprocate in their views. I have to congratulate this county that in it religion is no longer the battlefield of political controversy. I am the advocate of civil and religious liberty and of every measure to promote the prosperity of Ireland. I will have Ireland as she ought to be ...'Great, glorious and free, First flower of the earth and first gem of the sea'. I look forward to the regeneration of Ireland, and that England, notwithstanding the vituperative language of its press, will consider it but just to sympathise fully in the present affliction of Ireland, and to consider that awful famine which has visited our shores as a national calamity, should be met by national resources. Mendicancy and confiscation of property are near at hand. I shall expect on the meeting of parliament that the First Minister of the Crown will advise her gracious Majesty to announce from the throne that England shall fully and alike share in Ireland's woes, Ireland that has contributed to England's glory. I admit that the government has encountered famine an occurrence of no ordinary character. I am willing to make certain allowances for the embarrassing situation in which they have been placed, still I do think they should have hearkened not only to the voice of the landed proprietor but even the poorest inhabitant of this country, as to the mode of expenditure of the large sums of money that have been lavished on works chiefly of a useless description. If I shall have the honour of a seat in parliament I shall feel it my duty to procure a railway to Galway. Galway must become a packet station with America, such is necessary to advance the interest of Great Britain as well as Ireland. The fisheries of Ireland should be regarded as Nature's bountiful gifts to Ireland and must be properly appreciated. I consider that the education of the inhabitants of this country should be attended to. It is education which permits man to raise himself in society. Providence has afforded the humblest individual I now address, power of discrimination, if not equal but probably superior to my own –"*

"I think it's a great speech, Mama, don't you?" William interrupted.

"Indeed," said Honnie. "It goes on to say ... '*He demanded that education be administered to all classes of society in this country. As in the conformation of the human form, the blood which by arteries issues from the human heart, therefore returns by means of veins, so must Irish freedom. He would not sanction Ireland's resources to be in foreign climes dissipated by Irish proprietors. He would not admit of absenteeism. He trusted he should find Irish representatives acting in the next parliament differently from what they had done. They must stand together, and in a body contend for the interest of the country. He expressed to the candidates of this day his very great respect and regard, and that, no matter how this contest may terminate, he would entertain sentiments of esteem for all those whom he had the honour to address.'"*

"Mama, it says that there was a lot of hectoring at the hustings – what does hectoring mean, Mama?"

"Hectoring? Hectoring means that people who disagree with what is being said shout out their disagreements."

"So why were they were shouting at Papa? I think he said an awful lot of good things. Why would people disagree with the good things he wanted for this country? And who is Martin Cosgrave? People said he had been evicted, that Papa should be made answer for what he did. Did Papa evict him, Mama?"

"You'll have to ask your father about that," said Honnie. "Now it's almost your dinner time, for which you are nearly always late. Run along and get cleaned up. They get cross in the kitchen if food has to stand there, and get cold because you've gone off somewhere and don't remember the time, and nobody can find you."

Christopher was duly elected as Tory member for Galway County on August 11th.

On August 25th Christopher told Honnie he would be going to Connemara again.

Honnie looked at him coldly.

"Is it for a few more evictions?" she said. "From what I hear you've been busy in that area."

"If that's what you've heard you've been misinformed. The only person I've evicted so far is Martin Cosgrave. The trouble with you, Honnie, is that you've heard too much and you know too little. As I told you before, there are squatters on our land, and my tenants say they will not pay rent until I get rid of the squatters. I wouldn't call getting rid of squatters an eviction, since they've no right to be there in the first place. I'm not quite the monster you seem to think I am, and I won't evict anybody without good reason."

"Like Martin Cosgrave?" said Honnie.

His face hardened. "I don't want to hear that man's name mentioned again," he said, and walked out the door.

A very weary Christopher came back from Connemara three days later. He looked exhausted and his face was grim. Honnie felt a momentary flicker of sympathy for him, then thought of the Cosgrave family, and squashed any sympathetic feelings very firmly.

He flung himself into an armchair beside the fire in the drawing-room and said he was truly glad to be home.

"I can never get my head around Connemara," he said, "and these have been some of the grimmest days I've ever spent there."

"Well, you hardly expected it to be a picnic, did you?" said Honnie tartly. "So how many people did you evict?"

Christopher sat up straight. Suddenly he was very angry.

"Do you know something, Honnie? I'm heartily sick of you preaching at me, when half the time you don't know what you're talking about. So I want you to listen carefully to what I am going to tell you – the *true* story of my visit to Connemara. Yes, I found my estates in chaos. And my tenants, over 600 of them, were indeed in a bad way. They told me that people had come from other districts, from all parts of Ireland, to squat on my lands. Tenants came pleading with me to hear their story, plucking at my coat, beseeching with me to listen. They told me that upwards of 800 sheep had existed between all the various tenants, and not one now remained. They told me cows had been carried off and killed, and other goods had been taken as well. And the local priest, Father Patrick Horan, confirmed that everything they said was true. He said nothing could exceed the depredations of the squatters. The two dames said they hadn't paid me any rent because the tenants hadn't paid them any rent. The tenants said they hadn't paid any rent because the dames had done nothing to get rid of the squatters. I am owed a year-and-a-half's rent, about £1,500, and other monies besides. I told the tenants that if they paid me £400 within three months, I would remit the rest. The tenants agreed to do so if I got rid of the squatters and other bad characters. The tenants and Father Horan considered my offer most liberal. Things were bad, but they were bad chiefly because of the neglect of Mesdames O'Flaherty and O'Shaughnessy."

"And maybe a bit of neglect on the part of their landlord," said Honnie, and knew the minute she said it that she should have kept her mouth shut.

"Honnie, there are times when it seems you want to think the very worst of me," he said.

Honnie was taken aback. "*That's just not true*," she said vehemently. "It's not true. I want to think the very *best* of you."

"My story is true," said Christopher. "Honnie, what was I to do? These are people who shouldn't be there in the first place, people who came from all over the country to squat on my lands, who robbed my tenants. If these people came and squatted all around Tyrone, would you be happy? Would you tell them to stay, and welcome? Or would you ask me to get rid of them? I have to get them off my lands, and I will make no apology for it. My tenants have suffered greatly. I haven't enough resources to give them all the help they need. I can only do my best. As I have said, my tenants owe me £1,500 and I have told them they need only give me £400 in three months' time, and I will forget the rest. But I don't seriously expect to get £400 from them in three months' time – where are they going to get it from? I have borrowed £6,000 under the Land Improvement Act, and I am appropriating £1,500 to Lettermore, and £1,000 to the rest of Connemara. But this money is going to help my own people, not squatters. It isn't going to be an easy task to get rid of the troublemakers, but it must be done."

Looking at Christopher, Honnie began to see that he was very weary, his face haggard and drawn. He looked almost ... defeated.

She was still standing there, lost for words, with her head buzzing, when Lizzie came into the room to tell her that William had fallen off his horse.

"He's not badly hurt but he is quite bruised and shaken," said Lizzie. "He's calling for you."

Honnie looked at Christopher, but he was sitting, gazing into space, as though he hadn't heard anything.

"I'll come straight away," she said to Lizzie.

That night in bed Honnie lay awake a long time. Her brain swirled over her years with Christopher. There had been so much happiness, so much loving, so much fun. Of course there had been arguments as there would be in any marriage. But some of their arguments had been very serious, and her criticisms had been sharp. As in the case of John Heathers, the Ordnance Survey man. Honnie had felt that if Christopher employed bullyboys who carried out this kind of attack, then he was partly responsible as well. Christopher said that the man who actually carried out the attack had only been in his employment for a few months, and he had no reason to believe he was violent. And to be fair, he seemed almost as upset by young Heathers' death as she was.

Martin Cosrave was a different matter. She had never thought of Christopher as a vengeful man. Hot-tempered, quick to fire up, yes, but not mean-minded, not cruel. What had happened that bleak November day over in Connemara, the day of his first altercation with Martin Cosgrave, when he felt he had been taunted and publicly humiliated in front of all his tenantry, had sown in him a black, blind desire for vengeance.

But this was not the Christopher she knew, the Christopher who had married her against the wishes of his family, against the horror and opprobrium of many of his friends and acquaintances, the Christopher who installed her as mistress of Tyrone, not caring what people might think or say.

Then she remembered his speech on the occasion of the election. William was right. It had been a good speech, a sincere speech.

In her head she went over his account of his visit to Connemara. She had been quick to judge, and not so quick to listen. Clearly the problems were immense, and Christopher had felt very distressed about the state of his tenants. He had borrowed £2,500 to try to help them.

She could see that the squatters had to go. Drastic

problems demanded drastic solutions. But it wouldn't be easy.

She was beginning to understand why Christopher looked so beaten, so broken, when he came home. And she had to admit that, on occasions, she herself had been too judgmental, too harsh in her criticisms.

Over the next days they were wary of each other, but much kinder to each other. No harsh words were exchanged.

Meanwhile the Government had decided that soup kitchens were to cease altogether at the end of September.

"*Even though everybody knows that there is nothing like enough potatoes this year to feed people,*" said Honnie, once again writing to William, "*it seems that the Chancellor of the Exchequer, Mr. Charles Wood, thinks that the Irish must rely on their own resources. What resources? The Poor Law system is to be maintained by whatever can be extracted from landlords and stronger farmers. But they have no money either. Many of them are completely bankrupt. And now the Relief Commission operations are to be wound up. People are starving all over the country.*"

She quoted the words of William Forster, a Quaker, writing from Galway. "*It was enough to have broken the stoutest heart to have seen the poor little children in the workhouse yesterday – their flesh hanging so loose from their bones that the physician took it in his hand and wrapped it round their legs.*"

And she told her own children the story, and said they should never, ever, forget how lucky they were, and that they should give thanks to the Lord every day.

At the end of October, the Church hierarchy spoke out against Britain's policy. Father Tom was delighted.

"I thought they'd never get around to it," he told Honnie. "They wrote to Lord Clarendon, the Lord Lieutenant, rejecting the view of the *Times* newspaper which said that the Famine was caused by the 'innate indolence' of the Irish people – what gall! And they went on to list what they see as the real causes of the famine. They demanded a fair arrangement between landlords and tenants, productive employment, and special government interventions. Archbishop MacHale has said that if something isn't done, social disorder will ensue, and that men enraged by hunger and despair threaten the derangement of society."

Then, at the beginning of November, the children got measles. William got it first. In the beginning it seemed just like a bad cold – a cough, a runny nose. But when his temperature went up and up, and he complained of sore eyes, she began to wonder. Then Lizzie told her that many of the children in the district were coming down with measles.

"And you know how William is always out and about, playing with one or other of them? I got measles when I was about ten years old," said Lizzie. "I was the first to get it, but soon it went right through the house. We should look for the spots."

"I had it too," said Honnie.

"Me too," said Hannah.

None of them mentioned that the disease could be fatal but they all thought it.

They found the spots, on his head, behind his ears, and within hours all over his body. He was a querulous patient. The spots were itchy. His eyes were sore.

"My eyes were very sore too," said Lizzie.

"I remember that as well," said Honnie. "He needs to be kept in a room with the curtains half drawn, so that he isn't in direct light, especially in direct sunlight. And I think my mother used a herbal recipe that Madge Shaughnessy gave her. It was made like tea. You put a good handful of a herb called *glanrosc* into a pint of boiling water, and when it cooled you used it to bathe the eyes. It worked very well."

"I think that was one of the remedies that Lady Harriet always had in store," said Hannah. "She called it eyebright. But where are we going to get eyebright in the month of November?"

"I think there's a good chance that Mairéad might have some put by," said Honnie. "I know she always dries herbs to have in the winter when there are no fresh herbs to be got. I'll send somebody over to Maree to ask her."

The next few weeks were hectic. One by one each of the children developed measles. Anne got it after William, then Mary, then James and Olivia, then Elizabeth and Nóra and finally little Matilda, who got it more lightly than any of the others.

Honnie, Lizzie and Hannah were on their feet every hour of every day, running up and down the stairs, bringing drinks to the invalids, trying to tempt their appetites as they started to get better, trying to calm them when they got fractious. And since they were once more without a cook, Honnie had to spend quite a lot of time in the kitchen.

It was Father Tom, visiting Honnie some days before Christmas, who told her about Captain Hellard.

"He's the Poor Law Inspector with the Galway Union, and he's a decent man, trying to do his best. He told me that there were over 1200 paupers in the Union. Outside the gates there were 140 people left unprovided for. Fever is increasing every day. One other thing he told me, Honnie, which is going to upset you. He said that just a few days ago he had seen no less than eleven boats, loaded with destitute persons, coming into Galway Harbour. He was told that most of them had come from Christopher's estates." Honnie's face paled. "Tom, they had to be the squatters. When Christopher went over to Connemara some months ago he found his estates in complete disarray."

She told him about the state of war between the tenants and the squatters, the sheep stolen, the cattle taken, and much other goods besides.

"Christopher had no choice, Tom. The tenants wouldn't pay any rents unless he got rid of the squatters, and I can understand that completely. The squatters had come from all over the country and they had beggared Christopher's tenants into the ground. The priest, your friend Father Horan, said nothing could exceed their depredations."

The Poor Law Commissioners began to sanction outdoor relief. Initially, able-bodied paupers in receipt of outdoor relief were expected to work at least eight hours a day. The Commissioners laid down the guidelines for this type of labour: "*It should be as repulsive as possible consistent with humanity, that is that paupers would rather do the work than starve.*"

The Commissioners were less than pleased with the

performance of the Guardians of the Galway Union, and unanimous in opposing all Captain Hellard's efforts to effect outdoor relief for the aged and the widowed. He wrote to the Commissioners on December 16th, to tell them that the Guardians were dragging their heels, that the distress throughout the Union was increasing to a fearful extent.

On December 28th the Commissioners issued an order dissolving the Board of Guardians. They planned to appoint paid officers to administer the affairs of the Union. In the meantime, Vice-Guardians would carry out these duties.

As the year drew to a close, people were now dying not just from famine and fever, but from exposure.

The Quakers decided to withdraw from providing direct relief. They were exhausted after their life-saving efforts, especially during the last spring when the government ordered the closure of the public works before the soup kitchens were in operation. The Friends, with their immense knowledge of the west and south, had realised that the Poor Law was incapable of relieving the starving masses in the remote parts of Ireland, where no workhouse existed for up to fifty miles. They said they would provide aid in the form of farm implements, seeds, and fishing tackle.

By Christmas the children in Tyrone were all well on the road to recovery, but still a bit pale and crotchety. The adults in the house were exhausted. It was hard to work up any appetite for a festive occasion. It was the bleakest Christmas Honnie could remember. And she was not looking forward to the New Year with any great hope.

Chapter 42

Charles Trevelyan's apologia, *The Irish Crisis*, was published in the first month of the New Year, 1848.

"Denis Daly got a copy of it," said Christopher.

"Well, don't bring it home here," said Honnie. "I can just imagine. It would put me in bad humour for a month of Sundays."

"Now that's a pity," said Christopher, flourishing a paper. "I have it right here. He again describes the Famine as '*a direct stroke of an all-wise and all-merciful Providence*'."

"That's enough!!" said Honnie. "More than enough."

"But I understand that Edward Twisleton, the Chief Poor Law Commissioner, has told Trevelyan a few home truths," said Christopher. "He said: '*It is wished that the Irish should not come upon the United Kingdom finances for the relief of their destitute. It is also wished that deaths from starvation should not take place. But these wishes are as unreasonable as if you ask us to make beer without malt, or to fly without wings.'"*

In the first week of January Martin Cosgrave was released from gaol, where he had languished for over six months. And Captain Hellard died of a fever.

In the middle of January Christopher came home one evening to find a letter with an English stamp waiting for him.

"I don't recognise the handwriting. Now who could that be from?" he said, holding the envelope up and looking at it.

"One way to find out would be to open the envelope," said Honnie.

As he read the letter, Honnie could see his face changing.

"It's from Caroline – you remember, the cousin Anne went to stay with in Rome? She gave this letter to a friend who was going to England to post, as the surest way of reaching me. It seems Anne is seriously ill. Caroline writes that she has a malignant tumour in her breast, and the cancer is quite advanced. Poor Anne! I may have had my differences with her in the past, but I don't like to think of her sick and far from home, with none of her own family near her. It must be terrifying to be sick in a strange country, with people who don't even speak your own language. I must go to her, Honnie."

"Of course you must," said Honnie, reaching out and putting her arms around him.

"It will take a bit of planning," said Christopher, "and there are affairs I have to settle up here before I go – hopefully in a few weeks' time, at the beginning or middle of next month."

But events were to overtake him.

By the 29th of the month, the Commissioners, while expressing regret at the recent death of Captain Hellard, wrote to say that they proposed at once to appoint a Major M'Kie as Temporary Poor Law Inspector, and he would be immediately proceeding to Galway.

Also on the 29th, a report of ejectments on the St. George estates appeared in the *Galway Mercury.*

Honnie showed Christopher the report and said the word was that the Commissioners wanted an inquiry.

Christopher had already seen the report, and was predictably furious.

"It is beyond my understanding why these people are taken seriously. They call themselves journalists. They are mere scribblers. They get hold of a few facts and they make up the rest – it's much easier to write fiction than find out facts. And their fictions sell papers. I've nothing but contempt for them. I cannot forget what they did to me and my family, and particularly my poor father, back in 1841, when Heathers, the Ordnance Survey man died. Do you remember the stories that appeared in the *Tuam Herald,* and the *Dublin Monitor,* and the *Morning Chronicle* in London? It was even suggested that my *father* was responsible, and that he had been arrested for murder. And all three of those papers had to make a grovelling apology."

"So will you be able to go to Rome?" asked Honnie.

"I intend to go to Rome as soon as I can, but if there is an inquiry ... I have to be here for it."

The Commissioners asked Major M'Kie to hold an inquiry. At the beginning of February he proceeded, as directed, to Connemara where he took evidence from a great number of witnesses with various claims. Only two of them concerned Christopher.

On the 16th of February Christopher went in to the offices of the Poor Law Guardians, to make application to the Guardians for a revaluation of his property. He found Major M'Kie was also in the Guardians' office where the notes of the evidence he had taken in Connemara were being copied by a clerk.

Christopher told Honnie about it when he came home.

"M'Kie came up to me and asked me would I like to look at the evidence he had collected, before he wrote his report. I said not particularly, since I never placed much credence on the information recorded in newspapers. I just glanced over it, but I thought it sensible to leave one of my men to make a copy of it. And I told M'Kie that I was not going to get into a squabble with a newspaper. If I have to defend myself for this affair, and for the other charges that have been levelled against me, I will do so in the House of Commons."

There was more to come. At the end of February Christopher got notification that he would have to appear in court to defend his treatment of Martin Cosgrave. It was clear that Martin had good friends who felt he had been very badly treated, and who were intent on bringing Christopher to justice.

Christopher waved the notice at Honnie.

"So, Honnie, are you pleased? Do you feel I am getting my come-uppance?"

"Of course I'm not pleased," said Honnie. "I'm just sad that somehow you lost your head and got yourself into this situation. I think you know what you did wasn't right, but your pride wouldn't let you admit it. When is the case to come up?"

"I don't know yet," said Christopher. "Some time later in the year."

And no more was said.

He was still planning to go to Rome, "when things have settled down," he said. But it turned out that there would be no immediate necessity for him to go to Rome. Another letter arrived from Caroline.

Honnie saw him wince – then he read the letter out to her.

"'I have sad news. Anne died here just three days ago. Poor woman, she suffered much in those last weeks, and it was heartbreaking to watch her in pain. But we had a good doctor who tried to relieve her pain as much as he could and helped us to make her as comfortable as possible. She talked quite a lot about you, Christopher, and said she regretted that you two were at daggers drawn so often. She wanted you to know that she loved you very much, and she hoped you are happy.

She was only with us for a short few years, but we will miss her greatly.'"

"Oh Christopher, I am so very, very sorry," said Honnie, and put her arms around him. She could see that he was near to tears. He clung to her tightly for a few minutes.

"I feel so badly about it, Honnie, so guilty. I should have gone the minute I got Caroline's first letter, but there seemed to be so much happening here. I didn't realise she was so very sick. I thought she was probably going to die, but not for a while."

Father Tom had heard about Anne's death and came over to sympathise with Christopher.

"He's gone off on horseback somewhere, I'm not sure where," said Honnie. "He isn't talking much about it, but I know he's very cut up about Anne's death, and blames himself for not going over immediately."

"And the charges against him are gaining ground," said Tom. "You know that back in December, a month before he died, Captain Hellard had written to the Commissioners, and had mentioned the large numbers of destitute people coming into Galway. He had been told that they came from Christopher's estates. You and I talked about it the last time we met. Major M'Kie will have seen that report and now he is writing his own report on his recent visit to Connemara. Only two cases involve Christopher, involving people called M'Donough. The Commissioners are looking for answers."

Honnie watched as Christopher got more and more irate with each new report that reached him. But it was March 25th before he received a letter from Tom Redington who was the Under-Secretary for Ireland and a near neighbour of Christopher's. The letter drew his attention to the report of the Poor Law Commissioners respecting ejectments in the Galway Union, and requesting to know if he was desirous of making observations to the Government on that document.

Christopher waved the letter furiously at Honnie.

"Am I desirous of making observations? Am I desirous of making observations? *Yes*, most certainly I am desirous of making observations. How was it that I wasn't consulted before Major M'Kie – a Poor Law

Inspector only in Galway a few short weeks – sent his report to London? Sent it to London where it was recorded in the Blue Book in the House of Parliament. And I wasn't even given the opportunity to rebut these aspersions. Did he ask me for information, for my account of what happened?"

"Well, you have to admit that Major M'Kie asked you if you would like to look over his notes that day you met him in the Guardians' Office," said Honnie mildly.

"He didn't tell me that he was going to send his report to the Commissioners without giving me any chance to rebut it," said Christopher. "He didn't tell me that it was all going to go on record in the House of Commons, did he? This letter today is the first official communication upon this subject which I have received. Yes, I'll write to Tom Redington, and give him my observations on the whole affair. But I will also defend myself and my reputation in the House of Commons. I have been grossly misunderstood and misrepresented."

Over the next few days Christopher closeted himself in his study, working on his reply to Tom Redington, and the speech he intended to give in the House of Commons. He wrote, crossed out, rewrote, late into the night. Draft after draft fluttered to the floor. He didn't even appear at mealtimes, but absent-mindedly ate whatever refreshments Honnie brought him. With each day Honnie's heart grew more sore for him. First had come the news about Anne, then word about the expected case being brought by Martin Cosgrave, and now this latest blow.

On the third night, when there was no sign of him coming to bed long after midnight, she went down to the study. She found him hunched over his desk, looking grimly at the latest draft of his statement. The pile of crumpled sheets of paper on the floor had grown and grown. He didn't seem to hear her come into the room

She went up behind him, and tentatively put her hands on his shoulders, and was surprised when – without looking round at her – he reached up and gripped her hands fiercely.

"Do you still love me, Honnie?" he said.

She was stunned into silence for a few moments. Then she spoke.

"Amn't I still with you?"

"But do you still love me?" he said again.

"Of course I still love you," she said. "There may have been times when I haven't liked you very much, and times when I found it hard to recognise the man I married. But I've *always* loved you."

Christopher turned around and buried his head against her breast, and held her fiercely. Honnie was surprised by her body's reaction. Then again, even when they were at odds with each other, Christopher had almost always been able to break down her defences.

"You're very tired and so am I," said Honnie. "And it's very late. Tomorrow is another day. Tomorrow you can show me what you have written, your final draft, and we will send it off. Let's go to bed."

The next morning they looked at his letter together.

"I'll read it out to you," Christopher said. "The handwriting is careless. I will have to make a fair copy. Very well – *'I beg to observe, in relation to your letter of the 25th instant, that I am of the opinion that the Poor*

Law Commissioner should have communicated with me at the time, February 3rd, of sending the Inspector, Major M'Kie, to investigate into the statement of the Galway Mercury of January 29th. The Poor Law Commissioners should have acted impartially: they would have more amply vindicated the interests they are concerned for, by affording an opportunity to the accused, as well as the accusers, to be present at the Inquiry at Costello Bay. They have thought fit, in a most unbecoming manner, to be lavish of the character of an individual fully as respectable as themselves, by inserting, without one precaution, statements unsupported for the most part by facts. Because I have not entered onto a newspaper squabble, the allegations of certain journalists are supposed to be true.'" He stopped. "I don't have to read out the whole letter to you, Honnie. I then have gone on to thank the Lord Lieutenant for the courtesy he has shown me, which exhibits a glaring contrast with the Poor Law Commissioners of Ireland. Then I have set out for him all the history and problems relating to my estates in Connemara. I have told him about the part played – or rather not played – by the Mesdames O'Flaherty and O'Shaughnessy to whom my father had leased the land in 1846. I have told him about the squatters, and the depredations they had wreaked on my tenants. I have said that I have not received any rents, and I have paid an immense poor rate. I have admitted that my tenants in Connemara were in a bad way but I have been doing my best to sort out the problems. I have got rid of the Mesdames. I have told the people who owe me £1500 rent, that if they pay me £400 in three months' time that I will remit the rest. That I don't expect to get any money. That I have borrowed money under the Land Improvement Act and plan to appropriate £2500 to Connemara. I have remarked that in Queen's County and in other parts of Galway, my property is in a fairly wholesome condition. I have said that I pay weekly between £50 and £60 for the employment of my tenants."

"What about the M'Donoughs who complained about you to Major M'Kie?" said Honnie.

"Major M'Kie took evidence from a great number of witnesses," said Christopher, "and only two of them concerned me. No such occurrence as that described by Thomas M'Donough ever took place and the statement by Michael M'Donough that his house had been taken down was untrue. I can produce an affidavit made by my agent, Linnane, that their charges are unfounded and devoid of truth. Read it over yourself, Honnie, and tell me what you think."

Honnie read it over slowly.

"You seem to have covered everything," she said. "I think you've done well. I think it is a good letter and an honest letter. Is this what you are going to say when you speak in the House of Commons?"

"Yes, that is the sum of what I'm going to say," said Christopher.

On April 5th, the *Times* newspaper carried a complete account of his speech.

The case being brought by Martin Cosgrave was waiting in the wings.

At the end of June Christopher appeared in the court of the Queen's Bench before the Lord Chief Justice and a special jury to answer the charges made against him. It was an action of trespass and the pleadings contained counts for false imprisonment – Martin Cosgrave had been in Galway Gaol for six months and eleven days, at a time when pestilence was raging there to such a fearful extent that sixteen deaths a day were commonplace – and for the unlawful taking of the plaintiff's crops. Damages were laid at £1,000. Christopher pleaded provocation.

After an hour's deliberation the jury returned a verdict for the plaintiff of £434 damages and 6d costs, £350 for false imprisonment, and the remainder for the value of the wheat.

Chapter 43

The first half of 1848 had been nerve-shattering. The second half was quieter. Honnie was expecting her ninth child. She was up in Rathbride when baby Harriet decided to make an early appearance at the beginning of March. After the baby's birth she decided to stay on in Kildare for a few weeks until she felt stronger to face the journey home to Tyrone.

She was dozing beside the fire, with baby Harriet asleep in her arms, when Christopher came back in high good spirits from a visit to Dublin. He waved a piece of paper at her. She glanced at it with sleepy eyes.

"What is it?" she asked.

"Take a good look at it," he said, a grave look in his eye.

Honnie sat up straight and looked.

"A marriage license," Honnie said. "What on earth are you doing with a marriage licence?"

"I'm asking you to marry me," said Christopher.

"What do you mean?" said Honnie. "We're married already. Are you saying we are not married?"

"No, of course not," said Christopher. "But I'd like to marry you in my own church, legally."

"But we were married by Father Tom. We are married in the eyes of God. If I married you in your church that's as good as saying that our first marriage wasn't a real marriage. I'll not do it."

The arguments went back and forth, until Honnie refused to discuss the matter any further.

Life in Tyrone turned to a more even course. And the passing of the Encumbered Estates' Act in 1848/49 brought Christopher huge relief from the worst of his financial woes. This Act facilitated the sale of Irish estates whose owners were in severe debt because of the Famine. It allowed the sale of land, even if was entailed, in order to distribute the proceeds among creditors. Christopher was able to sell off land and property to the tune of £70,000, still not the full £100,000 that was probably owed, but getting rid of two thirds of the debts.

Cooks had come and gone a number of times in Tyrone since Mrs. Dunne had left. Then one night Christopher came with the news that he had found a brilliant cook – or rather his friend, Denis Daly, had found a brilliant cook. Honnie looked sceptical. She had heard of brilliant cooks before. But Mrs. Jeffries, when she came, lived up to her reputation. She was a truly brilliant cook. She was also enormously fat. Christopher had a special chair made for her. He said it was worth every penny it cost, for all the enjoyment and pleasure Mrs. Jeffries' food gave them.

One more daughter was born, Louisa in 1851 – and there were two more yet to come: Katherine in 1853, and Josephine in 1855. But before these last two births a certain momentous event took place.

Since Christopher's unexpected second proposal in early 1848, the idea of marriage continued to be bandied around.

Honnie's answer was always the same: "No – because we are already married."

Then one evening, when the subject came up again, she asked, "But exactly *why* do you want to marry me again?"

"Because I love you, you silly goose," said Christopher, taking her in arms and kissing her hard. "Because I want to get married in my faith the way you wanted to get married in yours. Because being married twice seems better to me than being married just once. Because –"

"Because this time I'm saying yes," said Honnie.

On the 15th of December, 1852, Honnie and Christopher were married again, in St. Ann's Church in Dawson Street, Dublin.

The End

Author's Note

Over fifty years ago, just two months after my own wedding, I went down to a wedding in Galway. A close friend of my husband was getting married. At the wedding breakfast I was sitting beside the father of the groom. He asked me had I any Galway connections? I said I had a grandmother from Galway, Mary Anne St. George, but she had died before I was born, and I knew very little about her.

He turned out to be a solicitor, and his firm had looked after the St. George affairs for many years. He went on to tell me about the St. George family, who lived in Tyrone House near Clarenbridge in the nineteenth century and owned close on 30,000 acres of land, spread over Galway, Queen's County and Roscommon. He told me that my grandmother Mary Anne was the daughter of William, son of Christopher St. George.

Over the following years I met Gordon Mark St. George, an American, who had done a lot of research on the family, and who had written a pamphlet about the St. Georges and Tyrone for the Irish Georgian Society. His mother had grown up In Tyrone. I met his cousin, Mary

Keegan, whose father had also grown up in Tyrone, who had accumulated a lot of family material, and was most generous in making it available to me. I was able to make a copy of a handwritten book of family recipes from another St. George descendant. And I acquired a copy of the memoires of Elizabeth Lahiff who had emigrated to America with her husband and two young children in 1906 – her father too had grown up in Tyrone.

I spent a great deal of time in the National Library, leafing through old newspapers on micro fiche. But it took me some time to get down to writing the novel I could hear in my head. Seven children and working full-time as a freelance journalist was quite demanding.

My novel is made up of historical facts and a great deal of imagination. Christopher St. George fell in love with Honoria Kane, a local girl. Family lore says she was a cook. So I have placed her in the Tyrone kitchens. They were married by a childhood friend of Honnie's, Tom Kelly – family lore again. By marrying a Catholic girl to a Protestant man Father Tom was exposing himself to prosecution. Such a marriage was illegal until 1871.

It seems Christopher always did what Christopher wanted to do. After their marriage he and Honnie set up house in Drumacoo – which took a lot of neck given that it was only a mile or so from Tyrone and his family. This was described as "*St. George's scandalous domestic arrangements*" by a contemporary. Honnie said that as far as she was concerned she was married in the eyes of God and that was all that mattered to her.

Christopher was very active in Galway county. He was one of the founders of the Galway Blazers, a famous hunt. He was instrumental in setting up Galway race course, and later the race course in Killarney. He was a successful breeder of horses. He was a steward of the Turf Club and had his own stables at the Curragh.

He was a Member of Parliament for one term, and when he was accused of evicting people from his estates in 1848 he defended himself very effectively in the House of Commons, and his speech was printed in *The Times* in London. He was never an absentee landlord.

Honnie and Christopher lived through the Night of the Big Wind, and the horror of the Famine years. Together they had twelve children, ten daughters and two sons. They were married a second time in 1852, in a Protestant Church, St. Ann's in Dawson Street in Dublin.

Like most Irish landlords in the nineteenth century, the St. George family were debt-ridden. The bailiff was never far from the door. When Christopher inherited Tyrone after his father died, he also took on the debts of his father, and of his grandfather – another Christopher – as well.

Christopher died in 1877. For the last ten years of his life he was an invalid, after a fall off a horse from which he never really recovered. The funeral hearse, drawn by four black horses "richly caparisoned", was led by about 400 of the St. George estate tenants on horseback and 600 on foot marching three-deep. Next came a number of Catholic clergymen. Behind the hearse walked the chief mourners and many others, the procession covering three miles of road.

Honnie outlived him by almost thirty years, dying in 1905 at the age of 96, Mrs. St. George of Tyrone House.

28385749R00310

Printed in Great Britain
by Amazon